A BRIDE'S STORY

5

Kaoru Mori

TABLE OF
CONTENTS

CHAPTER 23
WEDDING BANQUET (PART 1)————003

CHAPTER 24
WEDDING BANQUET (PART 2)————035

CHAPTER 25
WEDDING BANQUET (PART 3)————079

CHAPTER 26
THE DAYLONG SONG ————117

SIDE STORY
QUEEN OF THE MOUNTAIN————141

CHAPTER 27
THE WOUNDED HAWK————149

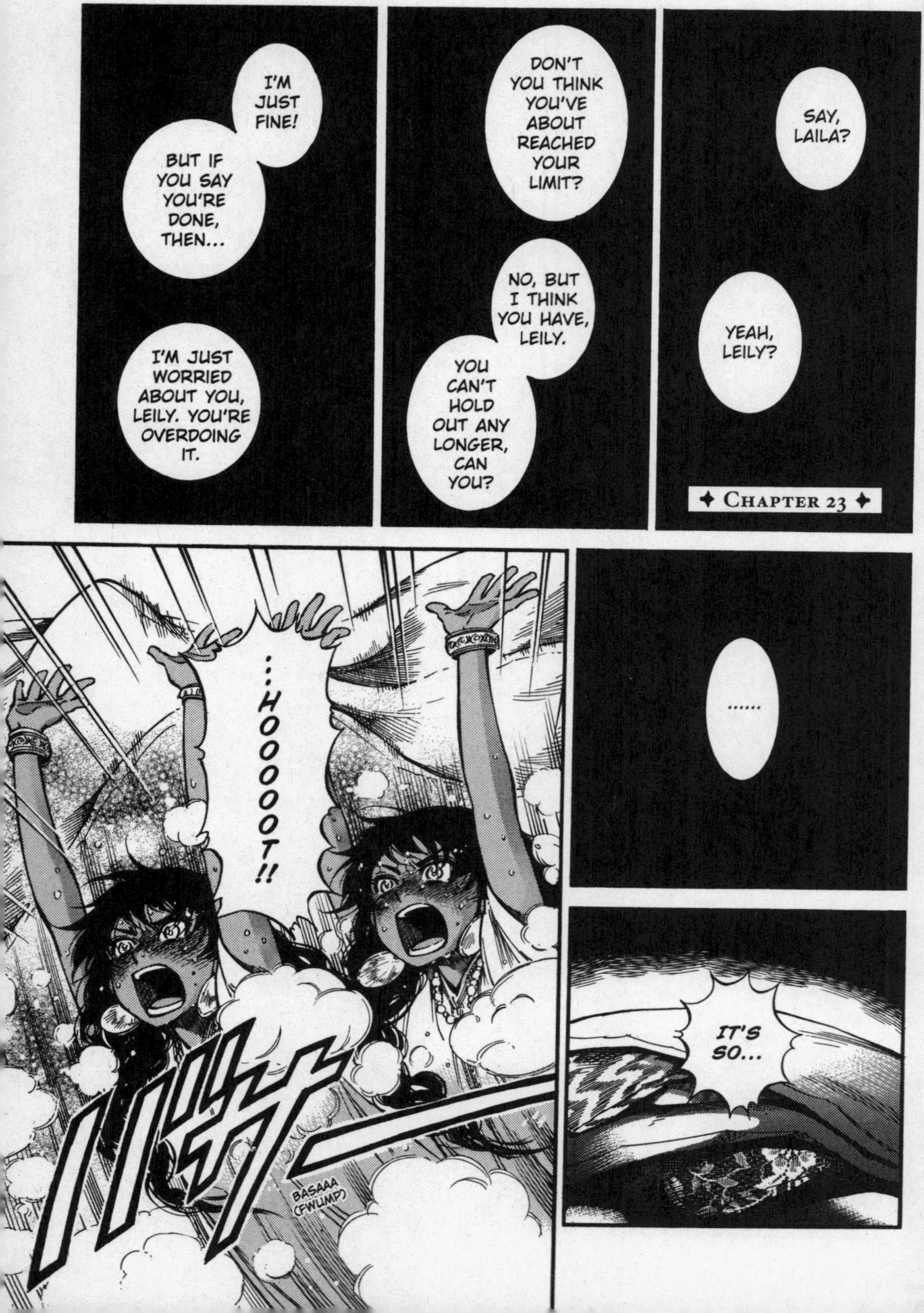
SAY, LAILA?
YEAH, LEILY?
✦ CHAPTER 23 ✦
DON'T YOU THINK YOU'VE ABOUT REACHED YOUR LIMIT?
NO, BUT I THINK YOU HAVE, LEILY.
YOU CAN'T HOLD OUT ANY LONGER, CAN YOU?
I'M JUST FINE!
BUT IF YOU SAY YOU'RE DONE, THEN...
I'M JUST WORRIED ABOUT YOU, LEILY. YOU'RE OVERDOING IT.
......
IT'S SO...
...HOOOOOOT!!
BASAAA (FWUMP)

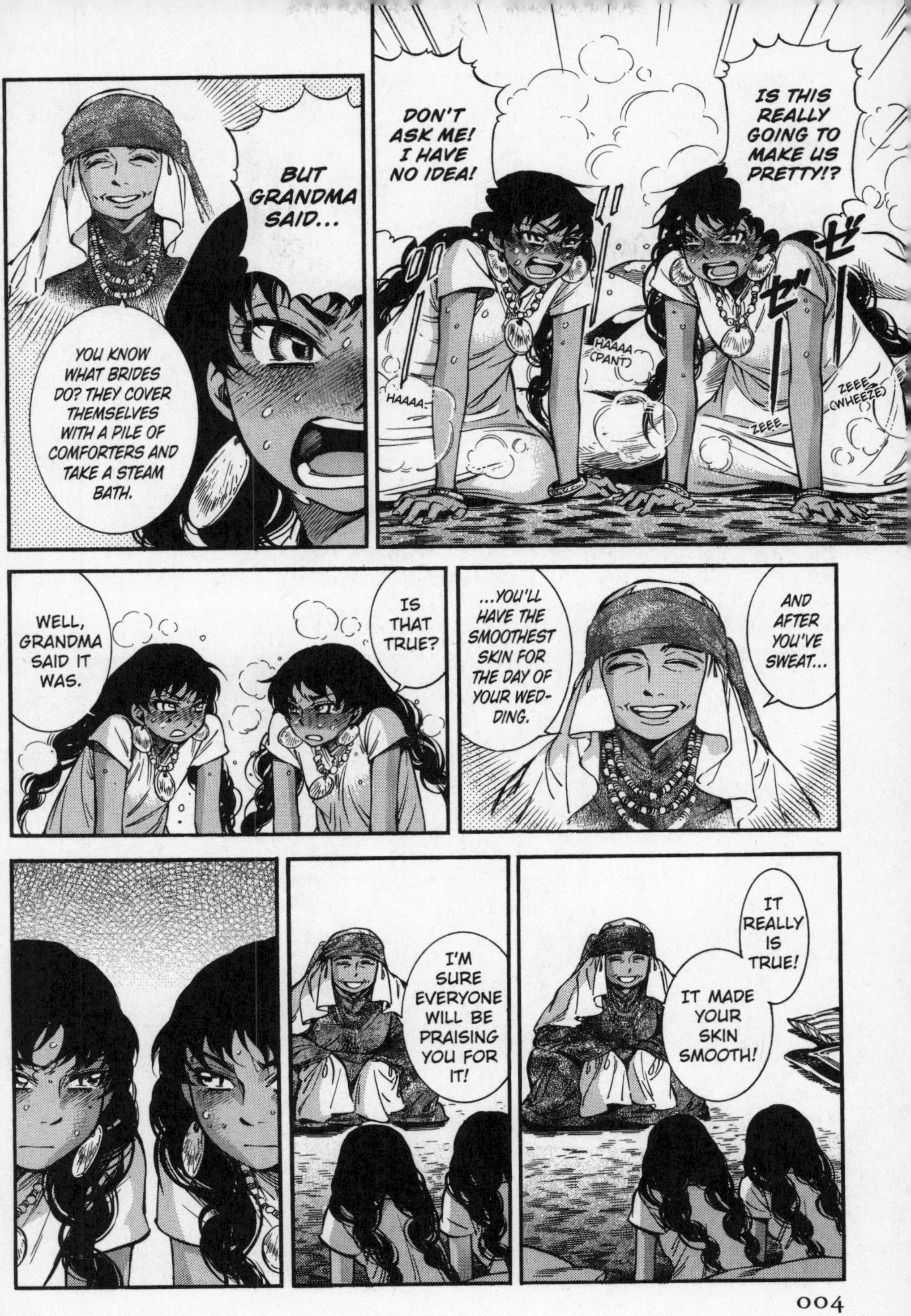
IS THIS REALLY GOING TO MAKE US PRETTY!?
DON'T ASK ME! I HAVE NO IDEA!
ゼ ゼ
ZEEE (WHEEZE)
ZEEE
HAAAA (PANT)
HAAAA
BUT GRANDMA SAID...
YOU KNOW WHAT BRIDES DO? THEY COVER THEMSELVES WITH A PILE OF COMFORTERS AND TAKE A STEAM BATH.
AND AFTER YOU'VE SWEAT...
...YOU'LL HAVE THE SMOOTHEST SKIN FOR THE DAY OF YOUR WEDDING.
IS THAT TRUE?
WELL, GRANDMA SAID IT WAS.
IT REALLY IS TRUE!
IT MADE YOUR SKIN SMOOTH!
I'M SURE EVERYONE WILL BE PRAISING YOU FOR IT!

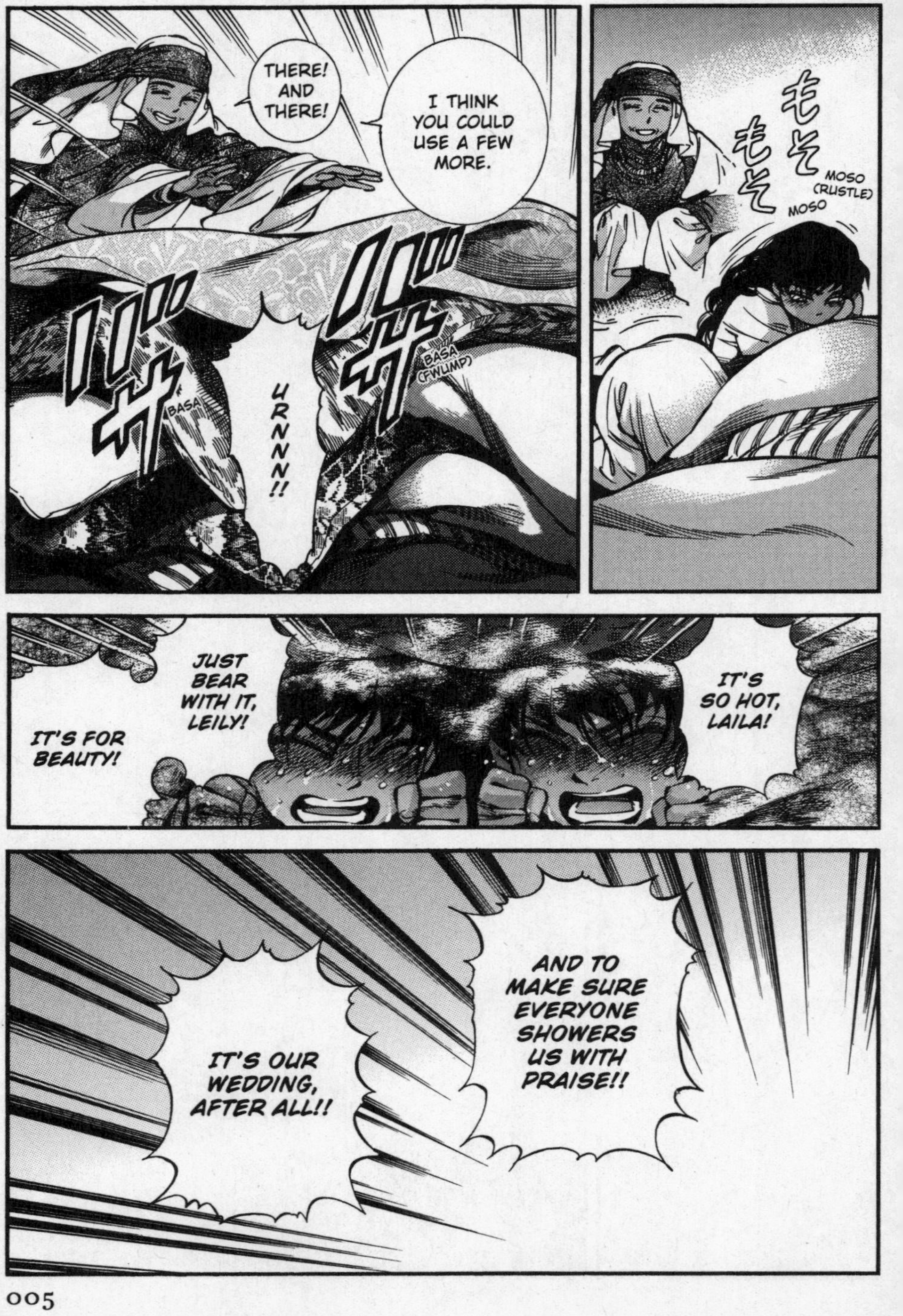

もそもそ
MOSO (RUSTLE) MOSO
I THINK YOU COULD USE A FEW MORE.
THERE! AND THERE!
バサ
BASA (FWUMP)
URNNN!!
バサ
BASA
IT'S SO HOT, LAILA!
JUST BEAR WITH IT, LEILY!
IT'S FOR BEAUTY!
AND TO MAKE SURE EVERYONE SHOWERS US WITH PRAISE!!
IT'S OUR WEDDING, AFTER ALL!!

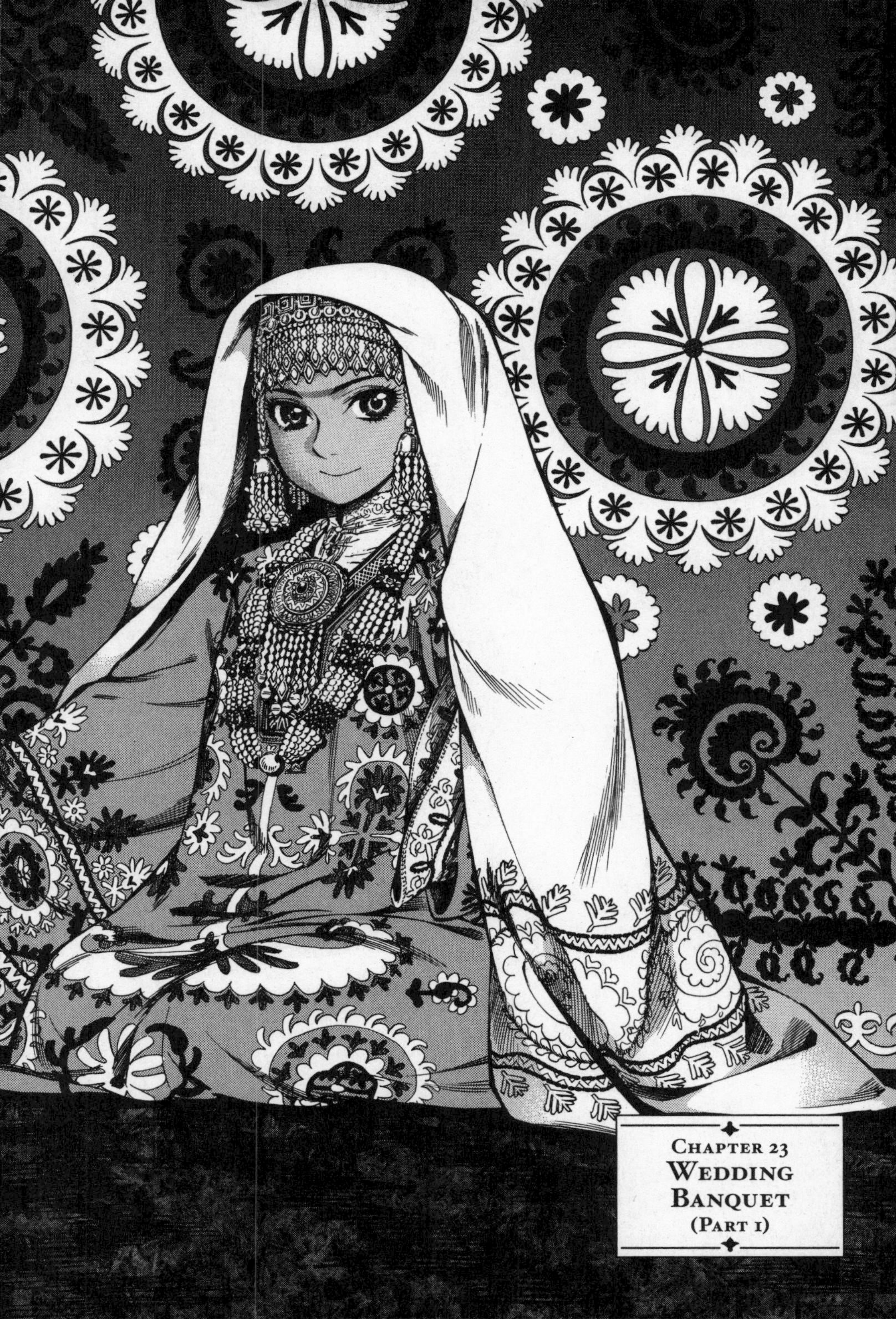

Chapter 23
Wedding Banquet
(Part 1)

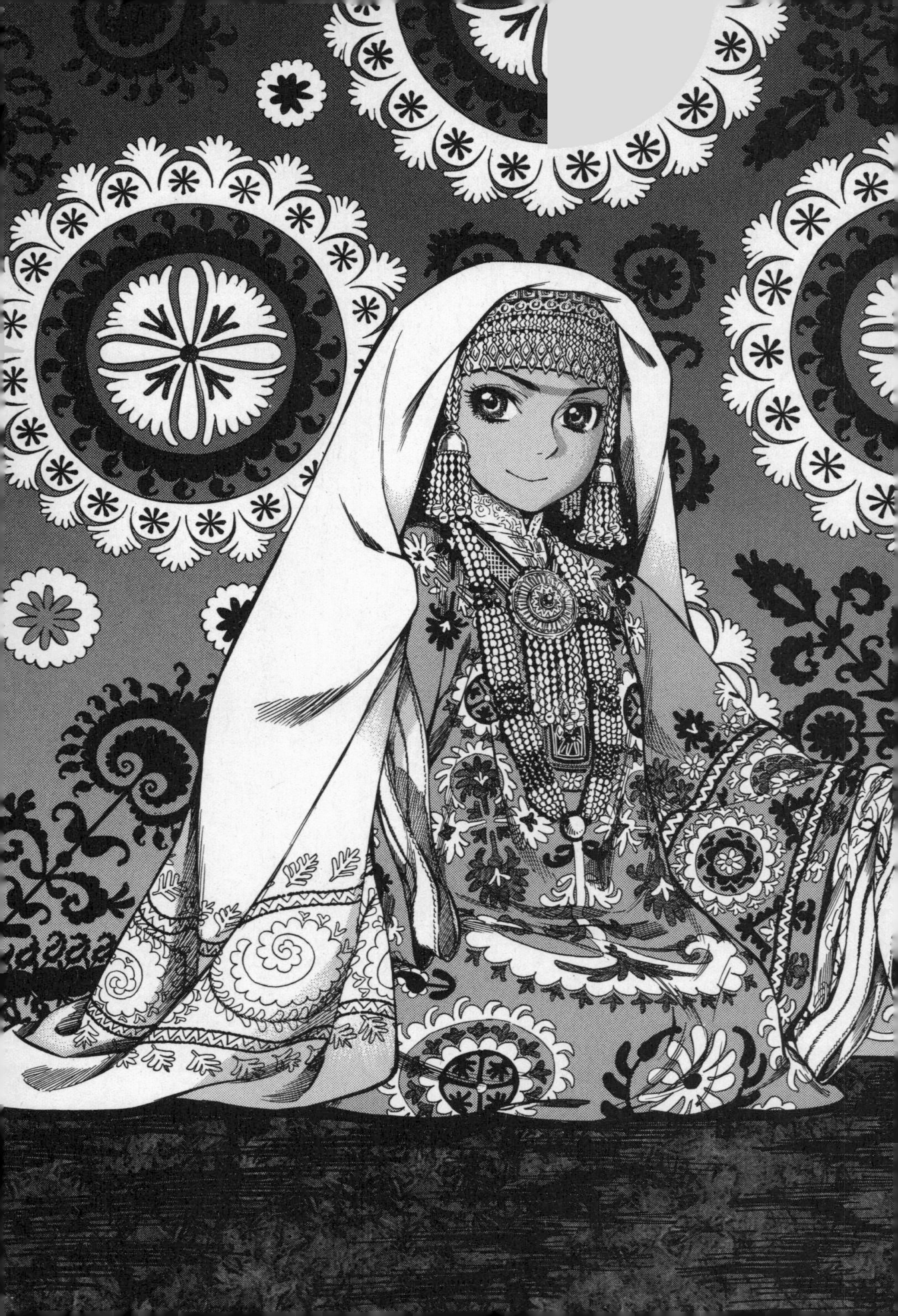

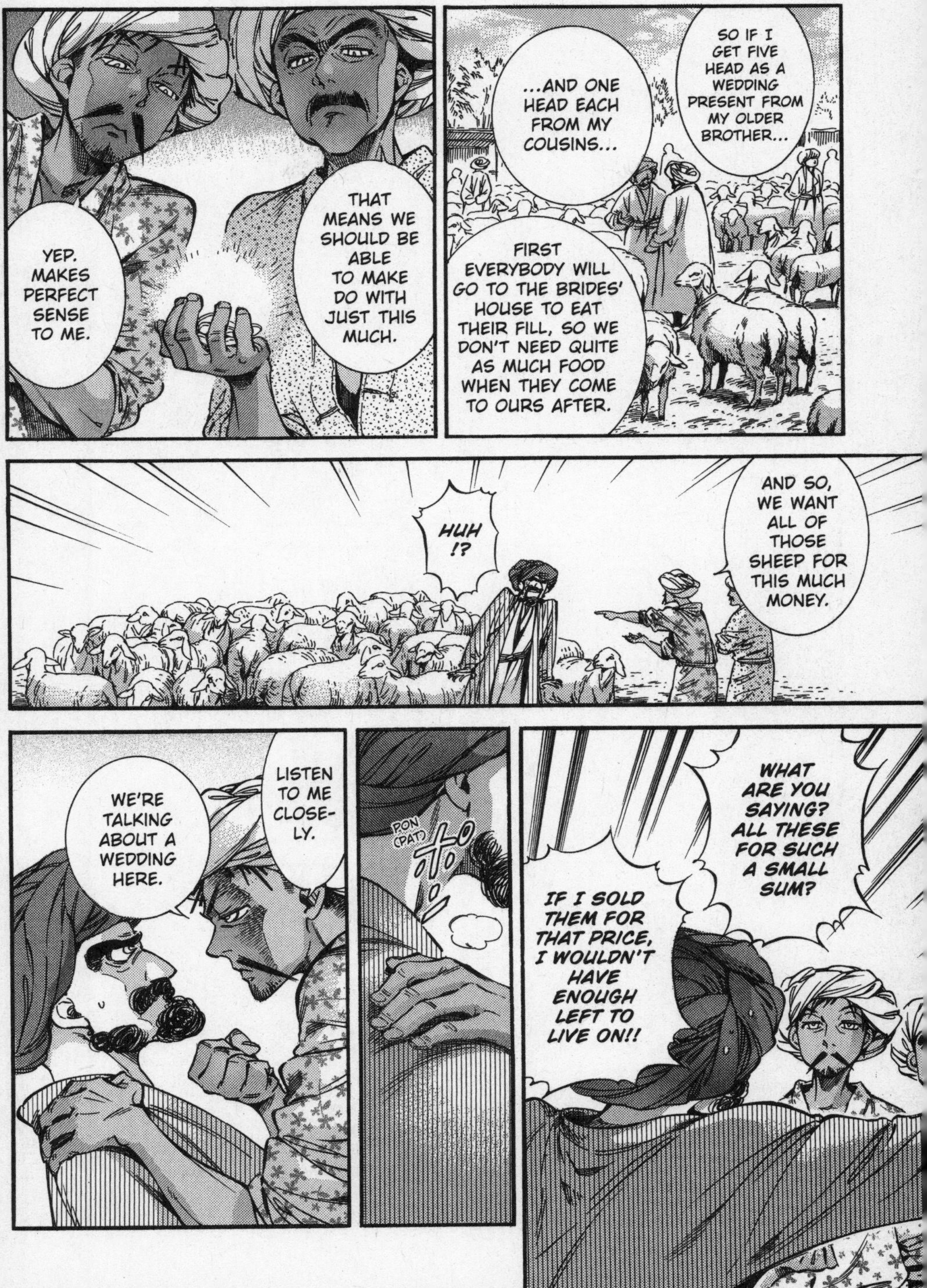
SO IF I GET FIVE HEAD AS A WEDDING PRESENT FROM MY OLDER BROTHER...
...AND ONE HEAD EACH FROM MY COUSINS...
FIRST EVERYBODY WILL GO TO THE BRIDES' HOUSE TO EAT THEIR FILL, SO WE DON'T NEED QUITE AS MUCH FOOD WHEN THEY COME TO OURS AFTER.
THAT MEANS WE SHOULD BE ABLE TO MAKE DO WITH JUST THIS MUCH.
YEP. MAKES PERFECT SENSE TO ME.
AND SO, WE WANT ALL OF THOSE SHEEP FOR THIS MUCH MONEY.
HUH!?
WHAT ARE YOU SAYING? ALL THESE FOR SUCH A SMALL SUM?
IF I SOLD THEM FOR THAT PRICE, I WOULDN'T HAVE ENOUGH LEFT TO LIVE ON!!
PON (PAT)
LISTEN TO ME CLOSE-LY.
WE'RE TALKING ABOUT A WEDDING HERE.

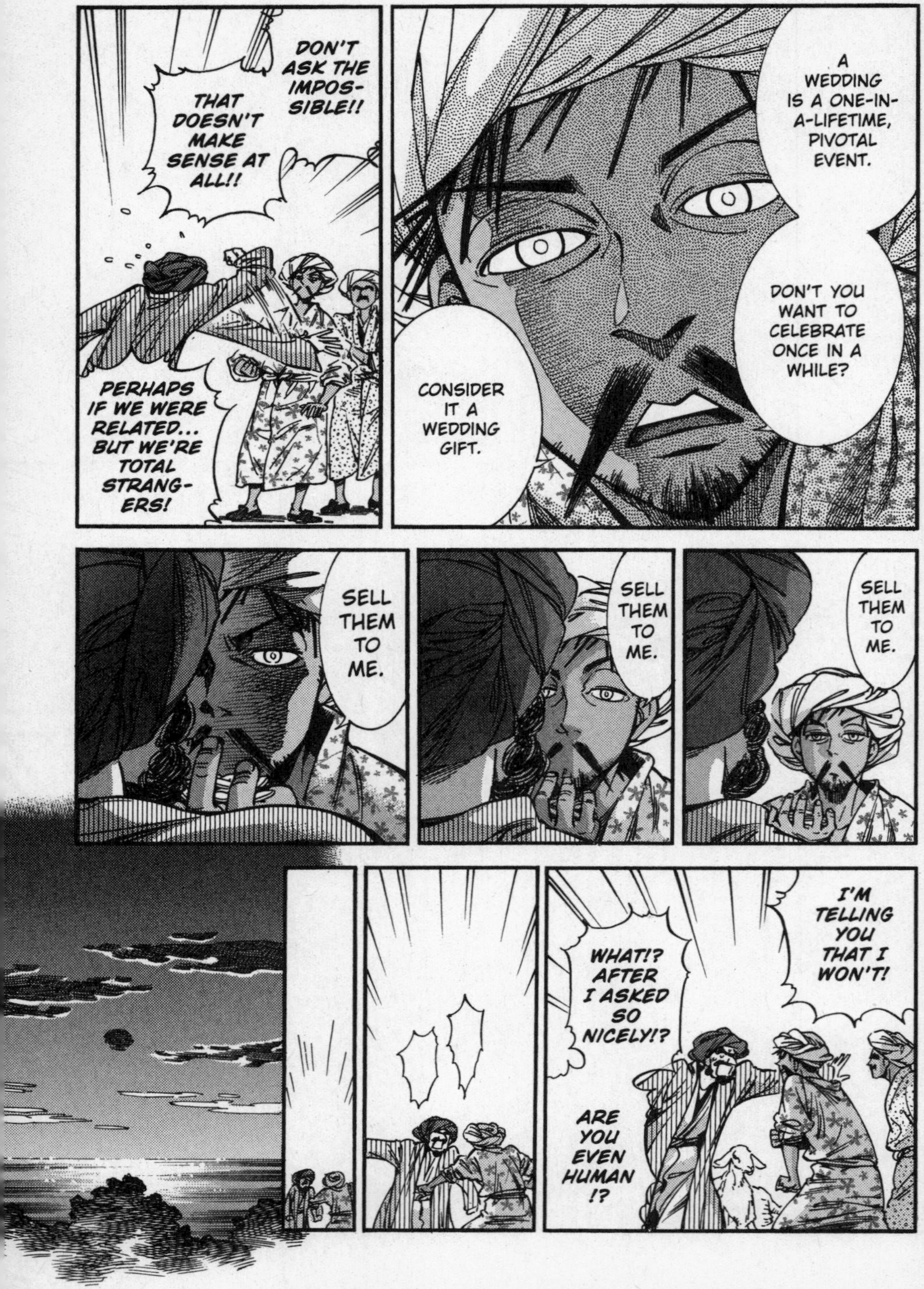
A WEDDING IS A ONE-IN-A-LIFETIME, PIVOTAL EVENT.
DON'T YOU WANT TO CELEBRATE ONCE IN A WHILE?
CONSIDER IT A WEDDING GIFT.
DON'T ASK THE IMPOSSIBLE!!
THAT DOESN'T MAKE SENSE AT ALL!!
PERHAPS IF WE WERE RELATED... BUT WE'RE TOTAL STRANGERS!
SELL THEM TO ME.
SELL THEM TO ME.
SELL THEM TO ME.
I'M TELLING YOU THAT I WON'T!
WHAT!? AFTER I ASKED SO NICELY!?
ARE YOU EVEN HUMAN !?

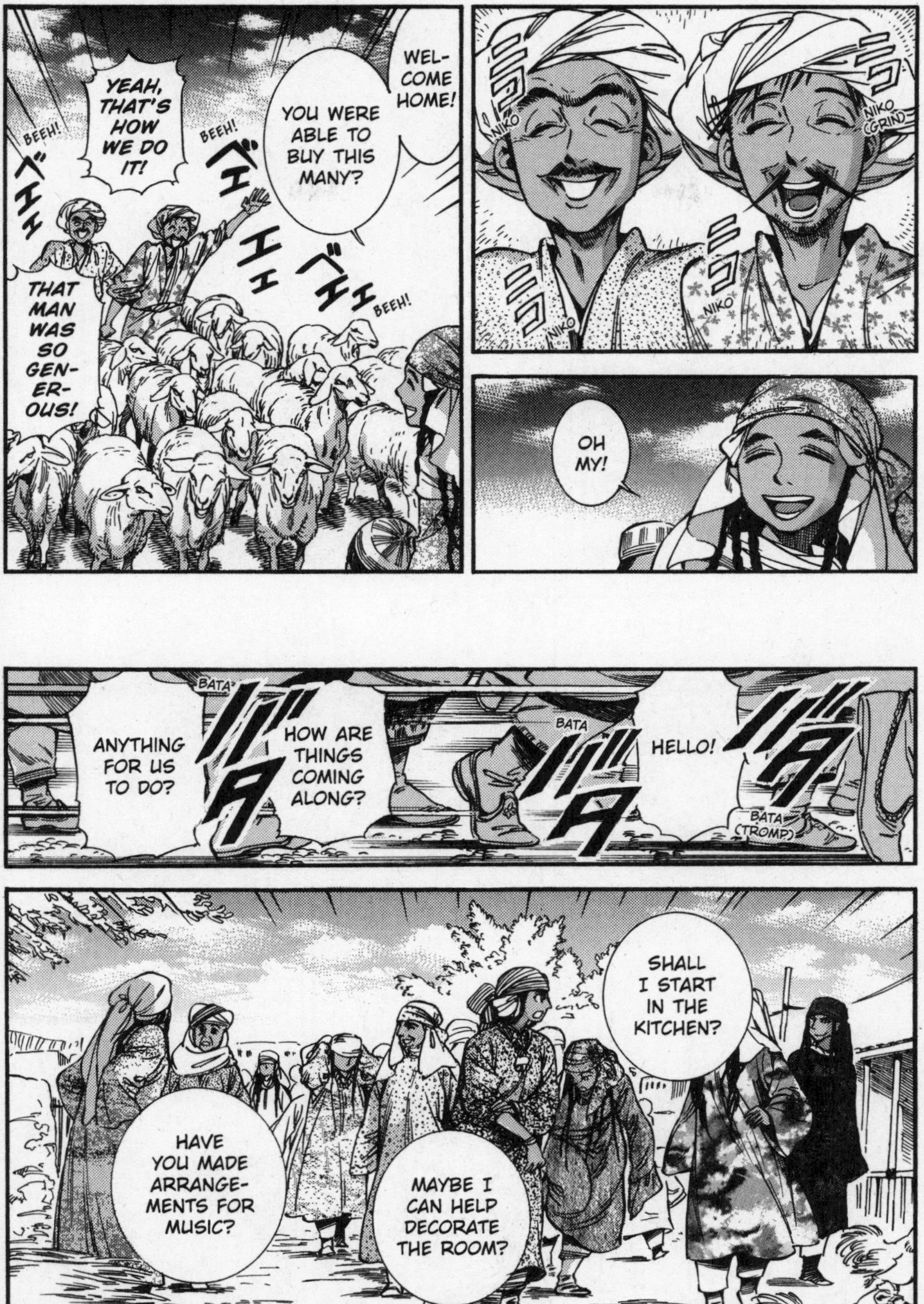
NIKO
NIKO (GRIN)
NIKO
NIKO
OH MY!
WEL-COME HOME!
YOU WERE ABLE TO BUY THIS MANY?
BEEH!
YEAH, THAT'S HOW WE DO IT!
BEEH!
BEEH!
THAT MAN WAS SO GEN-ER-OUS!
BATA (TROMP)
HELLO!
BATA
HOW ARE THINGS COMING ALONG?
BATA
ANYTHING FOR US TO DO?
SHALL I START IN THE KITCHEN?
MAYBE I CAN HELP DECORATE THE ROOM?
HAVE YOU MADE ARRANGE-MENTS FOR MUSIC?

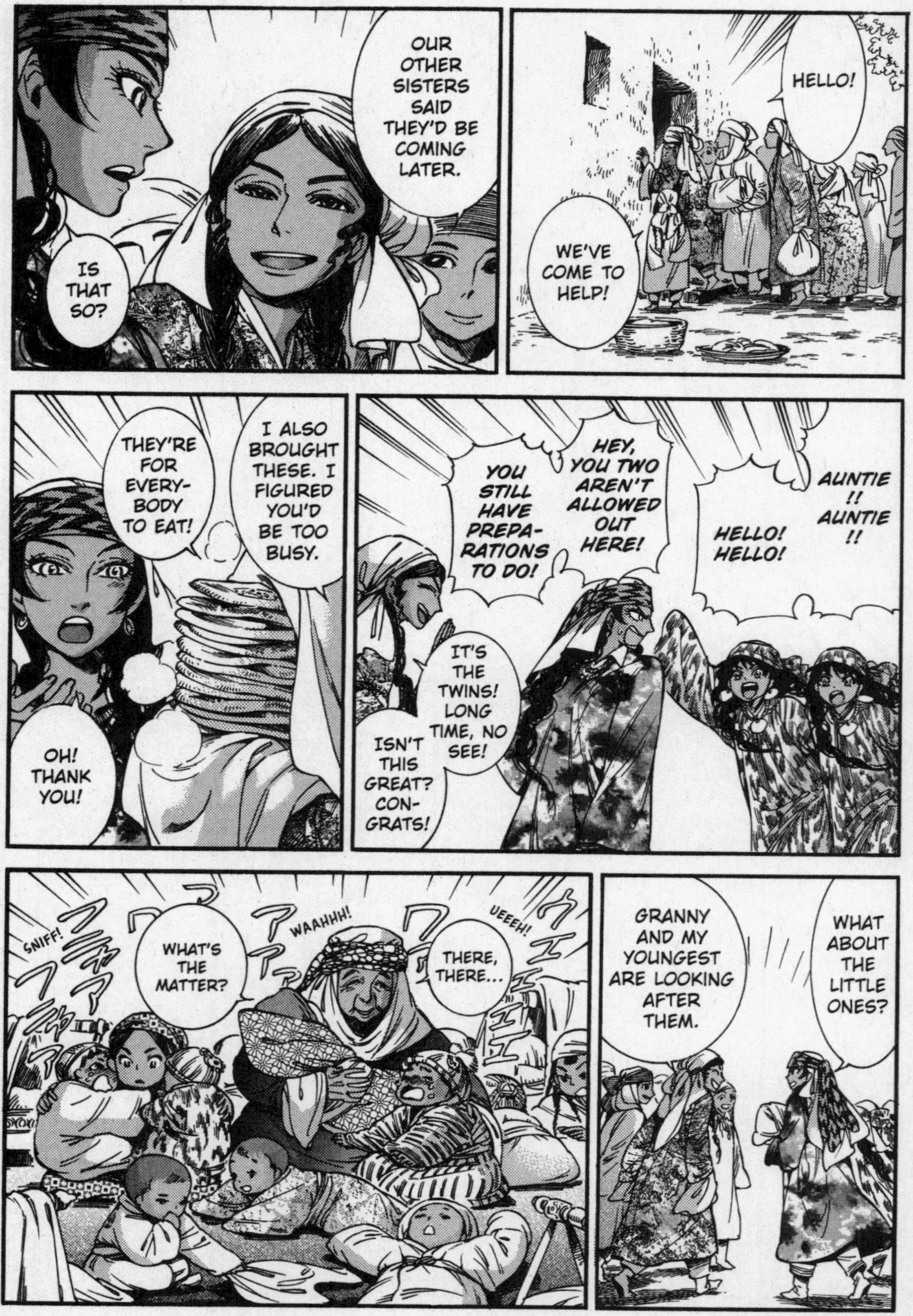
HELLO!
WE'VE COME TO HELP!
OUR OTHER SISTERS SAID THEY'D BE COMING LATER.
IS THAT SO?
AUNTIE!! AUNTIE!!
HELLO! HELLO!
HEY, YOU TWO AREN'T ALLOWED OUT HERE!
YOU STILL HAVE PREPARATIONS TO DO!
IT'S THE TWINS! LONG TIME, NO SEE!
ISN'T THIS GREAT? CONGRATS!
I ALSO BROUGHT THESE. I FIGURED YOU'D BE TOO BUSY.
THEY'RE FOR EVERYBODY TO EAT!
OH! THANK YOU!
WHAT ABOUT THE LITTLE ONES?
GRANNY AND MY YOUNGEST ARE LOOKING AFTER THEM.
UEEEH!
THERE, THERE...
WAAHHH!
WHAT'S THE MATTER?
SNIFF!

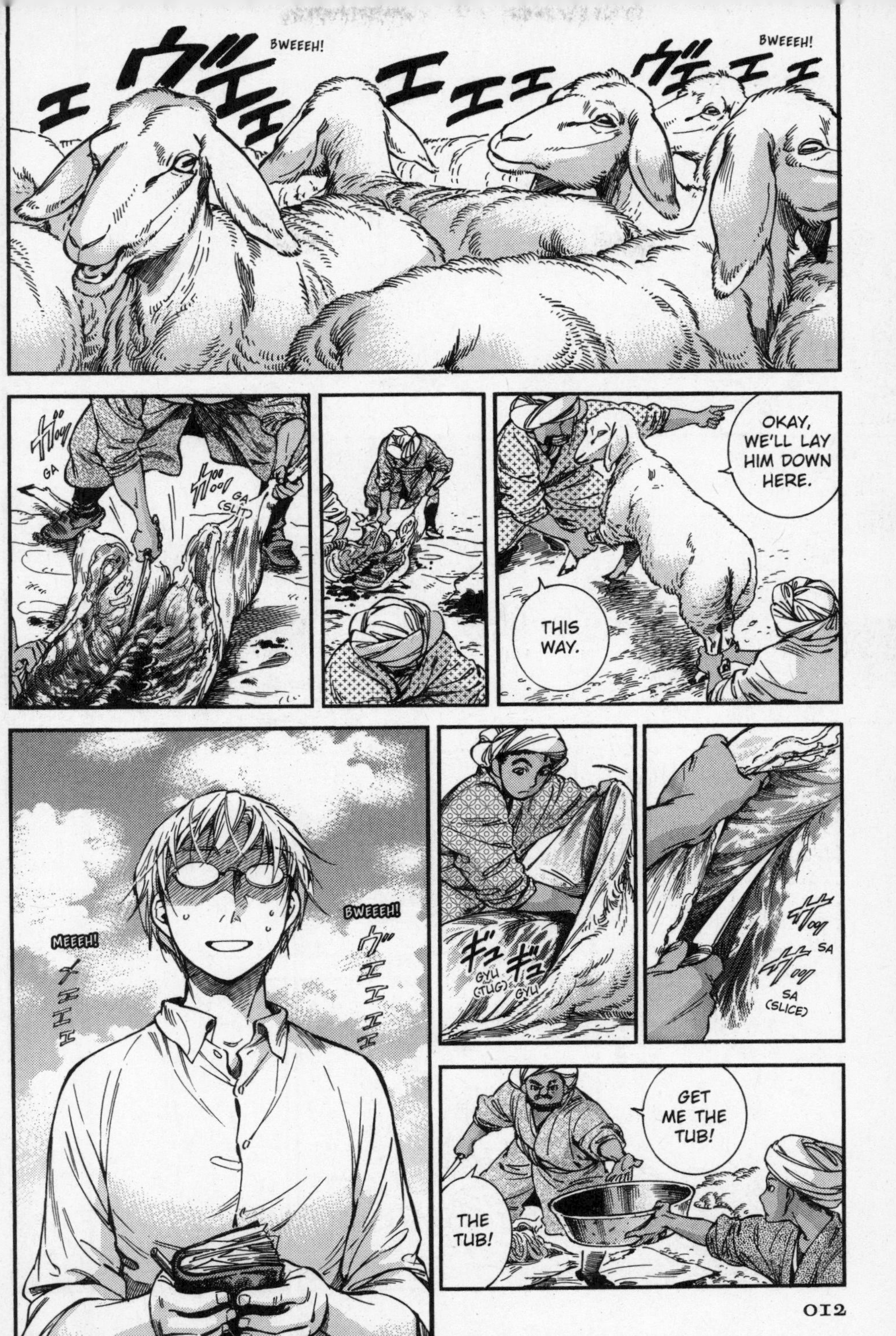

BWEEEH!
ヴェエェ
BWEEEH!
エヴェエェエェ
OKAY, WE'LL LAY HIM DOWN HERE.
THIS WAY.
ガッ
GA
ガッ
GA (SLIT)
ガッ
SA
ガッ
SA (SLICE)
ギュ ギュ
GYU (TUG) GYU
GET ME THE TUB!
THE TUB!
BWEEEH!
ヴェエエエ
MEEEH!
メェエエ

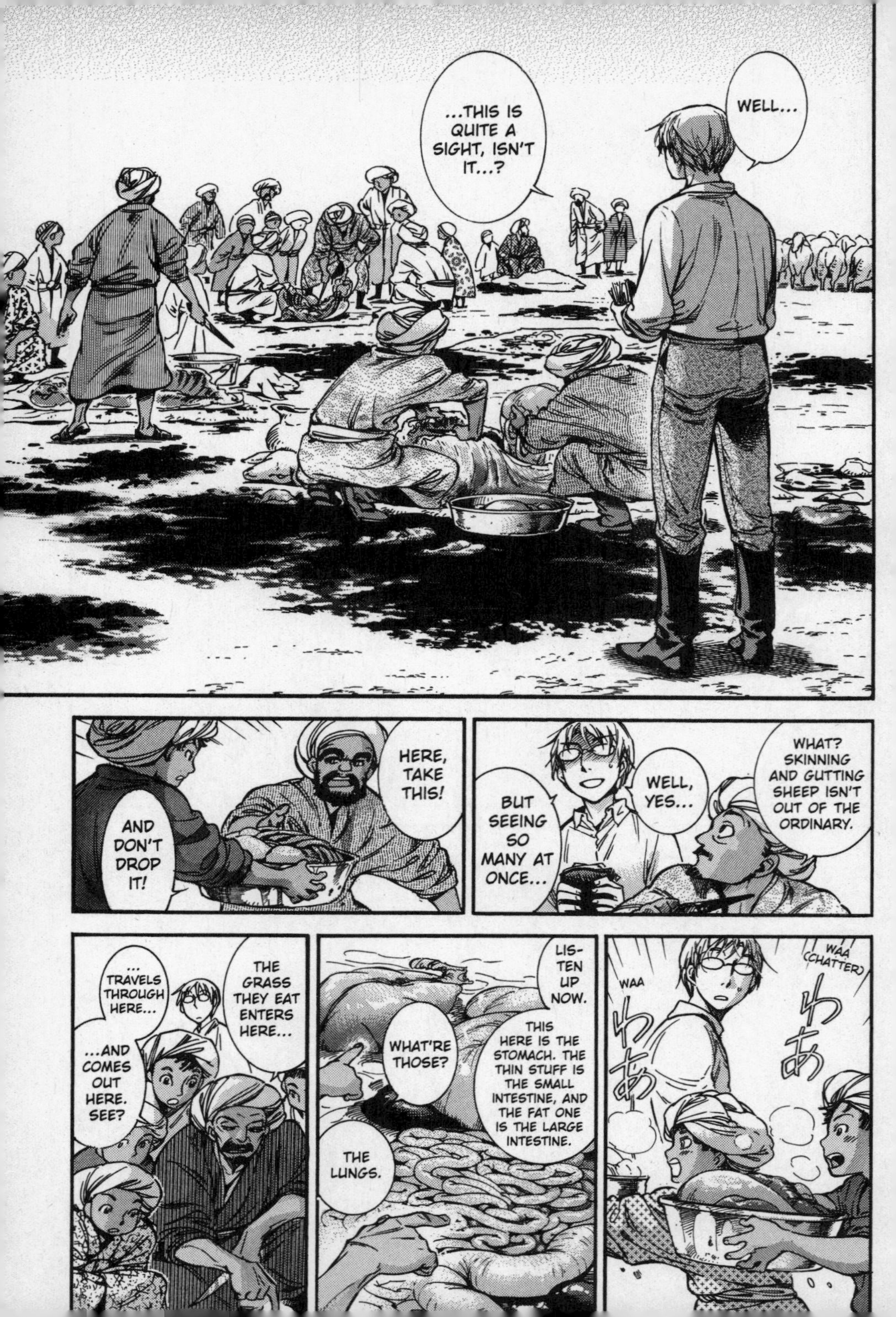
WELL...
...THIS IS QUITE A SIGHT, ISN'T IT...?
WHAT? SKINNING AND GUTTING SHEEP ISN'T OUT OF THE ORDINARY.
WELL, YES...
BUT SEEING SO MANY AT ONCE...
HERE, TAKE THIS!
AND DON'T DROP IT!
WAA (CHATTER)
わあ
WAA
わあ
LIS-TEN UP NOW.
THIS HERE IS THE STOMACH. THE THIN STUFF IS THE SMALL INTESTINE, AND THE FAT ONE IS THE LARGE INTESTINE.
WHAT'RE THOSE?
THE LUNGS.
THE GRASS THEY EAT ENTERS HERE...
... TRAVELS THROUGH HERE...
...AND COMES OUT HERE. SEE?

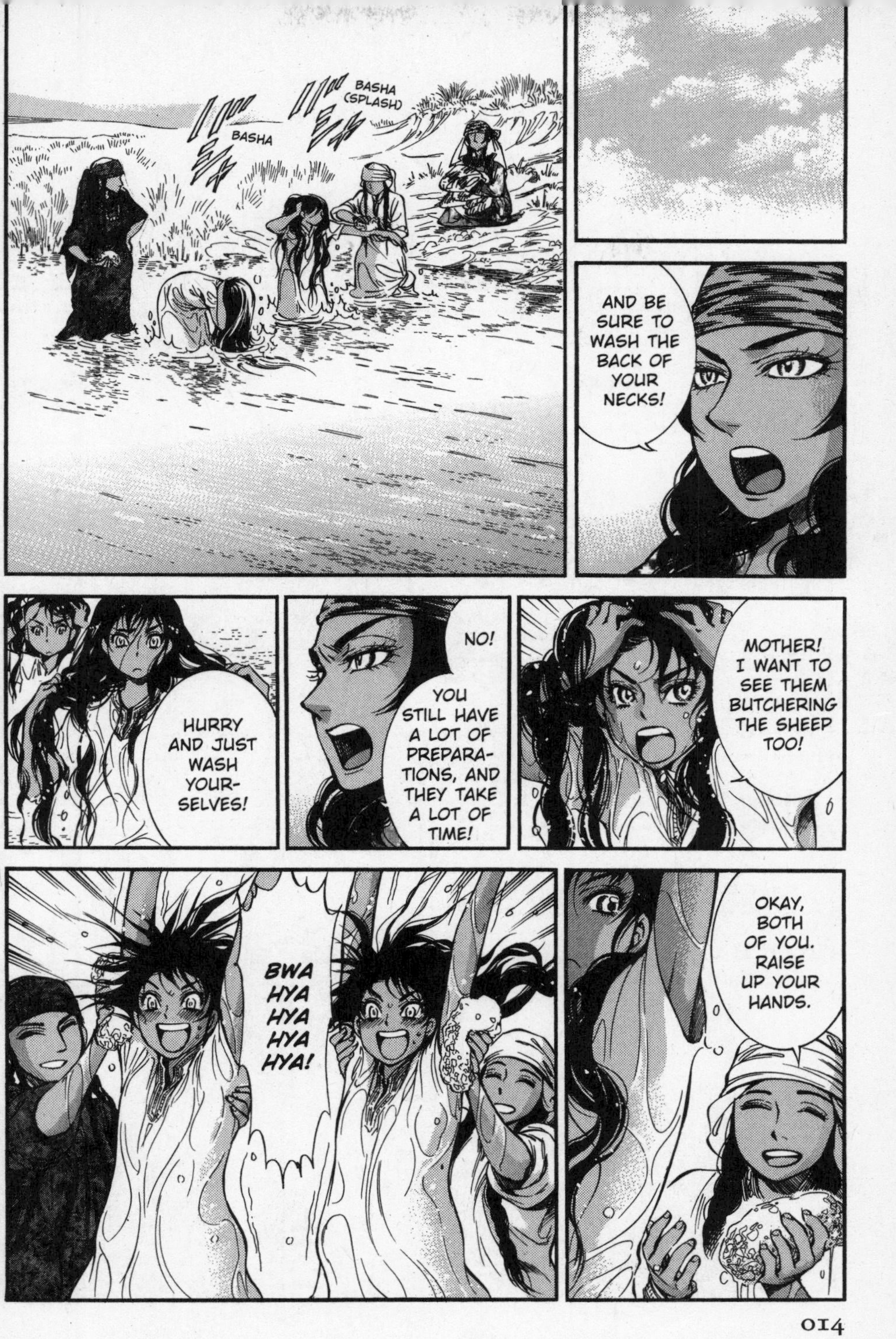
AND BE SURE TO WASH THE BACK OF YOUR NECKS!
BASHA (SPLASH)
BASHA
MOTHER! I WANT TO SEE THEM BUTCHERING THE SHEEP TOO!
NO!
YOU STILL HAVE A LOT OF PREPARATIONS, AND THEY TAKE A LOT OF TIME!
HURRY AND JUST WASH YOURSELVES!
OKAY, BOTH OF YOU. RAISE UP YOUR HANDS.
BWA HYA HYA HYA HYA!

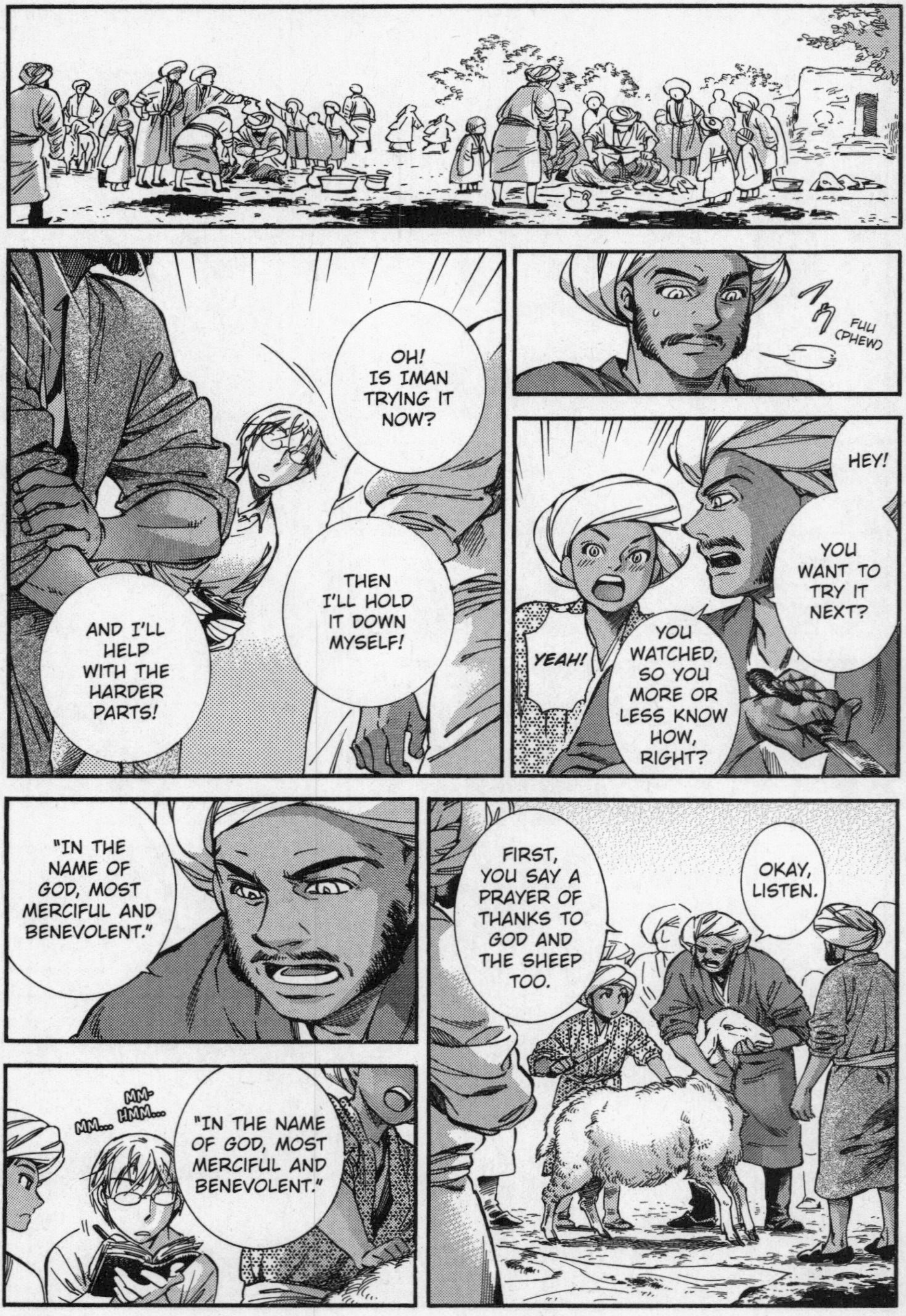
FUU (PHEW)
HEY!
YOU WANT TO TRY IT NEXT?
YOU WATCHED, SO YOU MORE OR LESS KNOW HOW, RIGHT?
YEAH!
OH! IS IMAN TRYING IT NOW?
THEN I'LL HOLD IT DOWN MYSELF!
AND I'LL HELP WITH THE HARDER PARTS!
OKAY, LISTEN.
FIRST, YOU SAY A PRAYER OF THANKS TO GOD AND THE SHEEP TOO.
"IN THE NAME OF GOD, MOST MERCIFUL AND BENEVOLENT."
"IN THE NAME OF GOD, MOST MERCIFUL AND BENEVOLENT."
MM-HMM...
MM...

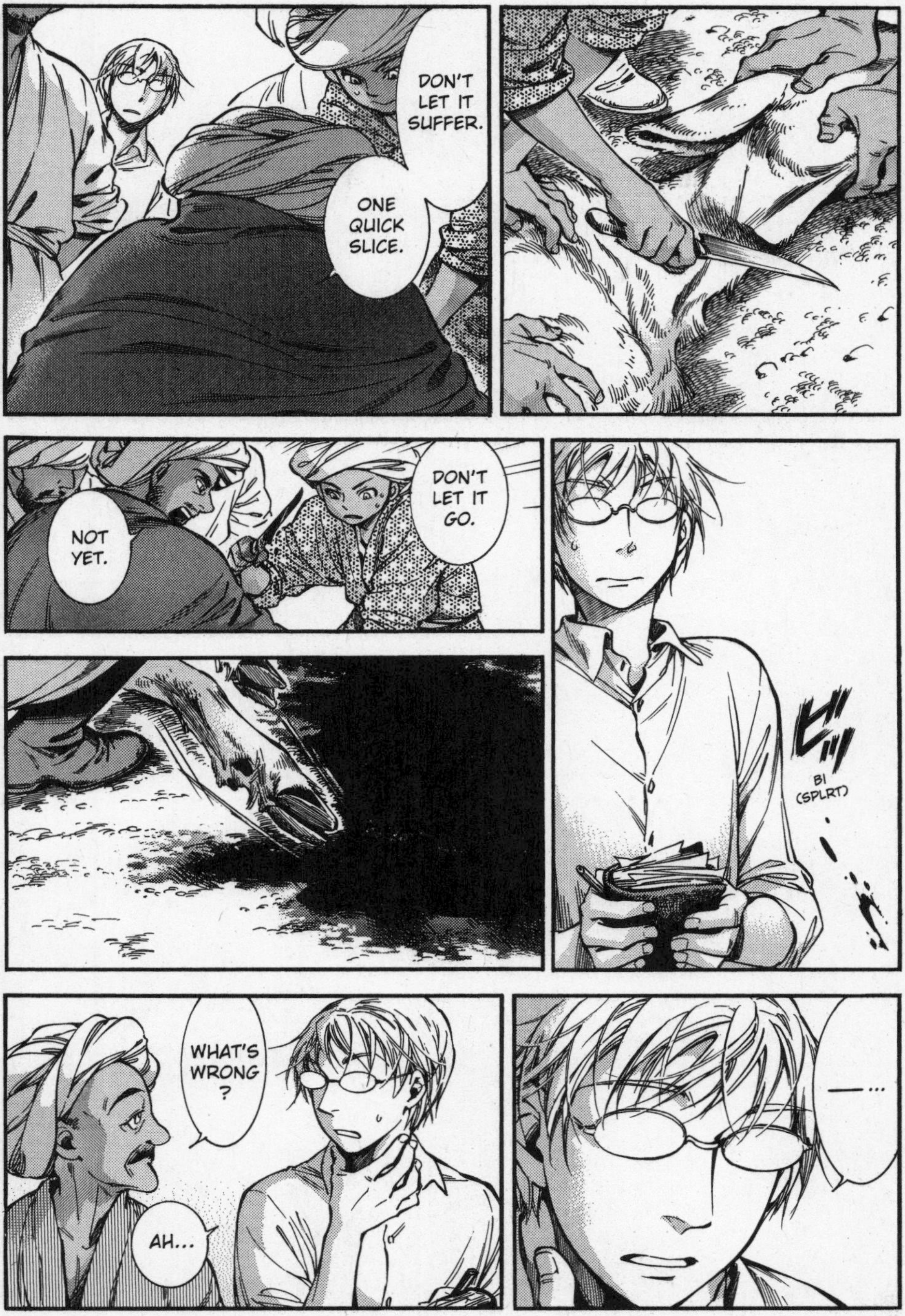
DON'T LET IT SUFFER.
ONE QUICK SLICE.
ビッ
BI (SPLRT)
DON'T LET IT GO.
NOT YET.
—...
WHAT'S WRONG?
AH...

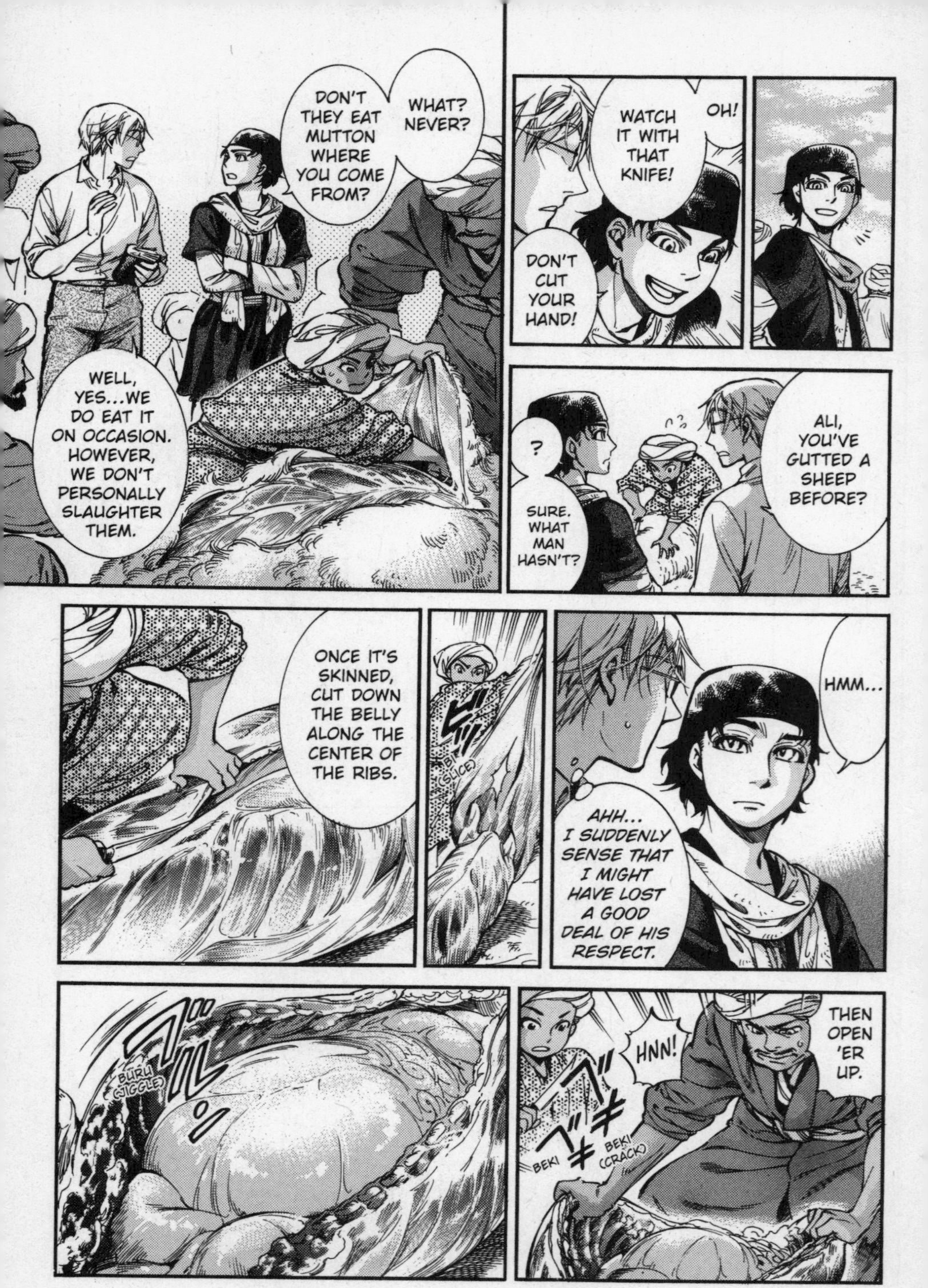
OH!
WATCH IT WITH THAT KNIFE!
DON'T CUT YOUR HAND!
ALI, YOU'VE GUTTED A SHEEP BEFORE?
?
SURE. WHAT MAN HASN'T?
WHAT? NEVER?
DON'T THEY EAT MUTTON WHERE YOU COME FROM?
WELL, YES...WE DO EAT IT ON OCCASION. HOWEVER, WE DON'T PERSONALLY SLAUGHTER THEM.
HMM...
AHH... I SUDDENLY SENSE THAT I MIGHT HAVE LOST A GOOD DEAL OF HIS RESPECT.
BI (SLICE)
ONCE IT'S SKINNED, CUT DOWN THE BELLY ALONG THE CENTER OF THE RIBS.
THEN OPEN 'ER UP.
HNN!
BEKI BEKI (CRACK)
BURU (JIGGLE)

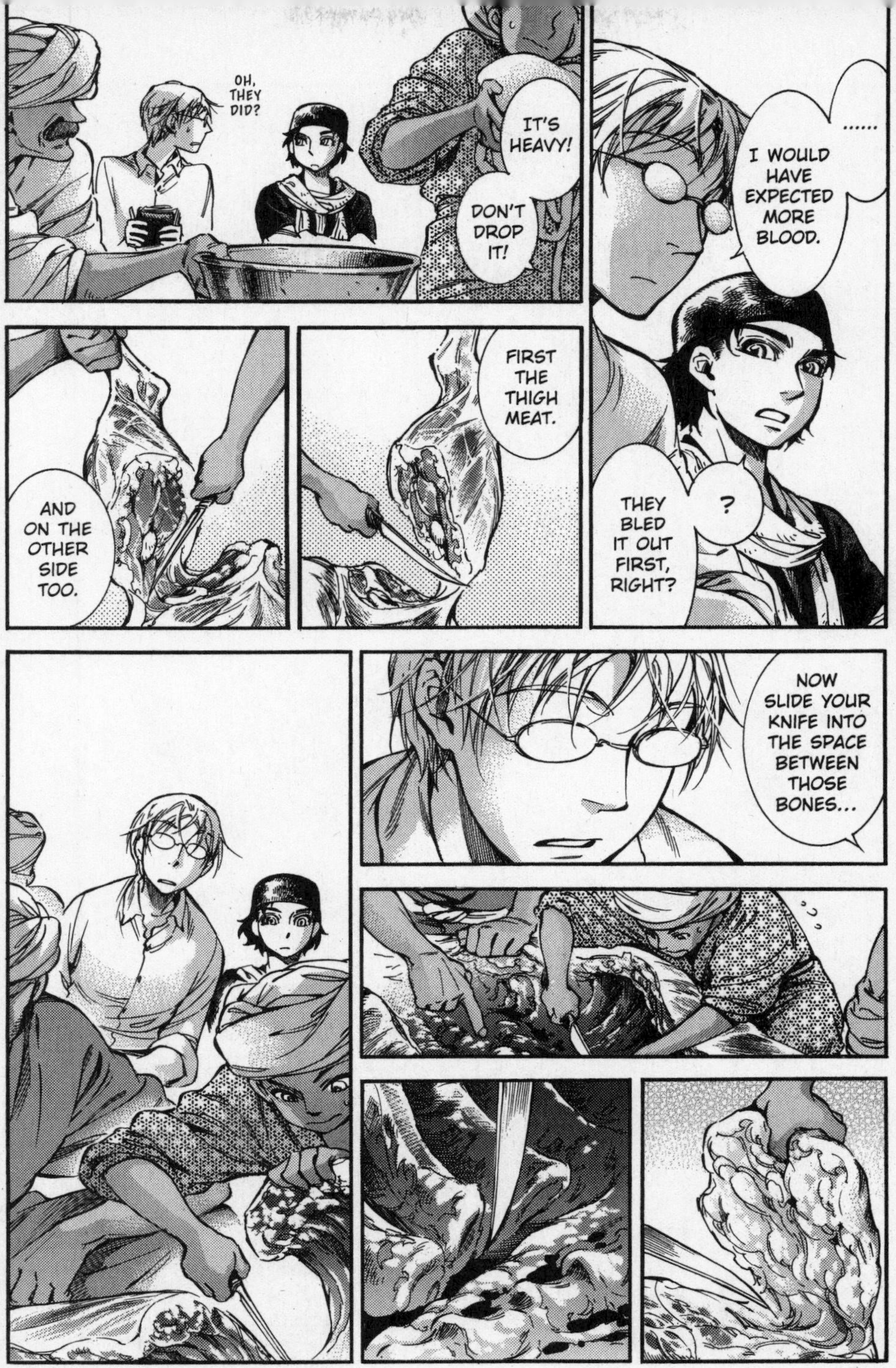
......
I WOULD HAVE EXPECTED MORE BLOOD.
?
THEY BLED IT OUT FIRST, RIGHT?
IT'S HEAVY!
DON'T DROP IT!
OH, THEY DID?
FIRST THE THIGH MEAT.
AND ON THE OTHER SIDE TOO.
NOW SLIDE YOUR KNIFE INTO THE SPACE BETWEEN THOSE BONES...

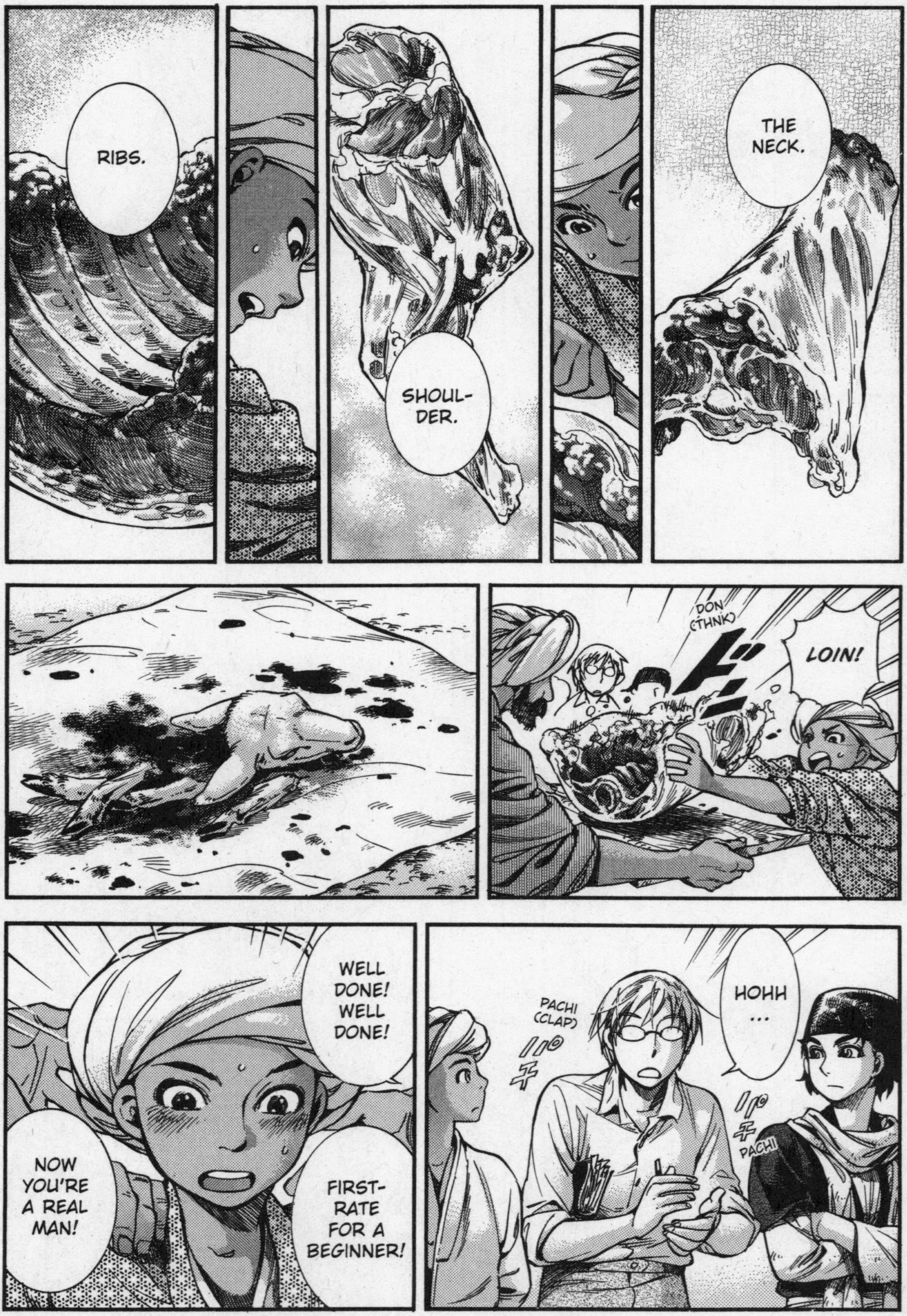
THE NECK.
SHOULDER.
RIBS.
DON (THNK)
LOIN!
HOHH ...
PACHI (CLAP)
PACHI
WELL DONE! WELL DONE!
FIRST-RATE FOR A BEGINNER!
NOW YOU'RE A REAL MAN!

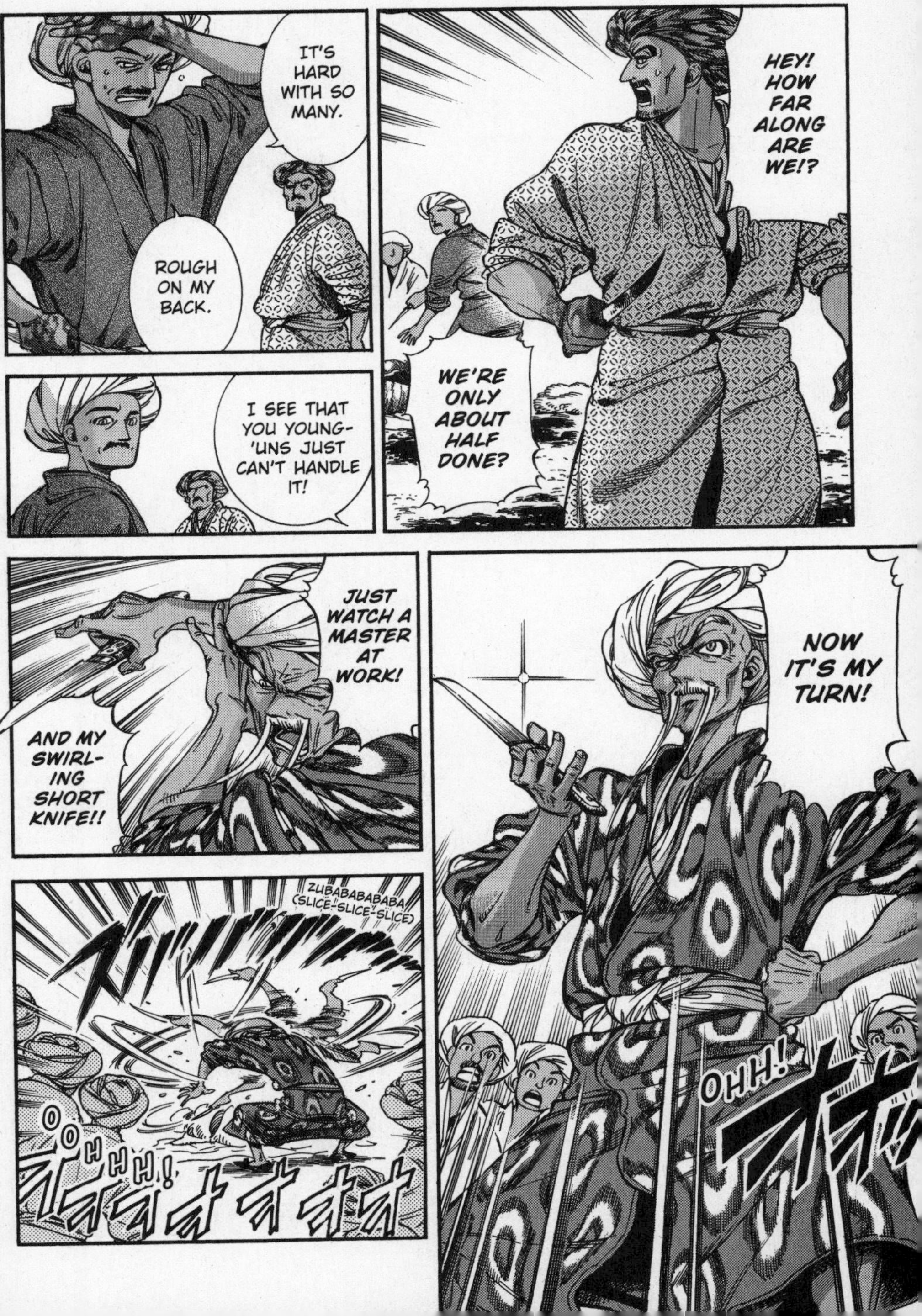
HEY! HOW FAR ALONG ARE WE!?
WE'RE ONLY ABOUT HALF DONE?
IT'S HARD WITH SO MANY.
ROUGH ON MY BACK.
I SEE THAT YOU YOUNG-'UNS JUST CAN'T HANDLE IT!
NOW IT'S MY TURN!
OHH!
JUST WATCH A MASTER AT WORK!
AND MY SWIRLING SHORT KNIFE!!
ZUBABABABABA (SLICE-SLICE-SLICE)
OOHHHH!

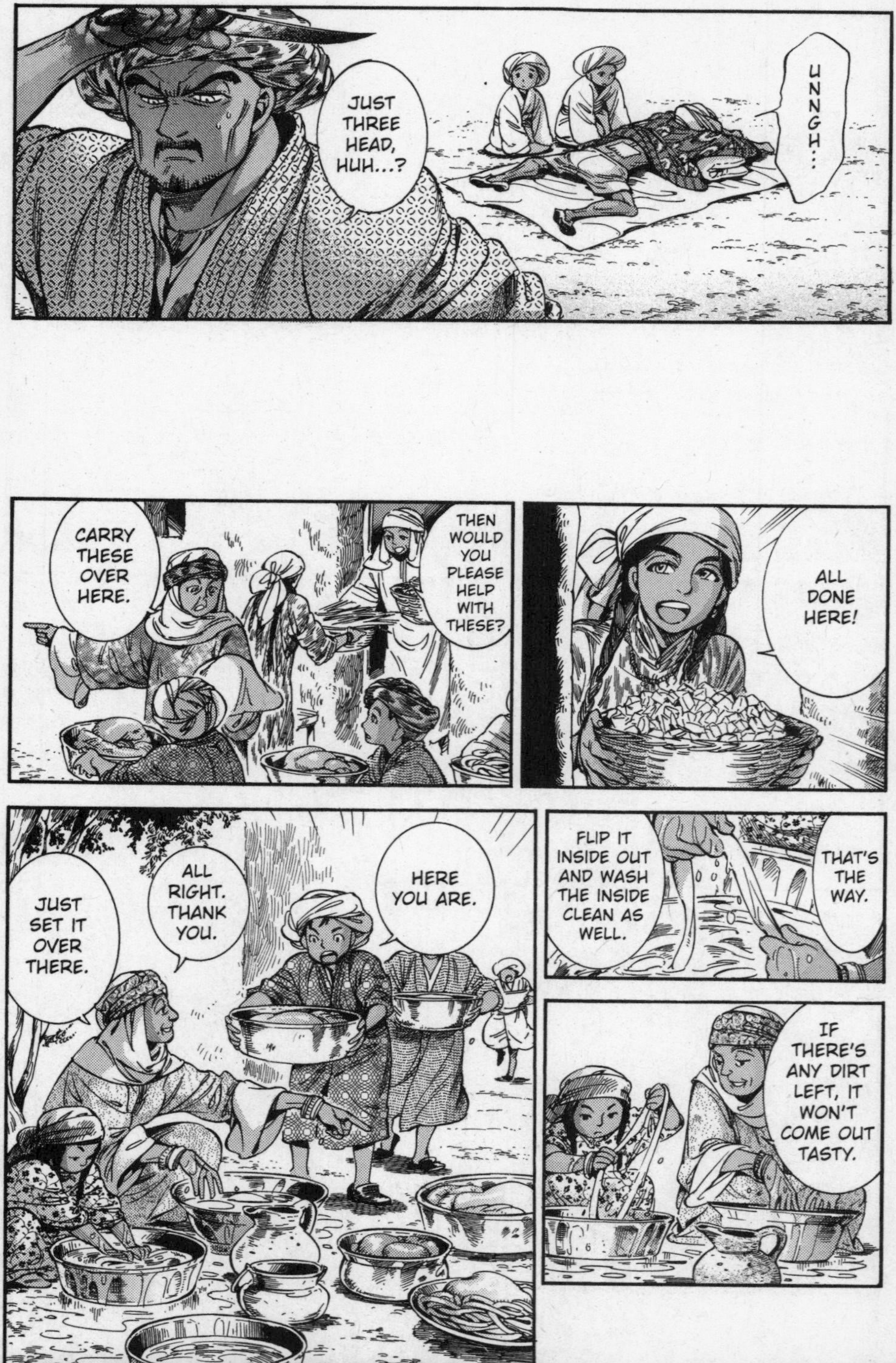
UNNGH...
JUST THREE HEAD, HUH...?
ALL DONE HERE!
THEN WOULD YOU PLEASE HELP WITH THESE?
CARRY THESE OVER HERE.
THAT'S THE WAY.
FLIP IT INSIDE OUT AND WASH THE INSIDE CLEAN AS WELL.
IF THERE'S ANY DIRT LEFT, IT WON'T COME OUT TASTY.
HERE YOU ARE.
ALL RIGHT. THANK YOU.
JUST SET IT OVER THERE.

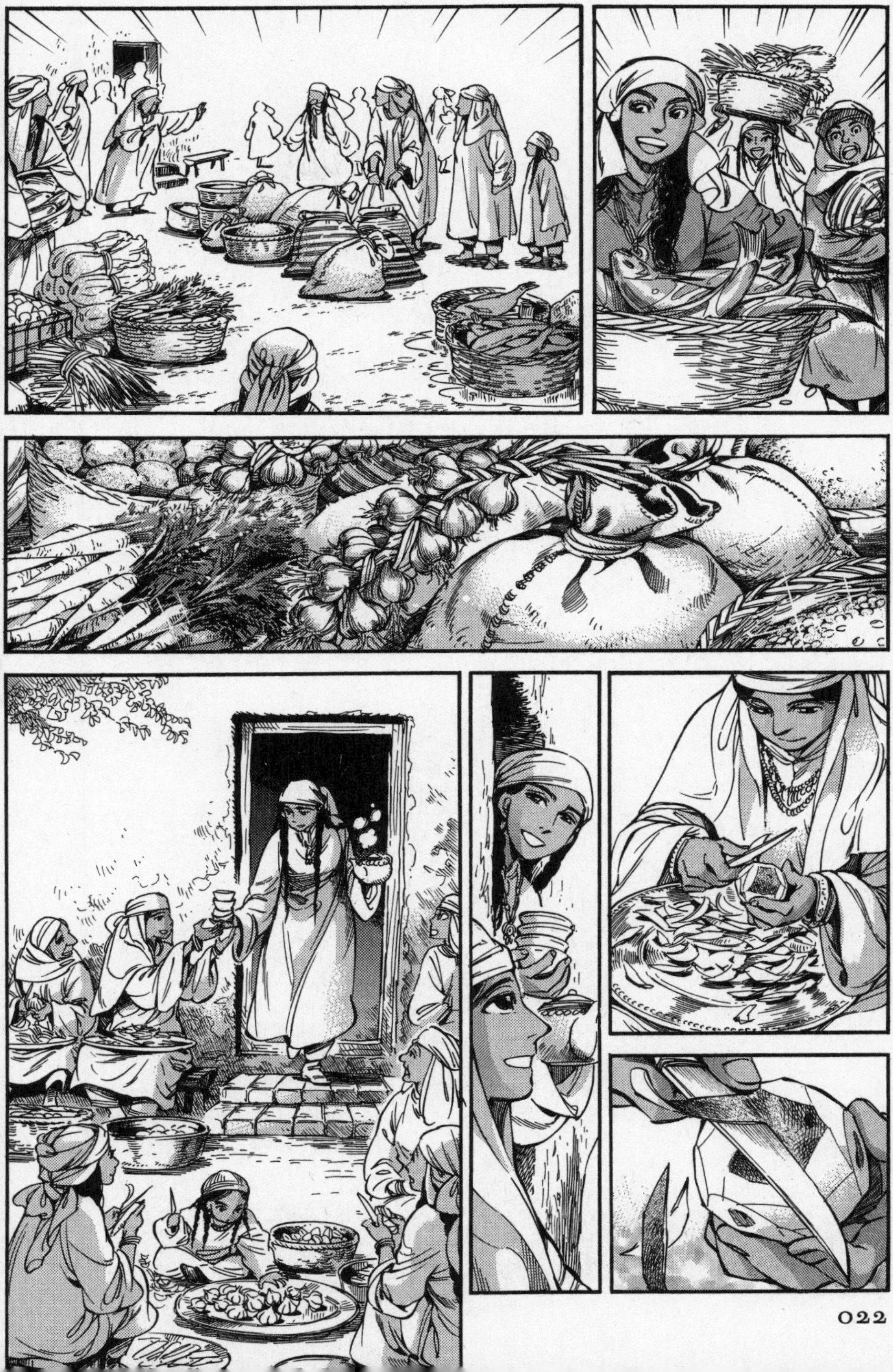

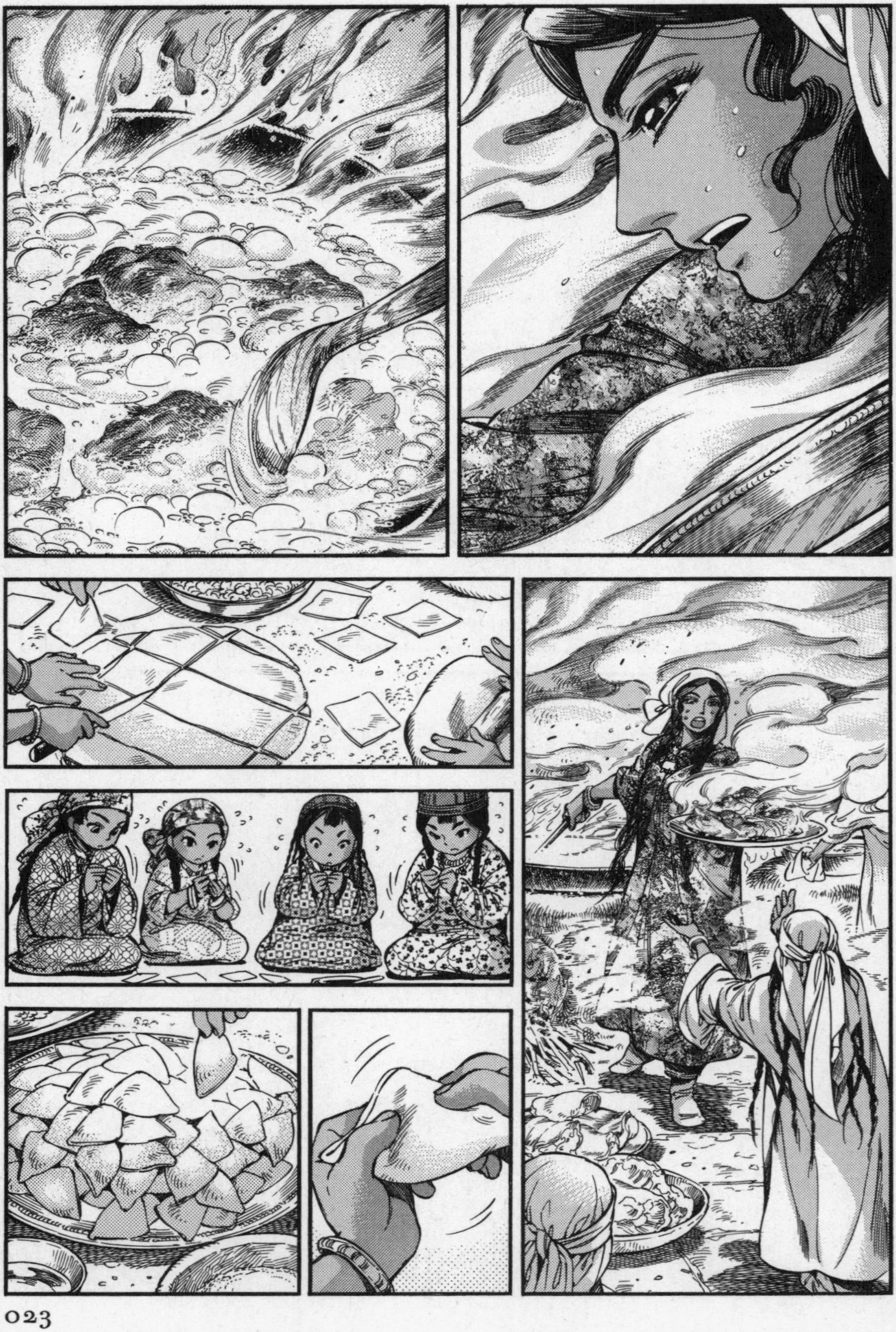

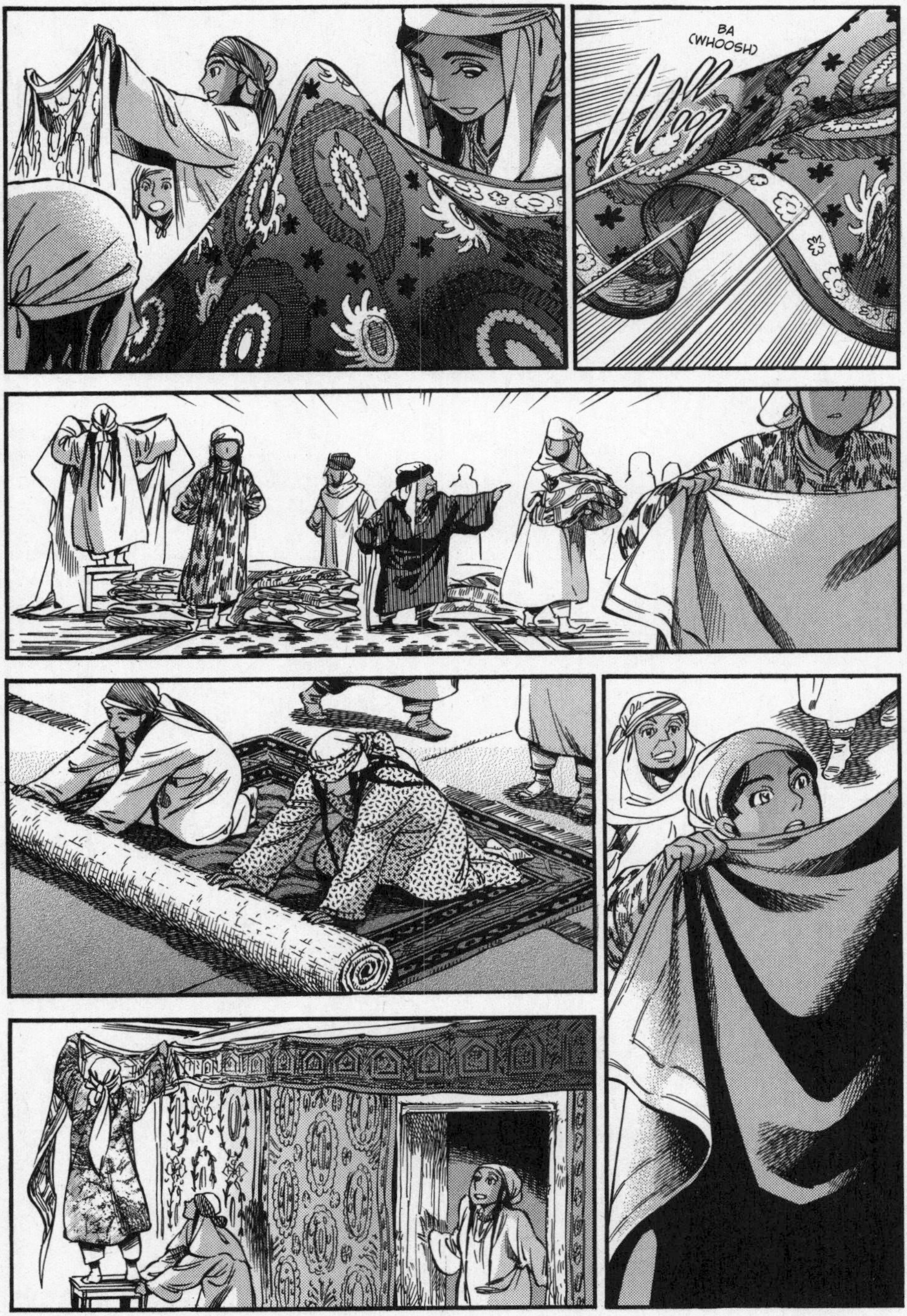
BA
(WHOOSH)

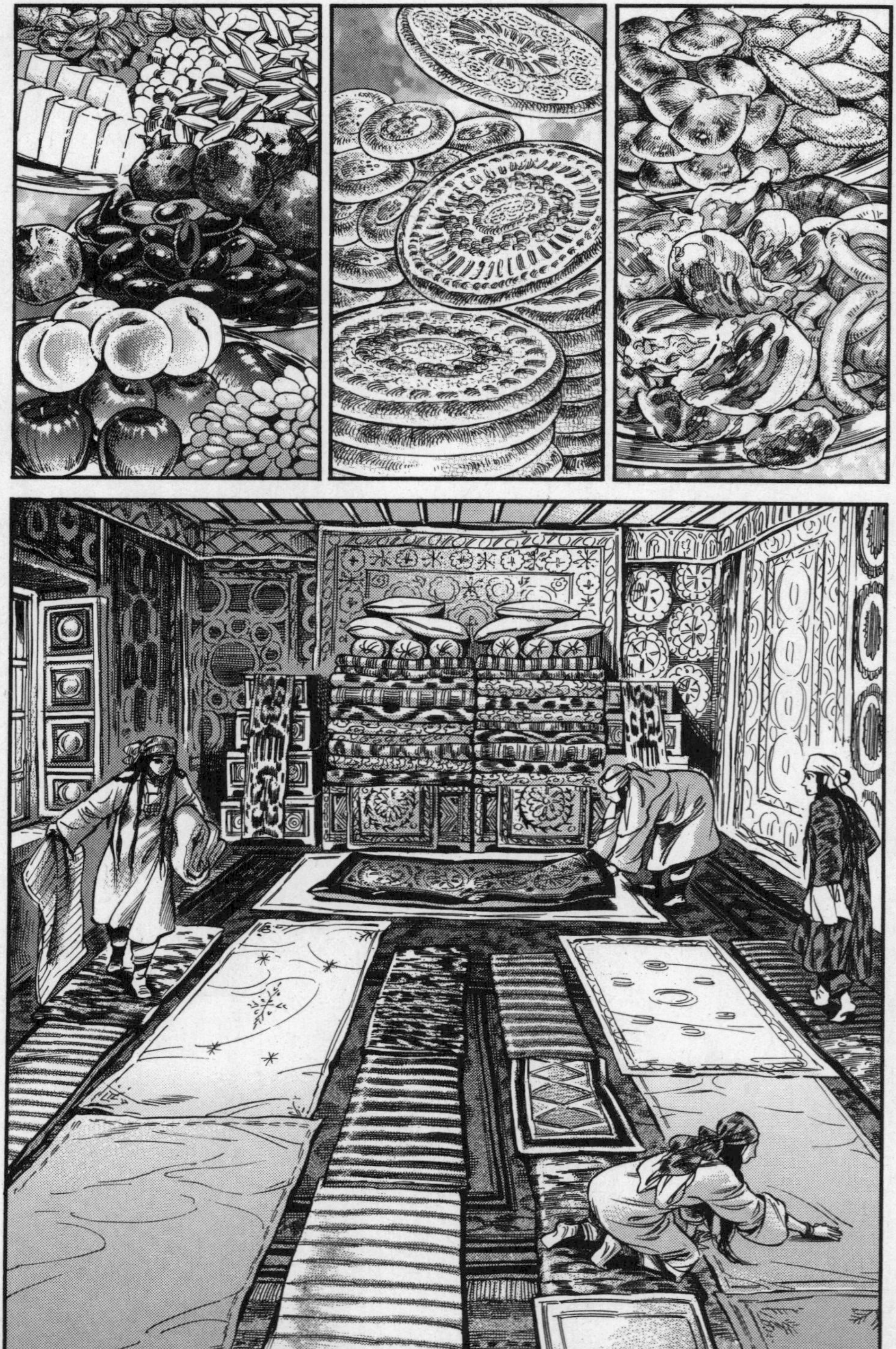

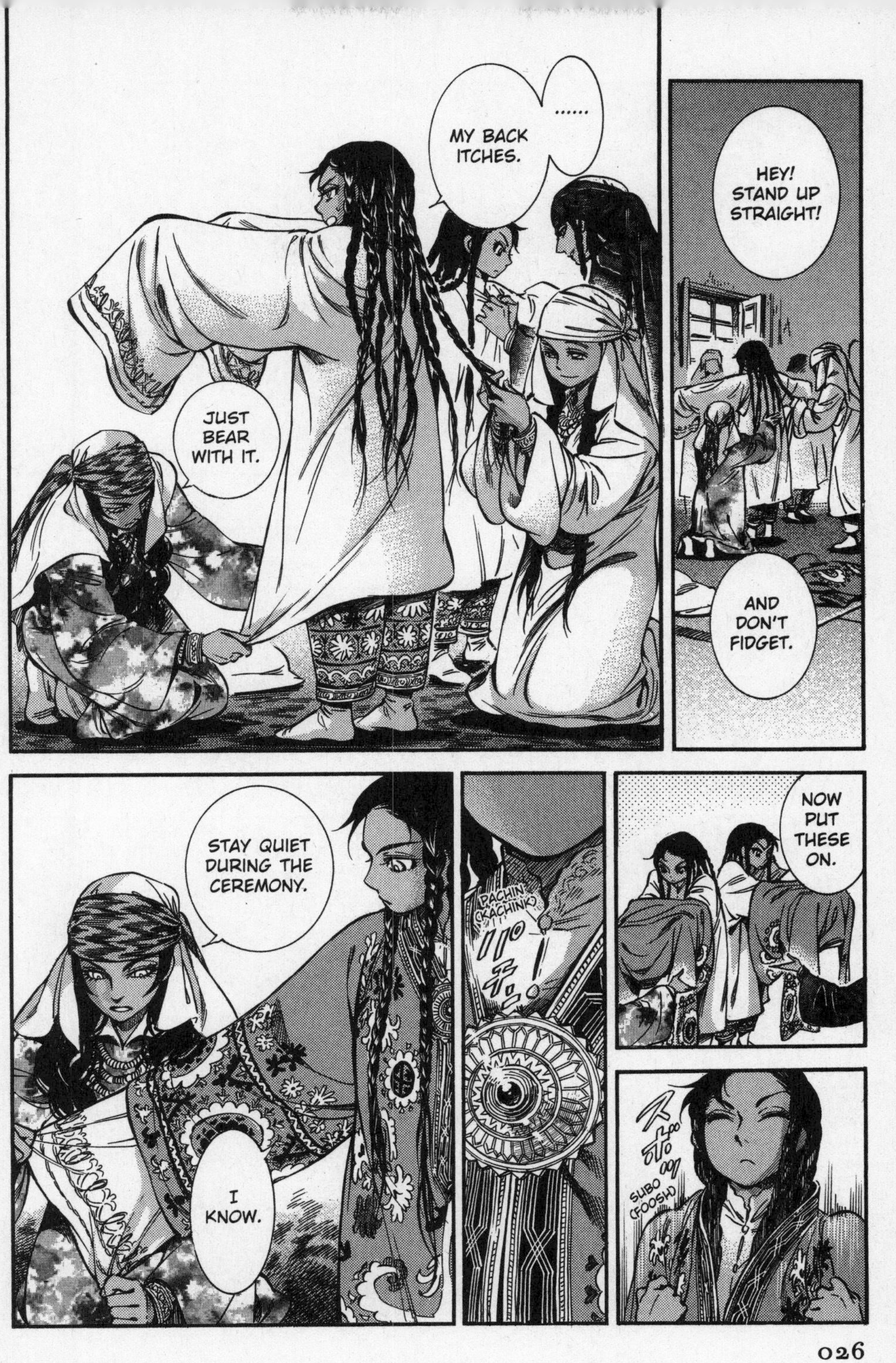
HEY! STAND UP STRAIGHT!
AND DON'T FIDGET.
MY BACK ITCHES.
......
JUST BEAR WITH IT.
NOW PUT THESE ON.
SUBO (FOOSH)
PACHIN (KACHINK)
STAY QUIET DURING THE CEREMONY.
I KNOW.

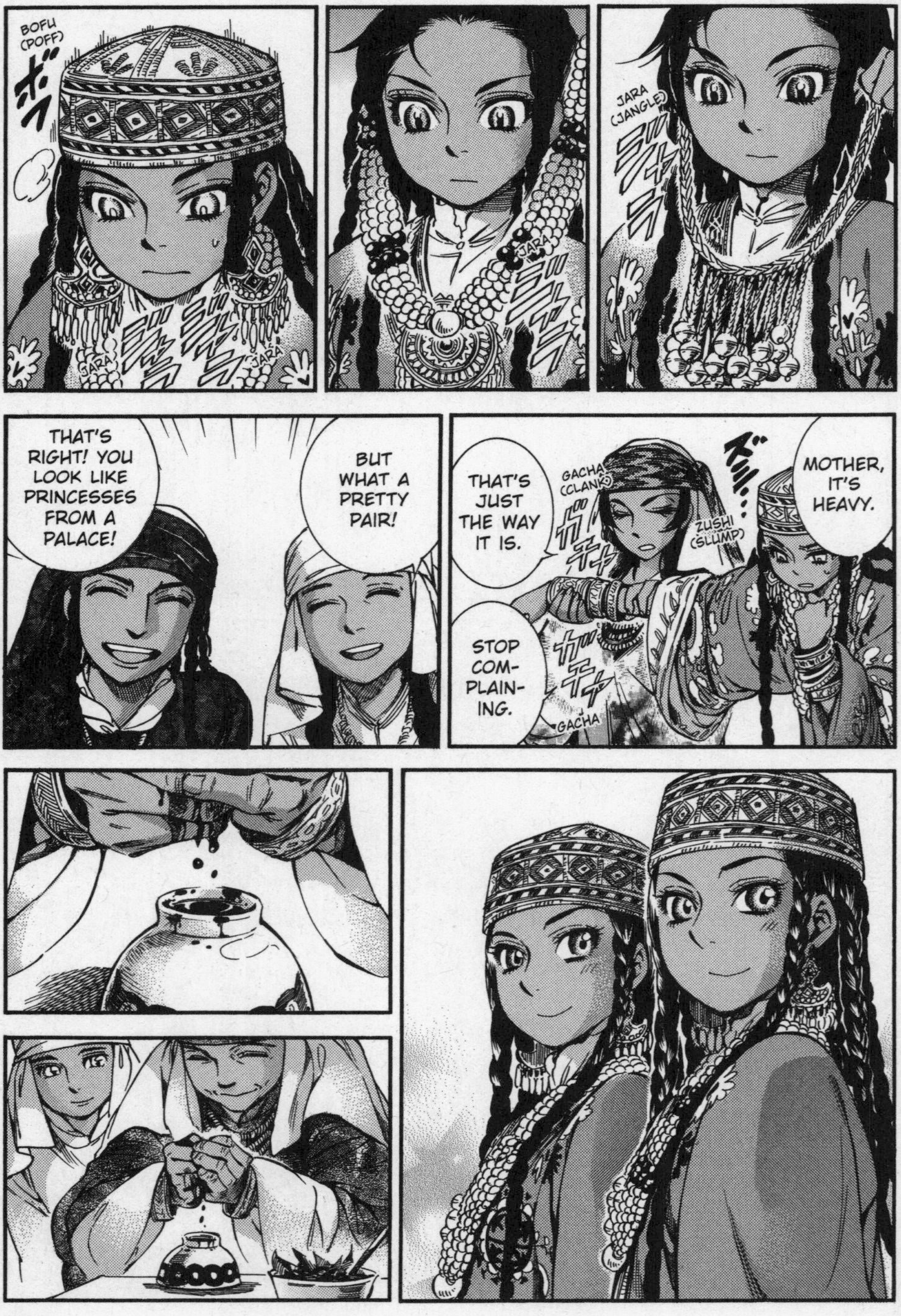
JARA (JANGLE)
JARA
BOFU (POFF)
JARA
JARA
MOTHER, IT'S HEAVY.
ZUSHI (SLUMP)
GACHA (CLANK)
THAT'S JUST THE WAY IT IS.
STOP COMPLAINING.
GACHA
BUT WHAT A PRETTY PAIR!
THAT'S RIGHT! YOU LOOK LIKE PRINCESSES FROM A PALACE!

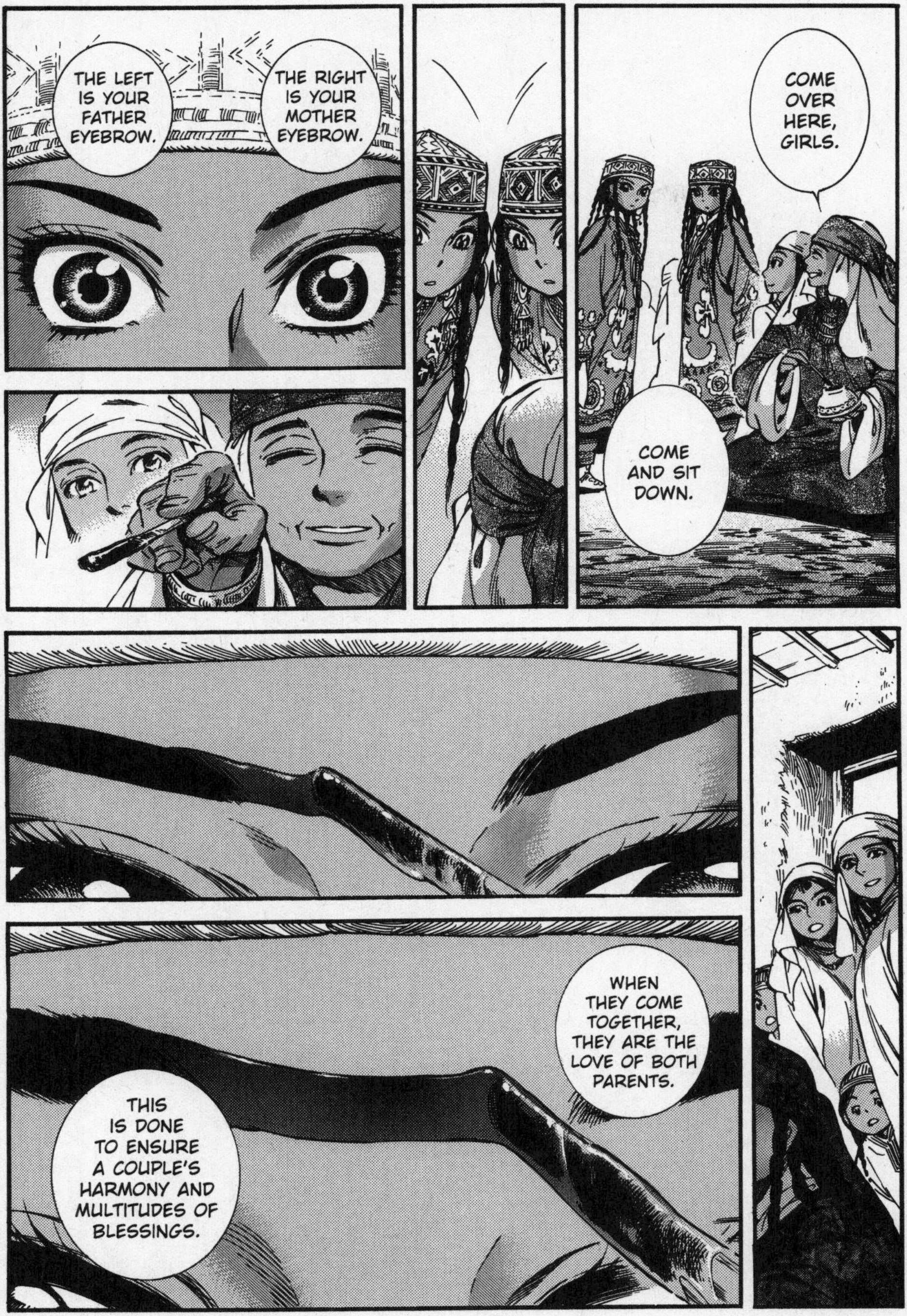
COME OVER HERE, GIRLS.
COME AND SIT DOWN.
THE RIGHT IS YOUR MOTHER EYEBROW.
THE LEFT IS YOUR FATHER EYEBROW.
WHEN THEY COME TOGETHER, THEY ARE THE LOVE OF BOTH PARENTS.
THIS IS DONE TO ENSURE A COUPLE'S HARMONY AND MULTITUDES OF BLESSINGS.

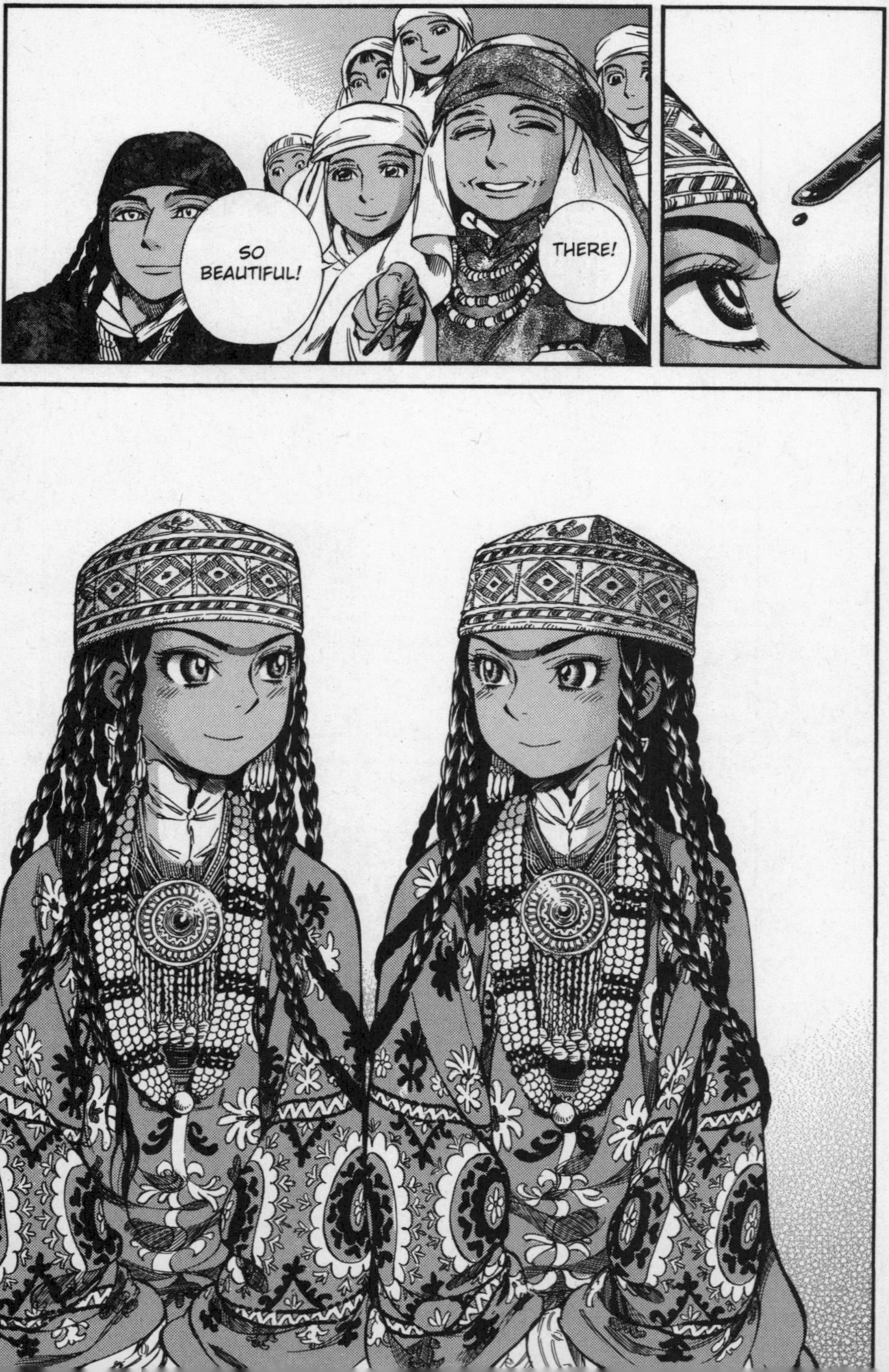
THERE!
SO BEAUTIFUL!

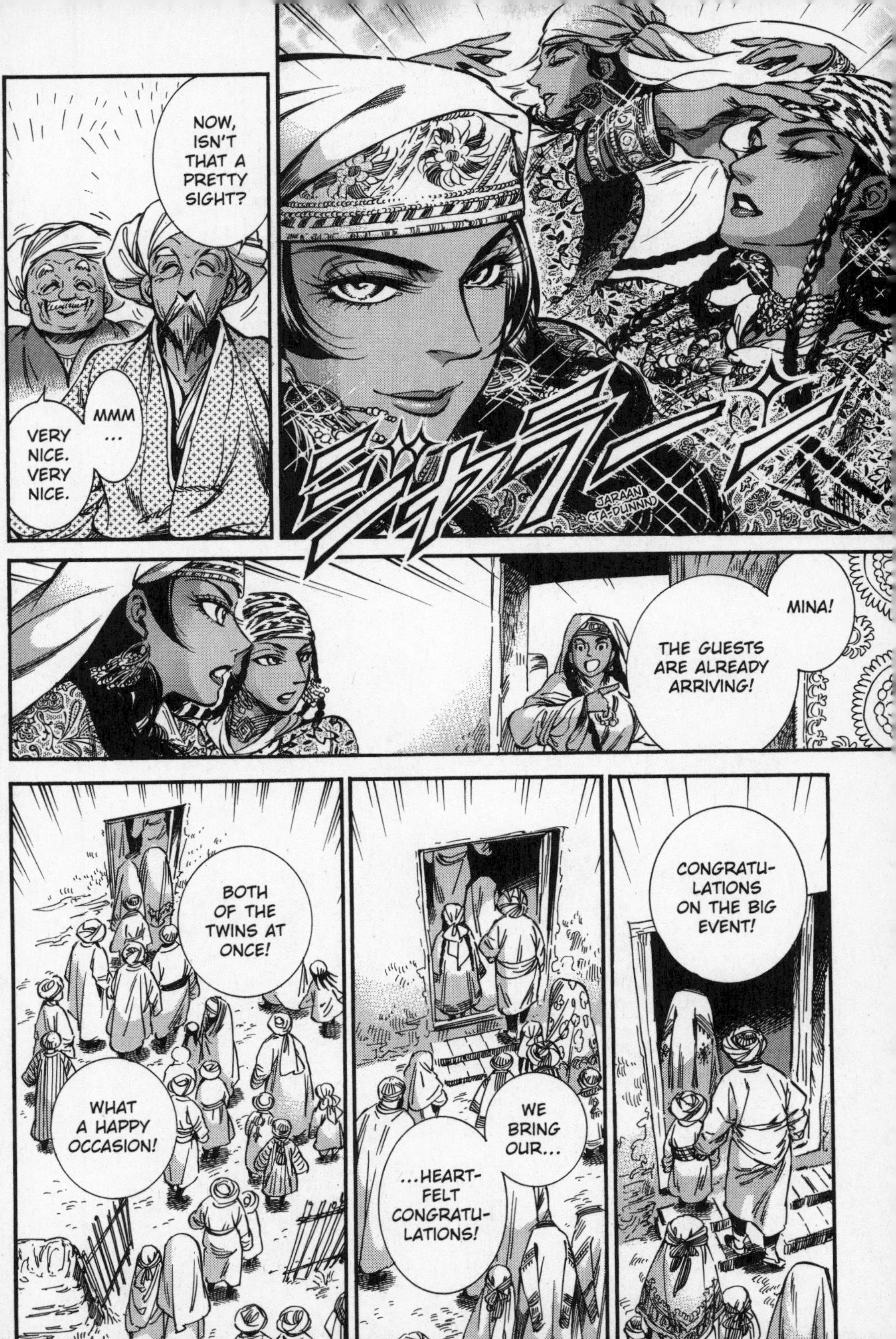
JARAAN (TA-DUNNN)
NOW, ISN'T THAT A PRETTY SIGHT?
MMM...
VERY NICE. VERY NICE.
MINA!
THE GUESTS ARE ALREADY ARRIVING!
CONGRATULATIONS ON THE BIG EVENT!
WE BRING OUR...
...HEARTFELT CONGRATULATIONS!
BOTH OF THE TWINS AT ONCE!
WHAT A HAPPY OCCASION!

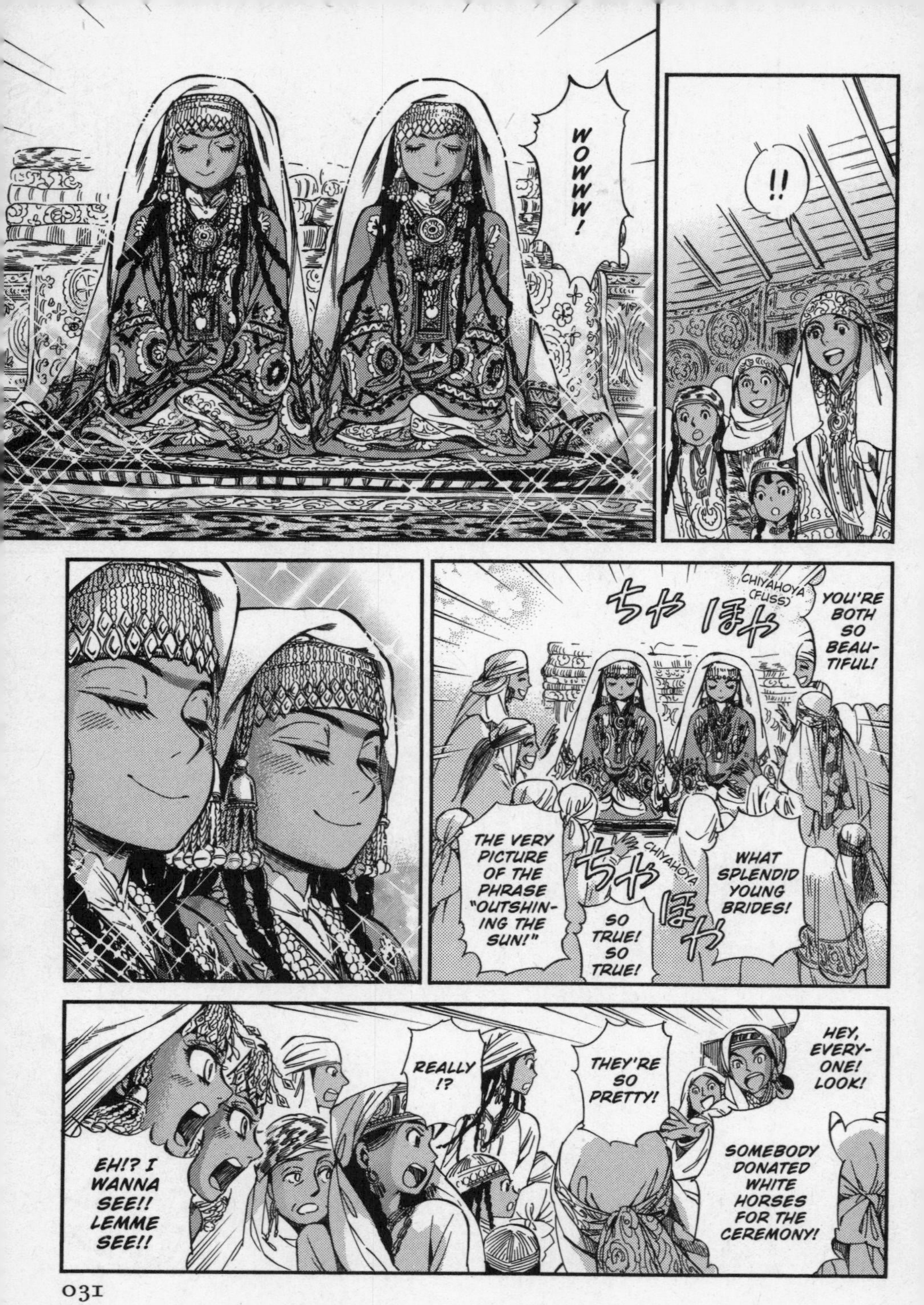
!!
WOWWW!
ちやほや
CHIYAHOYA (FUSS)
YOU'RE BOTH SO BEAUTIFUL!
WHAT SPLENDID YOUNG BRIDES!
ちやほや
CHIYAHOYA
THE VERY PICTURE OF THE PHRASE "OUTSHINING THE SUN!"
SO TRUE! SO TRUE!
HEY, EVERYONE! LOOK!
SOMEBODY DONATED WHITE HORSES FOR THE CEREMONY!
THEY'RE SO PRETTY!
REALLY!?
EH!? I WANNA SEE!! LEMME SEE!!

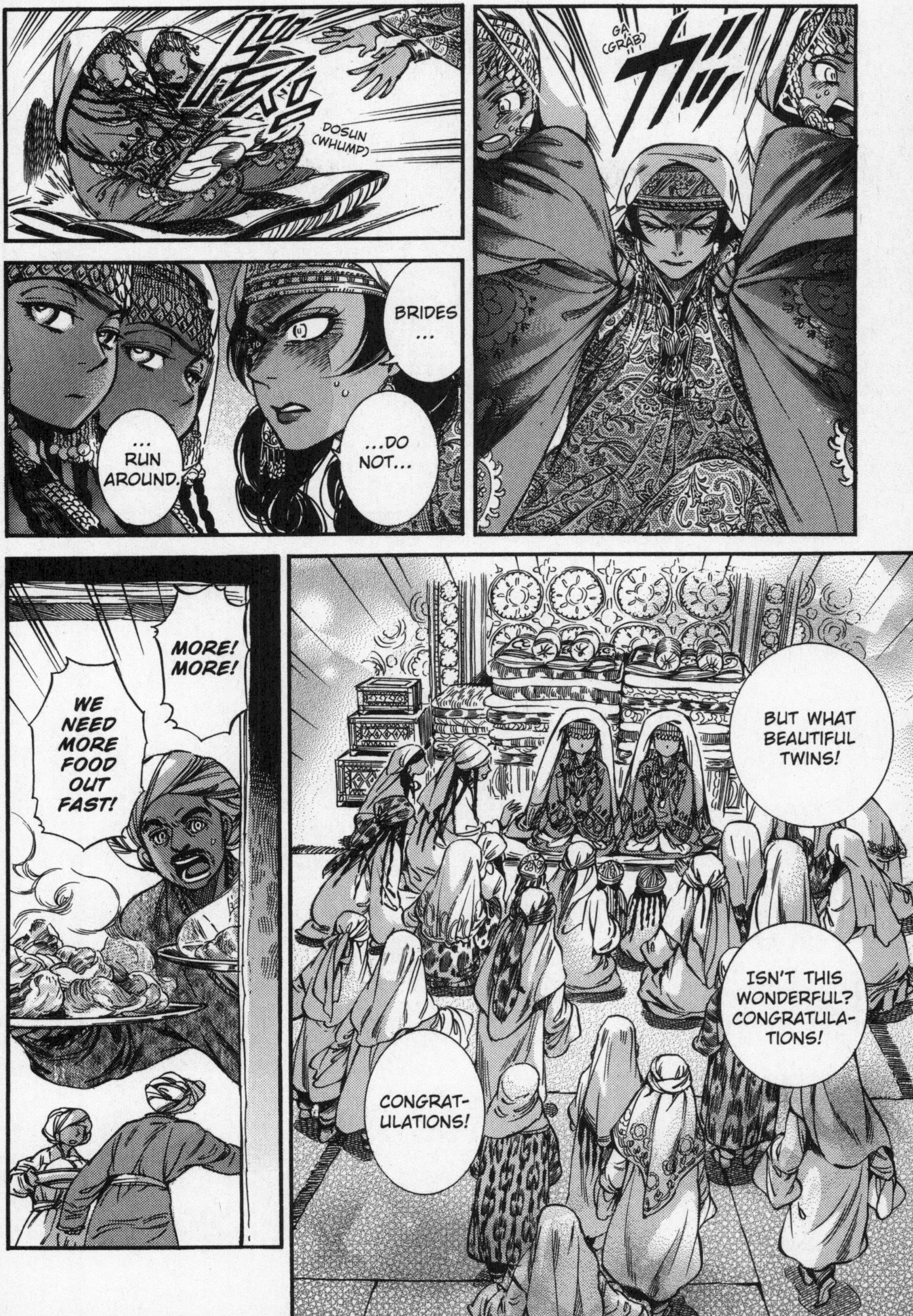
GA (GRAB)
DOSUN (WHUMP)
BRIDES ...
...DO NOT...
... RUN AROUND.
BUT WHAT BEAUTIFUL TWINS!
ISN'T THIS WONDERFUL? CONGRATULATIONS!
CONGRAT-ULATIONS!
MORE! MORE!
WE NEED MORE FOOD OUT FAST!

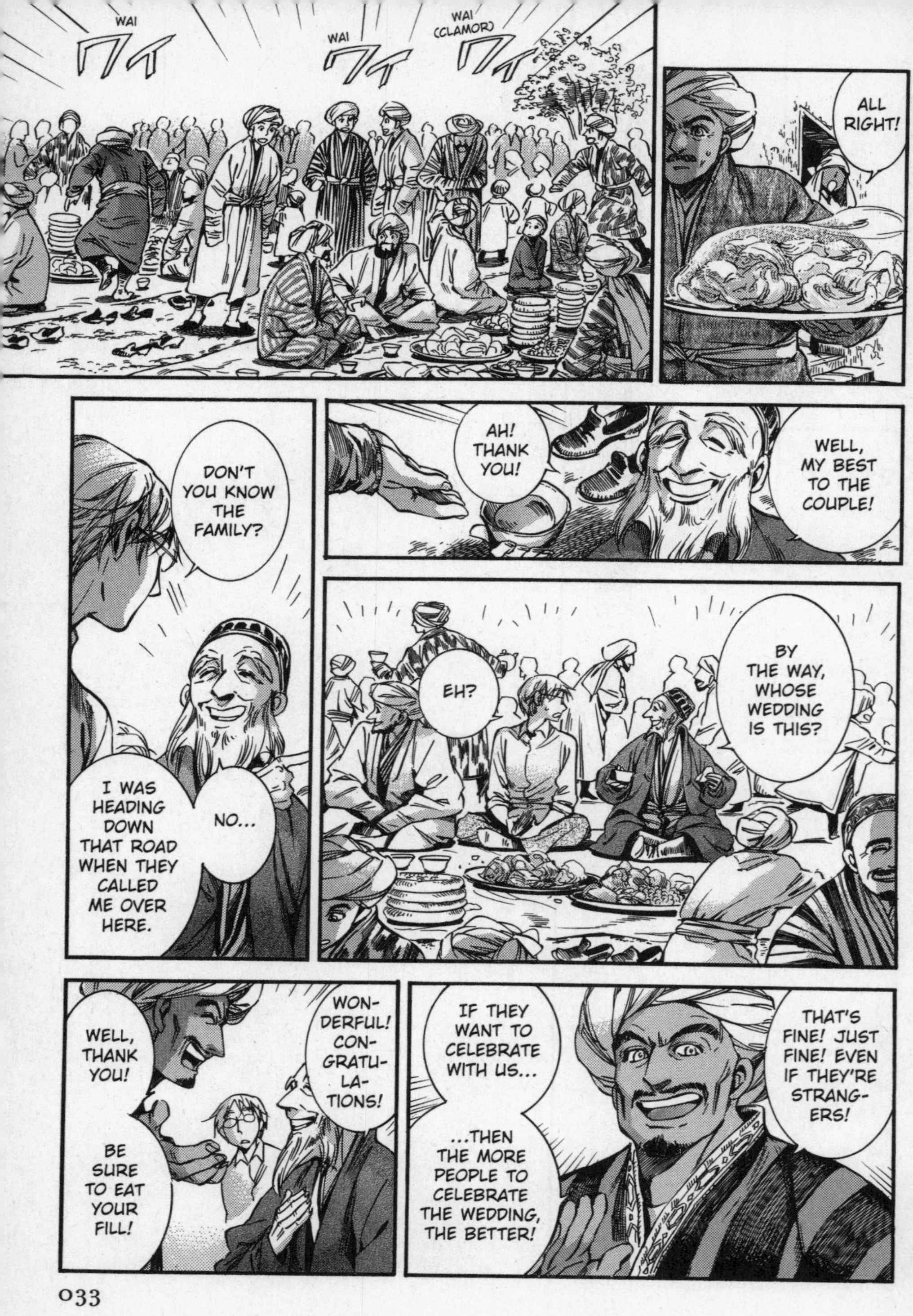
ALL RIGHT!
WAI
ワイ
WAI
ワイ
WAI (CLAMOR)
ワイ
WELL, MY BEST TO THE COUPLE!
AH! THANK YOU!
BY THE WAY, WHOSE WEDDING IS THIS?
EH?
DON'T YOU KNOW THE FAMILY?
NO...
I WAS HEADING DOWN THAT ROAD WHEN THEY CALLED ME OVER HERE.
THAT'S FINE! JUST FINE! EVEN IF THEY'RE STRANGERS!
IF THEY WANT TO CELEBRATE WITH US...
...THEN THE MORE PEOPLE TO CELEBRATE THE WEDDING, THE BETTER!
WON-DERFUL! CON-GRATU-LA-TIONS!
WELL, THANK YOU!
BE SURE TO EAT YOUR FILL!

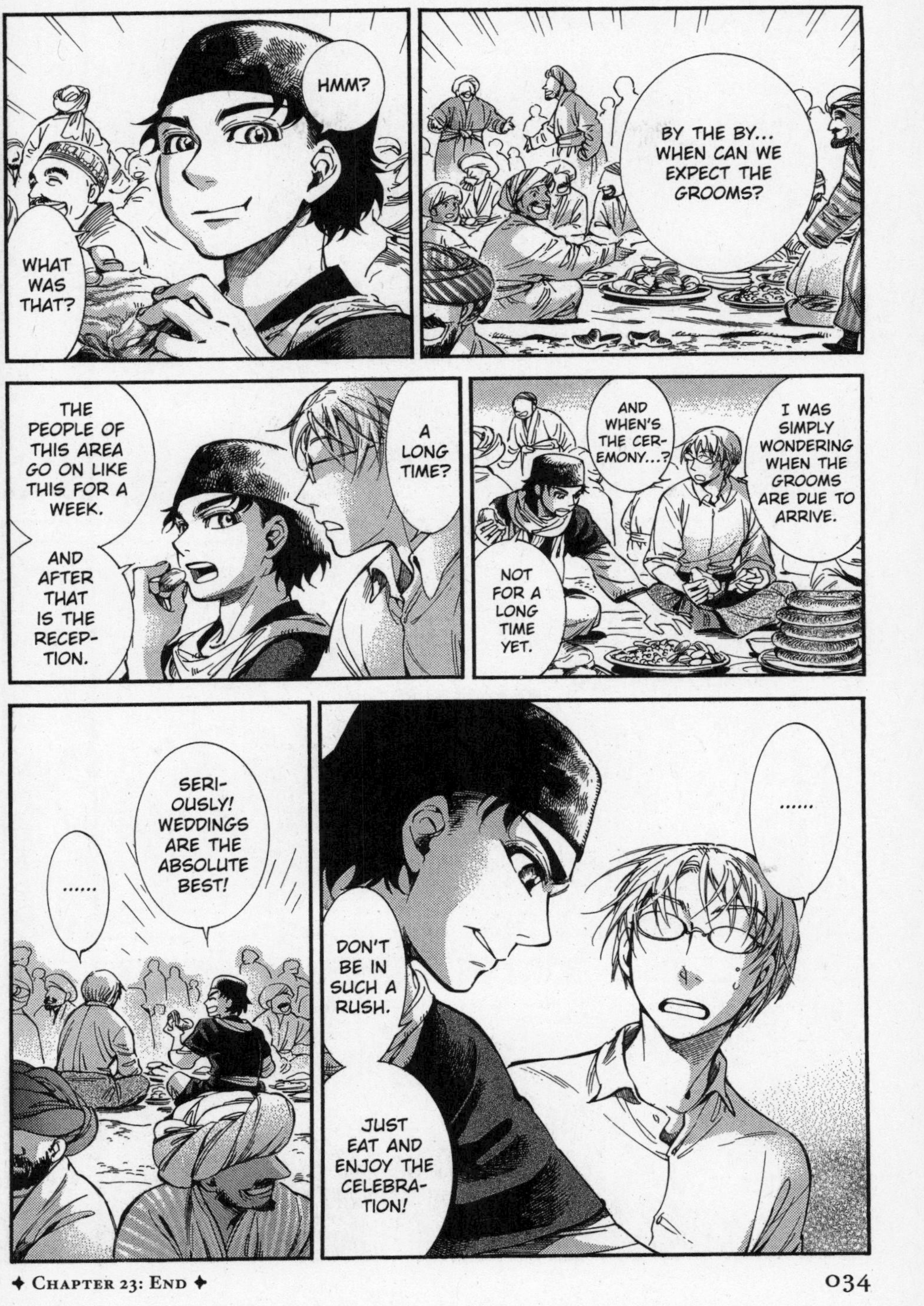
BY THE BY... WHEN CAN WE EXPECT THE GROOMS?
HMM?
WHAT WAS THAT?
I WAS SIMPLY WONDERING WHEN THE GROOMS ARE DUE TO ARRIVE.
AND WHEN'S THE CER-EMONY...?
NOT FOR A LONG TIME YET.
A LONG TIME?
THE PEOPLE OF THIS AREA GO ON LIKE THIS FOR A WEEK.
AND AFTER THAT IS THE RECEP-TION.
......
DON'T BE IN SUCH A RUSH.
JUST EAT AND ENJOY THE CELEBRA-TION!
SERI-OUSLY! WEDDINGS ARE THE ABSOLUTE BEST!
......

✦ Chapter 23: End ✦

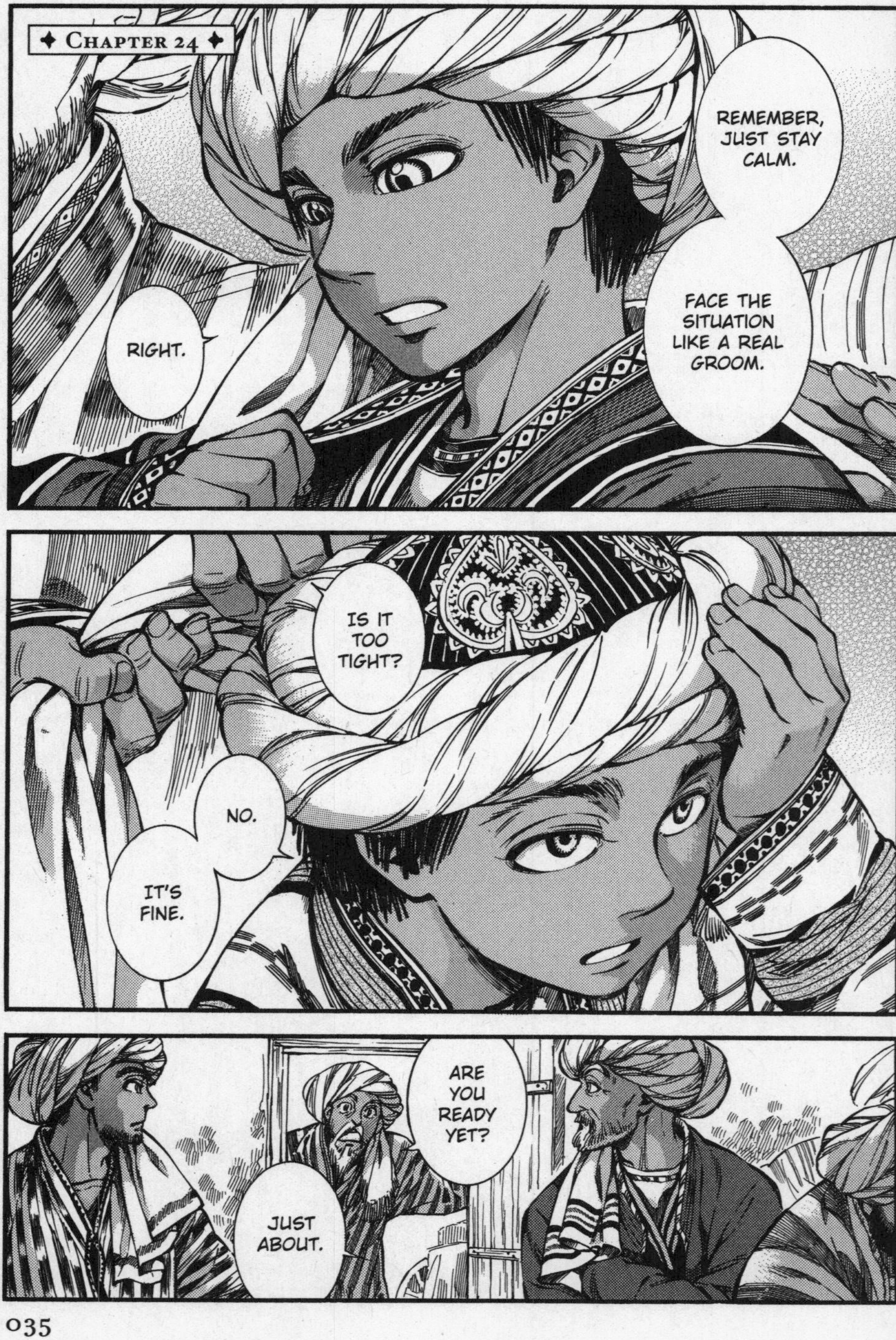
Chapter 24
REMEMBER, JUST STAY CALM.
FACE THE SITUATION LIKE A REAL GROOM.
RIGHT.
IS IT TOO TIGHT?
NO.
IT'S FINE.
ARE YOU READY YET?
JUST ABOUT.

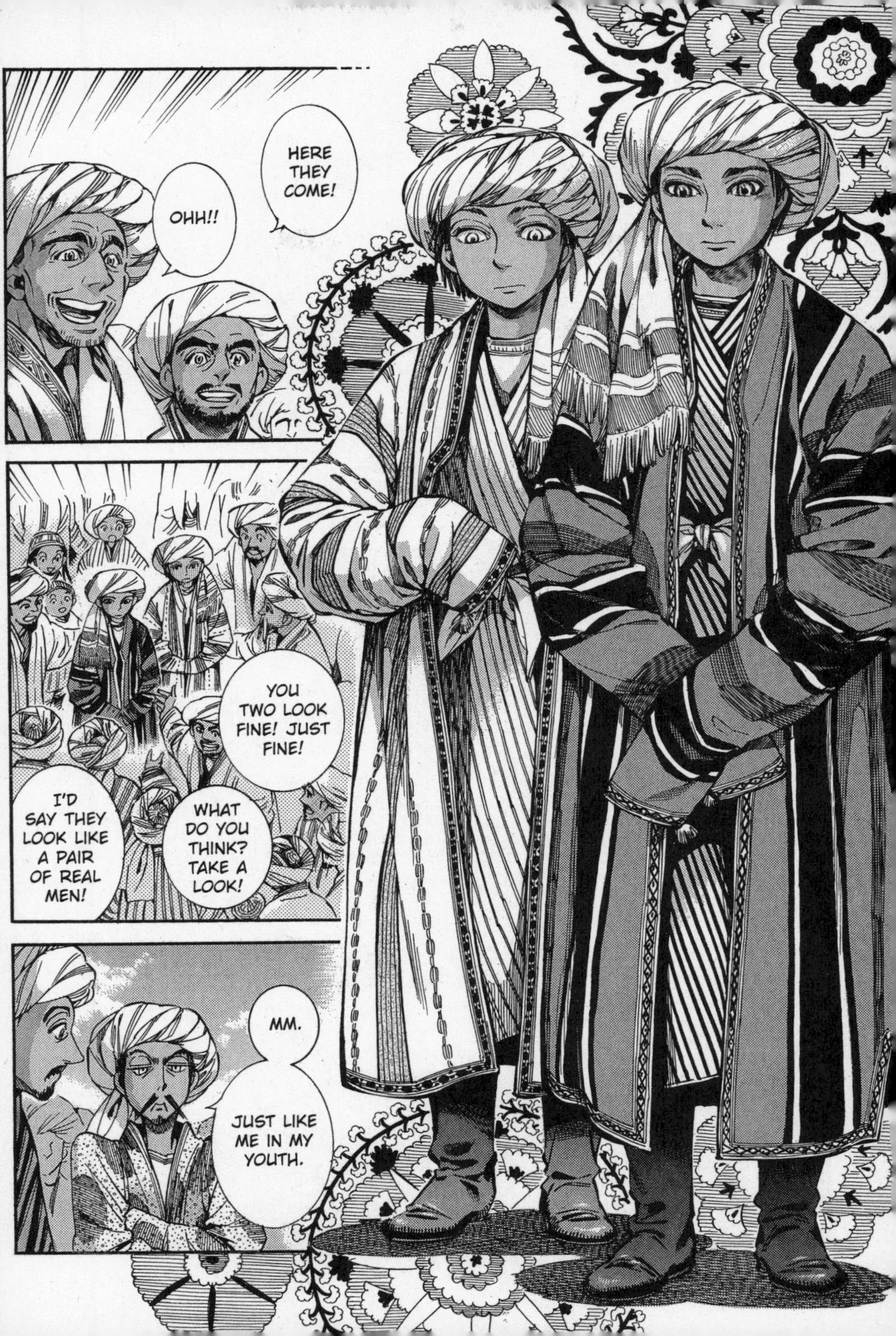
HERE THEY COME!
OHH!!
YOU TWO LOOK FINE! JUST FINE!
WHAT DO YOU THINK? TAKE A LOOK!
I'D SAY THEY LOOK LIKE A PAIR OF REAL MEN!
MM.
JUST LIKE ME IN MY YOUTH.

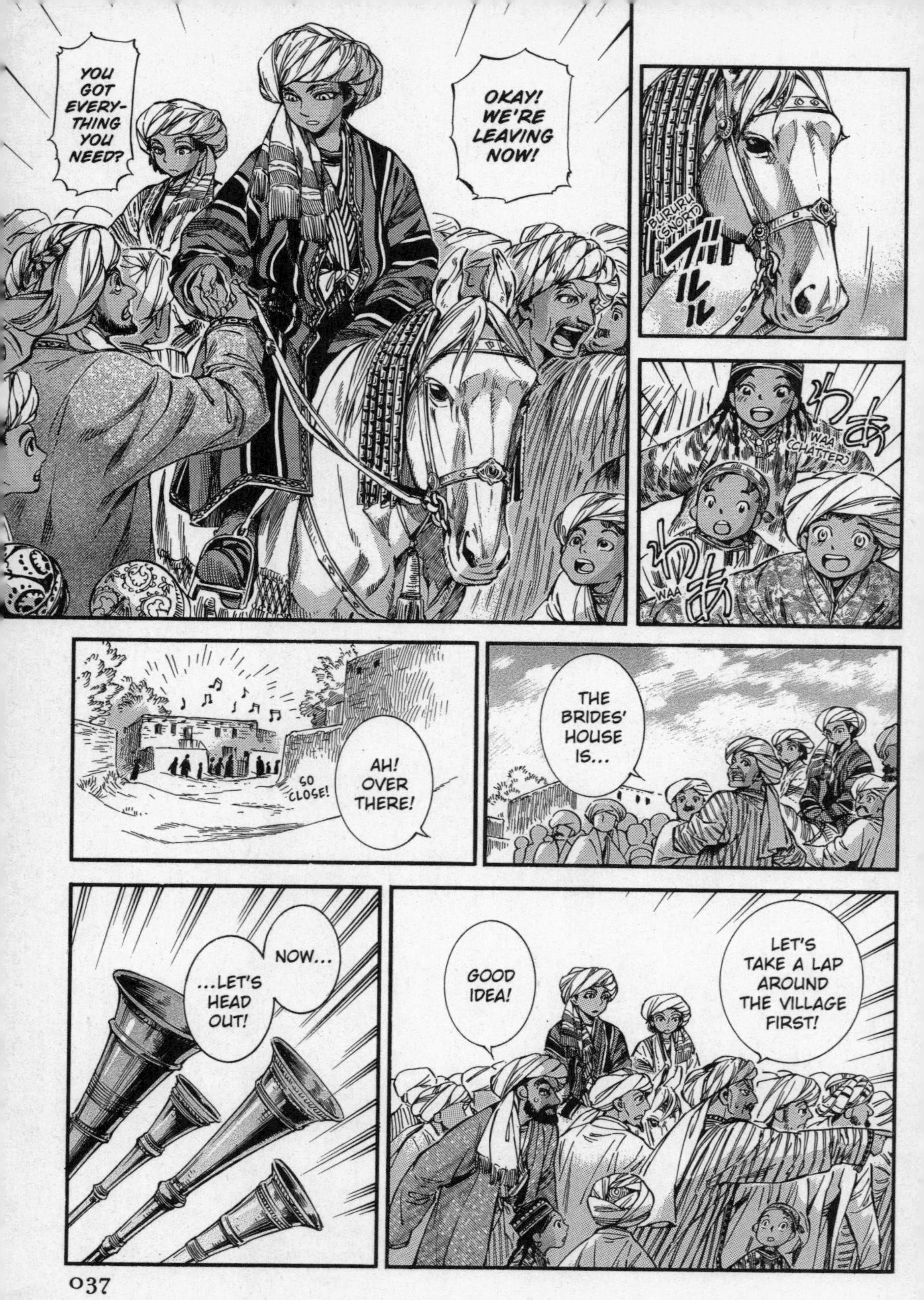
ブルル
BURURU (SNORT)
わあ
WAA (CHATTER)
わあ
WAA
OKAY! WE'RE LEAVING NOW!
YOU GOT EVERY-THING YOU NEED?
THE BRIDES' HOUSE IS...
AH! OVER THERE!
SO CLOSE!
LET'S TAKE A LAP AROUND THE VILLAGE FIRST!
GOOD IDEA!
NOW...
...LET'S HEAD OUT!

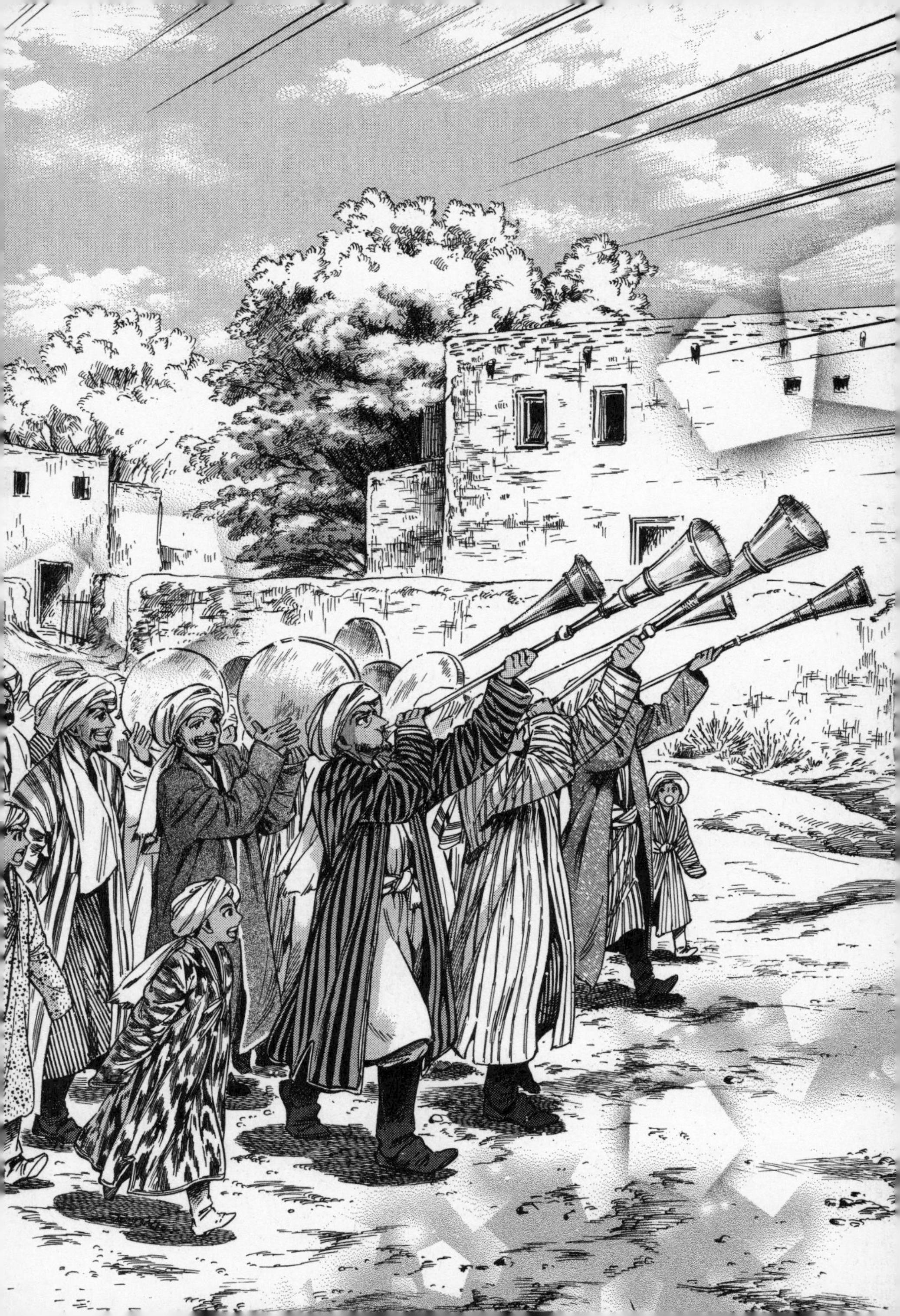

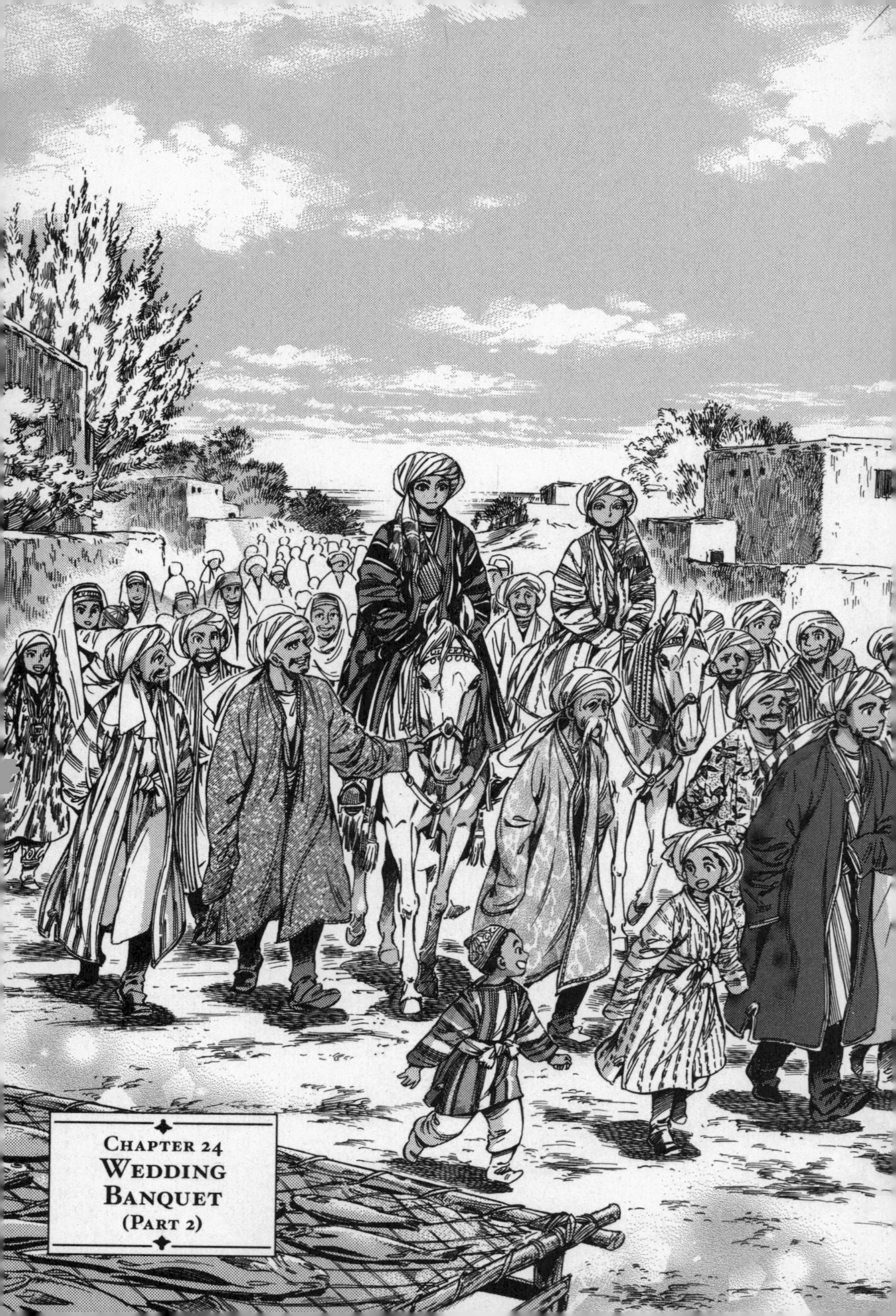
Chapter 24
Wedding Banquet
(Part 2)

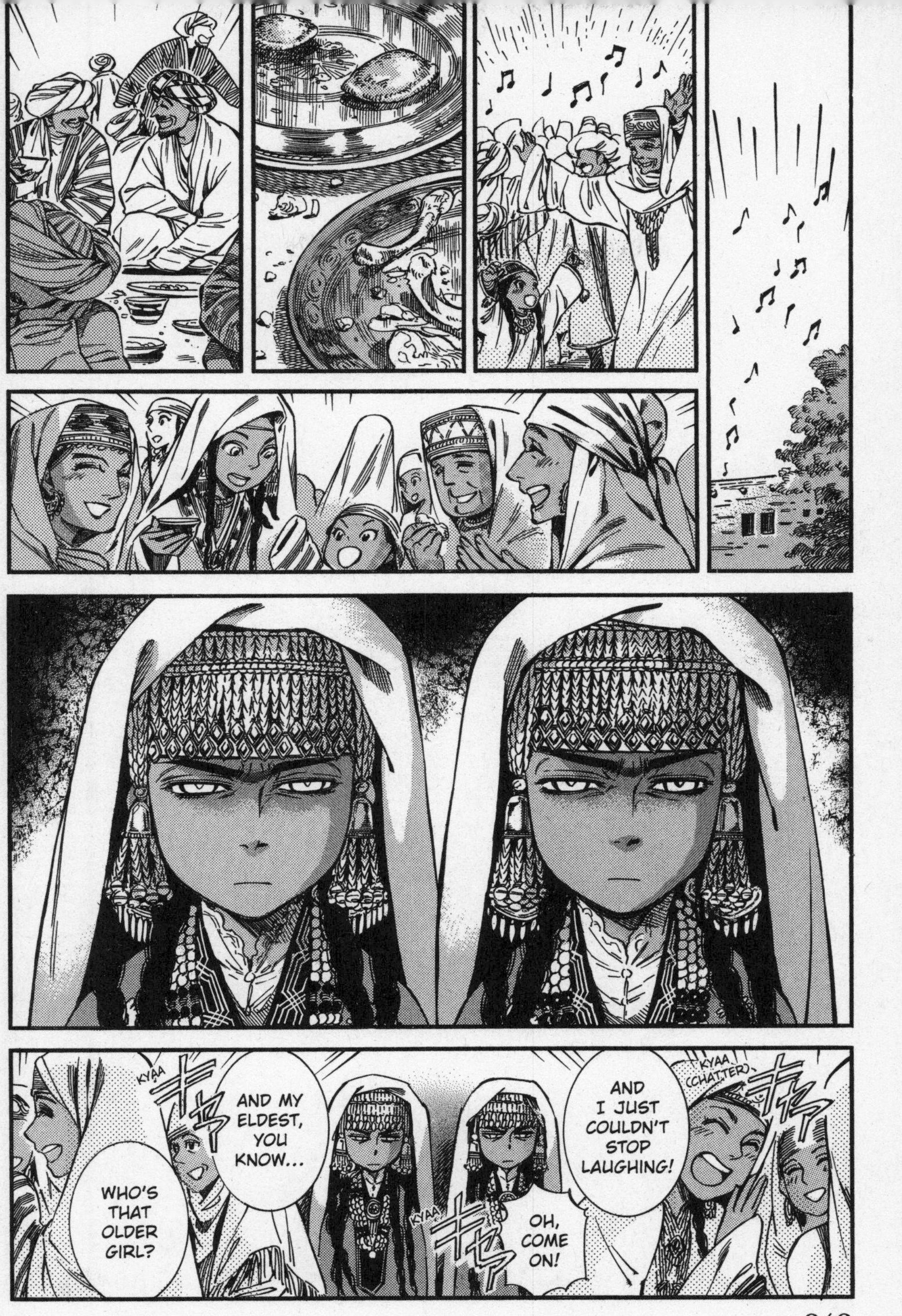
KYAA (CHATTER)
AND I JUST COULDN'T STOP LAUGHING!
OH, COME ON!
KYAA
AND MY ELDEST, YOU KNOW...
KYAA
WHO'S THAT OLDER GIRL?

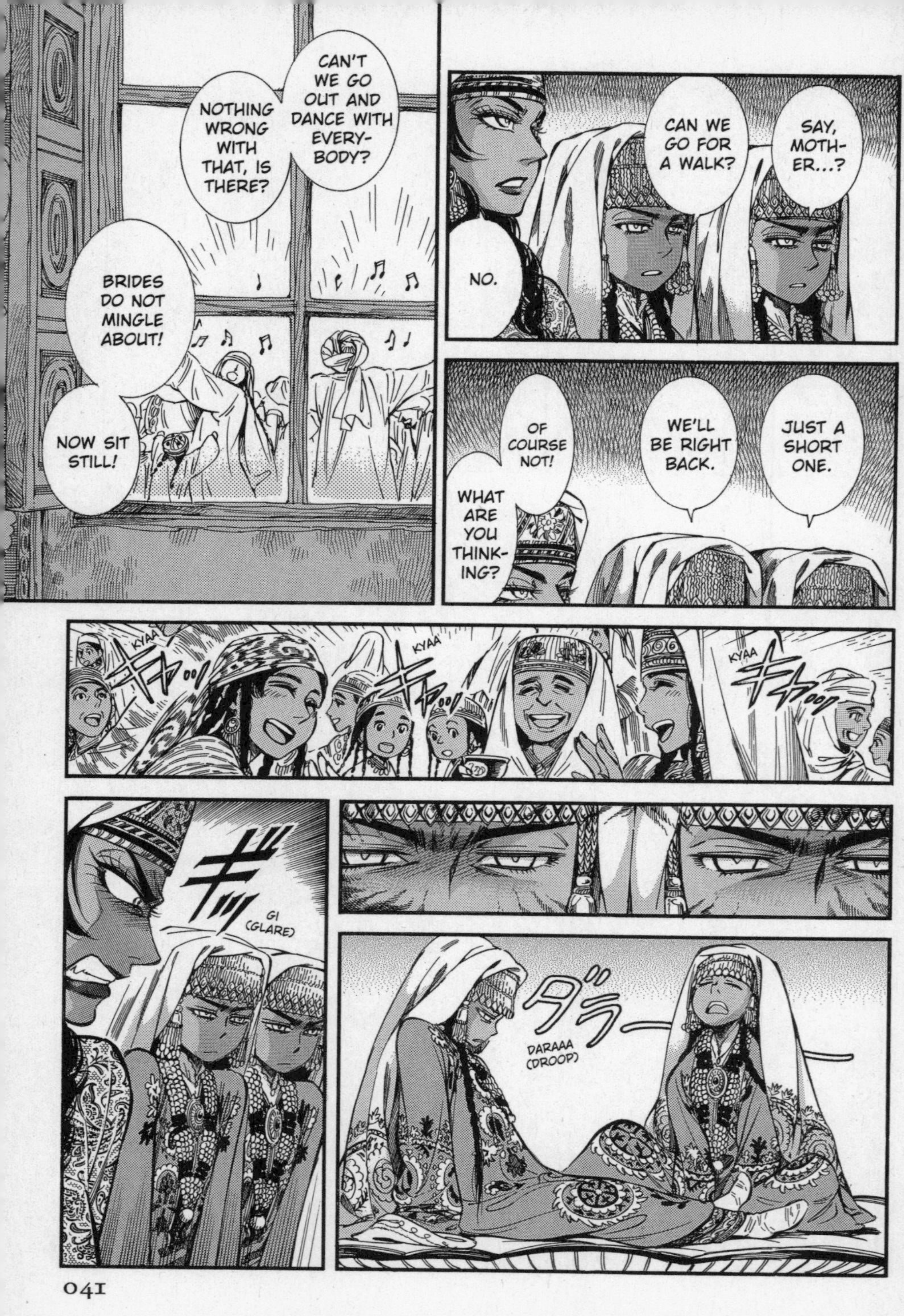
SAY, MOTHER...?
CAN WE GO FOR A WALK?
NO.
JUST A SHORT ONE.
WE'LL BE RIGHT BACK.
OF COURSE NOT!
WHAT ARE YOU THINKING?
CAN'T WE GO OUT AND DANCE WITH EVERY-BODY?
NOTHING WRONG WITH THAT, IS THERE?
BRIDES DO NOT MINGLE ABOUT!
NOW SIT STILL!
KYAA
KYAA
KYAA
DARAAA (DROOP)
GI (GLARE)

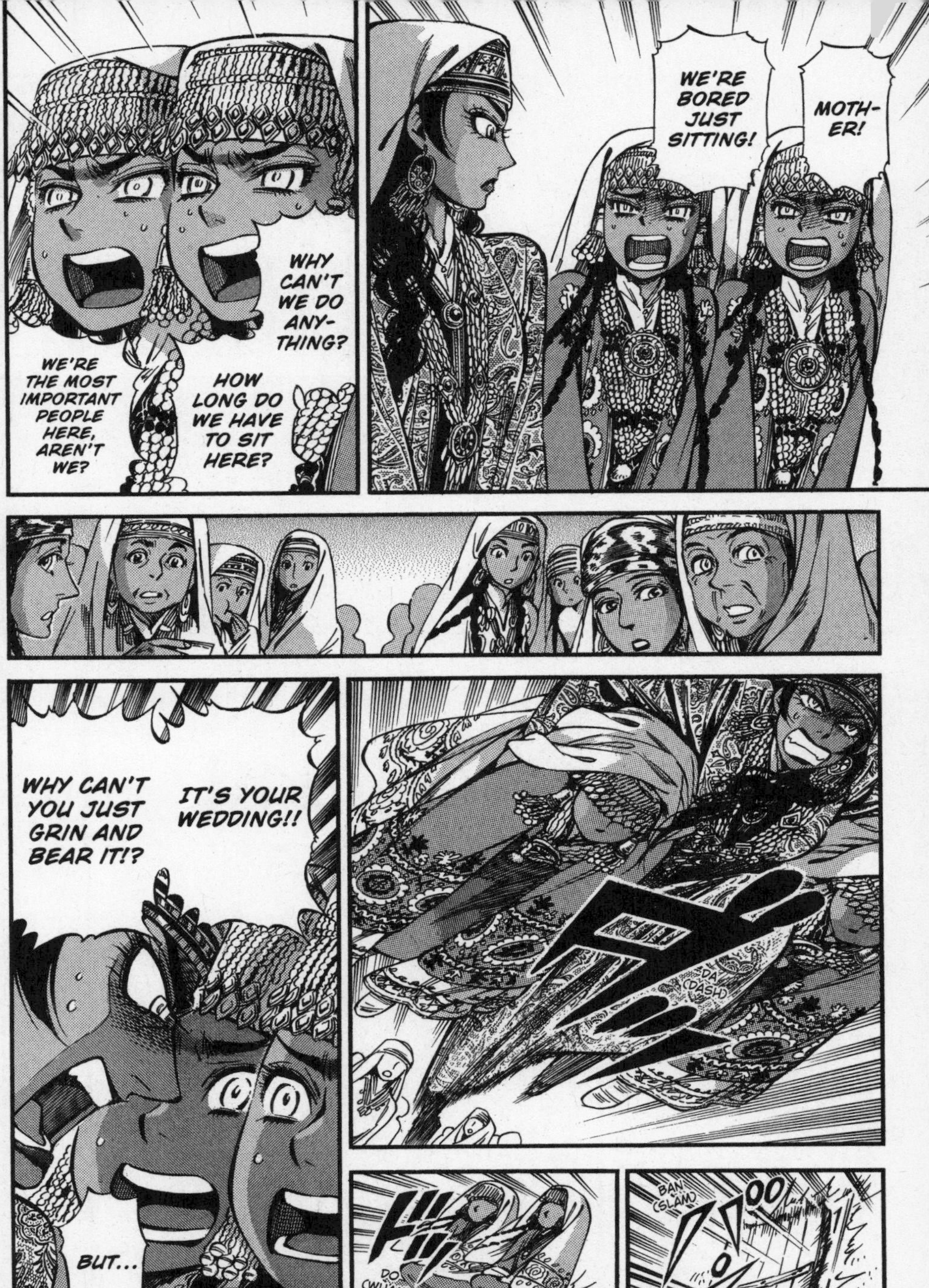
MOTH-ER!
WE'RE BORED JUST SITTING!
WHY CAN'T WE DO ANY-THING?
HOW LONG DO WE HAVE TO SIT HERE?
WE'RE THE MOST IMPORTANT PEOPLE HERE, AREN'T WE?
DA (DASH)
BAN (SLAM)
DO (WHAM)
IT'S YOUR WEDDING!!
WHY CAN'T YOU JUST GRIN AND BEAR IT!?
BUT...

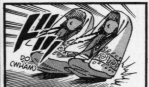

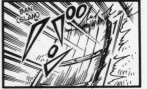

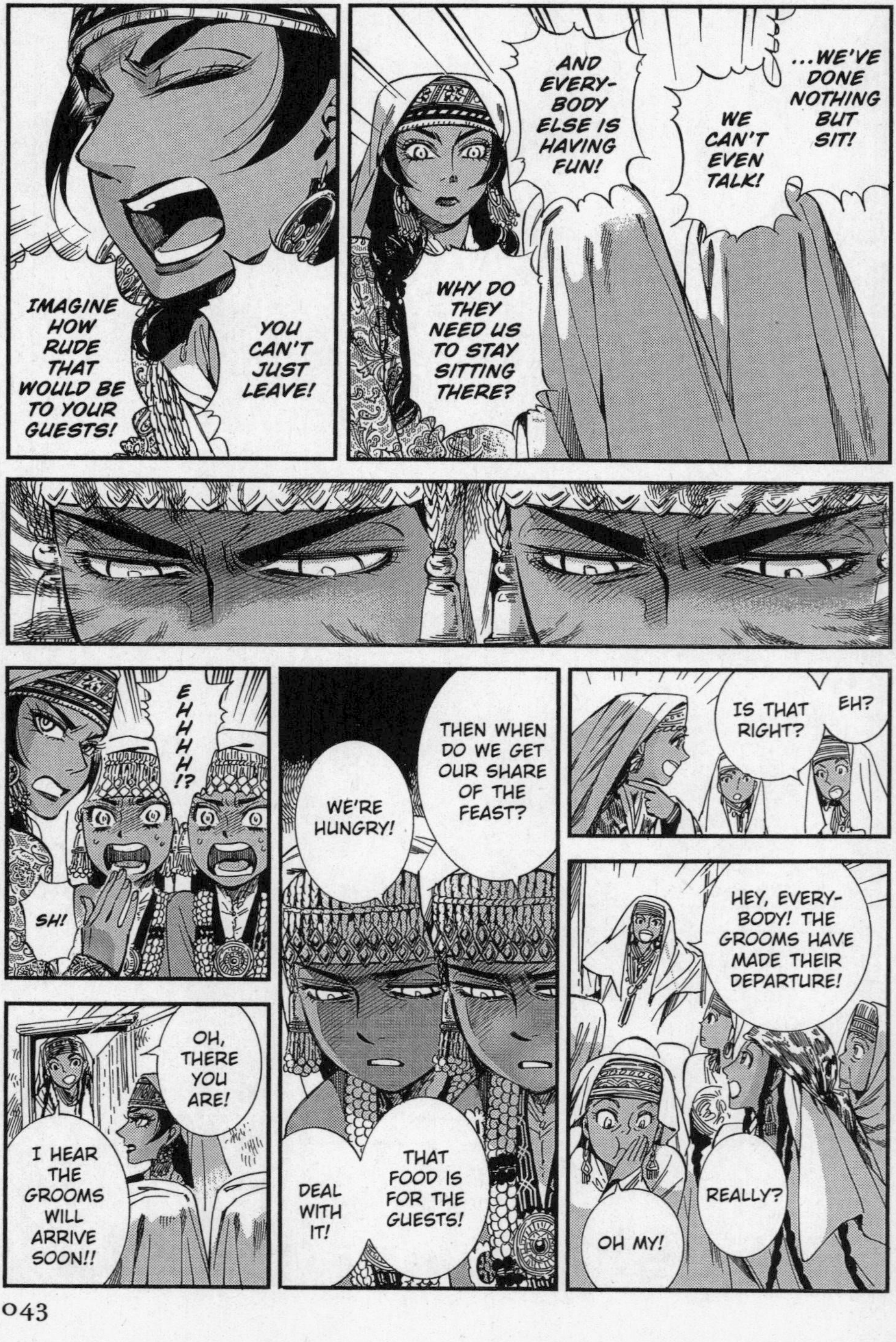
...WE'VE DONE NOTHING BUT SIT!
WE CAN'T EVEN TALK!
AND EVERY-BODY ELSE IS HAVING FUN!
WHY DO THEY NEED US TO STAY SITTING THERE?
YOU CAN'T JUST LEAVE!
IMAGINE HOW RUDE THAT WOULD BE TO YOUR GUESTS!
EH?
IS THAT RIGHT?
HEY, EVERY-BODY! THE GROOMS HAVE MADE THEIR DEPARTURE!
REALLY?
OH MY!
THEN WHEN DO WE GET OUR SHARE OF THE FEAST?
WE'RE HUNGRY!
THAT FOOD IS FOR THE GUESTS!
DEAL WITH IT!
EHHHH!?
SH!
OH, THERE YOU ARE!
I HEAR THE GROOMS WILL ARRIVE SOON!!

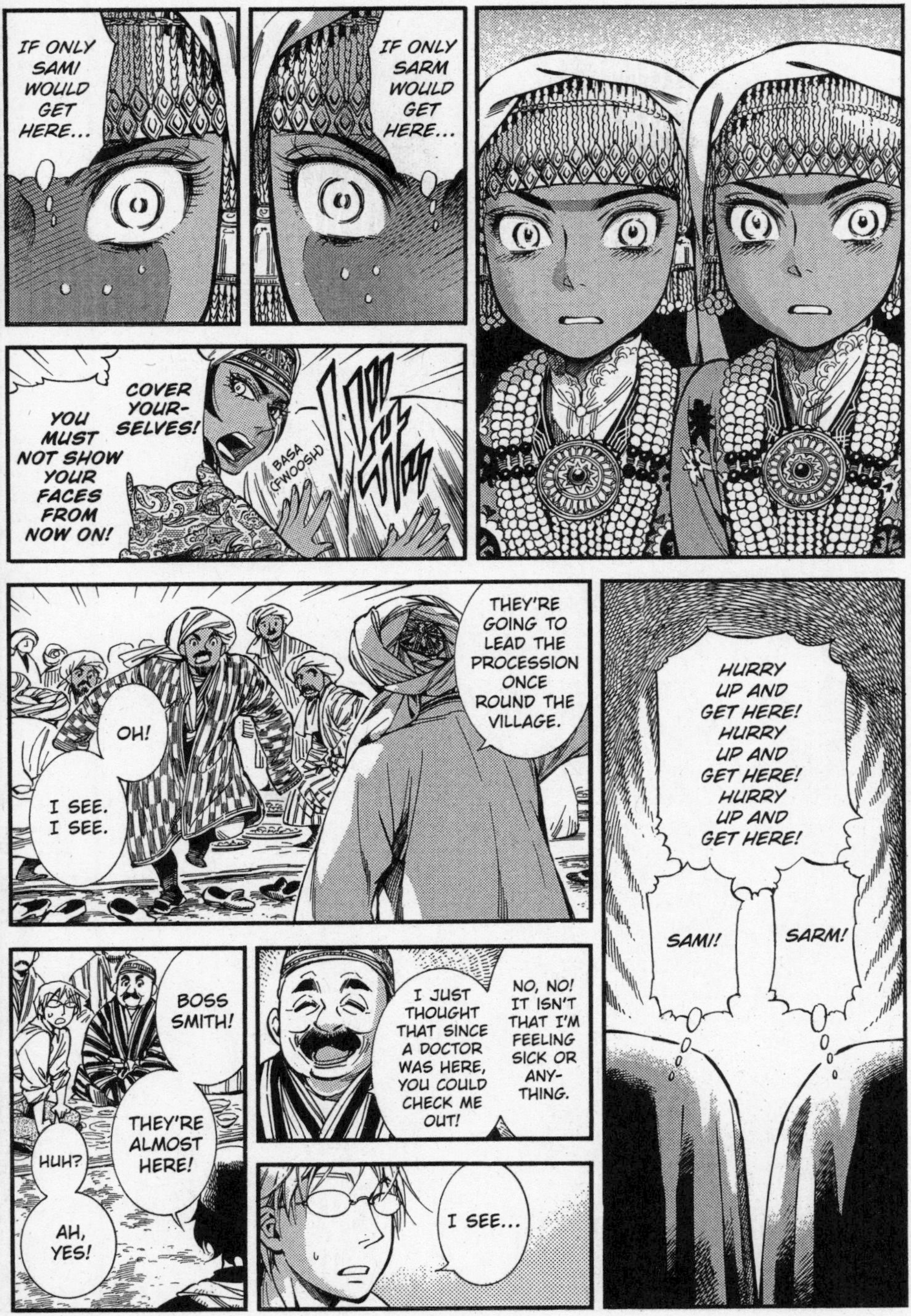
IF ONLY SARM WOULD GET HERE...
IF ONLY SAMI WOULD GET HERE...
COVER YOURSELVES!
YOU MUST NOT SHOW YOUR FACES FROM NOW ON!
BASA (FWOOSH)
HURRY UP AND GET HERE! HURRY UP AND GET HERE! HURRY UP AND GET HERE!
SARM!
SAMI!
THEY'RE GOING TO LEAD THE PROCESSION ONCE ROUND THE VILLAGE.
OH!
I SEE. I SEE.
NO, NO! IT ISN'T THAT I'M FEELING SICK OR ANYTHING.
I JUST THOUGHT THAT SINCE A DOCTOR WAS HERE, YOU COULD CHECK ME OUT!
I SEE...
BOSS SMITH!
THEY'RE ALMOST HERE!
HUH?
AH, YES!

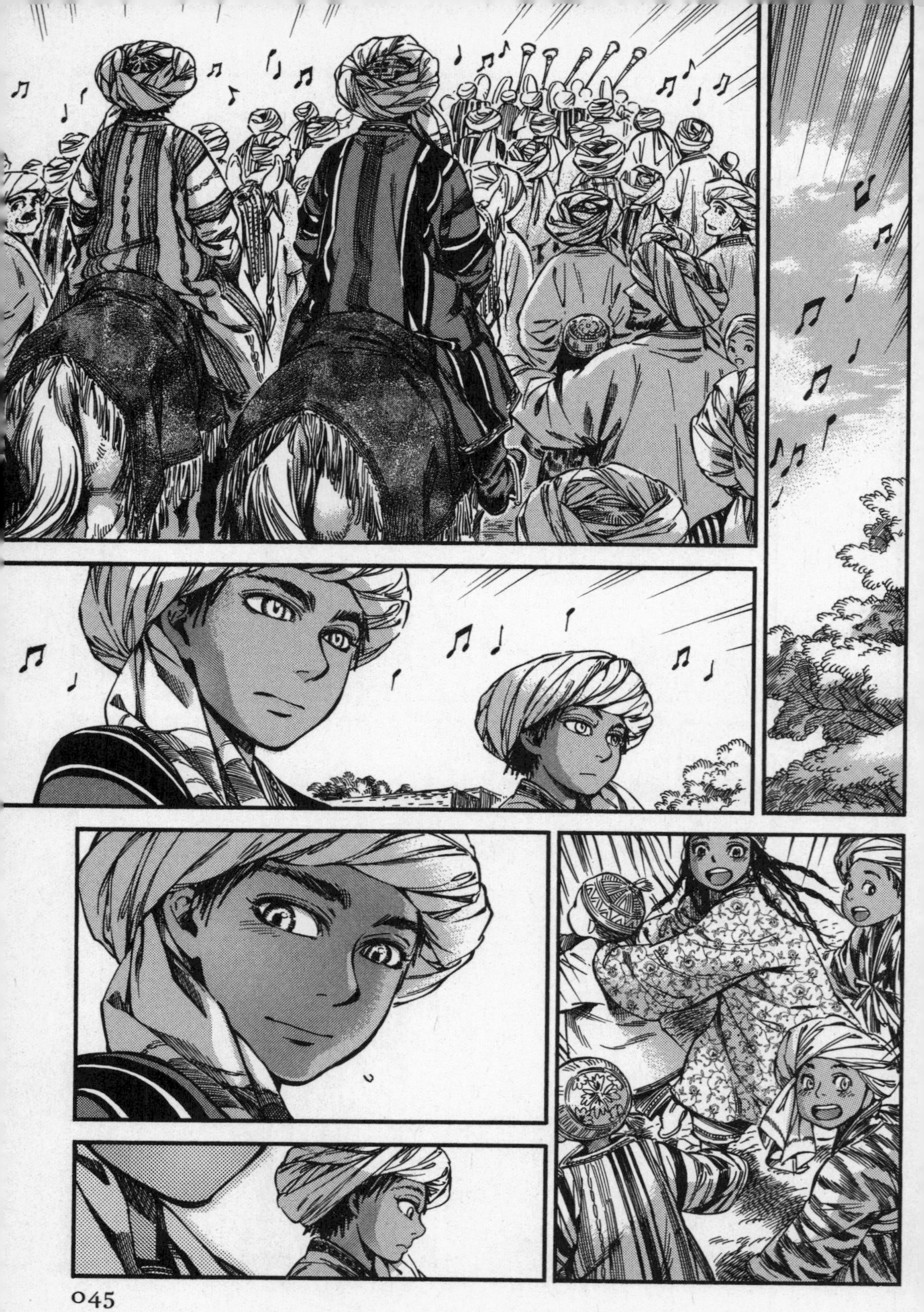

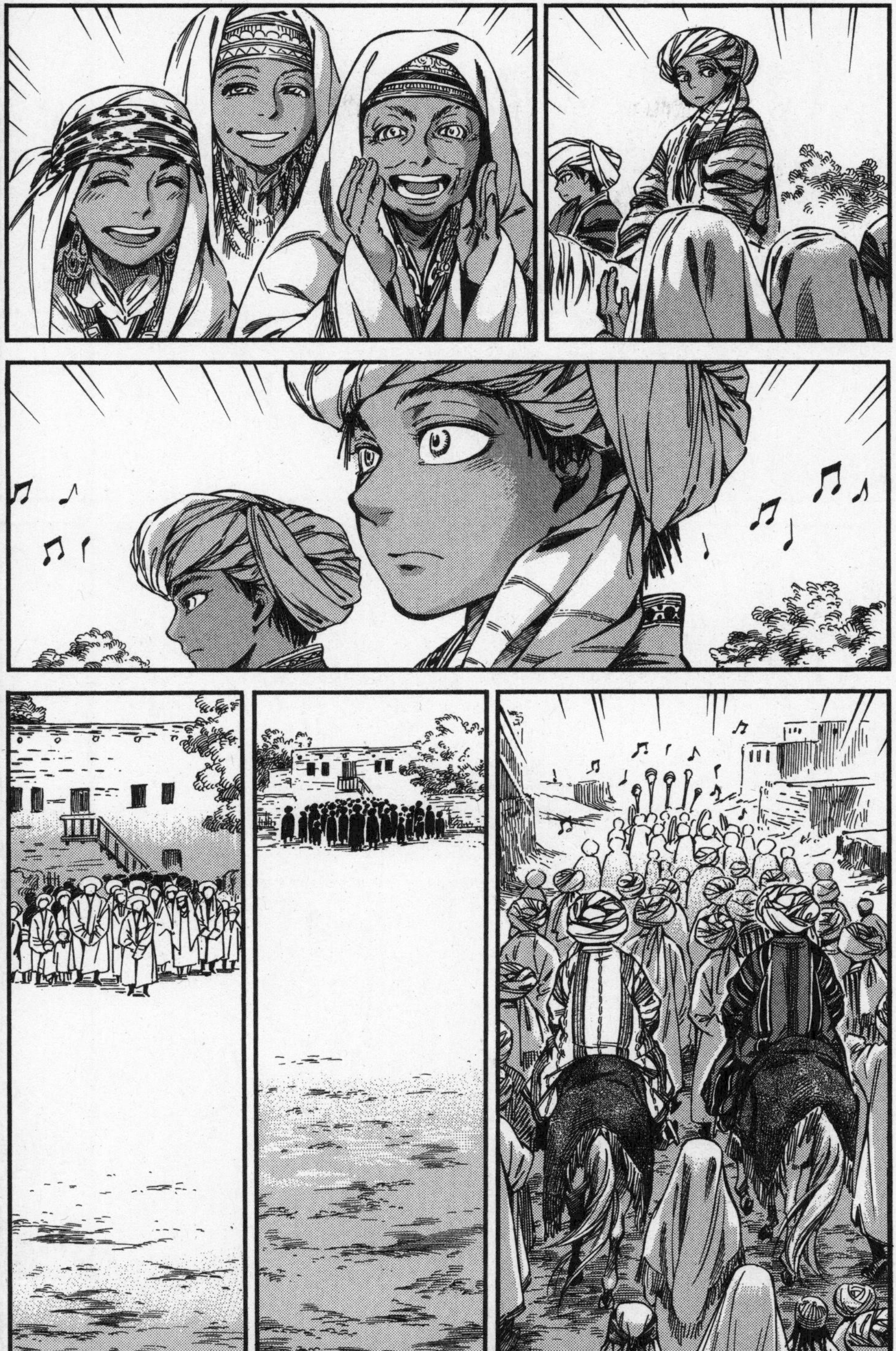

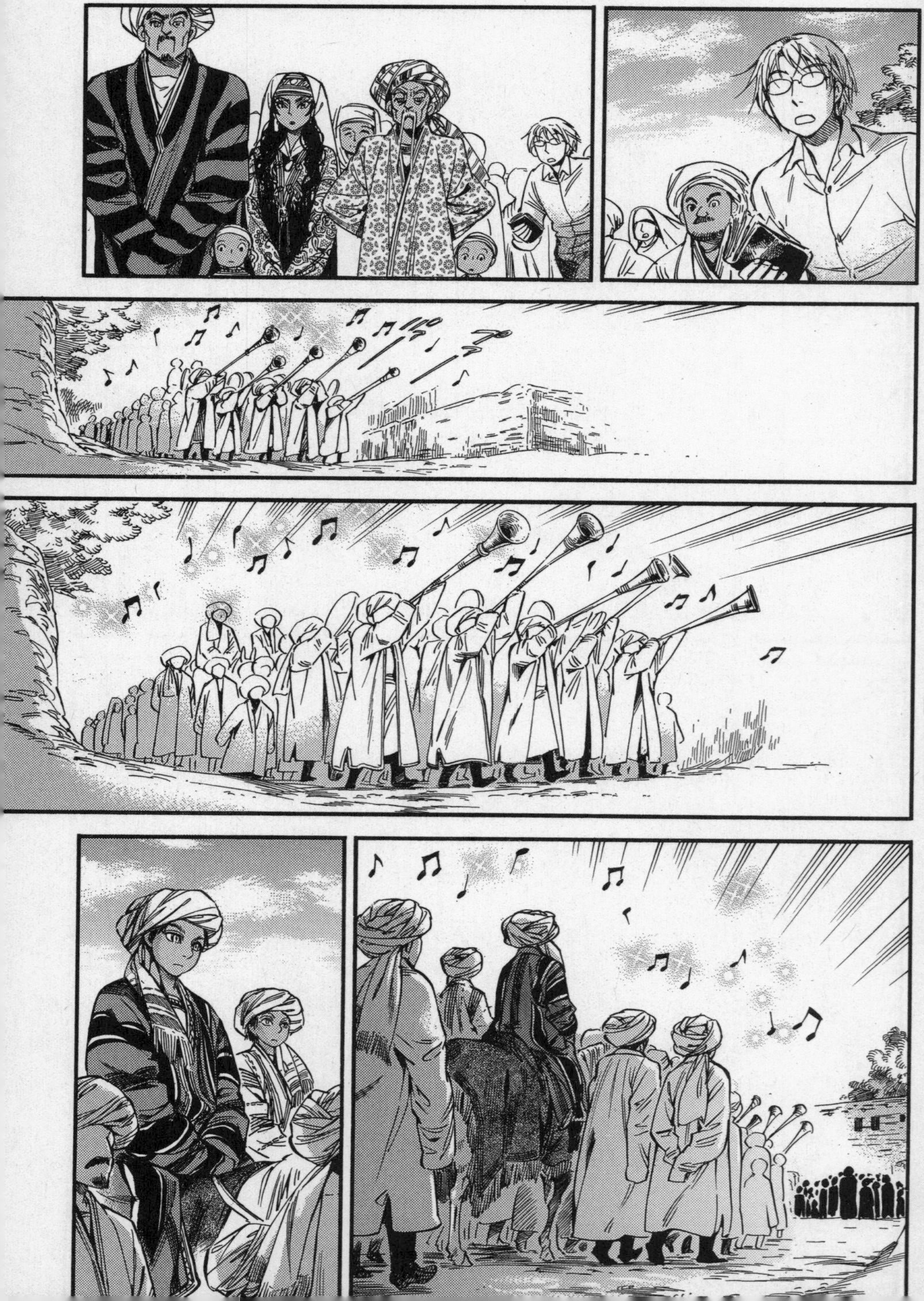

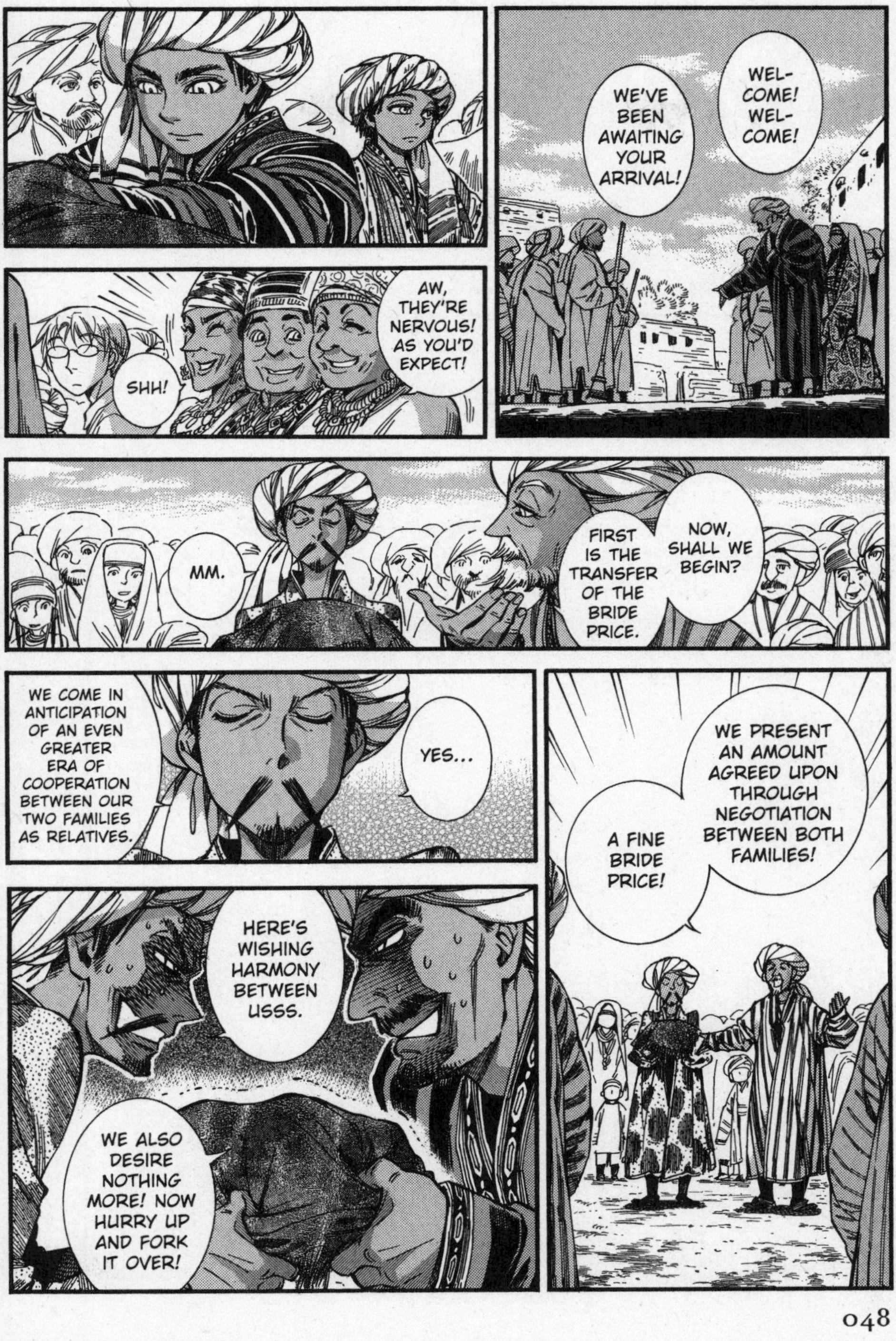
WEL-COME! WEL-COME!
WE'VE BEEN AWAITING YOUR ARRIVAL!
AW, THEY'RE NERVOUS! AS YOU'D EXPECT!
SHH!
NOW, SHALL WE BEGIN?
FIRST IS THE TRANSFER OF THE BRIDE PRICE.
MM.
WE PRESENT AN AMOUNT AGREED UPON THROUGH NEGOTIATION BETWEEN BOTH FAMILIES!
A FINE BRIDE PRICE!
YES...
WE COME IN ANTICIPATION OF AN EVEN GREATER ERA OF COOPERATION BETWEEN OUR TWO FAMILIES AS RELATIVES.
HERE'S WISHING HARMONY BETWEEN USSS.
WE ALSO DESIRE NOTHING MORE! NOW HURRY UP AND FORK IT OVER!

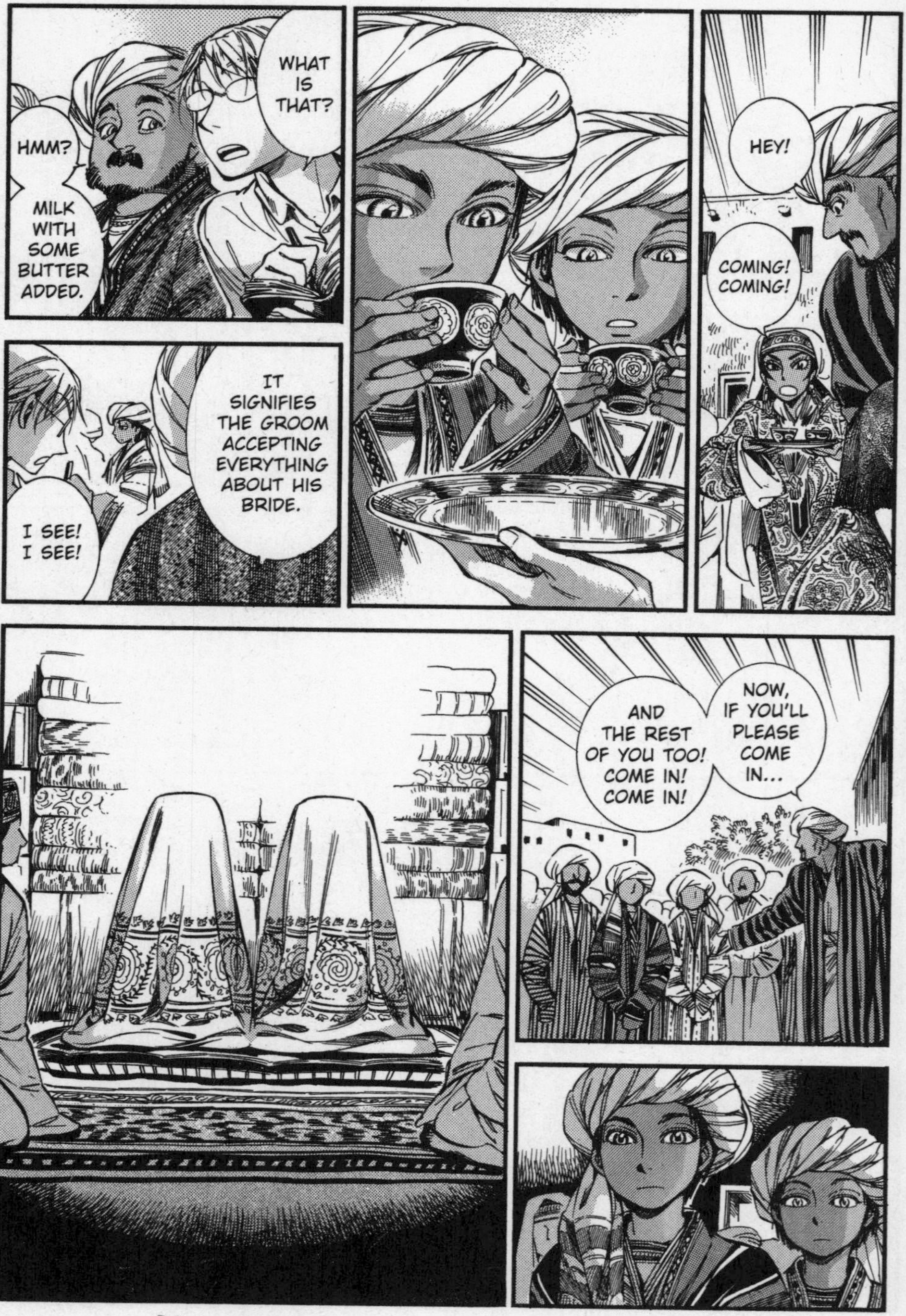
HEY!
COMING! COMING!
WHAT IS THAT?
HMM?
MILK WITH SOME BUTTER ADDED.
IT SIGNIFIES THE GROOM ACCEPTING EVERYTHING ABOUT HIS BRIDE.
I SEE! I SEE!
NOW, IF YOU'LL PLEASE COME IN...
AND THE REST OF YOU TOO! COME IN! COME IN!

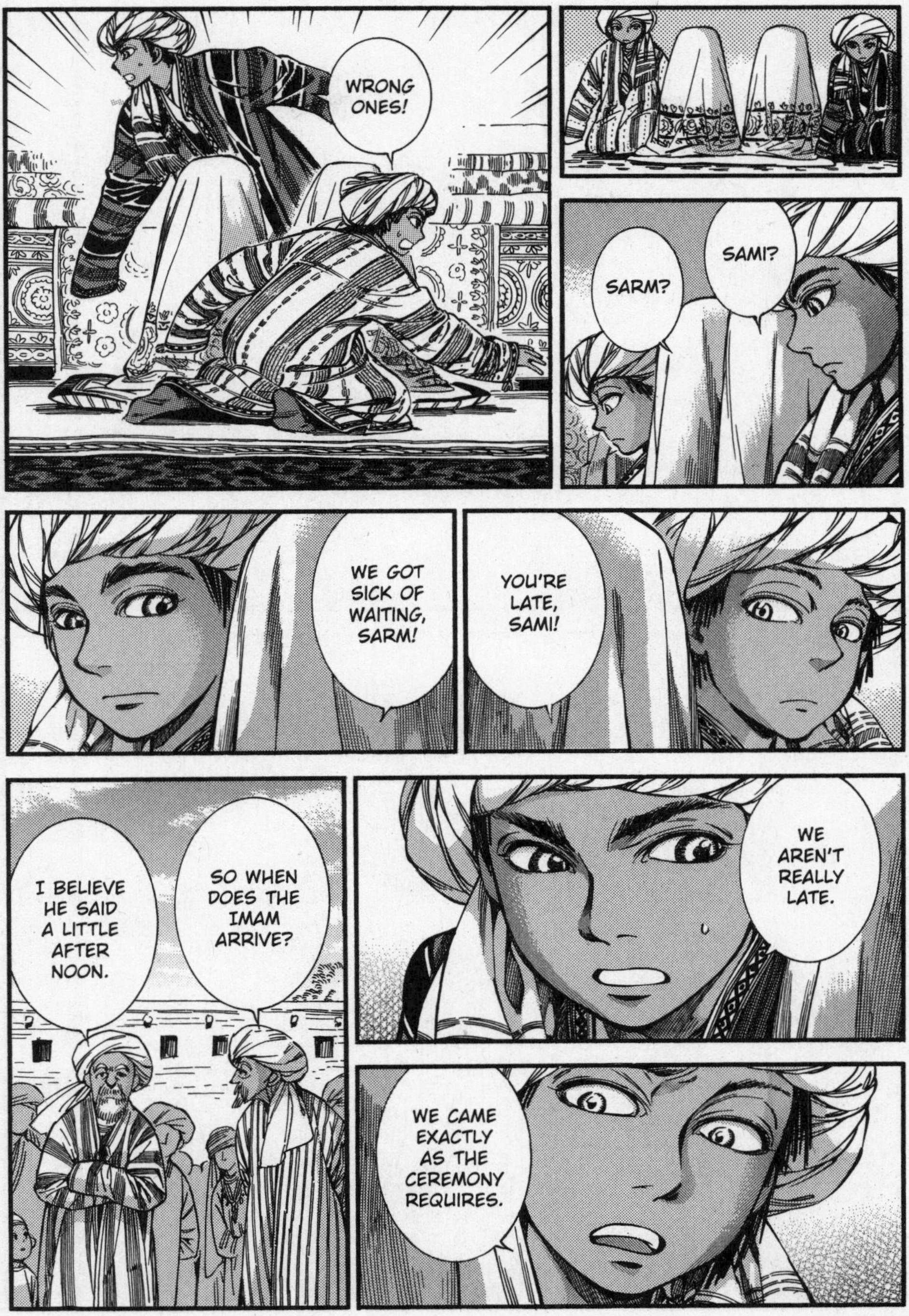
SAMI?
SARM?
WRONG ONES!
YOU'RE LATE, SAMI!
WE GOT SICK OF WAITING, SARM!
WE AREN'T REALLY LATE.
WE CAME EXACTLY AS THE CEREMONY REQUIRES.
SO WHEN DOES THE IMAM ARRIVE?
I BELIEVE HE SAID A LITTLE AFTER NOON.

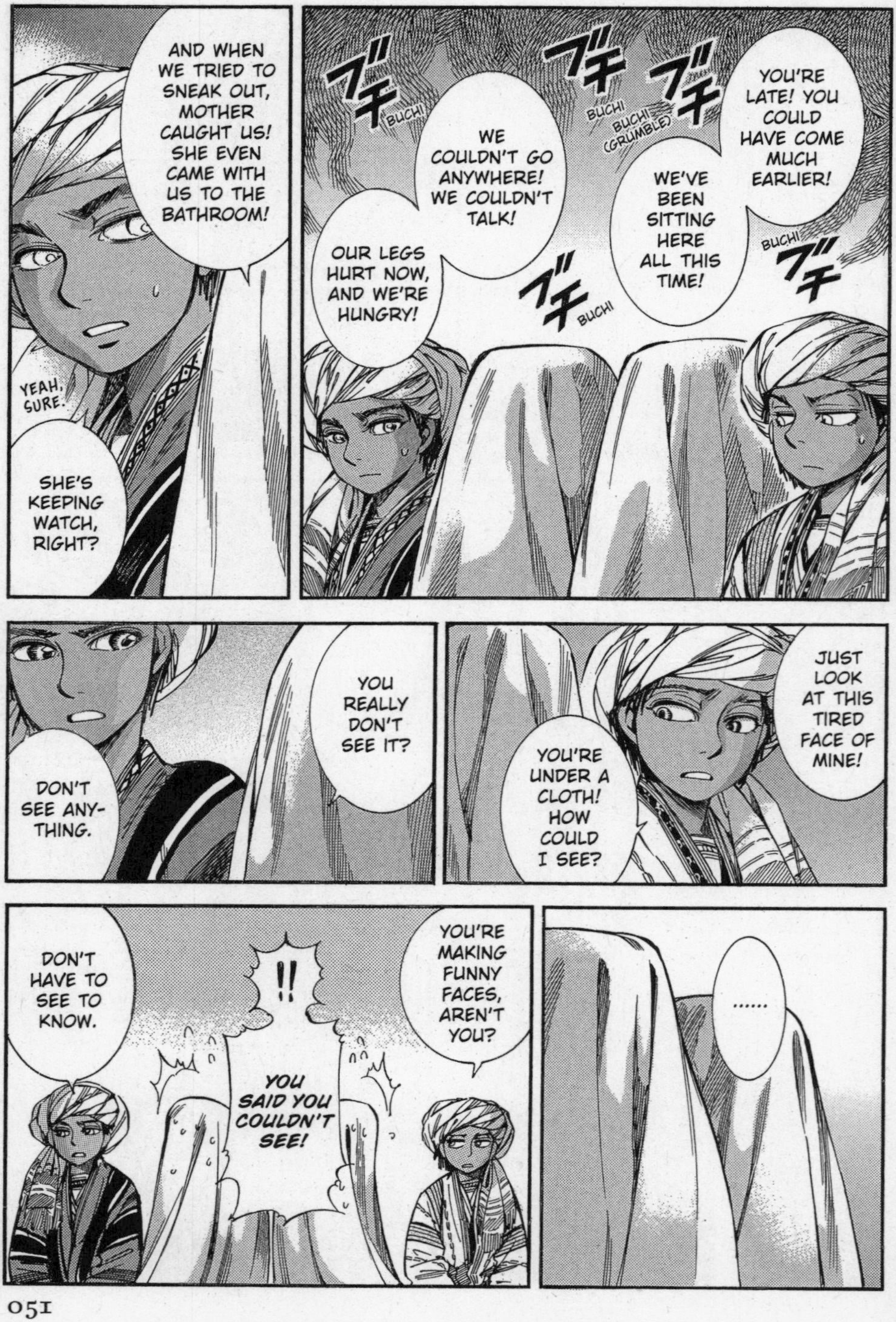
YOU'RE LATE! YOU COULD HAVE COME MUCH EARLIER!
BUCHI
BUCHI
BUCHI (GRUMBLE)
WE'VE BEEN SITTING HERE ALL THIS TIME!
BUCHI
WE COULDN'T GO ANYWHERE! WE COULDN'T TALK!
BUCHI
OUR LEGS HURT NOW, AND WE'RE HUNGRY!
AND WHEN WE TRIED TO SNEAK OUT, MOTHER CAUGHT US! SHE EVEN CAME WITH US TO THE BATHROOM!
YEAH, SURE.
SHE'S KEEPING WATCH, RIGHT?
JUST LOOK AT THIS TIRED FACE OF MINE!
YOU'RE UNDER A CLOTH! HOW COULD I SEE?
YOU REALLY DON'T SEE IT?
DON'T SEE ANYTHING.
......
YOU'RE MAKING FUNNY FACES, AREN'T YOU?
!!
YOU SAID YOU COULDN'T SEE!
DON'T HAVE TO SEE TO KNOW.

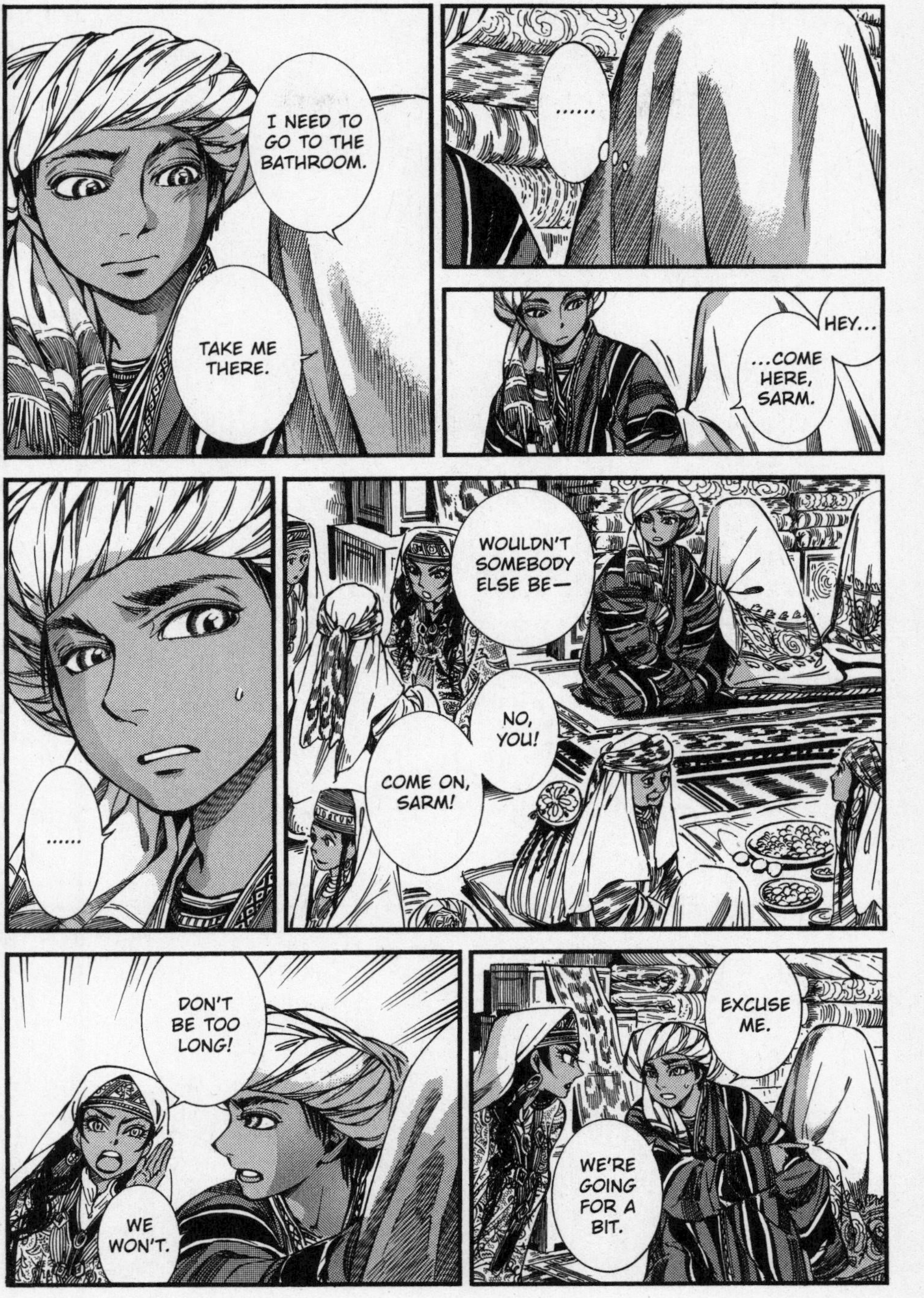
......
HEY...
...COME HERE, SARM.
I NEED TO GO TO THE BATHROOM.
TAKE ME THERE.
WOULDN'T SOMEBODY ELSE BE—
NO, YOU!
COME ON, SARM!
......
EXCUSE ME.
WE'RE GOING FOR A BIT.
DON'T BE TOO LONG!
WE WON'T.

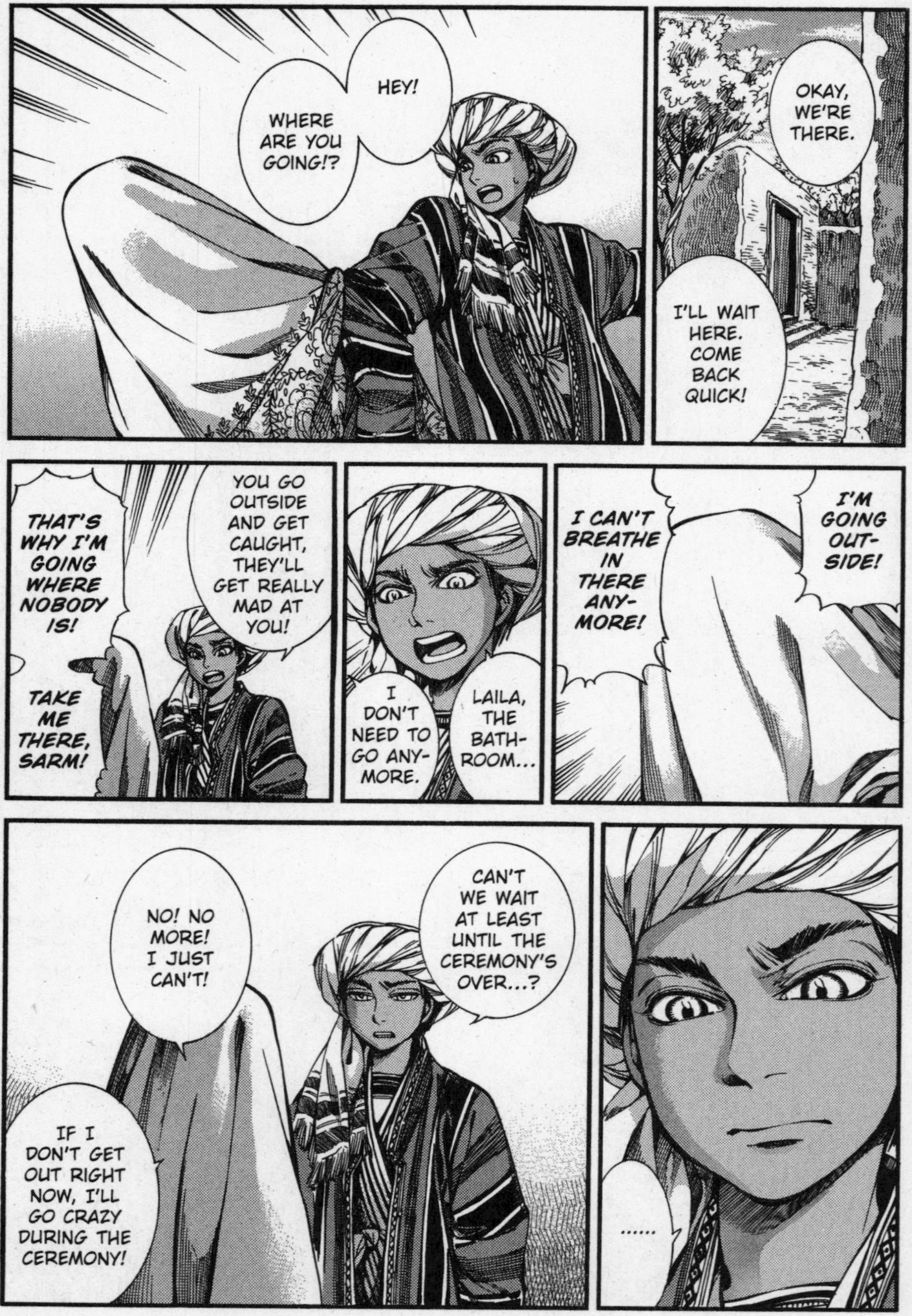
OKAY, WE'RE THERE.
I'LL WAIT HERE. COME BACK QUICK!
HEY!
WHERE ARE YOU GOING!?
I'M GOING OUT-SIDE!
I CAN'T BREATHE IN THERE ANY-MORE!
LAILA, THE BATH-ROOM...
I DON'T NEED TO GO ANY-MORE.
YOU GO OUTSIDE AND GET CAUGHT, THEY'LL GET REALLY MAD AT YOU!
THAT'S WHY I'M GOING WHERE NOBODY IS!
TAKE ME THERE, SARM!
......
CAN'T WE WAIT AT LEAST UNTIL THE CEREMONY'S OVER...?
NO! NO MORE! I JUST CAN'T!
IF I DON'T GET OUT RIGHT NOW, I'LL GO CRAZY DURING THE CEREMONY!

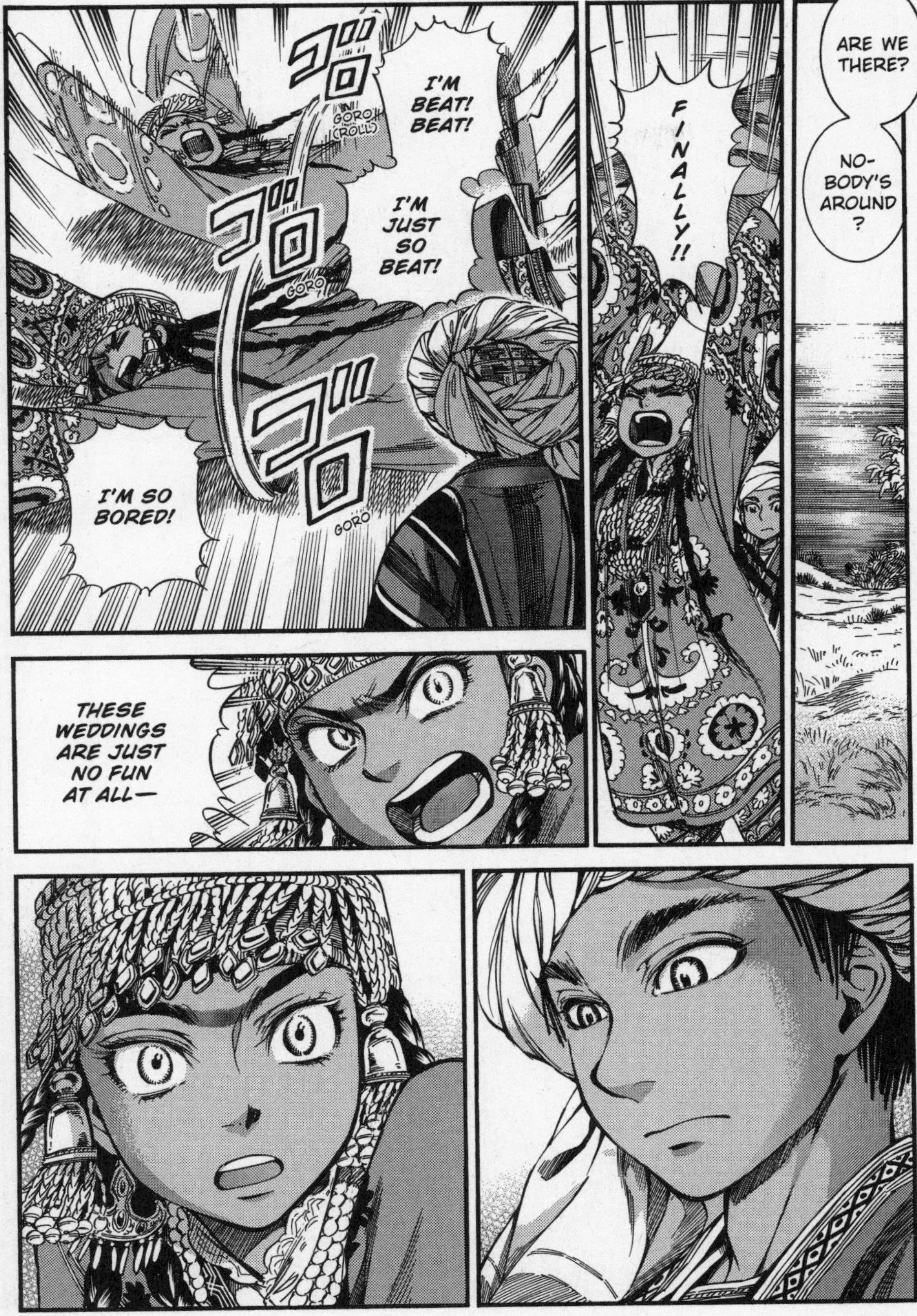
ARE WE THERE?
NO-BODY'S AROUND?
FINALLY!!
I'M BEAT! BEAT!
GORO (ROLL)
I'M JUST SO BEAT!
GORO
GORO
I'M SO BORED!
THESE WEDDINGS ARE JUST NO FUN AT ALL—

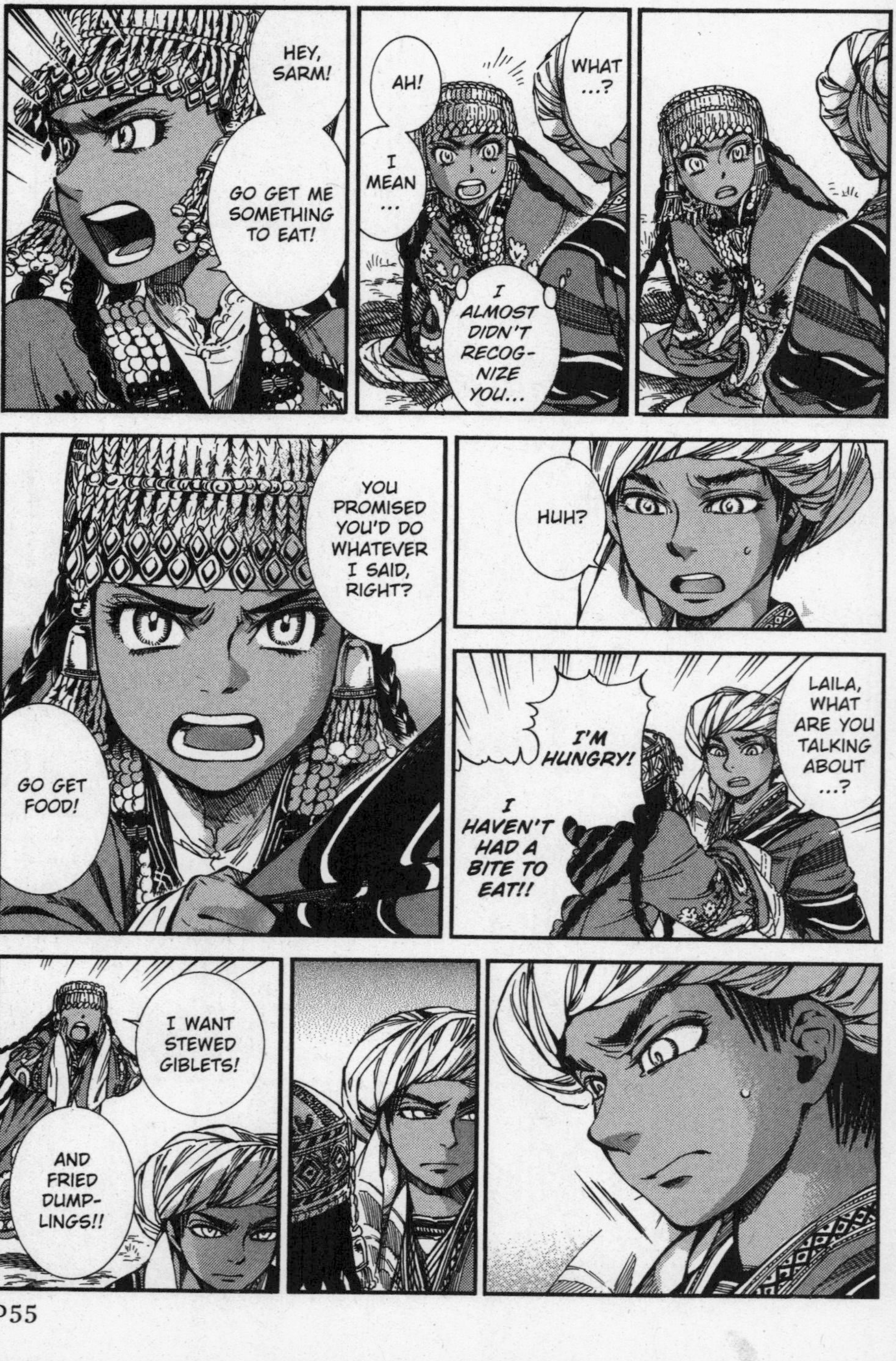
WHAT ...?
AH!
I MEAN ...
I ALMOST DIDN'T RECOGNIZE YOU...
HEY, SARM!
GO GET ME SOMETHING TO EAT!
HUH?
LAILA, WHAT ARE YOU TALKING ABOUT ...?
I'M HUNGRY!
I HAVEN'T HAD A BITE TO EAT!!
YOU PROMISED YOU'D DO WHATEVER I SAID, RIGHT?
GO GET FOOD!
I WANT STEWED GIBLETS!
AND FRIED DUMPLINGS!!

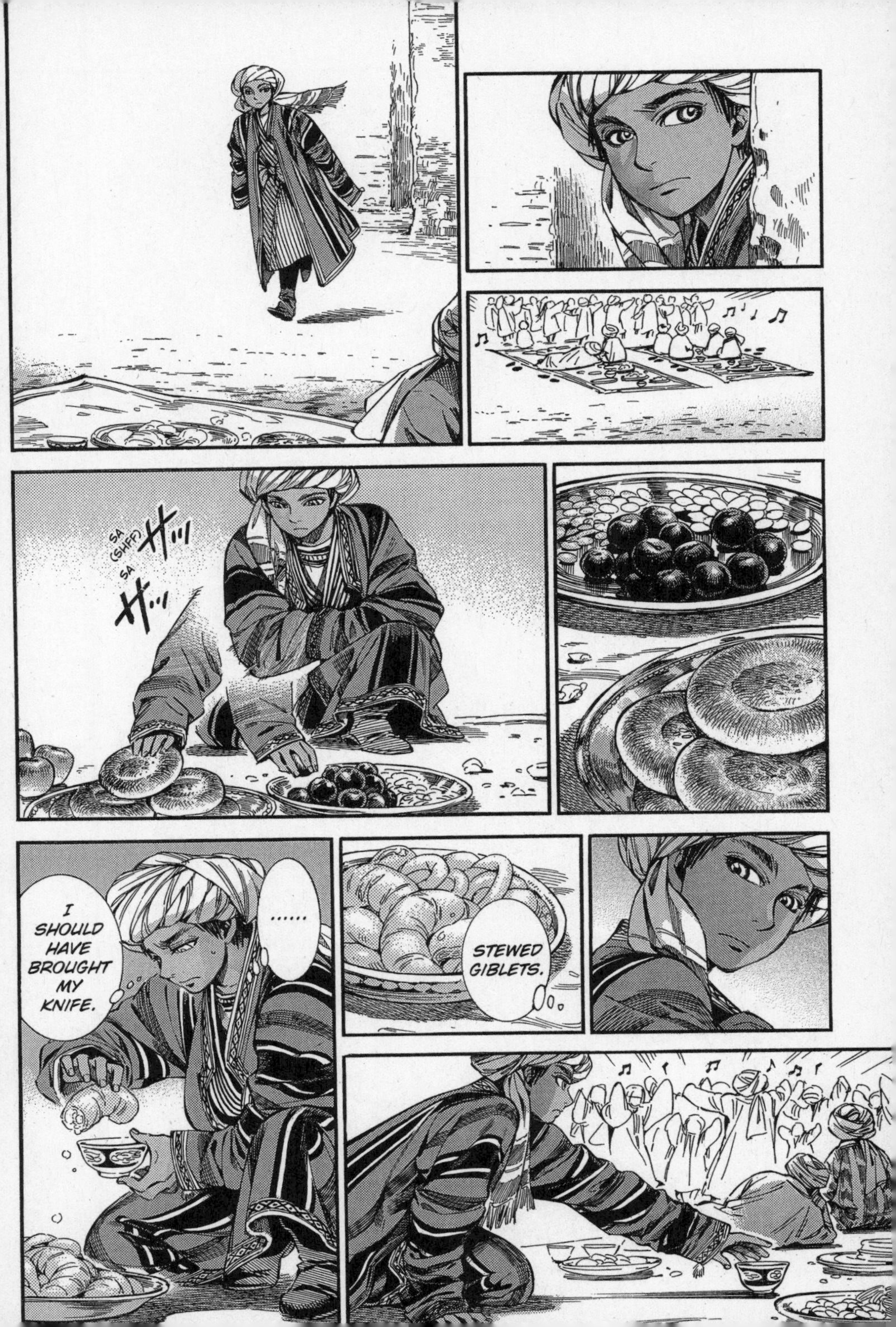
SA (SHFF)
SA
STEWED GIBLETS.
......
I SHOULD HAVE BROUGHT MY KNIFE.

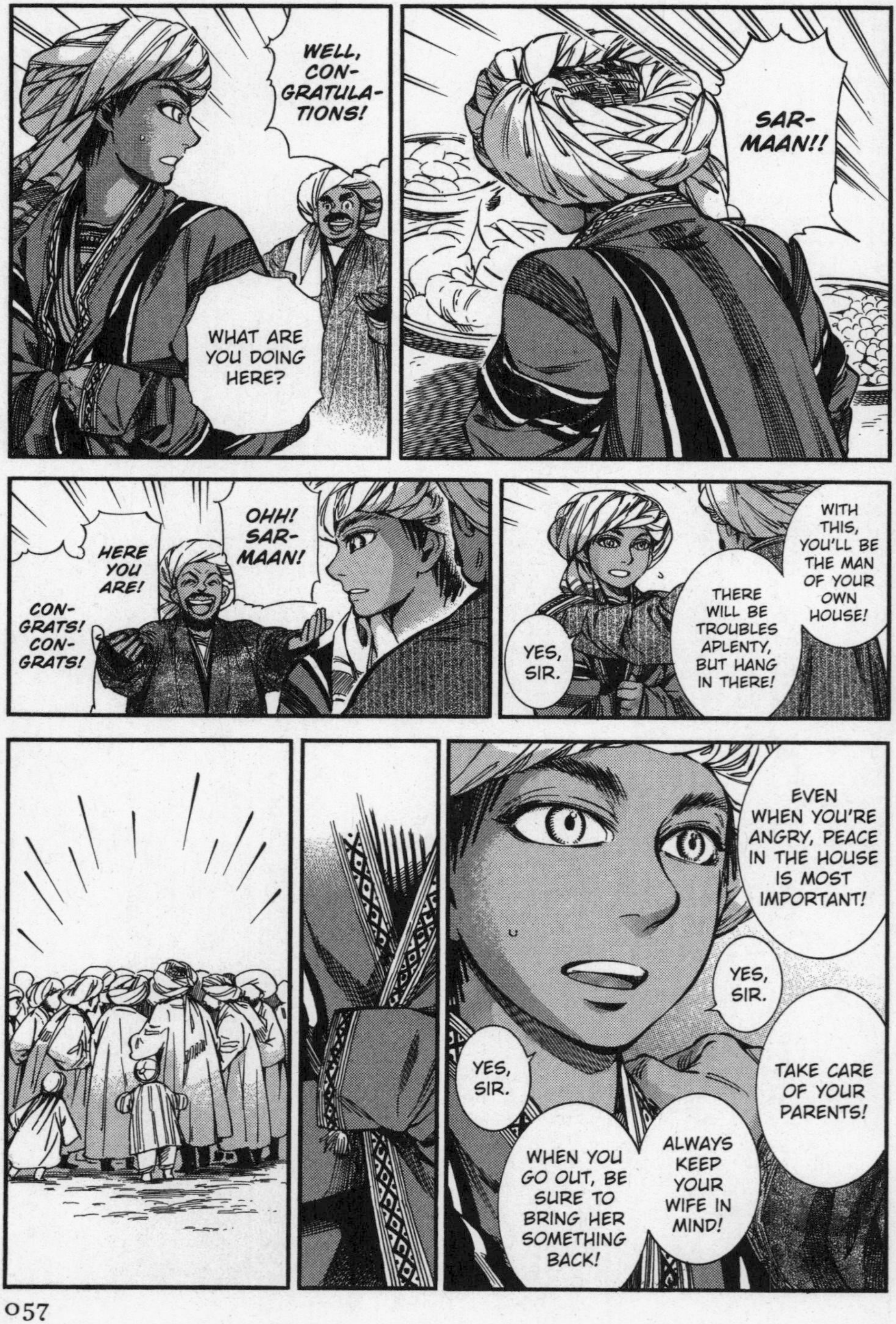
SAR-MAAN!!
WELL, CON-GRATULA-TIONS!
WHAT ARE YOU DOING HERE?
WITH THIS, YOU'LL BE THE MAN OF YOUR OWN HOUSE!
THERE WILL BE TROUBLES APLENTY, BUT HANG IN THERE!
YES, SIR.
OHH! SAR-MAAN!
HERE YOU ARE!
CON-GRATS! CON-GRATS!
EVEN WHEN YOU'RE ANGRY, PEACE IN THE HOUSE IS MOST IMPORTANT!
YES, SIR.
TAKE CARE OF YOUR PARENTS!
YES, SIR.
ALWAYS KEEP YOUR WIFE IN MIND!
WHEN YOU GO OUT, BE SURE TO BRING HER SOMETHING BACK!

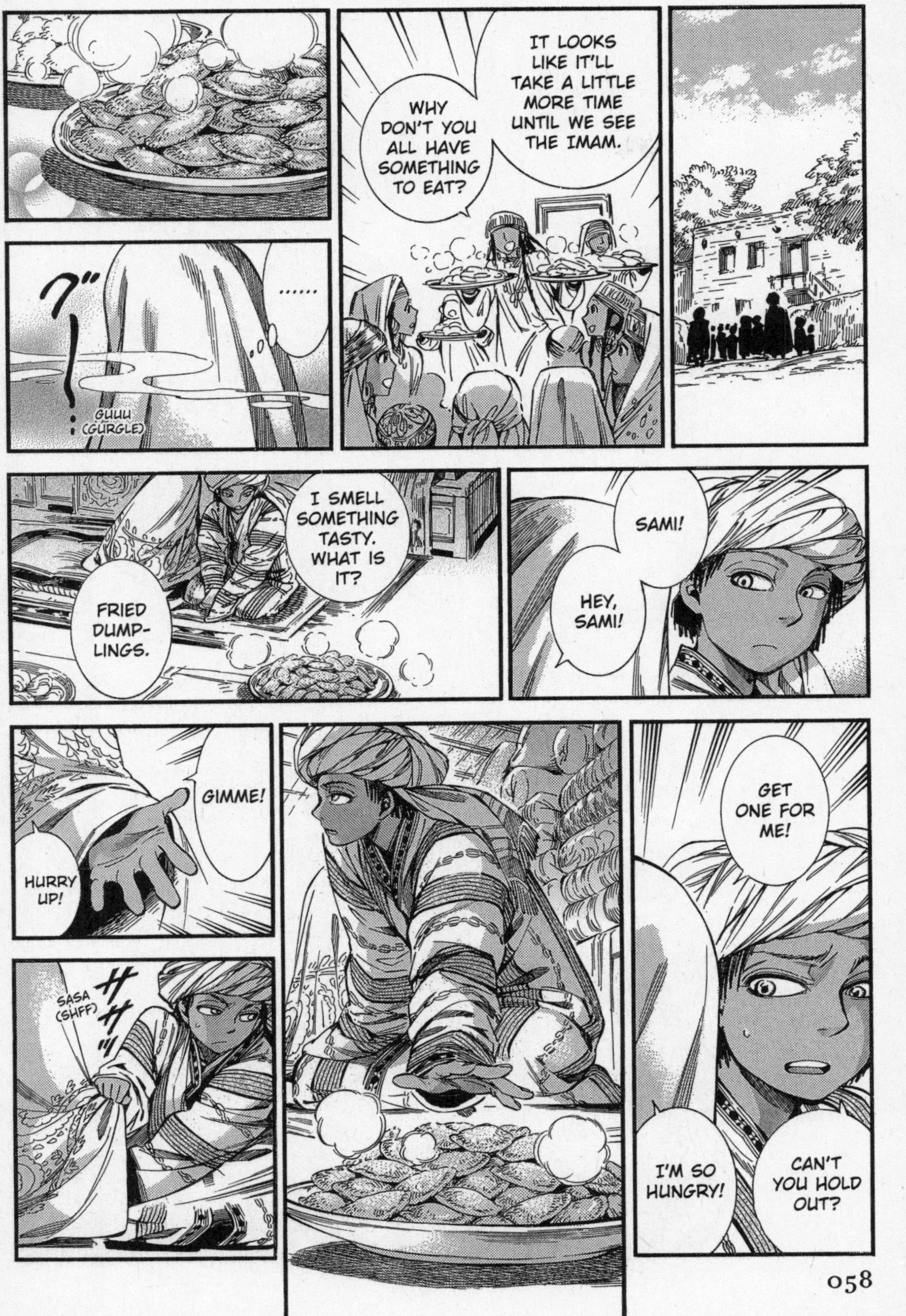
IT LOOKS LIKE IT'LL TAKE A LITTLE MORE TIME UNTIL WE SEE THE IMAM.
WHY DON'T YOU ALL HAVE SOMETHING TO EAT?
......
GUUU (GURGLE)
SAMI!
HEY, SAMI!
I SMELL SOMETHING TASTY. WHAT IS IT?
FRIED DUMP-LINGS.
GET ONE FOR ME!
CAN'T YOU HOLD OUT?
I'M SO HUNGRY!
GIMME!
HURRY UP!
SASA (SHFF)

SFX: SAKU (CRUNCH) SAKU SAKU SAKU SAKU SAKU
MOGU (MUNCH) MOGU MOGU MOGU

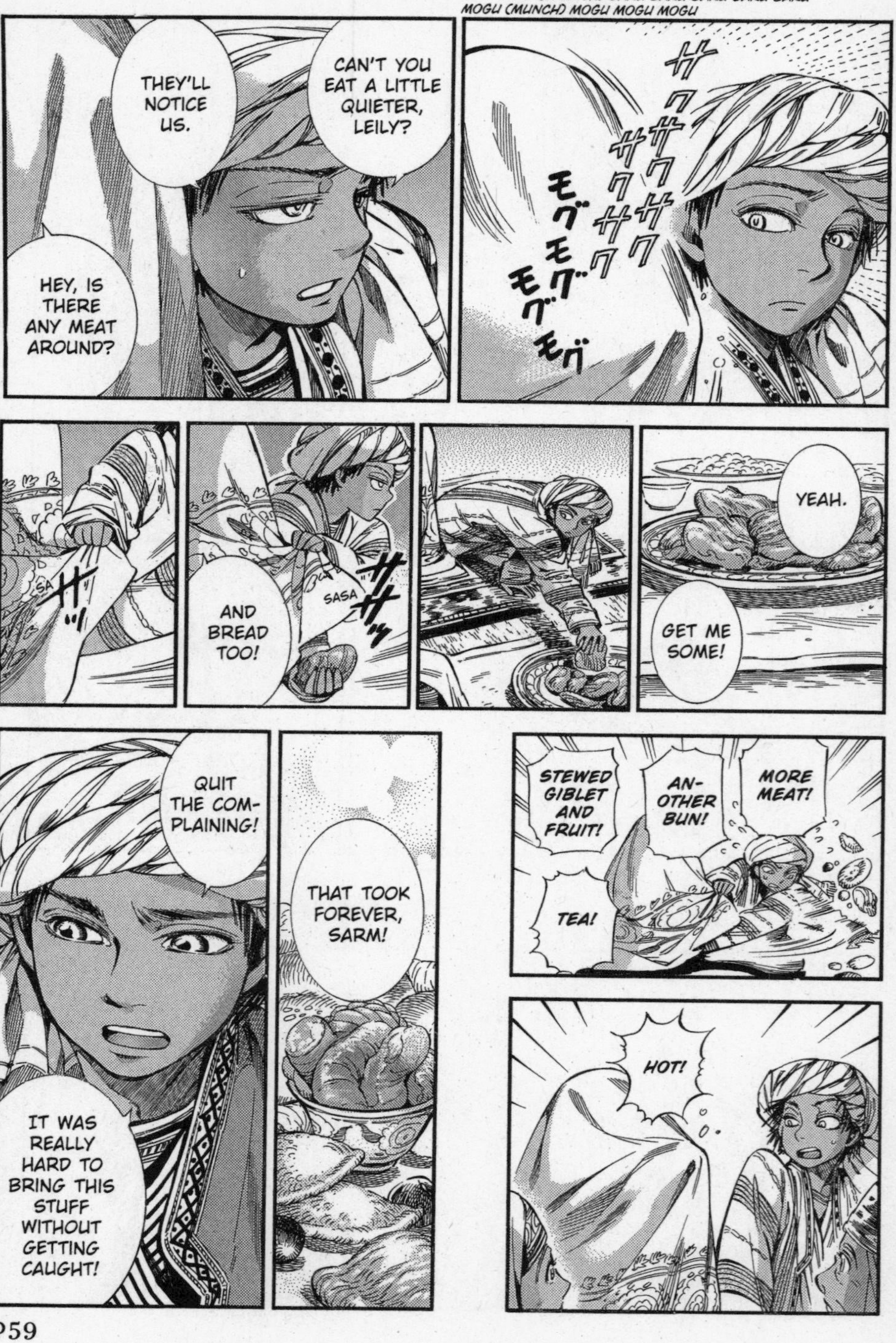
CAN'T YOU EAT A LITTLE QUIETER, LEILY?
THEY'LL NOTICE US.
HEY, IS THERE ANY MEAT AROUND?
YEAH.
GET ME SOME!
SASA
AND BREAD TOO!
SA
MORE MEAT!
AN-OTHER BUN!
STEWED GIBLET AND FRUIT!
TEA!
HOT!
THAT TOOK FOREVER, SARM!
QUIT THE COM-PLAINING!
IT WAS REALLY HARD TO BRING THIS STUFF WITHOUT GETTING CAUGHT!

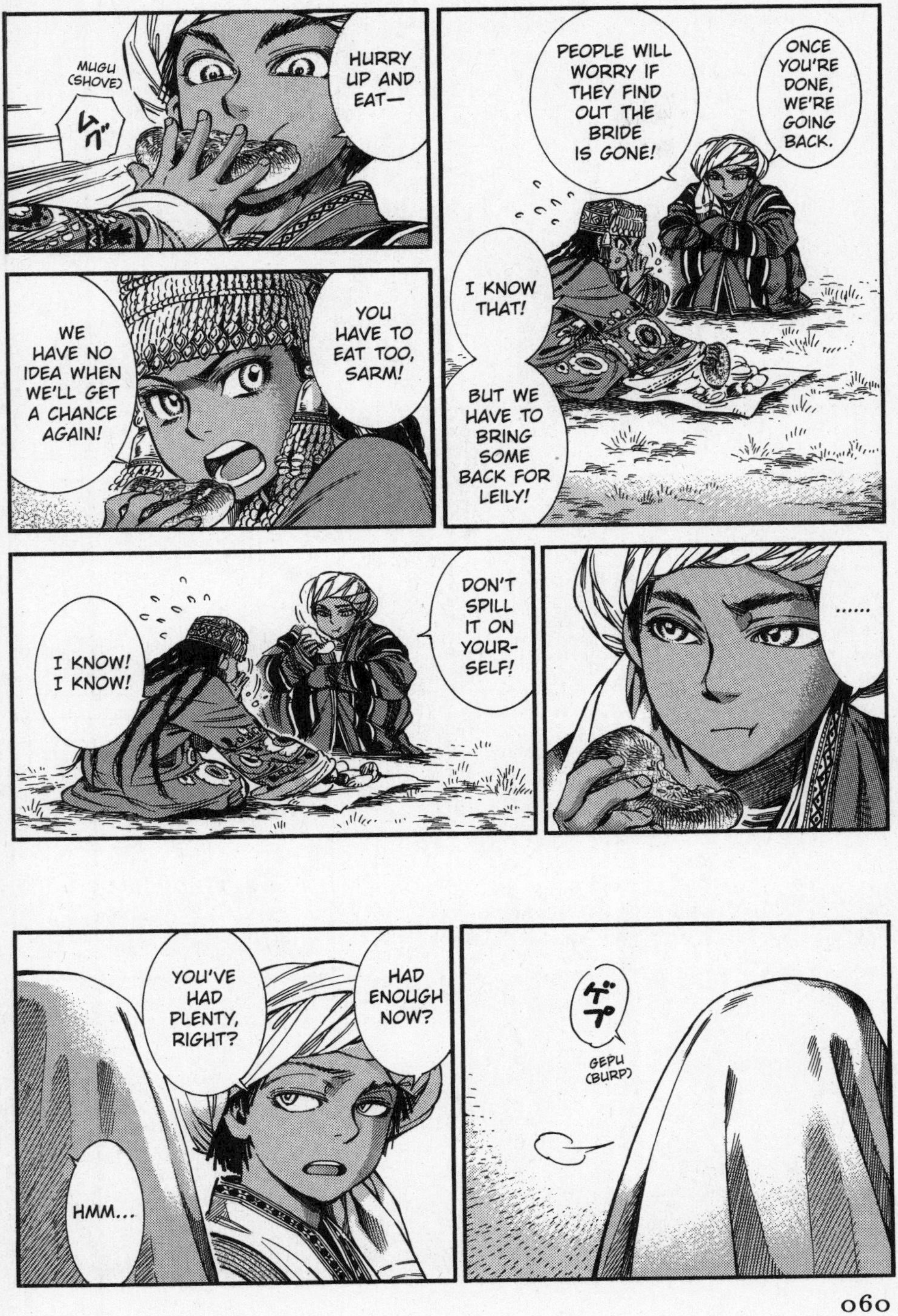
ONCE YOU'RE DONE, WE'RE GOING BACK.
PEOPLE WILL WORRY IF THEY FIND OUT THE BRIDE IS GONE!
I KNOW THAT!
BUT WE HAVE TO BRING SOME BACK FOR LEILY!
HURRY UP AND EAT—
ムグ
MUGU (SHOVE)
YOU HAVE TO EAT TOO, SARM!
WE HAVE NO IDEA WHEN WE'LL GET A CHANCE AGAIN!
......
DON'T SPILL IT ON YOURSELF!
I KNOW! I KNOW!
ゲプ
GEPU (BURP)
HAD ENOUGH NOW?
YOU'VE HAD PLENTY, RIGHT?
HMM...

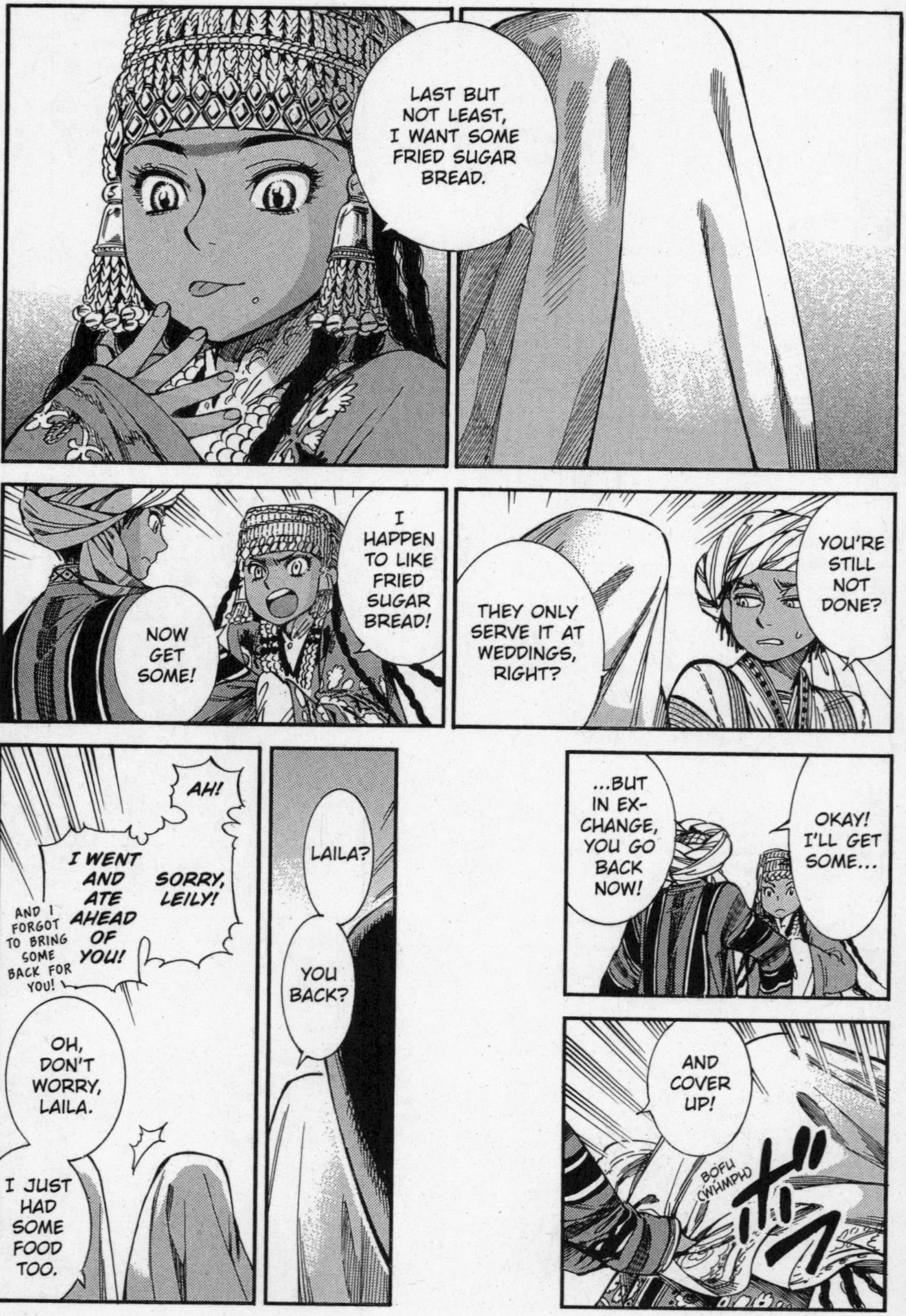
LAST BUT NOT LEAST, I WANT SOME FRIED SUGAR BREAD.
YOU'RE STILL NOT DONE?
THEY ONLY SERVE IT AT WEDDINGS, RIGHT?
I HAPPEN TO LIKE FRIED SUGAR BREAD!
NOW GET SOME!
OKAY! I'LL GET SOME...
...BUT IN EX-CHANGE, YOU GO BACK NOW!
AND COVER UP!
BOFU (WHMPH)
LAILA?
YOU BACK?
AH!
SORRY, LEILY!
I WENT AND ATE AHEAD OF YOU!
AND I FORGOT TO BRING SOME BACK FOR YOU!
OH, DON'T WORRY, LAILA.
I JUST HAD SOME FOOD TOO.

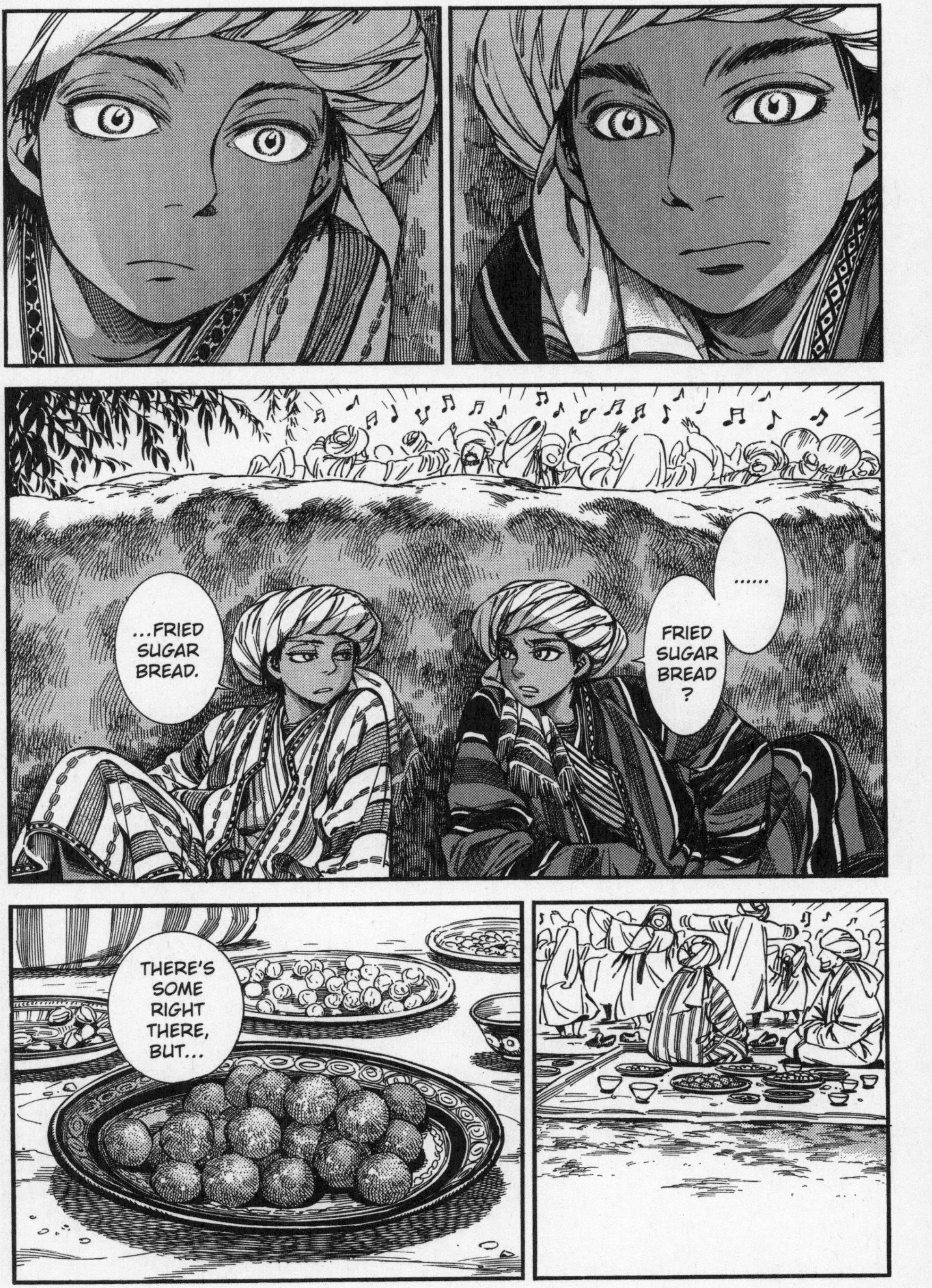
......
FRIED SUGAR BREAD?
...FRIED SUGAR BREAD.
THERE'S SOME RIGHT THERE, BUT...

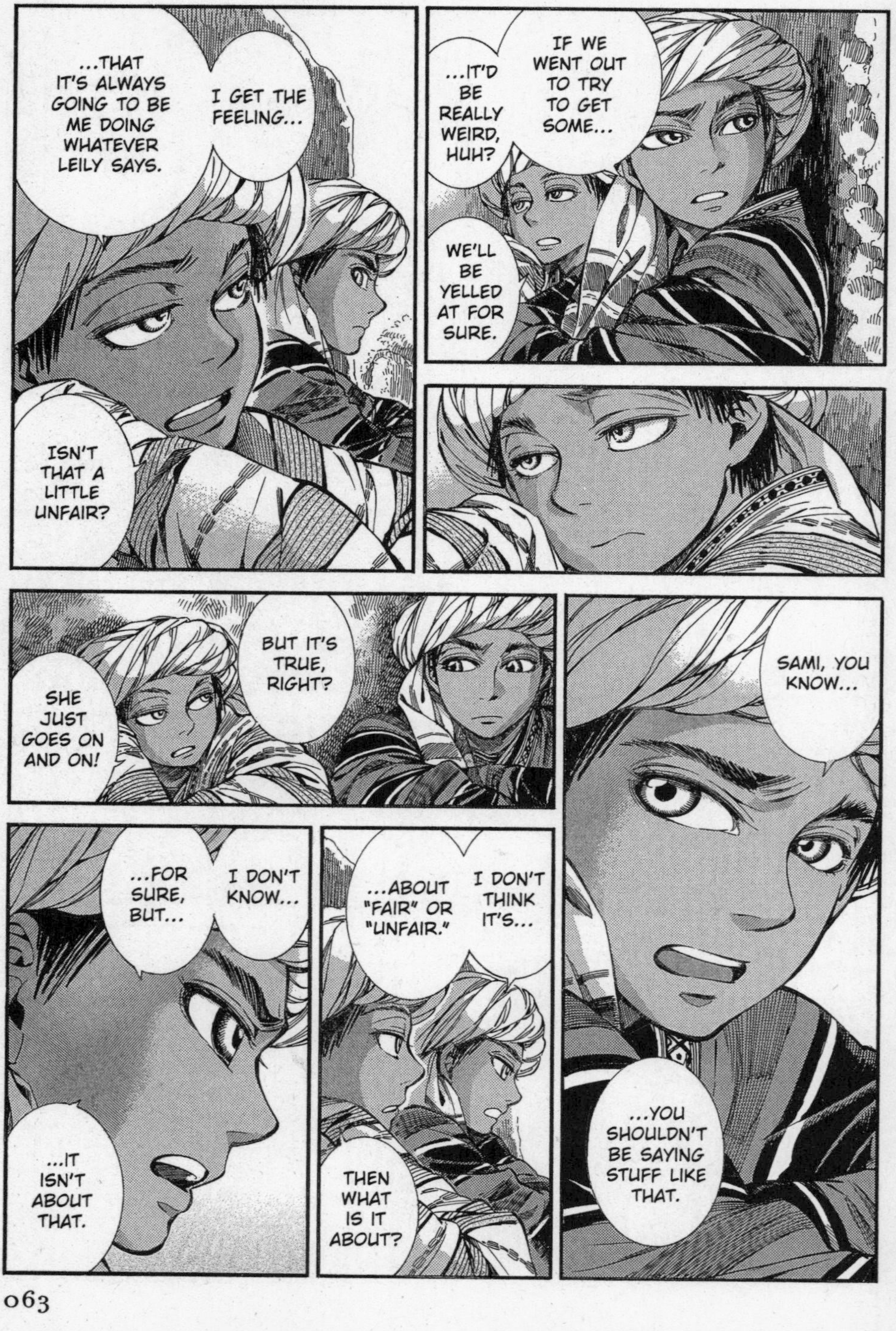
IF WE WENT OUT TO TRY TO GET SOME...
...IT'D BE REALLY WEIRD, HUH?
WE'LL BE YELLED AT FOR SURE.
I GET THE FEELING...
...THAT IT'S ALWAYS GOING TO BE ME DOING WHATEVER LEILY SAYS.
ISN'T THAT A LITTLE UNFAIR?
SAMI, YOU KNOW...
...YOU SHOULDN'T BE SAYING STUFF LIKE THAT.
BUT IT'S TRUE, RIGHT?
SHE JUST GOES ON AND ON!
I DON'T THINK IT'S...
...ABOUT "FAIR" OR "UNFAIR."
THEN WHAT IS IT ABOUT?
I DON'T KNOW...
...FOR SURE, BUT...
...IT ISN'T ABOUT THAT.

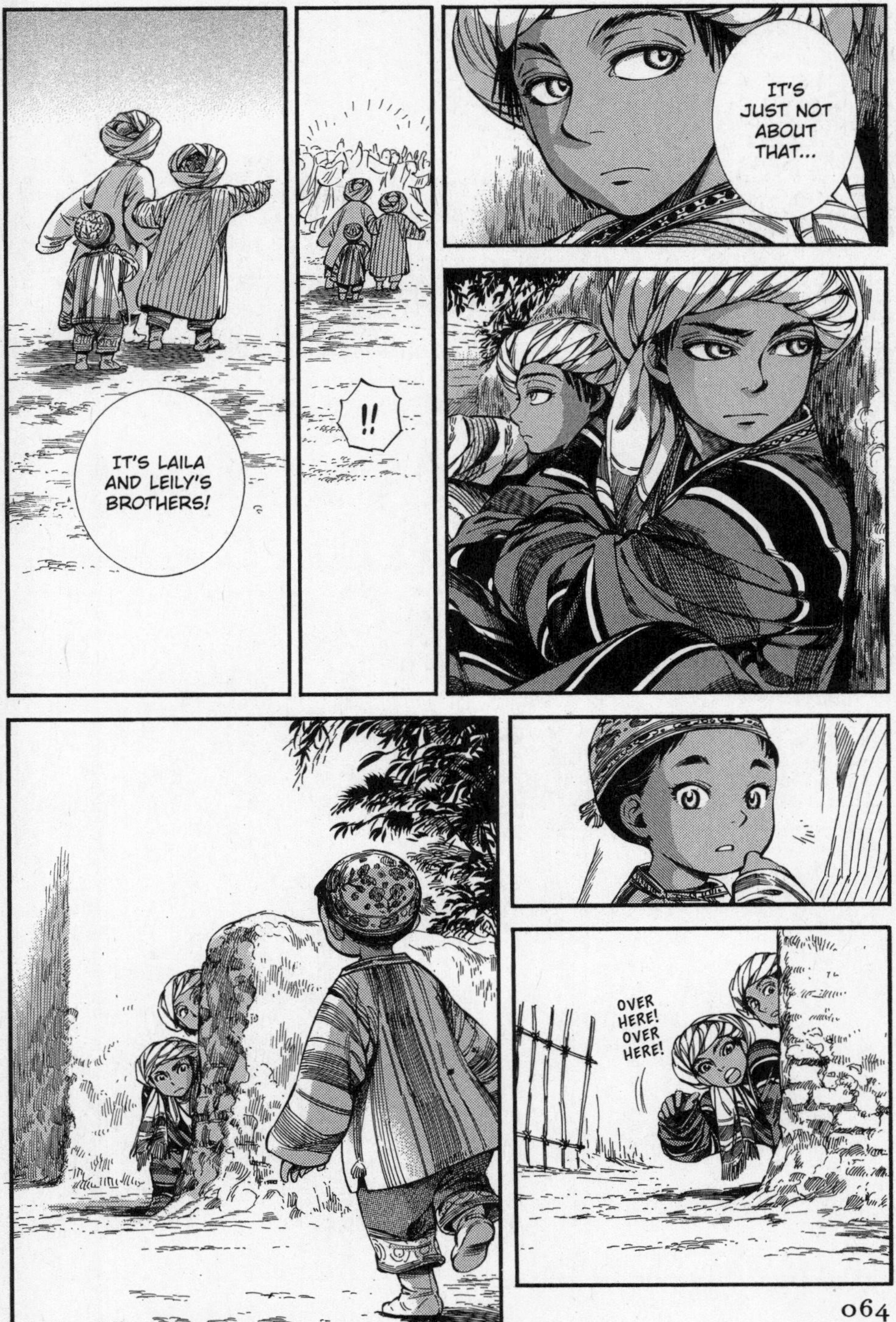
IT'S JUST NOT ABOUT THAT...
!!
IT'S LAILA AND LEILY'S BROTHERS!
OVER HERE! OVER HERE!

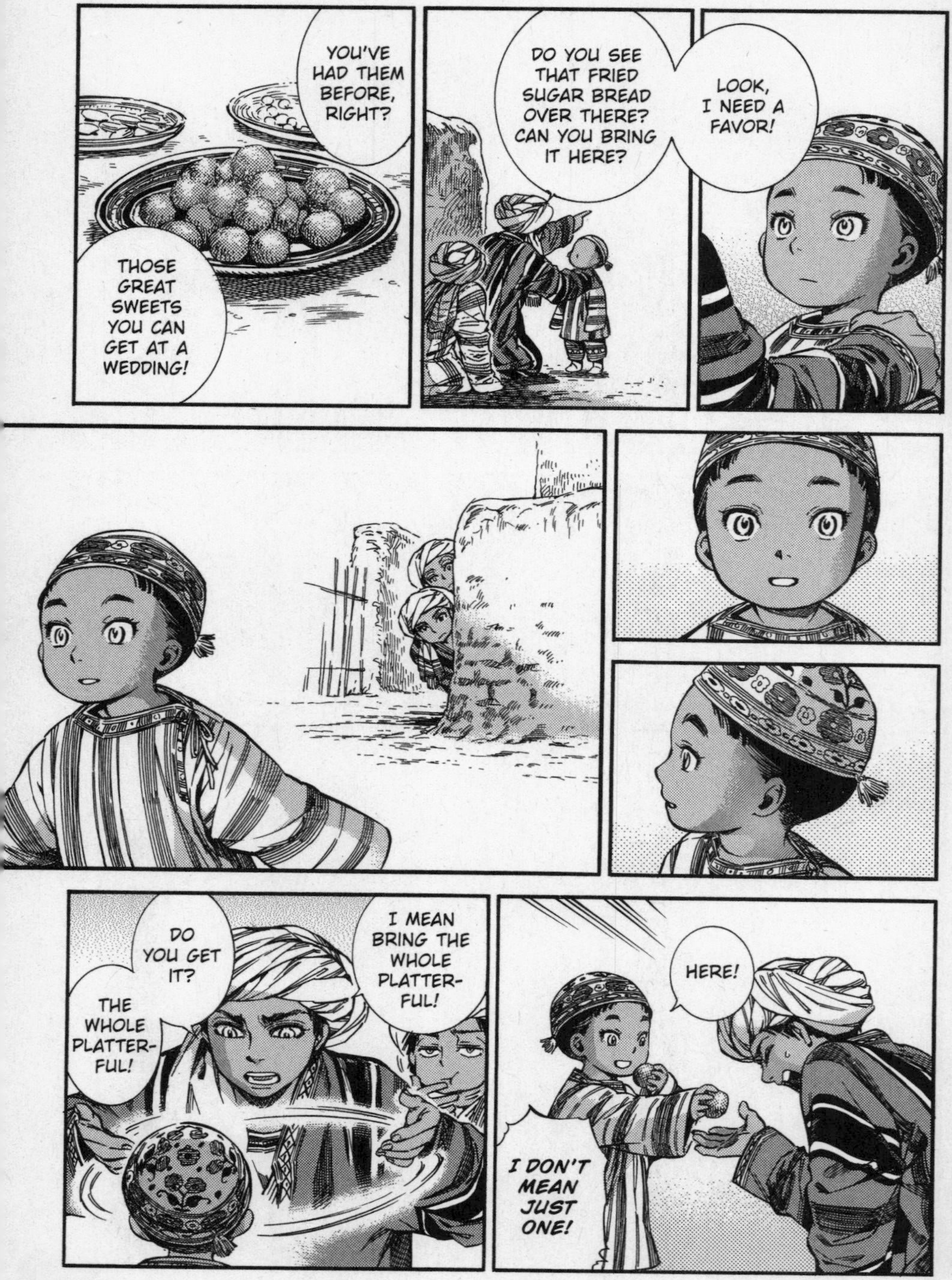
LOOK, I NEED A FAVOR!
DO YOU SEE THAT FRIED SUGAR BREAD OVER THERE? CAN YOU BRING IT HERE?
YOU'VE HAD THEM BEFORE, RIGHT?
THOSE GREAT SWEETS YOU CAN GET AT A WEDDING!
HERE!
I DON'T MEAN JUST ONE!
I MEAN BRING THE WHOLE PLATTER-FUL!
DO YOU GET IT?
THE WHOLE PLATTER-FUL!

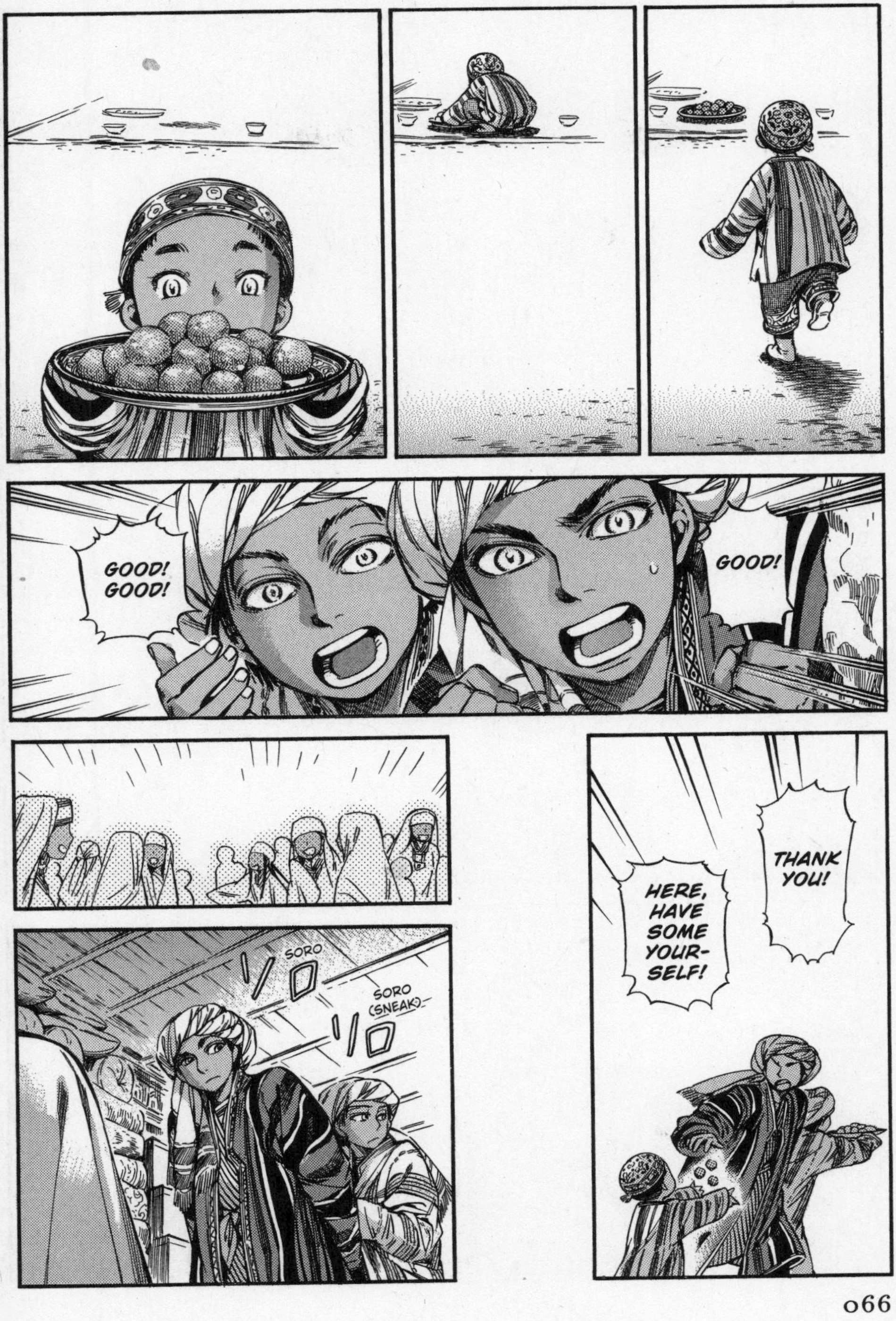
GOOD!
GOOD! GOOD!
THANK YOU!
HERE, HAVE SOME YOURSELF!
ソロ
SORO
ソロ
SORO (SNEAK)

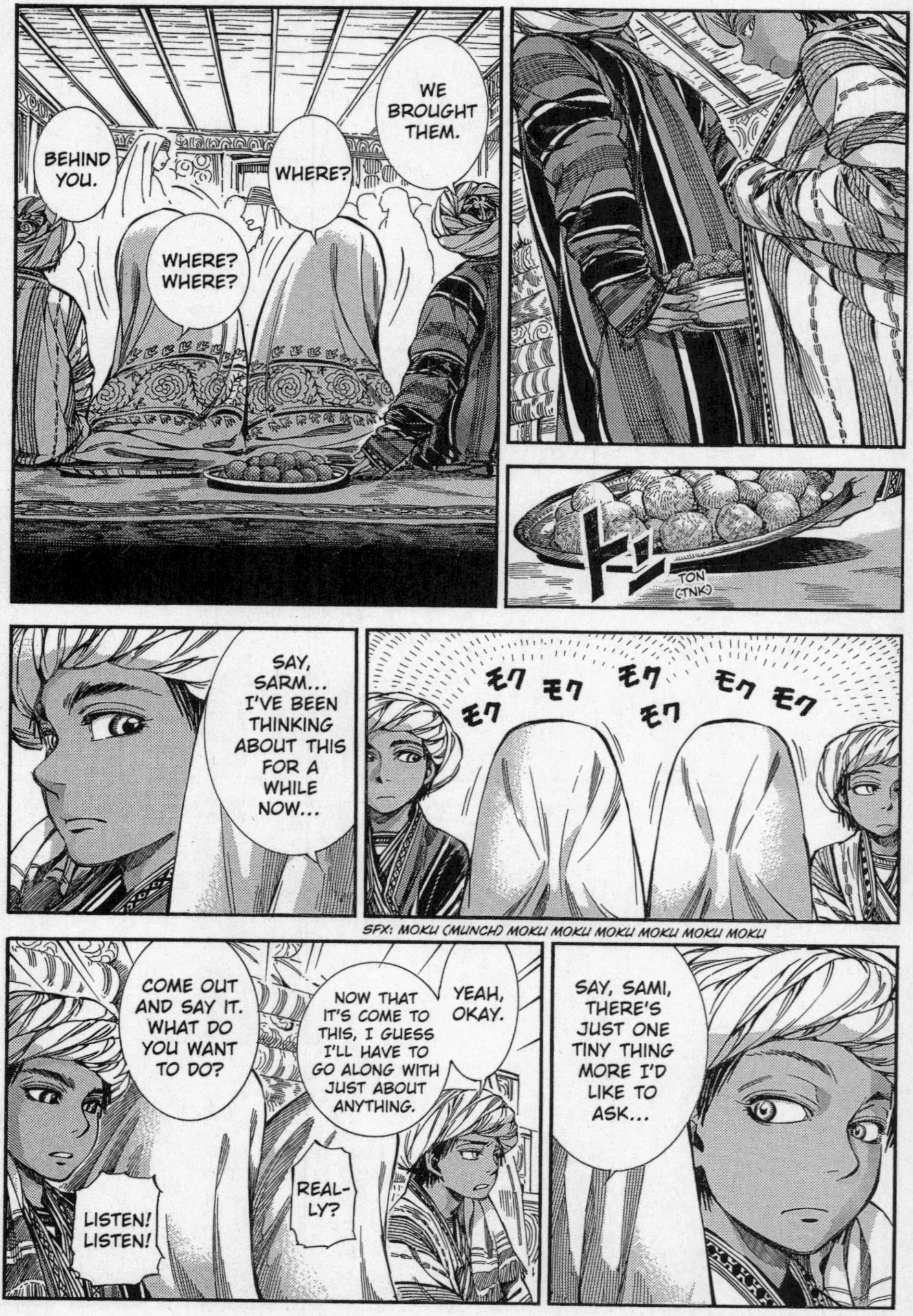
ドン
TON (TNK)
WE BROUGHT THEM.
WHERE?
BEHIND YOU.
WHERE? WHERE?
モク モク モク モク モク モク モク
SFX: MOKU (MUNCH) MOKU MOKU MOKU MOKU MOKU MOKU
SAY, SARM... I'VE BEEN THINKING ABOUT THIS FOR A WHILE NOW...
SAY, SAMI, THERE'S JUST ONE TINY THING MORE I'D LIKE TO ASK...
YEAH, OKAY.
NOW THAT IT'S COME TO THIS, I GUESS I'LL HAVE TO GO ALONG WITH JUST ABOUT ANYTHING.
COME OUT AND SAY IT. WHAT DO YOU WANT TO DO?
REAL-LY?
LISTEN! LISTEN!

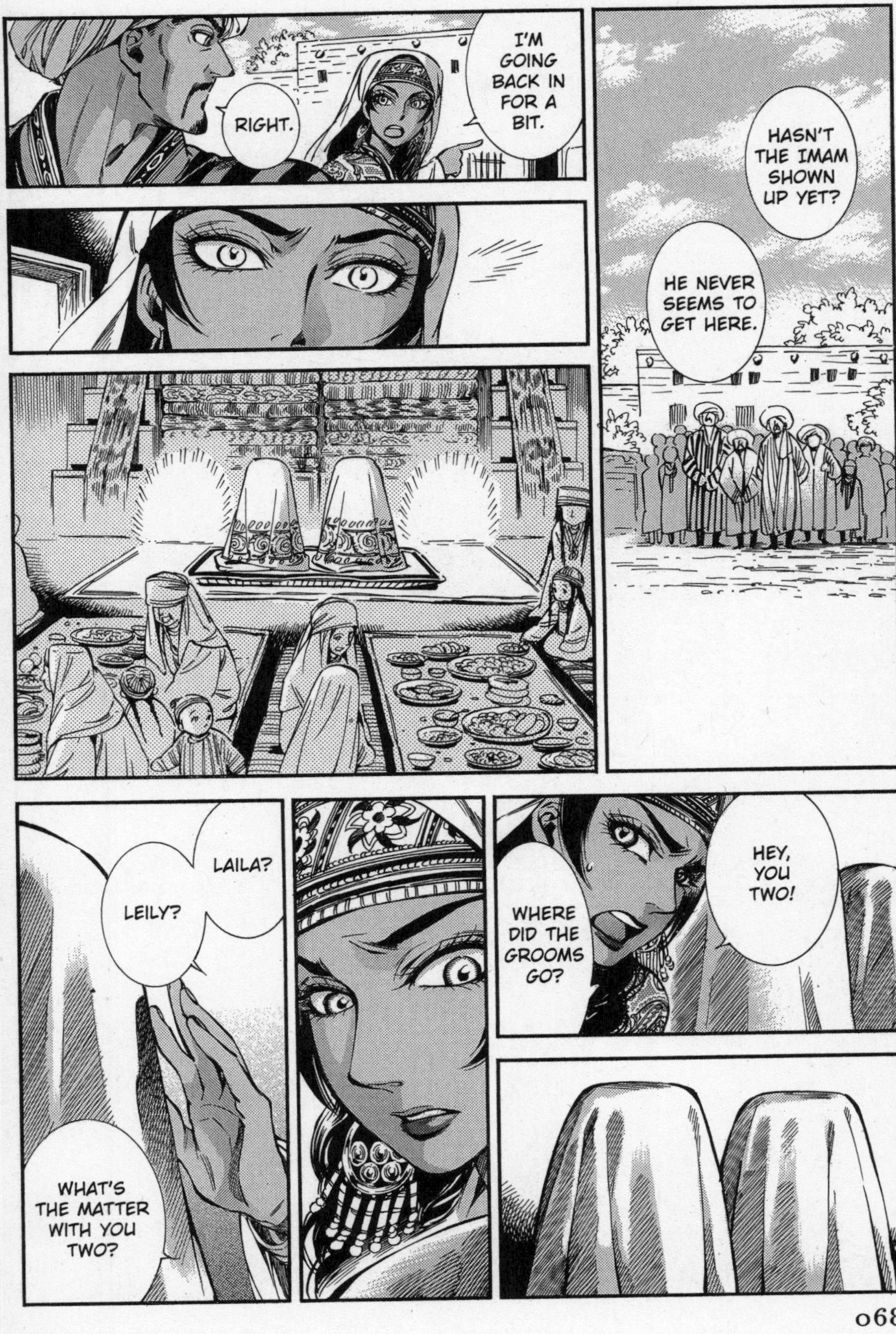

HASN'T THE IMAM SHOWN UP YET?
HE NEVER SEEMS TO GET HERE.
I'M GOING BACK IN FOR A BIT.
RIGHT.
HEY, YOU TWO!
WHERE DID THE GROOMS GO?
LAILA?
LEILY?
WHAT'S THE MATTER WITH YOU TWO?

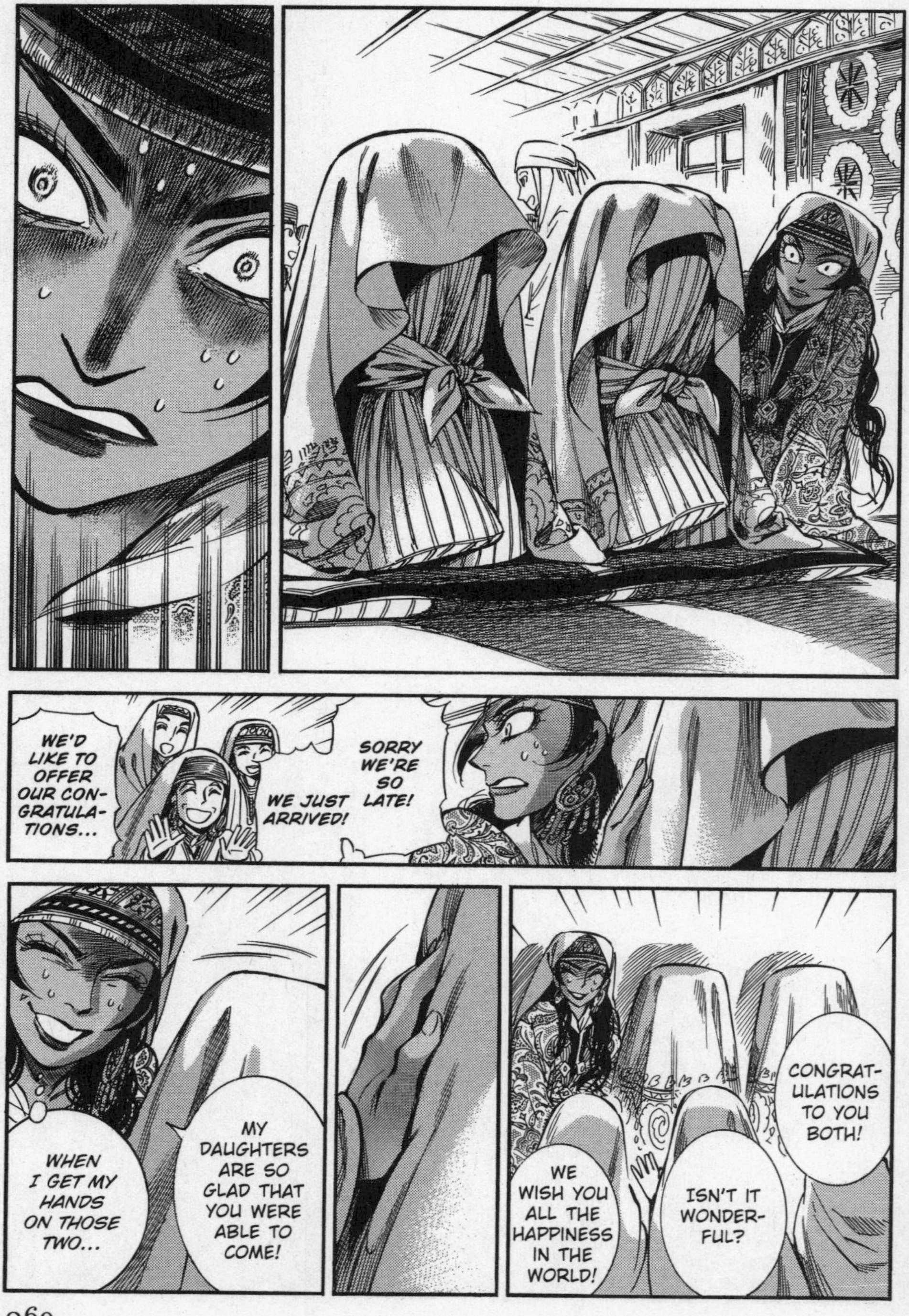
SORRY WE'RE SO LATE!
WE JUST ARRIVED!
WE'D LIKE TO OFFER OUR CONGRATULATIONS...
CONGRATULATIONS TO YOU BOTH!
ISN'T IT WONDERFUL?
WE WISH YOU ALL THE HAPPINESS IN THE WORLD!
MY DAUGHTERS ARE SO GLAD THAT YOU WERE ABLE TO COME!
WHEN I GET MY HANDS ON THOSE TWO...

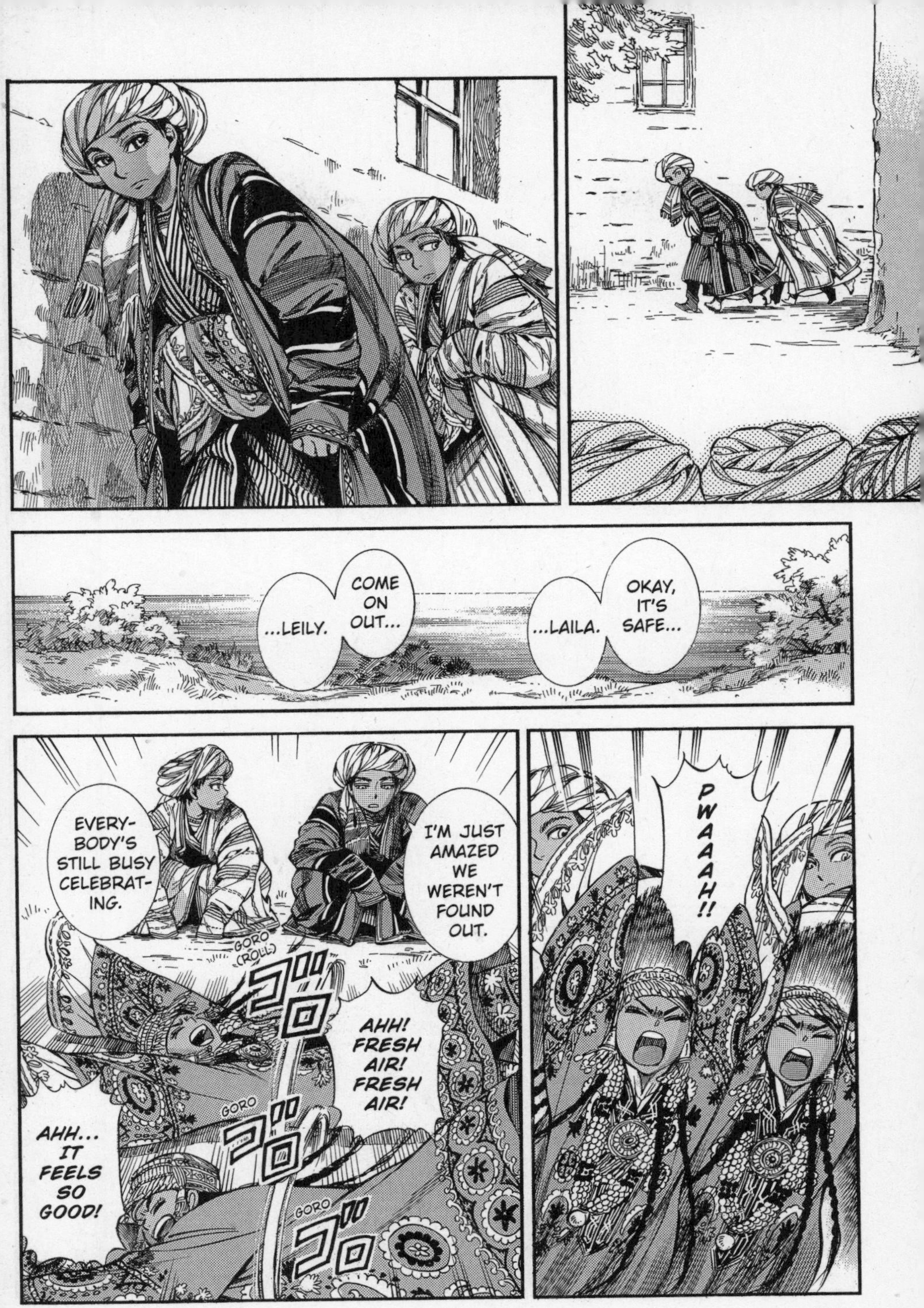
OKAY, IT'S SAFE...
...LAILA.
COME ON OUT...
...LEILY.
PWAAAAH!!
I'M JUST AMAZED WE WEREN'T FOUND OUT.
EVERY-BODY'S STILL BUSY CELEBRAT-ING.
GORO (ROLL)
AHH! FRESH AIR! FRESH AIR!
GORO
GORO
AHH... IT FEELS SO GOOD!

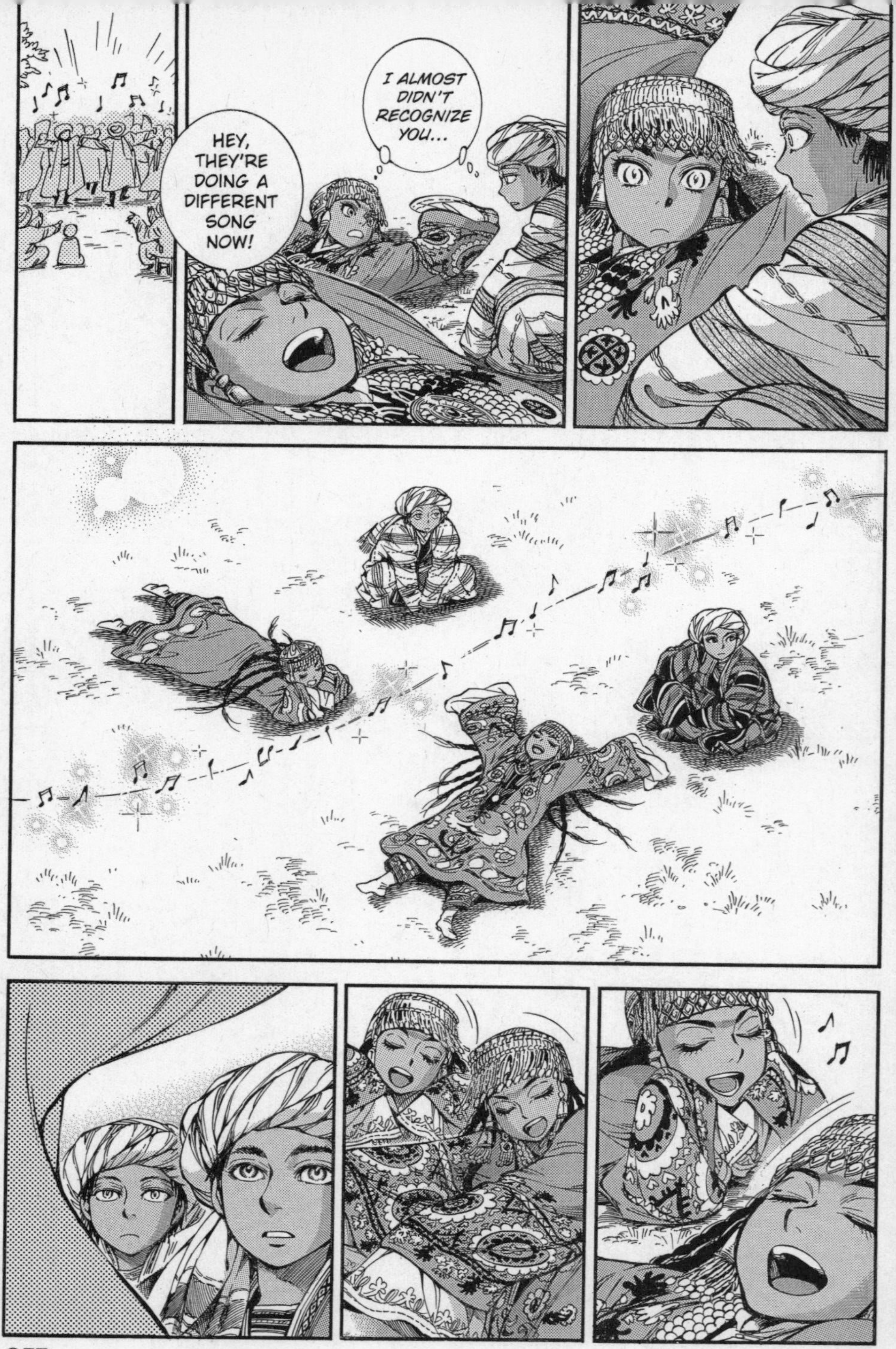
I ALMOST DIDN'T RECOGNIZE YOU...
HEY, THEY'RE DOING A DIFFERENT SONG NOW!

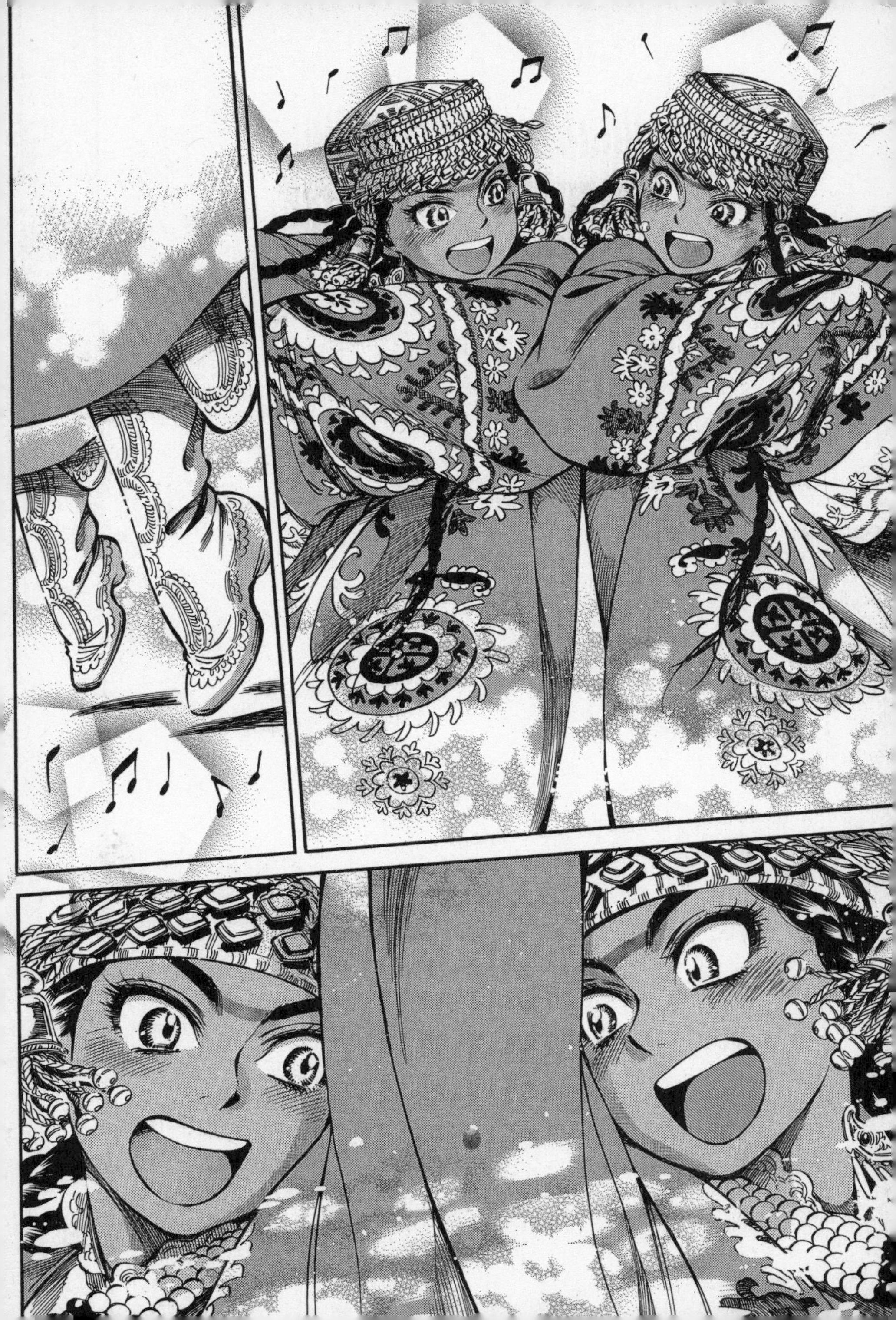

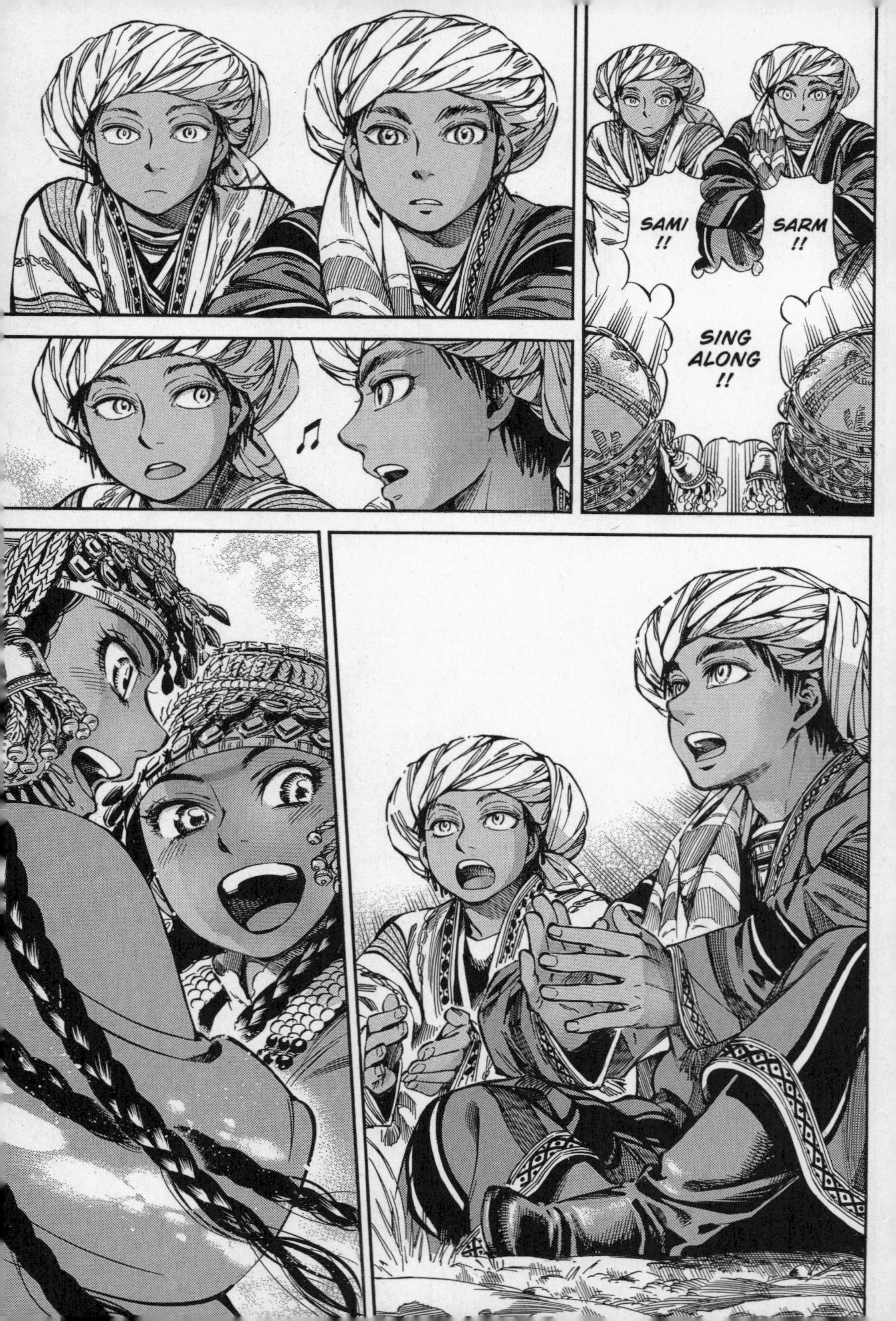
SAMI !!
SARM !!
SING ALONG !!

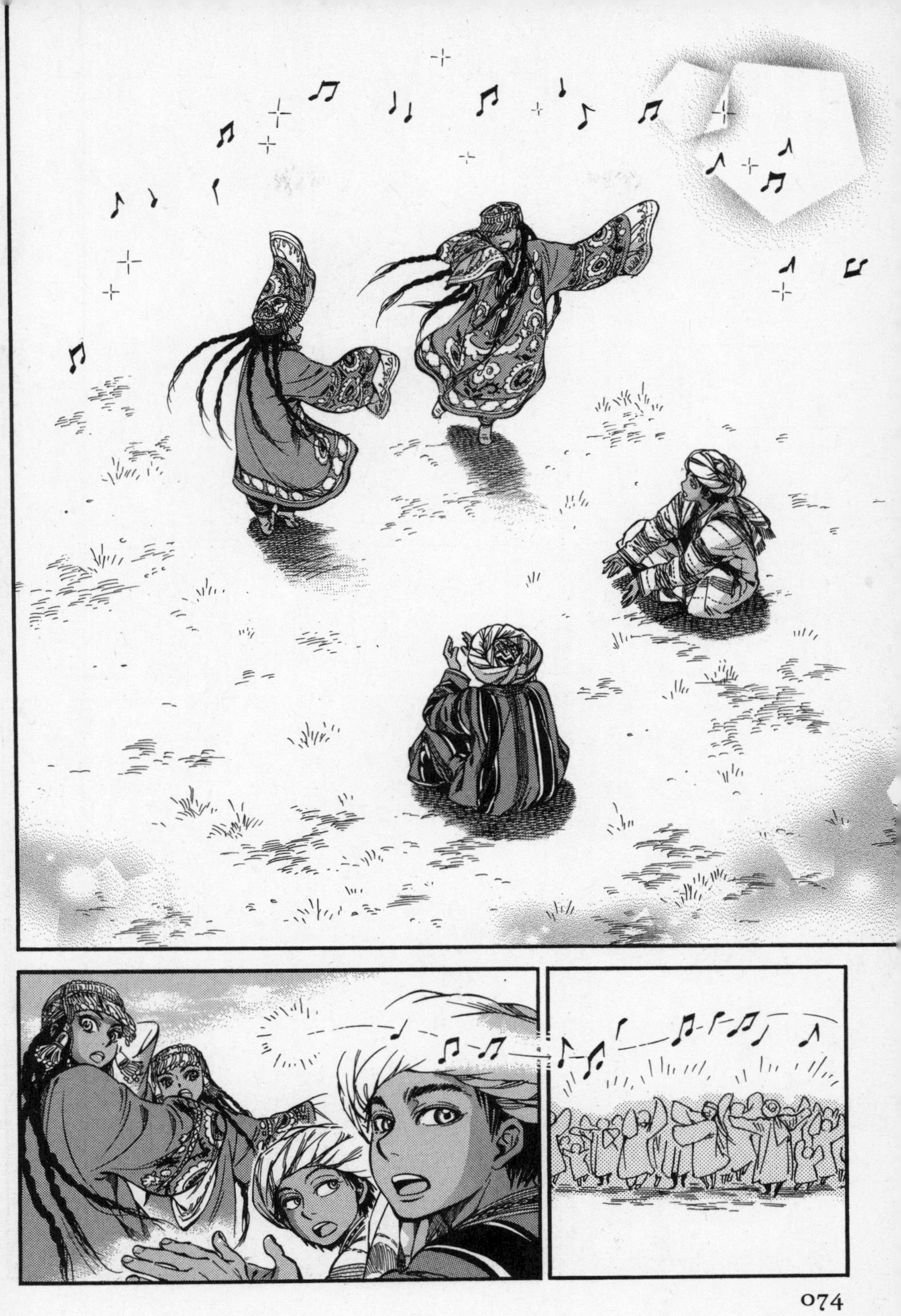

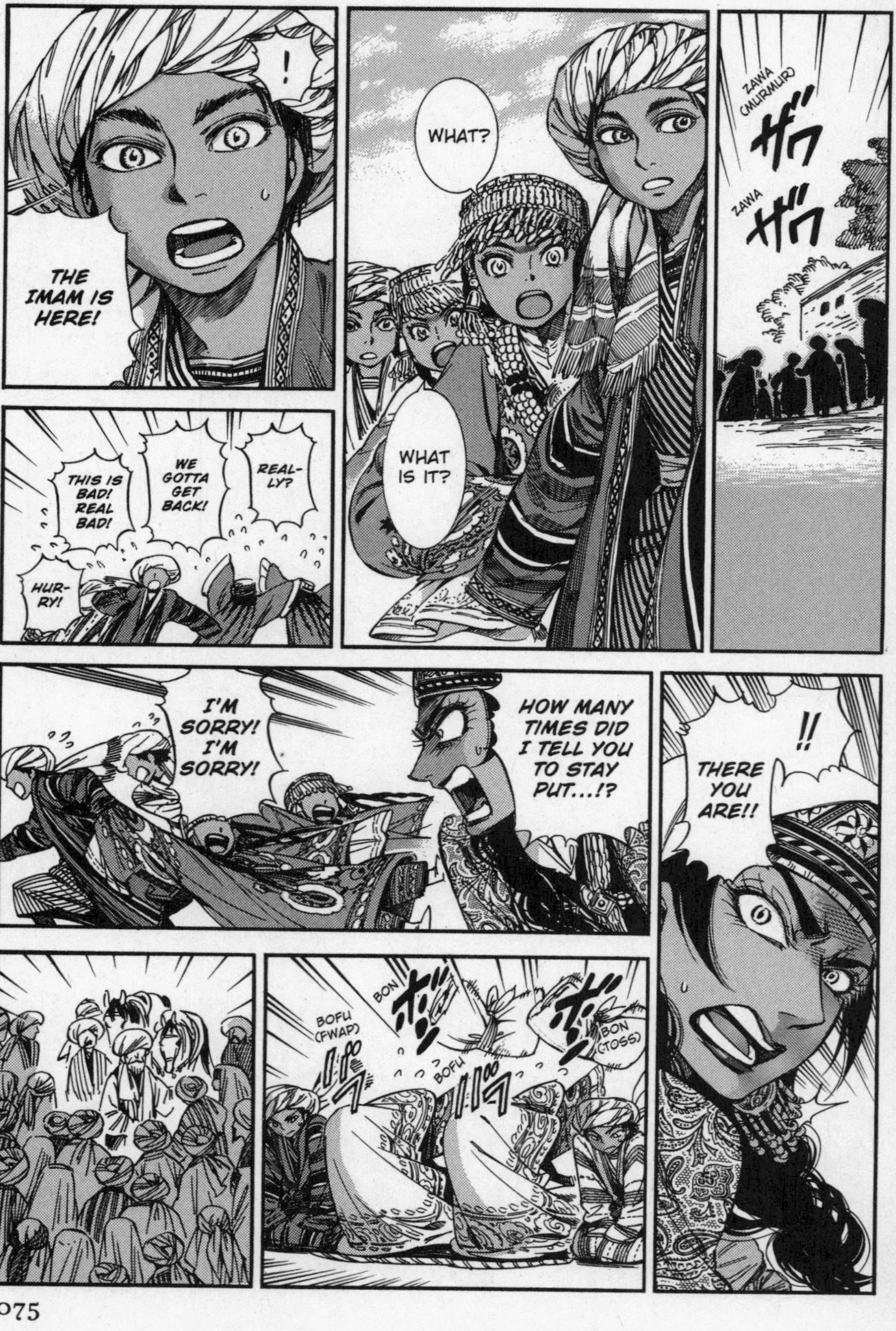

ZAWA (MURMUR)
ZAWA
WHAT?
WHAT IS IT?
!
THE IMAM IS HERE!
REAL-LY?
WE GOTTA GET BACK!
THIS IS BAD! REAL BAD!
HURRY!
!!
THERE YOU ARE!!
HOW MANY TIMES DID I TELL YOU TO STAY PUT...!?
I'M SORRY! I'M SORRY!
BON
BON (TOSS)
BOFU
BOFU (FWAP)

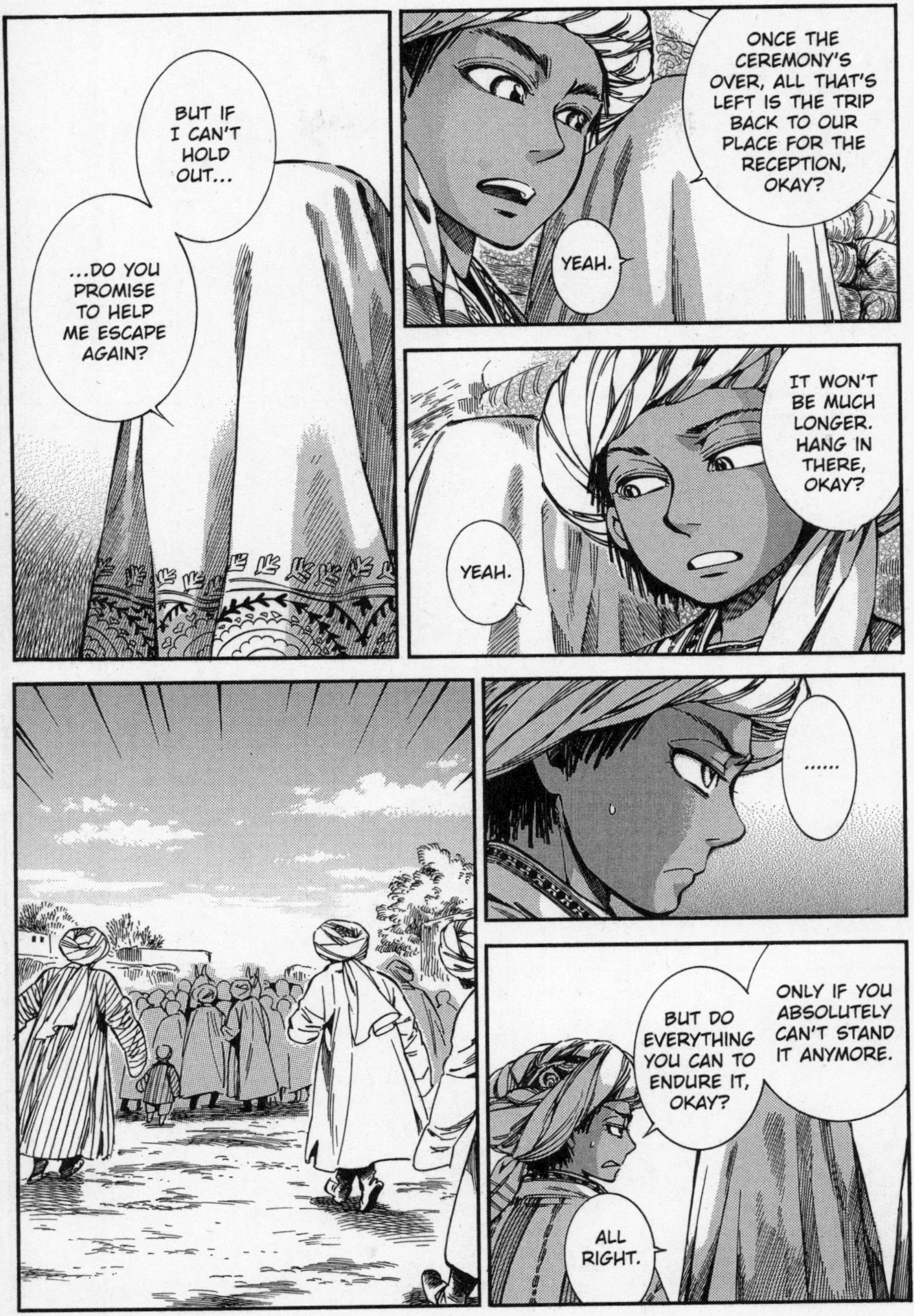
ONCE THE CEREMONY'S OVER, ALL THAT'S LEFT IS THE TRIP BACK TO OUR PLACE FOR THE RECEPTION, OKAY?
YEAH.
IT WON'T BE MUCH LONGER. HANG IN THERE, OKAY?
YEAH.
BUT IF I CAN'T HOLD OUT...
...DO YOU PROMISE TO HELP ME ESCAPE AGAIN?
......
ONLY IF YOU ABSOLUTELY CAN'T STAND IT ANYMORE.
BUT DO EVERYTHING YOU CAN TO ENDURE IT, OKAY?
ALL RIGHT.

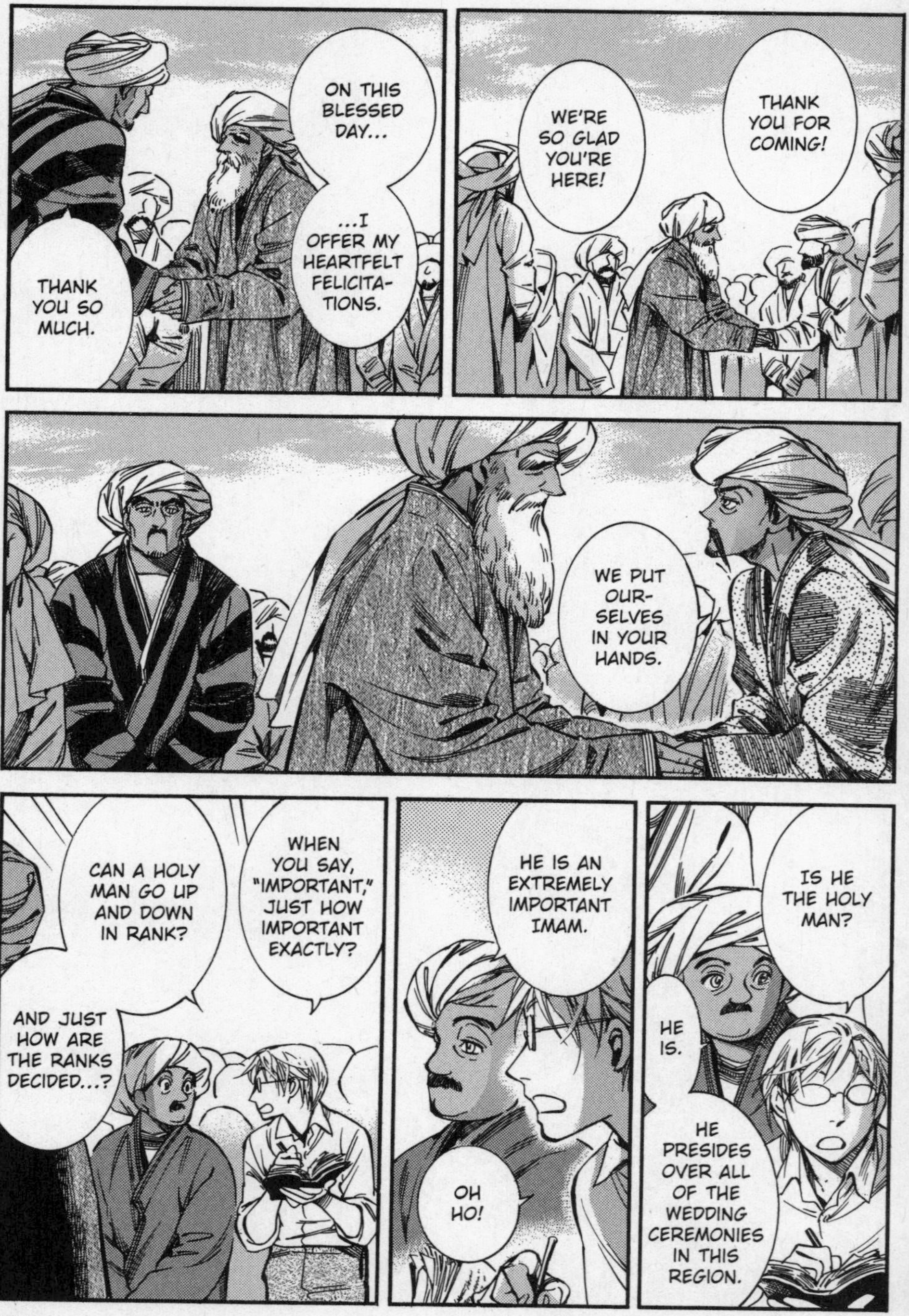
THANK YOU FOR COMING!
WE'RE SO GLAD YOU'RE HERE!
ON THIS BLESSED DAY...
...I OFFER MY HEARTFELT FELICITATIONS.
THANK YOU SO MUCH.
WE PUT OURSELVES IN YOUR HANDS.
IS HE THE HOLY MAN?
HE IS.
HE PRESIDES OVER ALL OF THE WEDDING CEREMONIES IN THIS REGION.
HE IS AN EXTREMELY IMPORTANT IMAM.
OH HO!
WHEN YOU SAY, "IMPORTANT," JUST HOW IMPORTANT EXACTLY?
CAN A HOLY MAN GO UP AND DOWN IN RANK?
AND JUST HOW ARE THE RANKS DECIDED...?

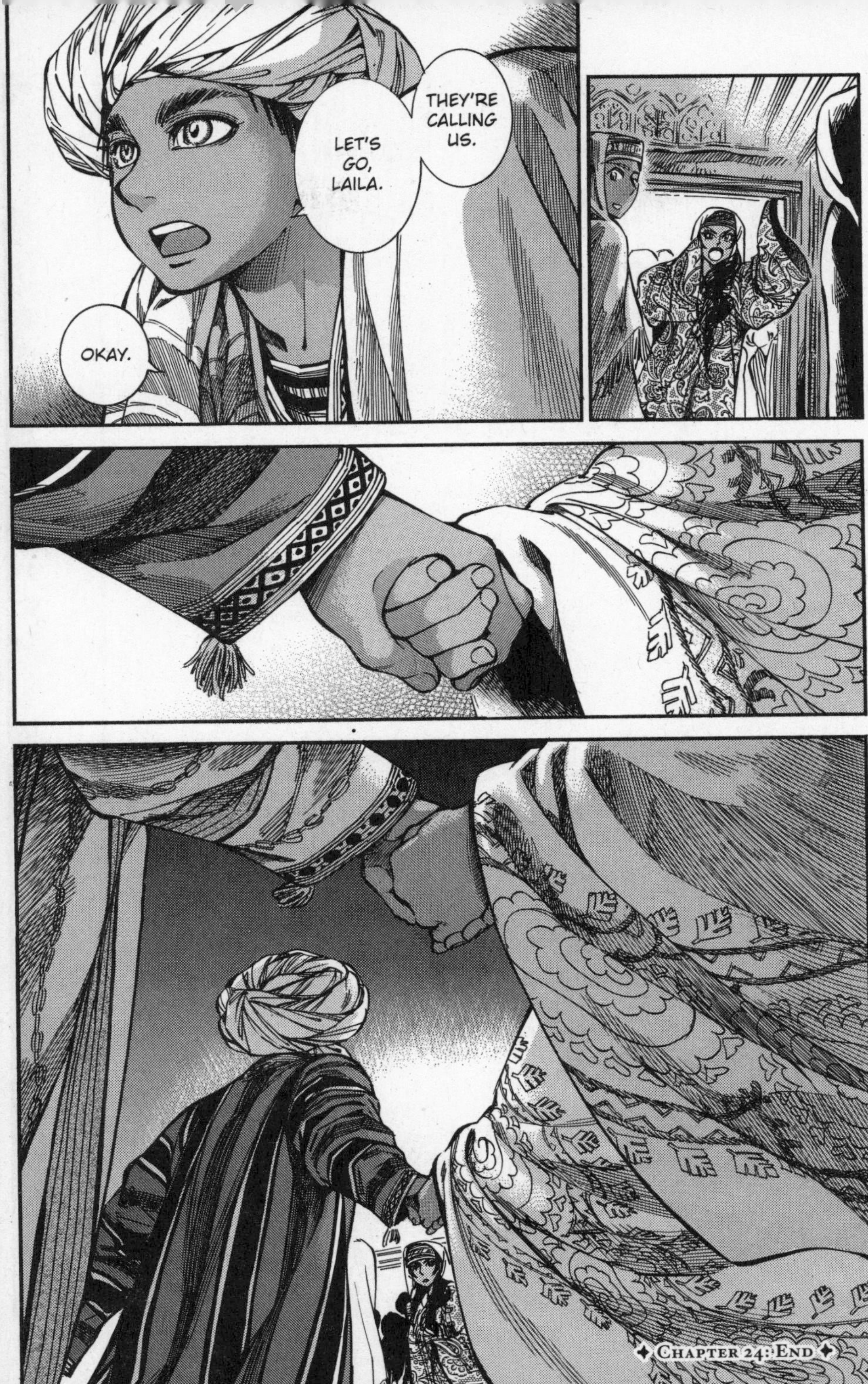
THEY'RE CALLING US.
LET'S GO, LAILA.
OKAY.
CHAPTER 24: END

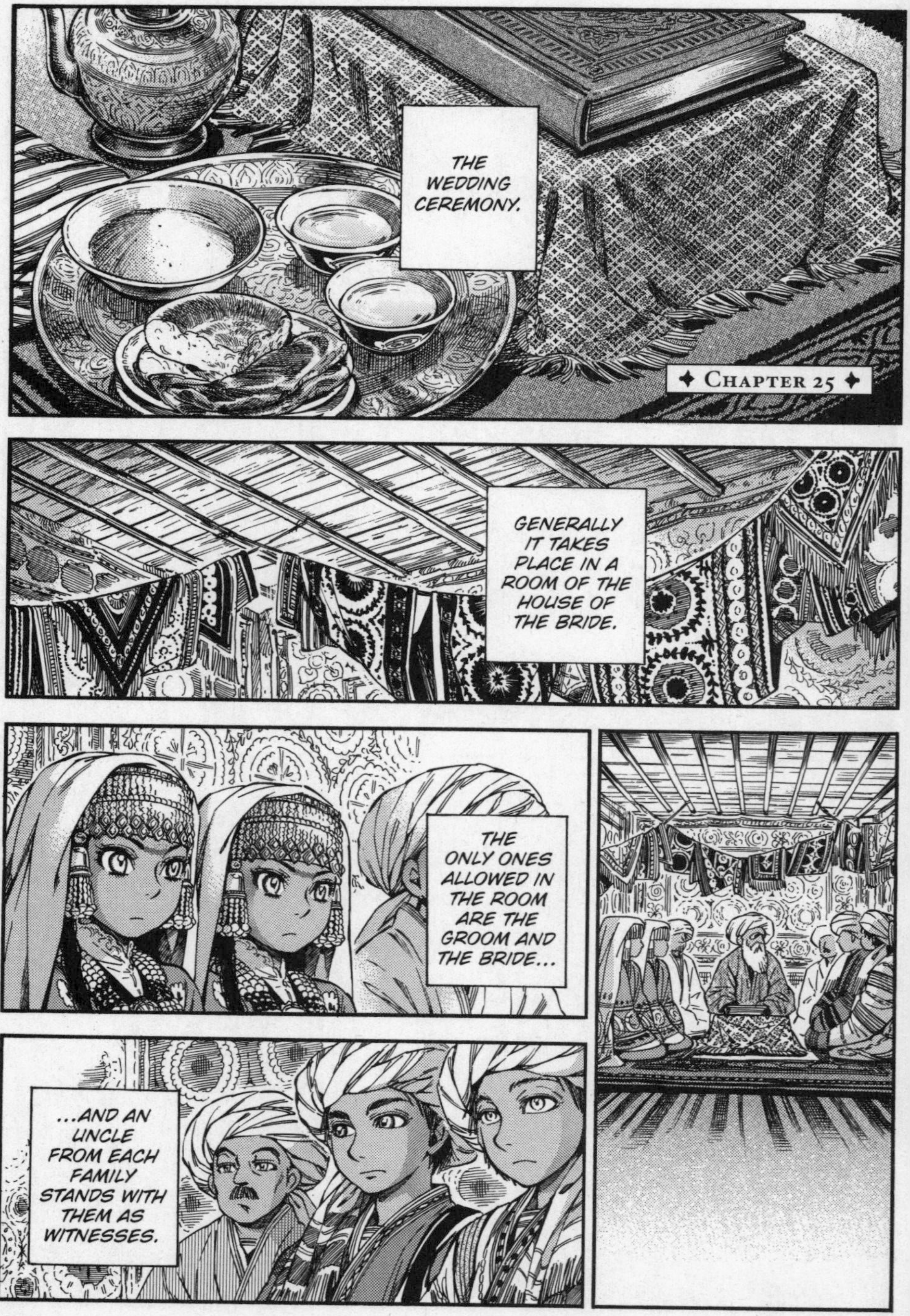
THE WEDDING CEREMONY.
✦ CHAPTER 25 ✦
GENERALLY IT TAKES PLACE IN A ROOM OF THE HOUSE OF THE BRIDE.
THE ONLY ONES ALLOWED IN THE ROOM ARE THE GROOM AND THE BRIDE...
...AND AN UNCLE FROM EACH FAMILY STANDS WITH THEM AS WITNESSES.

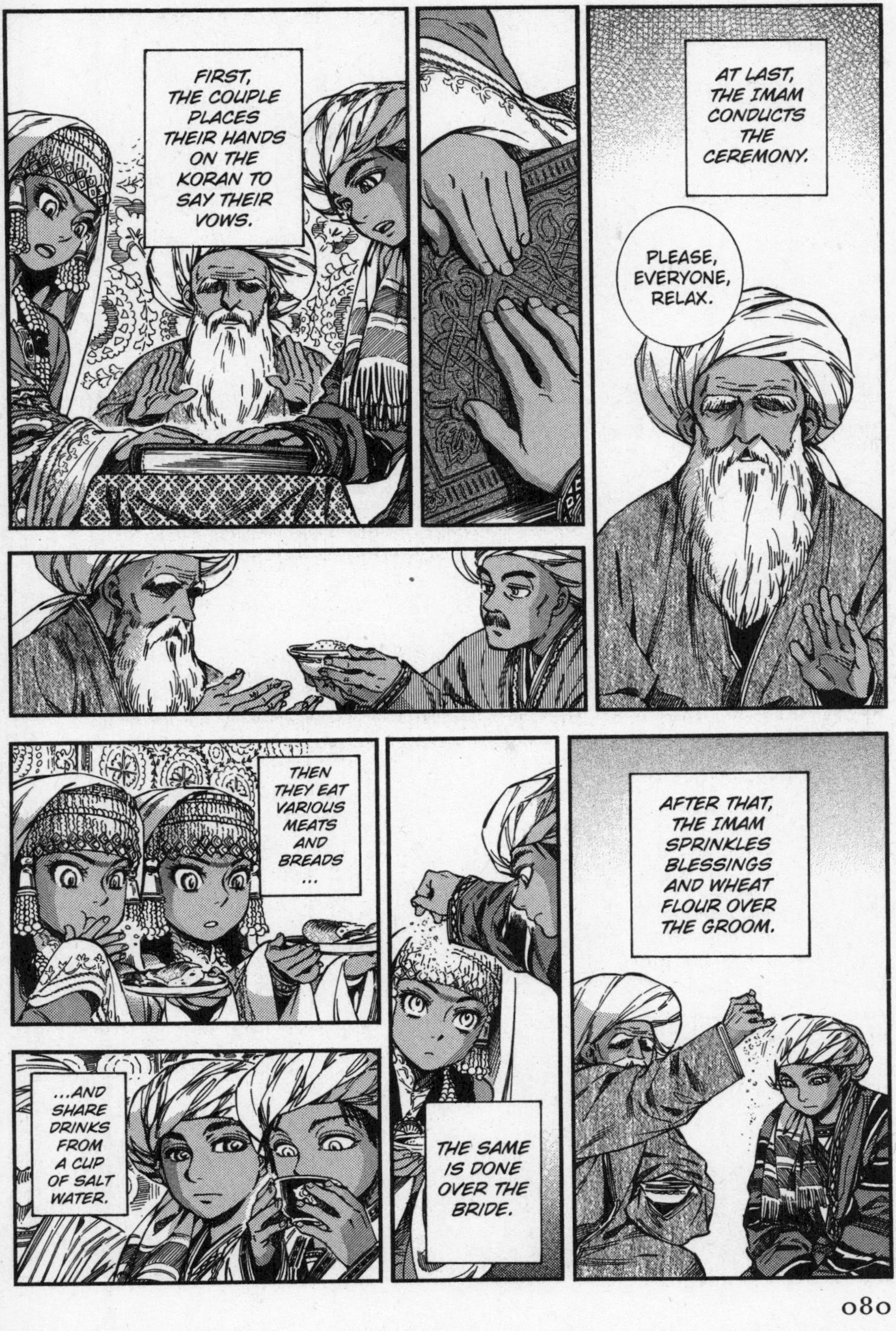
AT LAST, THE IMAM CONDUCTS THE CEREMONY.
PLEASE, EVERYONE, RELAX.
FIRST, THE COUPLE PLACES THEIR HANDS ON THE KORAN TO SAY THEIR VOWS.
AFTER THAT, THE IMAM SPRINKLES BLESSINGS AND WHEAT FLOUR OVER THE GROOM.
THE SAME IS DONE OVER THE BRIDE.
THEN THEY EAT VARIOUS MEATS AND BREADS ...
...AND SHARE DRINKS FROM A CUP OF SALT WATER.

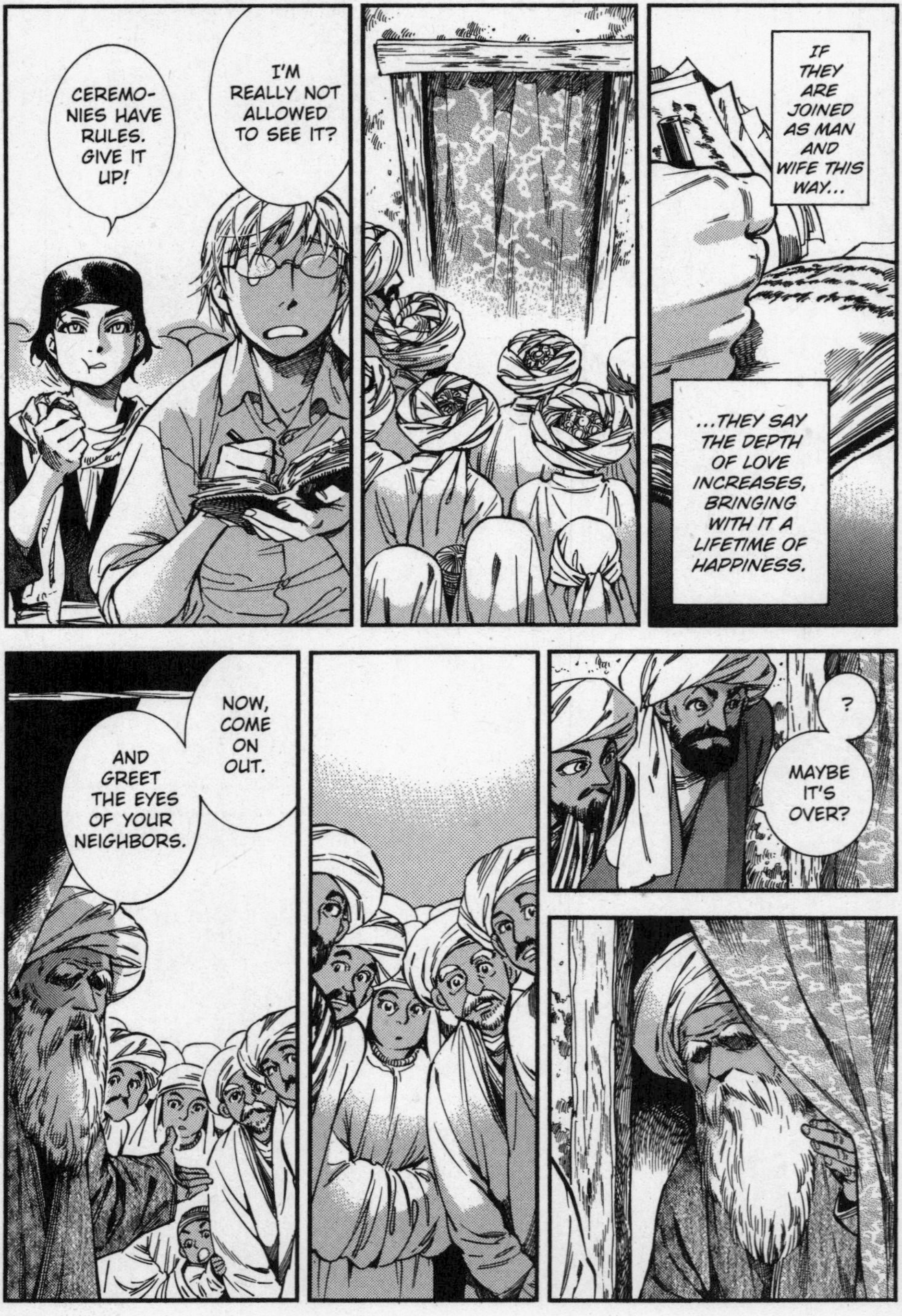
IF THEY ARE JOINED AS MAN AND WIFE THIS WAY...
...THEY SAY THE DEPTH OF LOVE INCREASES, BRINGING WITH IT A LIFETIME OF HAPPINESS.
I'M REALLY NOT ALLOWED TO SEE IT?
CEREMONIES HAVE RULES. GIVE IT UP!
?
MAYBE IT'S OVER?
NOW, COME ON OUT.
AND GREET THE EYES OF YOUR NEIGHBORS.

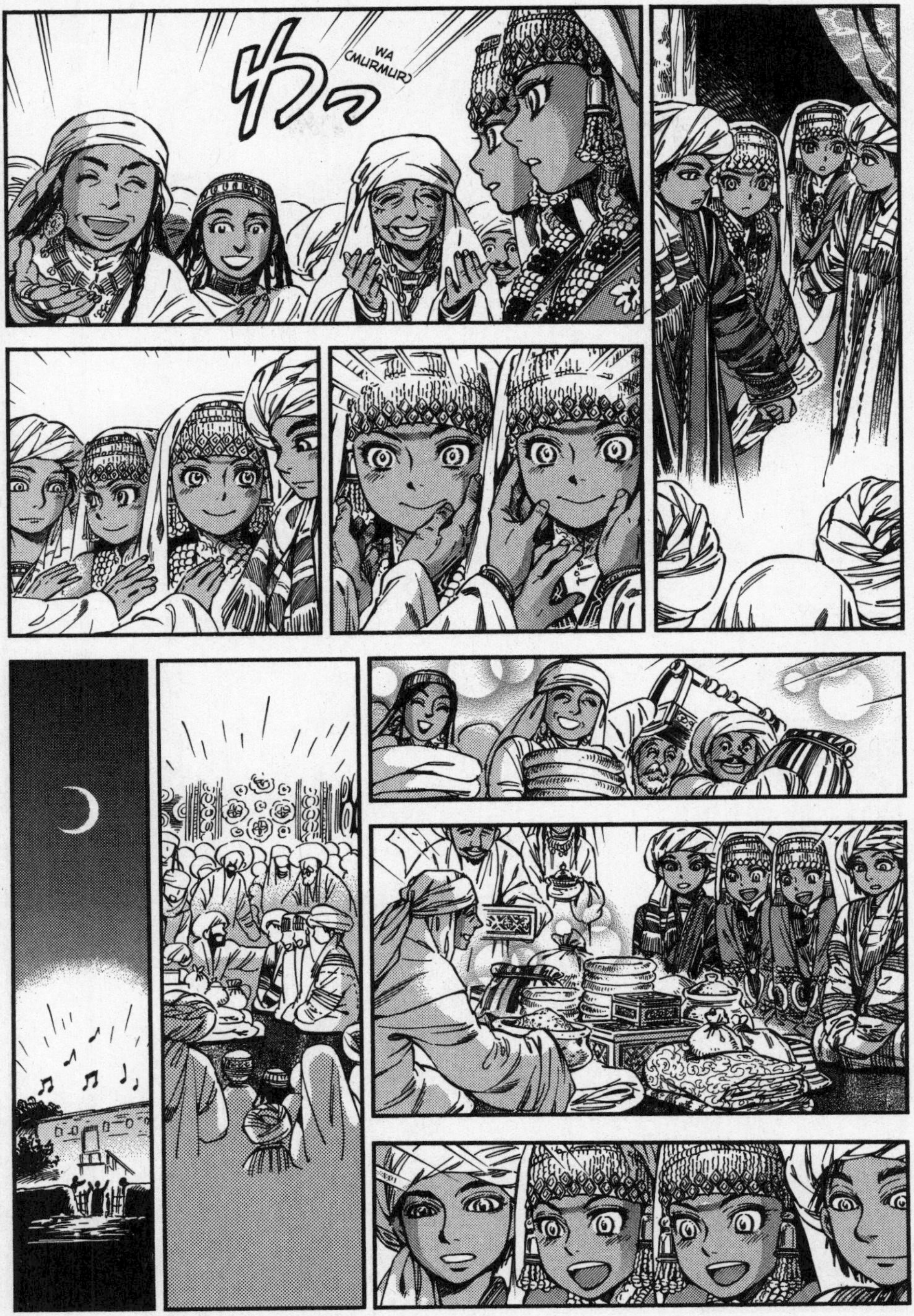
わっ
WA (MURMUR)

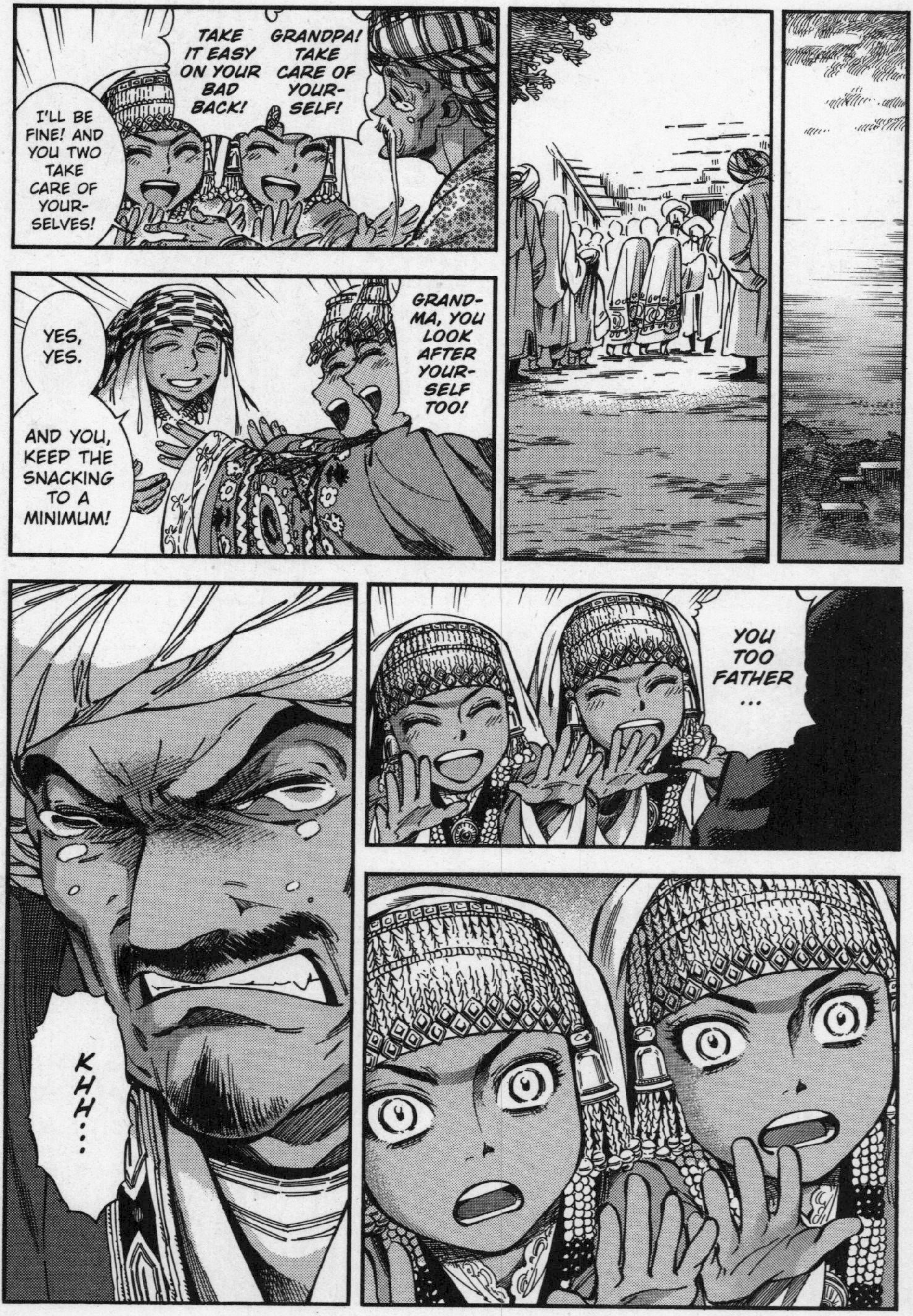
GRANDPA! TAKE CARE OF YOUR-SELF!
TAKE IT EASY ON YOUR BAD BACK!
I'LL BE FINE! AND YOU TWO TAKE CARE OF YOUR-SELVES!
GRAND-MA, YOU LOOK AFTER YOUR-SELF TOO!
YES, YES.
AND YOU, KEEP THE SNACKING TO A MINIMUM!
YOU TOO FATHER ...
KHH...

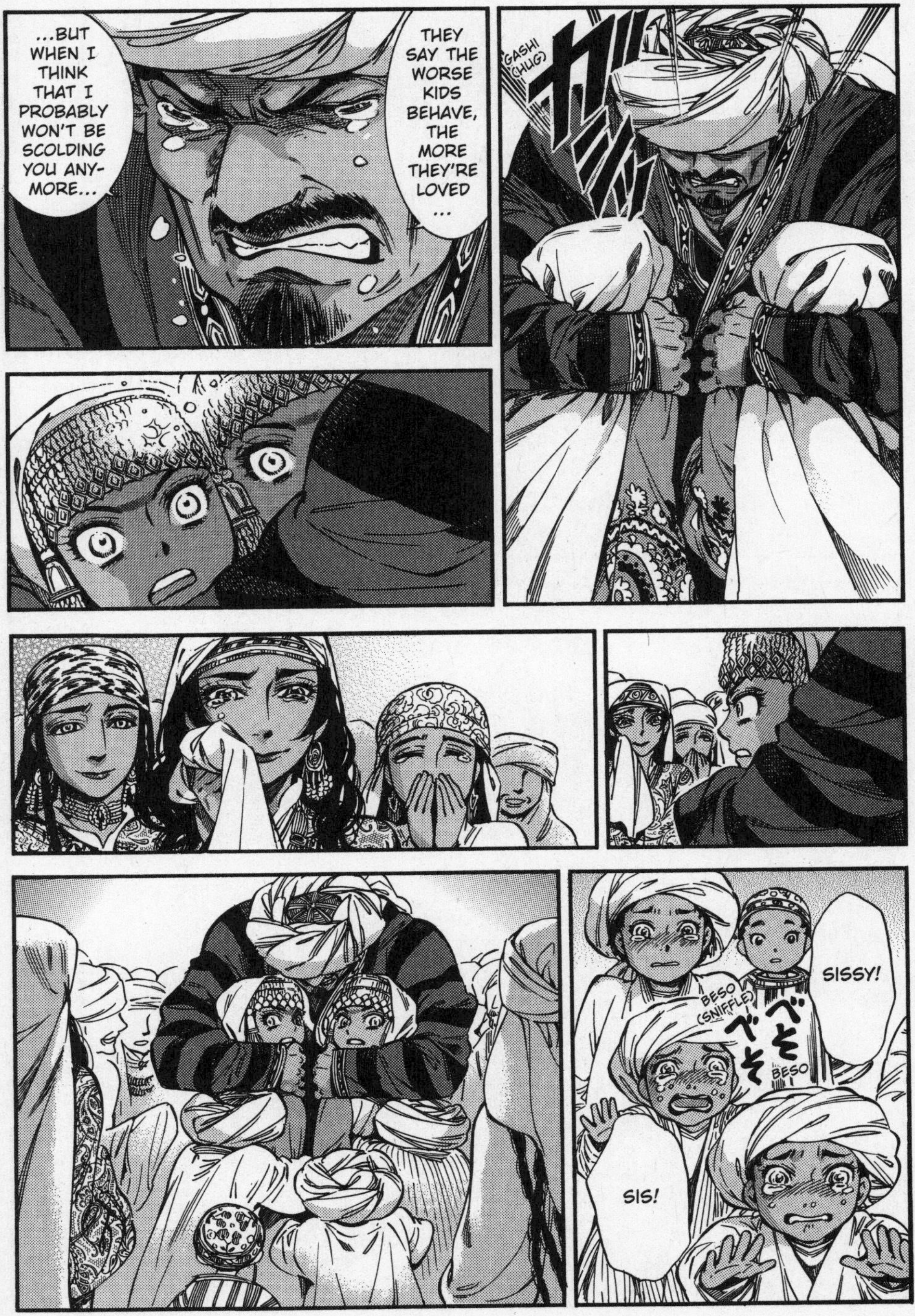
GASHI (HUG)
THEY SAY THE WORSE KIDS BEHAVE, THE MORE THEY'RE LOVED ...
...BUT WHEN I THINK THAT I PROBABLY WON'T BE SCOLDING YOU ANYMORE...
SISSY!
BESO (SNIFFLE)
べそべそ
BESO
SIS!

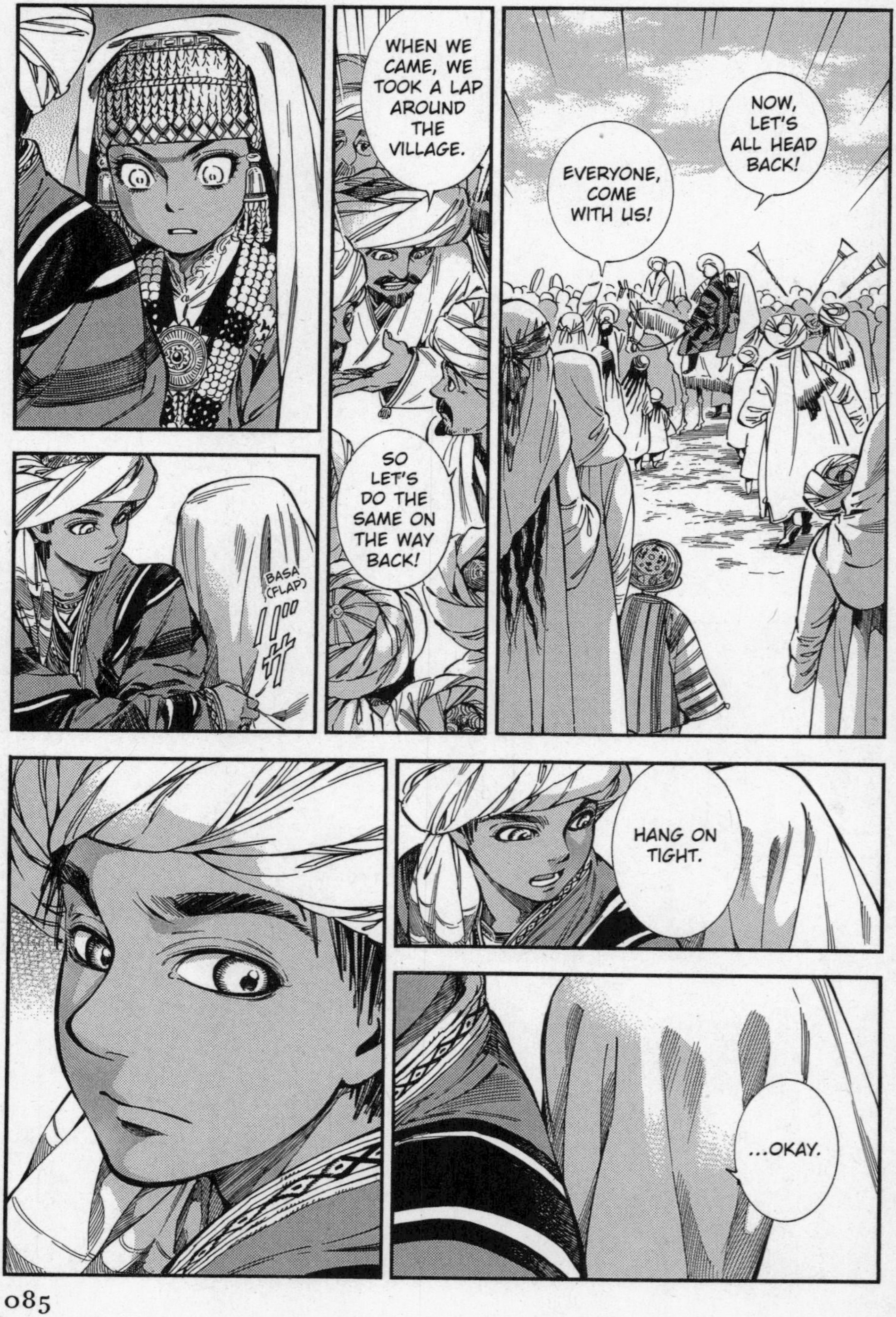
NOW, LET'S ALL HEAD BACK!
EVERYONE, COME WITH US!
WHEN WE CAME, WE TOOK A LAP AROUND THE VILLAGE.
SO LET'S DO THE SAME ON THE WAY BACK!
BASA (FLAP)
HANG ON TIGHT.
...OKAY.

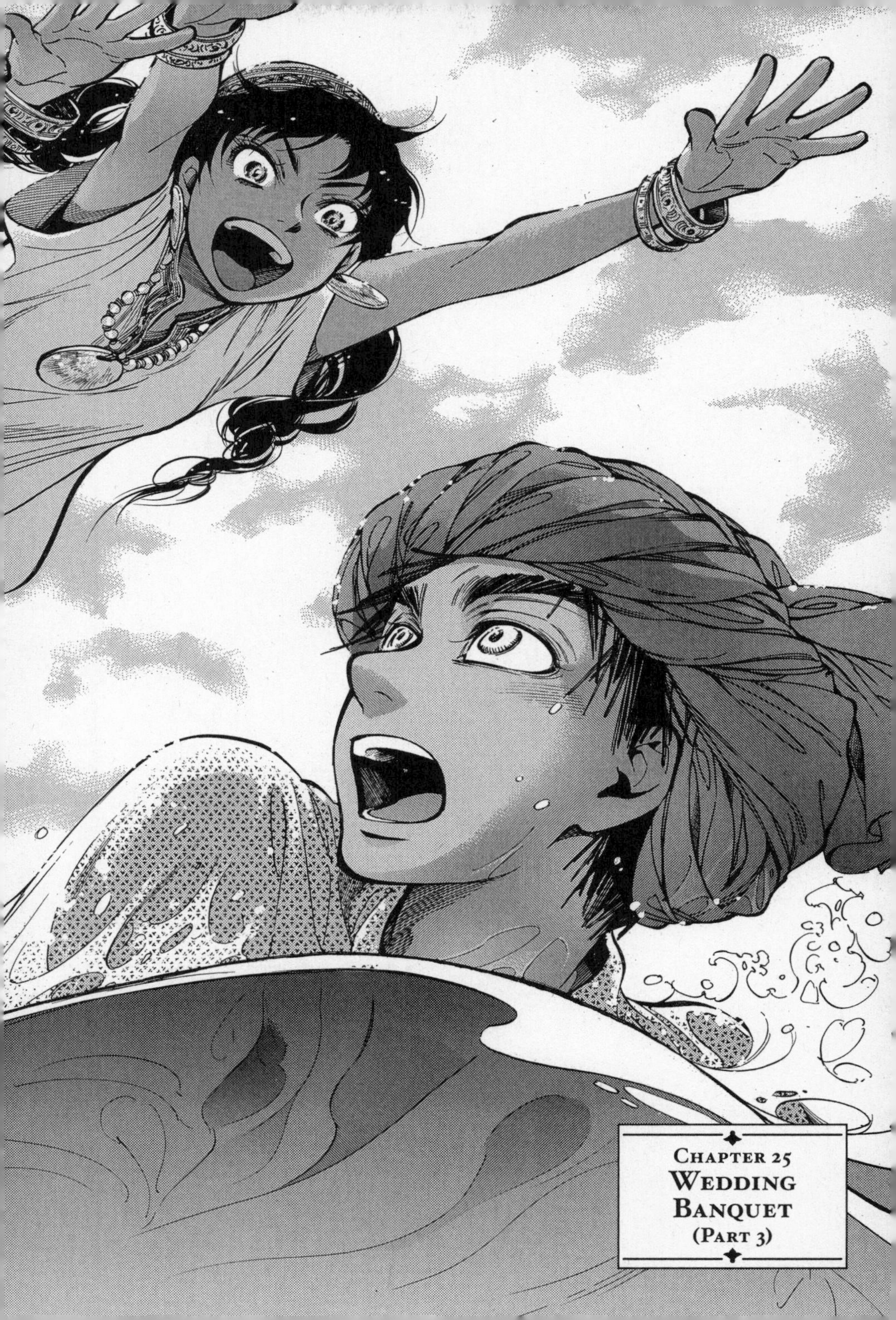

Chapter 25
Wedding Banquet
(Part 3)

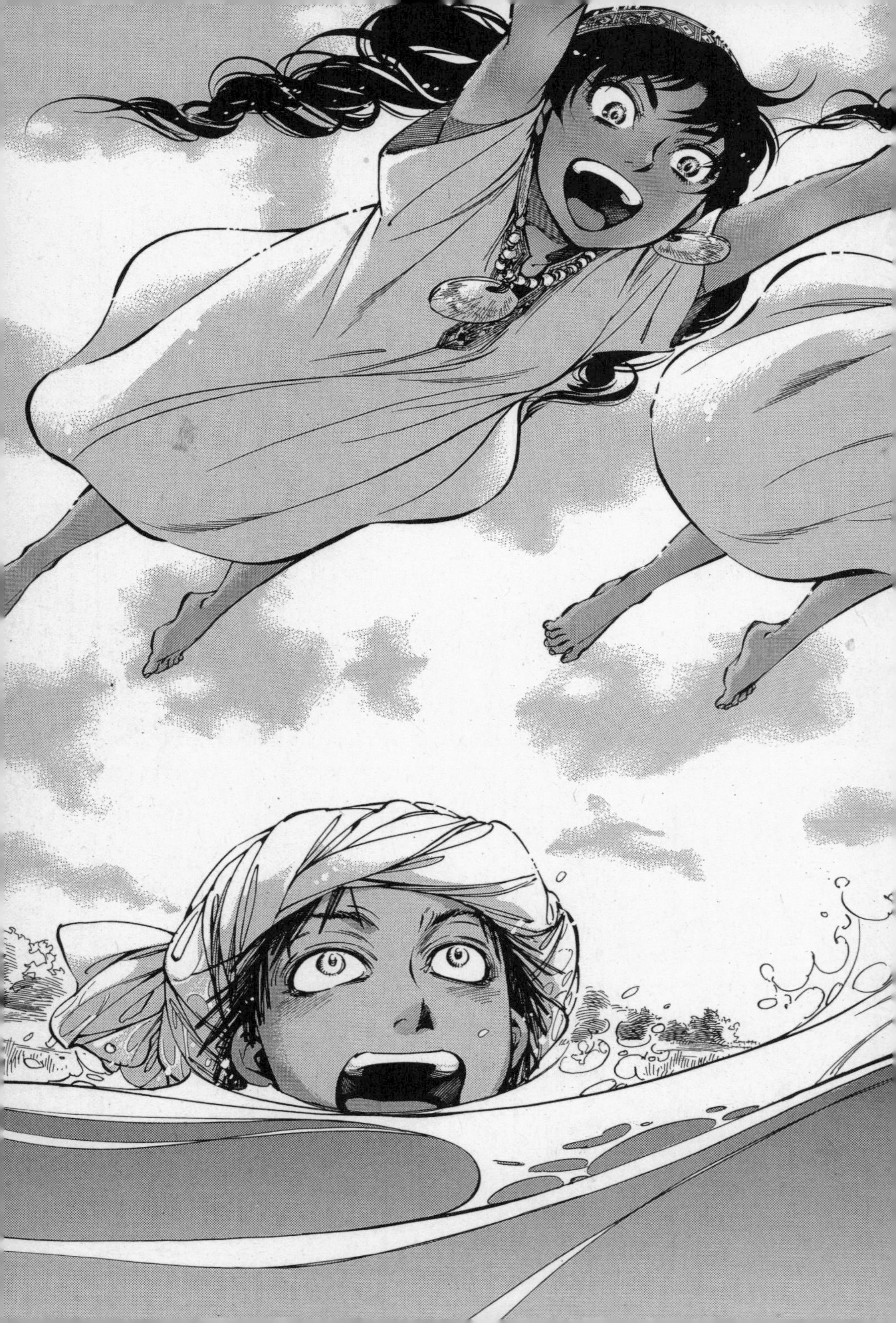

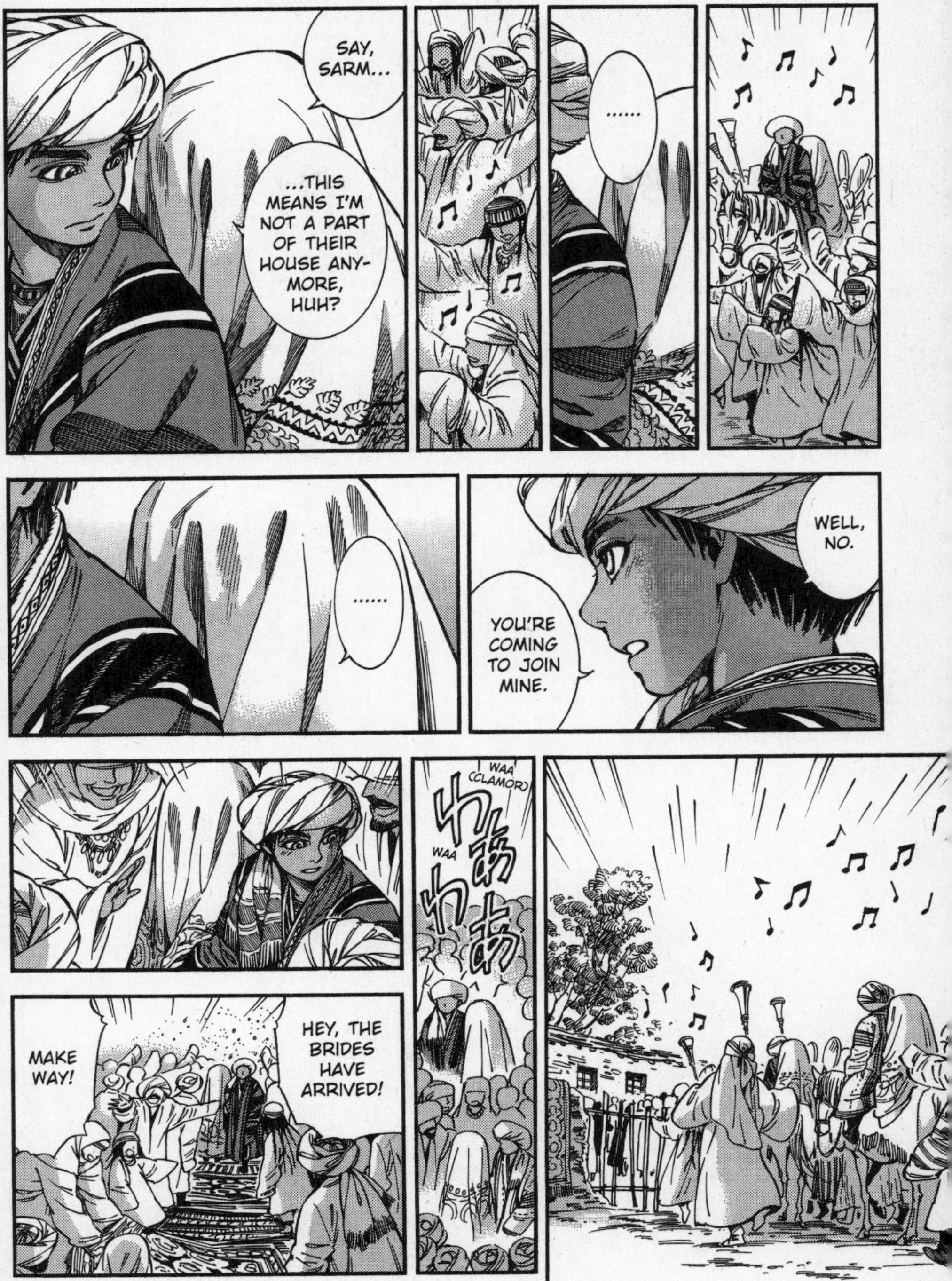
......
SAY, SARM...
...THIS MEANS I'M NOT A PART OF THEIR HOUSE ANYMORE, HUH?
WELL, NO.
YOU'RE COMING TO JOIN MINE.
......
WAA (CLAMOR)
わあ
WAA
わあ
HEY, THE BRIDES HAVE ARRIVED!
MAKE WAY!

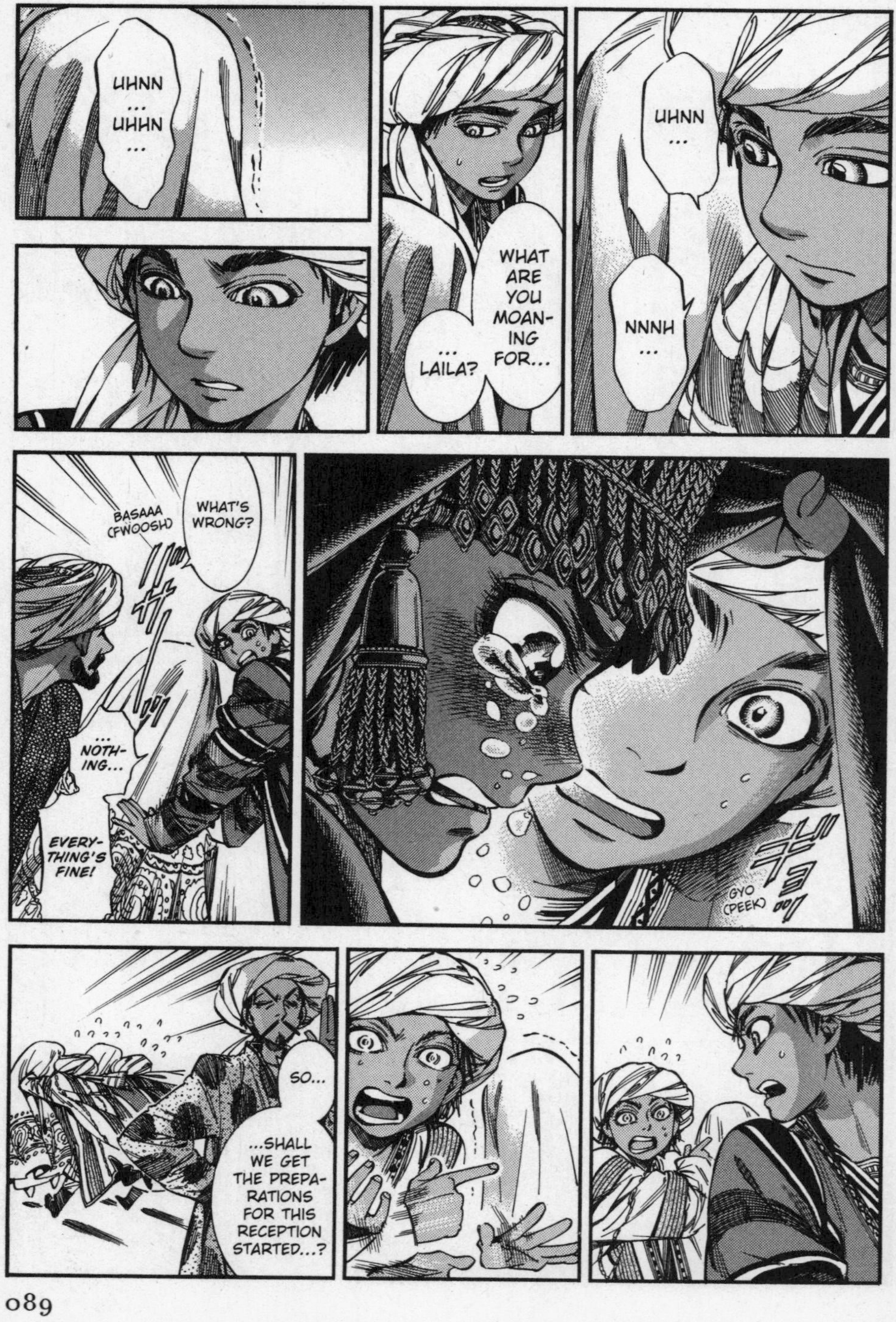
UHNN...
NNNH...
WHAT ARE YOU MOANING FOR...
...LAILA?
UHNN... UHHN...
GYO (PEEK)
WHAT'S WRONG?
BASAAA (FWOOSH)
...NOTHING...
EVERYTHING'S FINE!
SO...
...SHALL WE GET THE PREPARATIONS FOR THIS RECEPTION STARTED...?

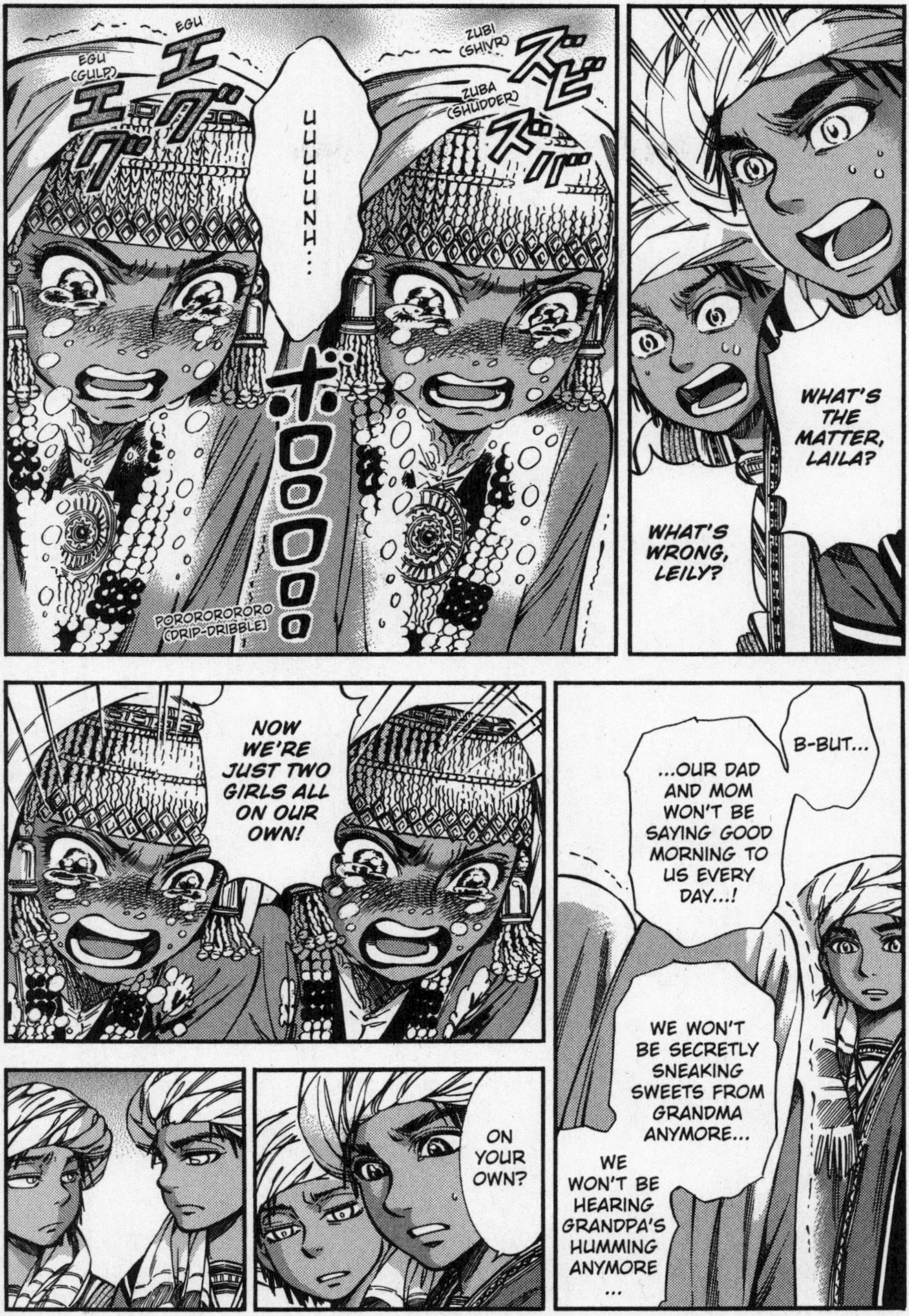
WHAT'S THE MATTER, LAILA?
WHAT'S WRONG, LEILY?
EGU (GULP)
EGU
ZUBI (SHIVR)
ZUBA (SHUDDER)
UUUUUUNH...
PORORORORORO (DRIP-DRIBBLE)
B-BUT...
...OUR DAD AND MOM WON'T BE SAYING GOOD MORNING TO US EVERY DAY...!
WE WON'T BE SECRETLY SNEAKING SWEETS FROM GRANDMA ANYMORE...
WE WON'T BE HEARING GRANDPA'S HUMMING ANYMORE ...
NOW WE'RE JUST TWO GIRLS ALL ON OUR OWN!
ON YOUR OWN?

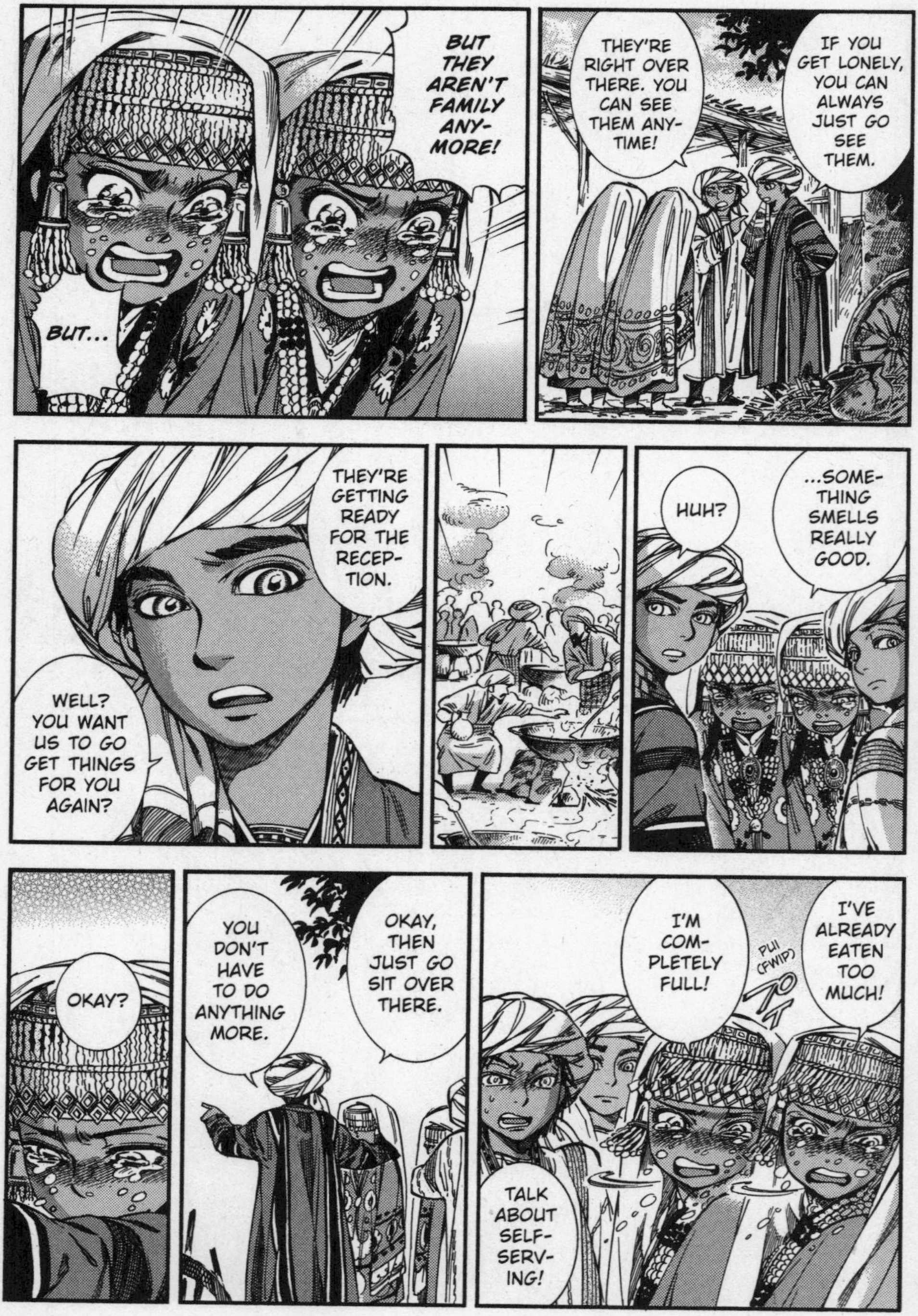
IF YOU GET LONELY, YOU CAN ALWAYS JUST GO SEE THEM.
THEY'RE RIGHT OVER THERE. YOU CAN SEE THEM ANY-TIME!
BUT THEY AREN'T FAMILY ANY-MORE!
BUT...
...SOME-THING SMELLS REALLY GOOD.
HUH?
THEY'RE GETTING READY FOR THE RECEP-TION.
WELL? YOU WANT US TO GO GET THINGS FOR YOU AGAIN?
I'VE ALREADY EATEN TOO MUCH!
PUI (FWIP)
I'M COM-PLETELY FULL!
TALK ABOUT SELF-SERV-ING!
OKAY, THEN JUST GO SIT OVER THERE.
YOU DON'T HAVE TO DO ANYTHING MORE.
OKAY?

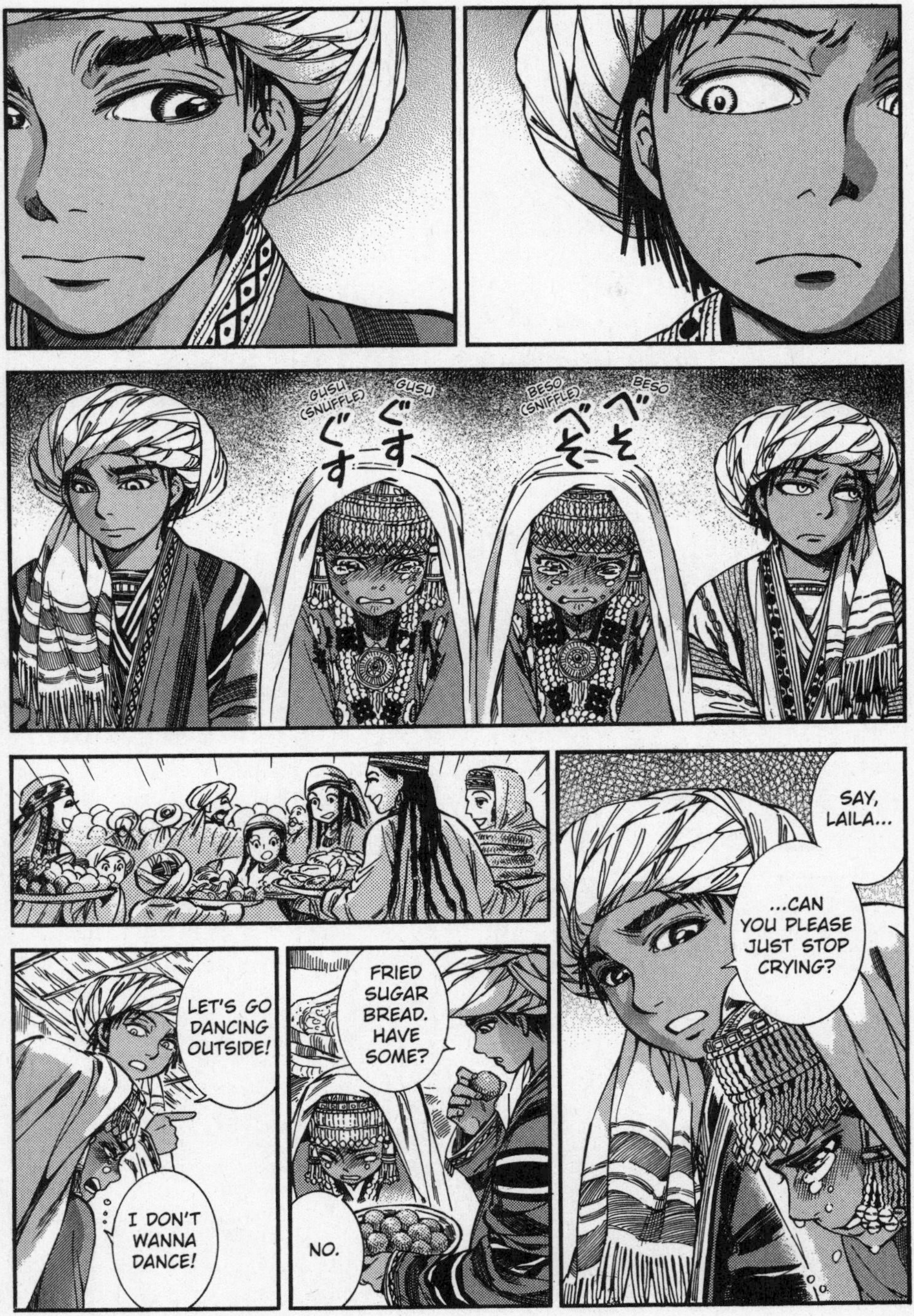
BESO
BESO (SNIFFLE)
べそ べそ
GUSU
GUSU (SNIFFLE)
ぐす ぐす
SAY, LAILA...
...CAN YOU PLEASE JUST STOP CRYING?
FRIED SUGAR BREAD. HAVE SOME?
NO.
LET'S GO DANCING OUTSIDE!
...
I DON'T WANNA DANCE!

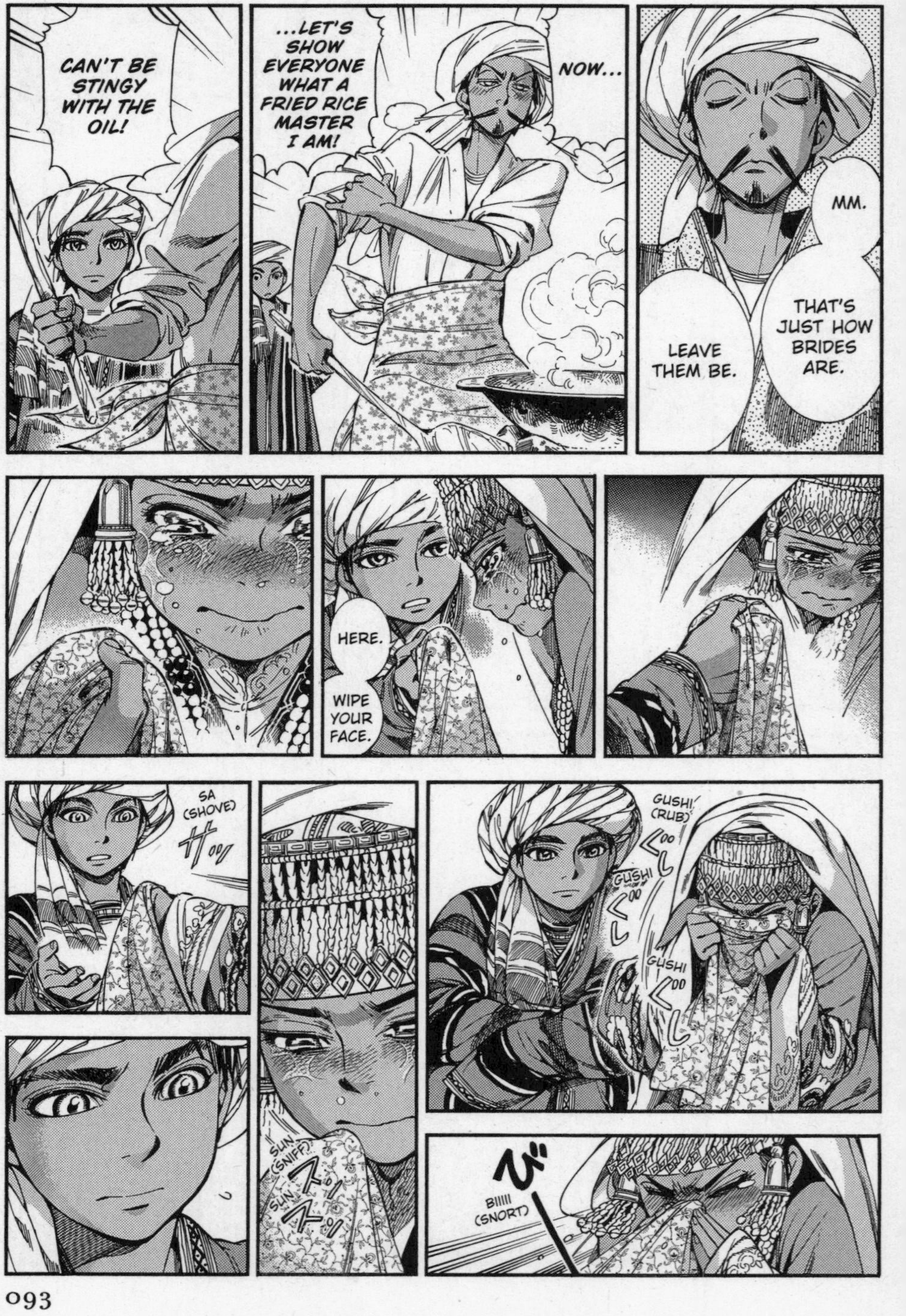
MM.
THAT'S JUST HOW BRIDES ARE.
LEAVE THEM BE.
NOW...
...LET'S SHOW EVERYONE WHAT A FRIED RICE MASTER I AM!
CAN'T BE STINGY WITH THE OIL!
HERE.
WIPE YOUR FACE.
GUSHI (RUB)
GUSHI
GUSHI
BIIIII (SNORT)
SUN (SNIFF)
SUN
SA (SHOVE)

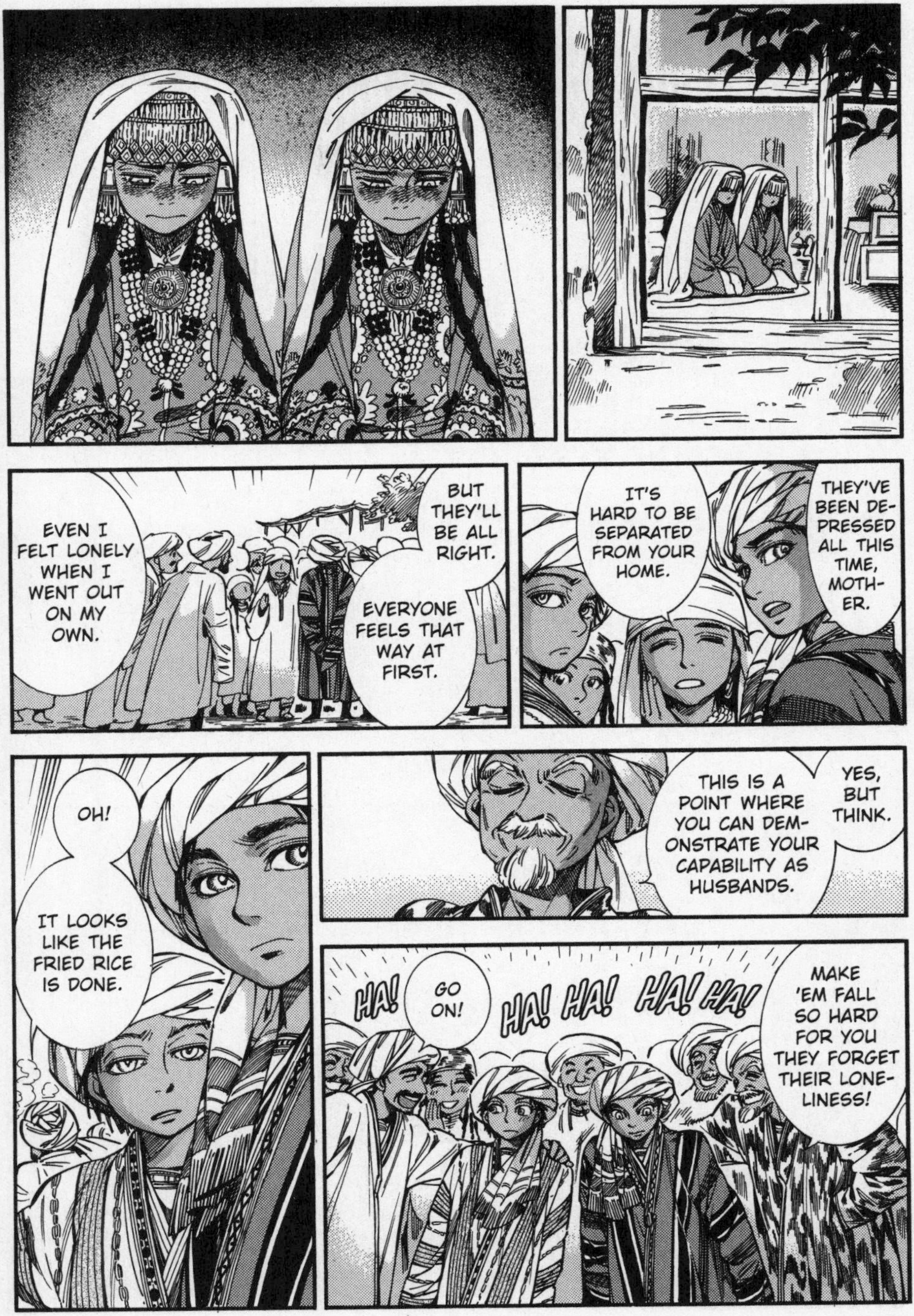
THEY'VE BEEN DE-PRESSED ALL THIS TIME, MOTH-ER.
IT'S HARD TO BE SEPARATED FROM YOUR HOME.
BUT THEY'LL BE ALL RIGHT.
EVERYONE FEELS THAT WAY AT FIRST.
EVEN I FELT LONELY WHEN I WENT OUT ON MY OWN.
YES, BUT THINK.
THIS IS A POINT WHERE YOU CAN DEM-ONSTRATE YOUR CAPABILITY AS HUSBANDS.
MAKE 'EM FALL SO HARD FOR YOU THEY FORGET THEIR LONE-LINESS!
HA! HA!
HA! HA!
GO ON!
HA!
OH!
IT LOOKS LIKE THE FRIED RICE IS DONE.

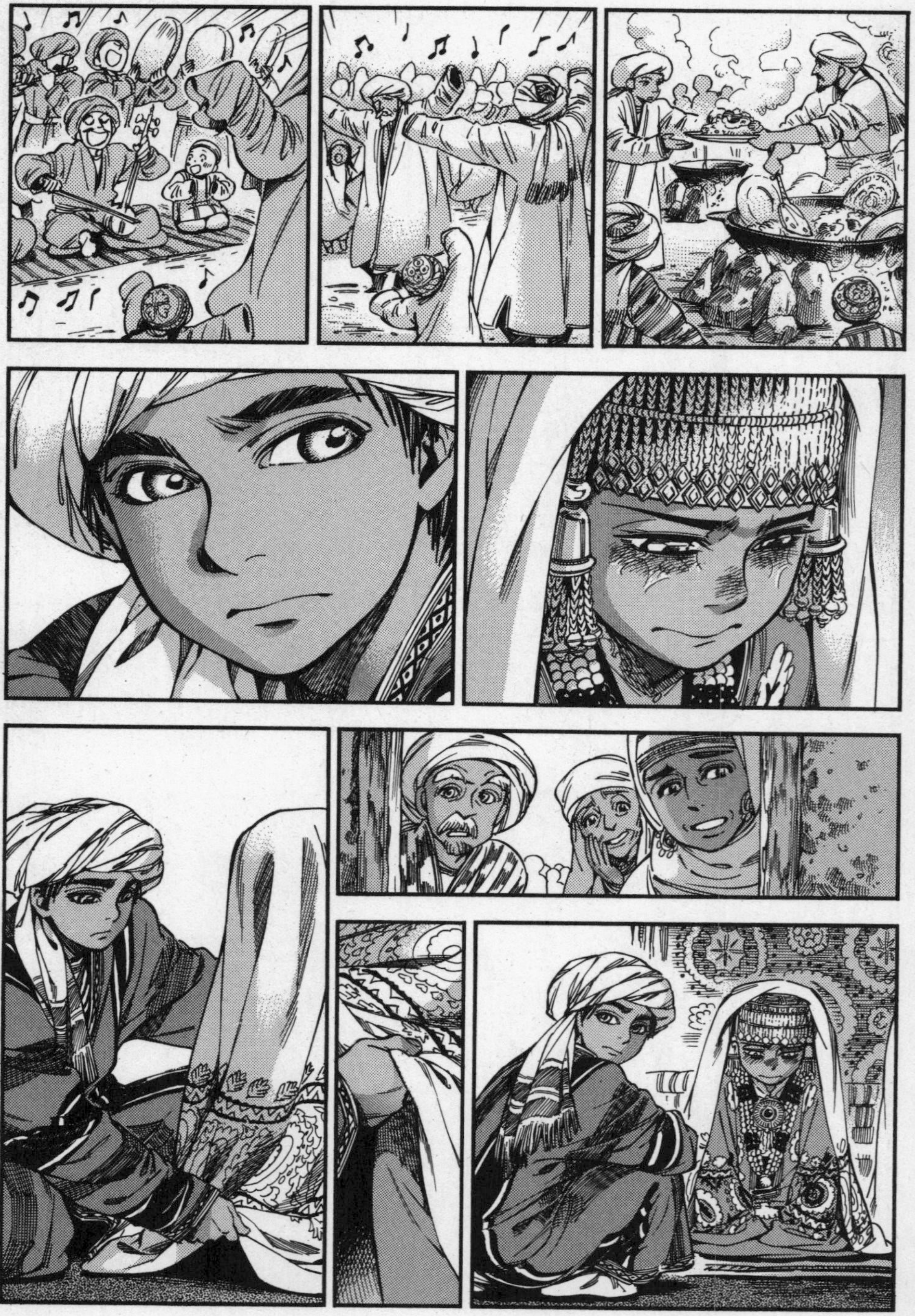

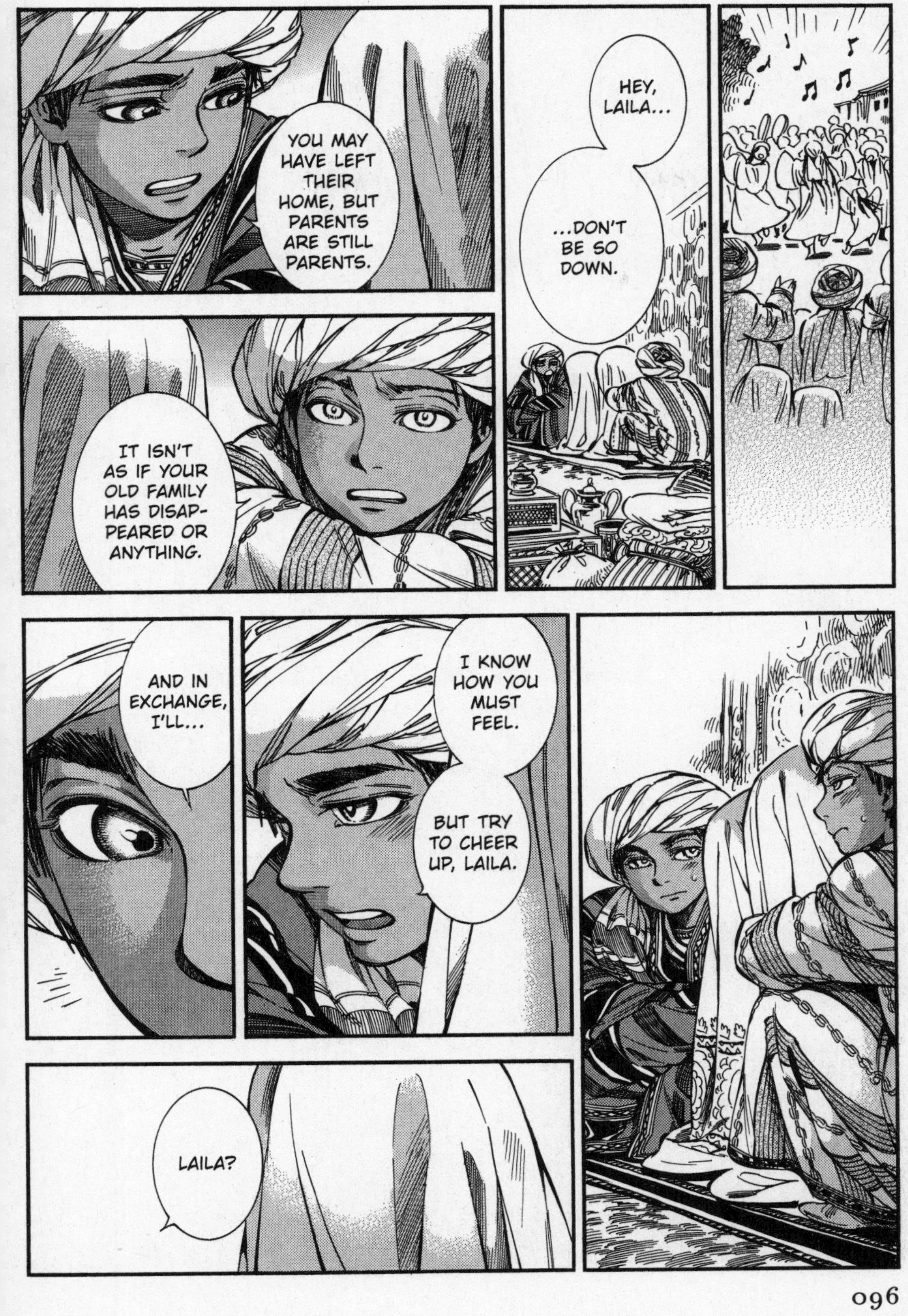
HEY, LAILA...
...DON'T BE SO DOWN.
YOU MAY HAVE LEFT THEIR HOME, BUT PARENTS ARE STILL PARENTS.
IT ISN'T AS IF YOUR OLD FAMILY HAS DISAP-PEARED OR ANYTHING.
I KNOW HOW YOU MUST FEEL.
BUT TRY TO CHEER UP, LAILA.
AND IN EXCHANGE, I'LL...
LAILA?

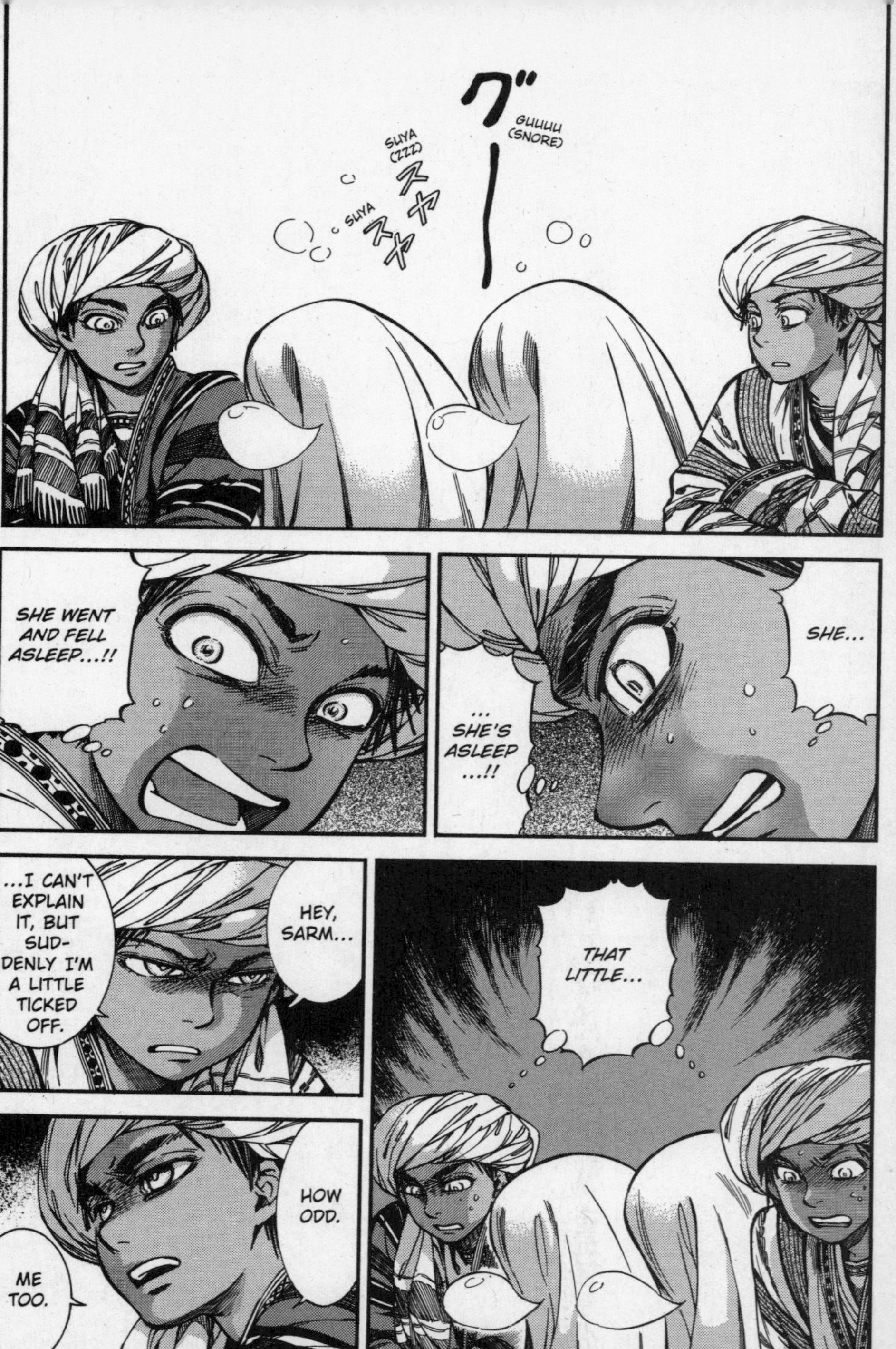
グー
GUUUU (SNORE)
スヤ
SUYA (ZZZ)
スヤ
SUYA
SHE...
...SHE'S ASLEEP...!!
SHE WENT AND FELL ASLEEP...!!
THAT LITTLE...
HEY, SARM...
...I CAN'T EXPLAIN IT, BUT SUD-DENLY I'M A LITTLE TICKED OFF.
HOW ODD.
ME TOO.

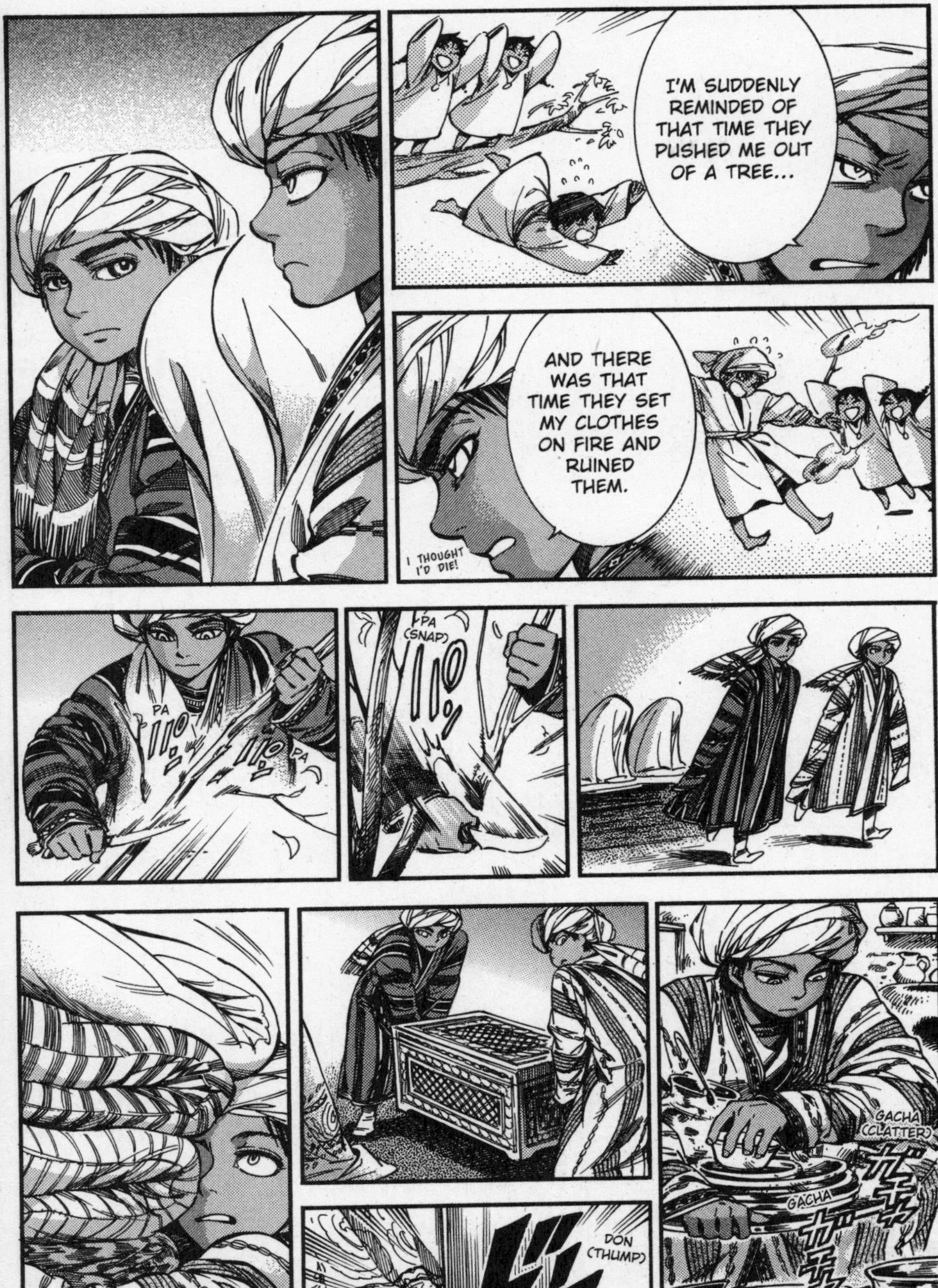
I'M SUDDENLY REMINDED OF THAT TIME THEY PUSHED ME OUT OF A TREE...
AND THERE WAS THAT TIME THEY SET MY CLOTHES ON FIRE AND RUINED THEM.
I THOUGHT I'D DIE!
PA (SNAP)
PA
PA
GACHA (CLATTER)
GACHA
DON (THUMP)

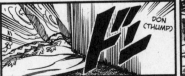

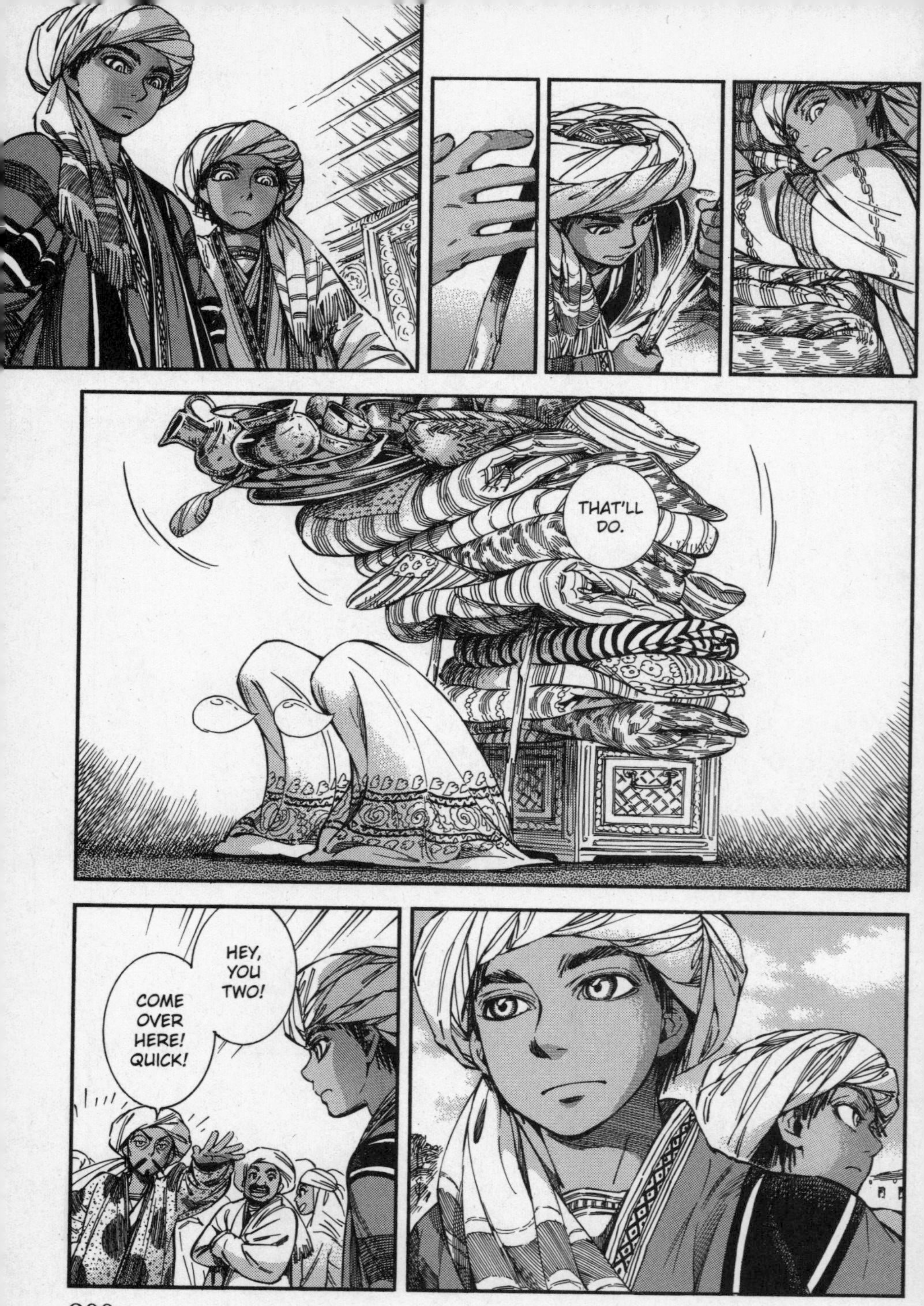
THAT'LL DO.
HEY, YOU TWO!
COME OVER HERE! QUICK!

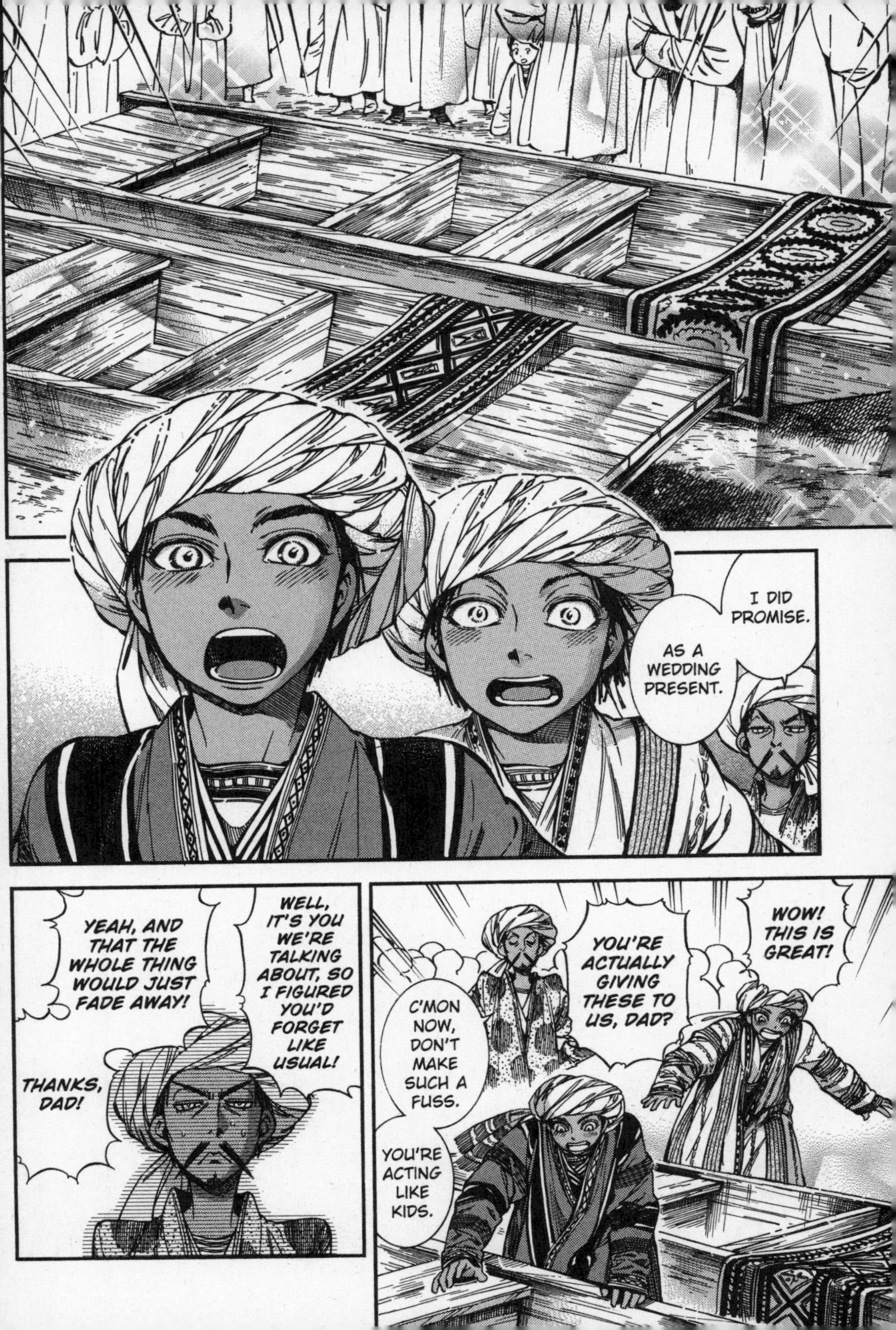
I DID PROMISE.
AS A WEDDING PRESENT.
WOW! THIS IS GREAT!
YOU'RE ACTUALLY GIVING THESE TO US, DAD?
C'MON NOW, DON'T MAKE SUCH A FUSS.
YOU'RE ACTING LIKE KIDS.
WELL, IT'S YOU WE'RE TALKING ABOUT, SO I FIGURED YOU'D FORGET LIKE USUAL!
YEAH, AND THAT THE WHOLE THING WOULD JUST FADE AWAY!
THANKS, DAD!

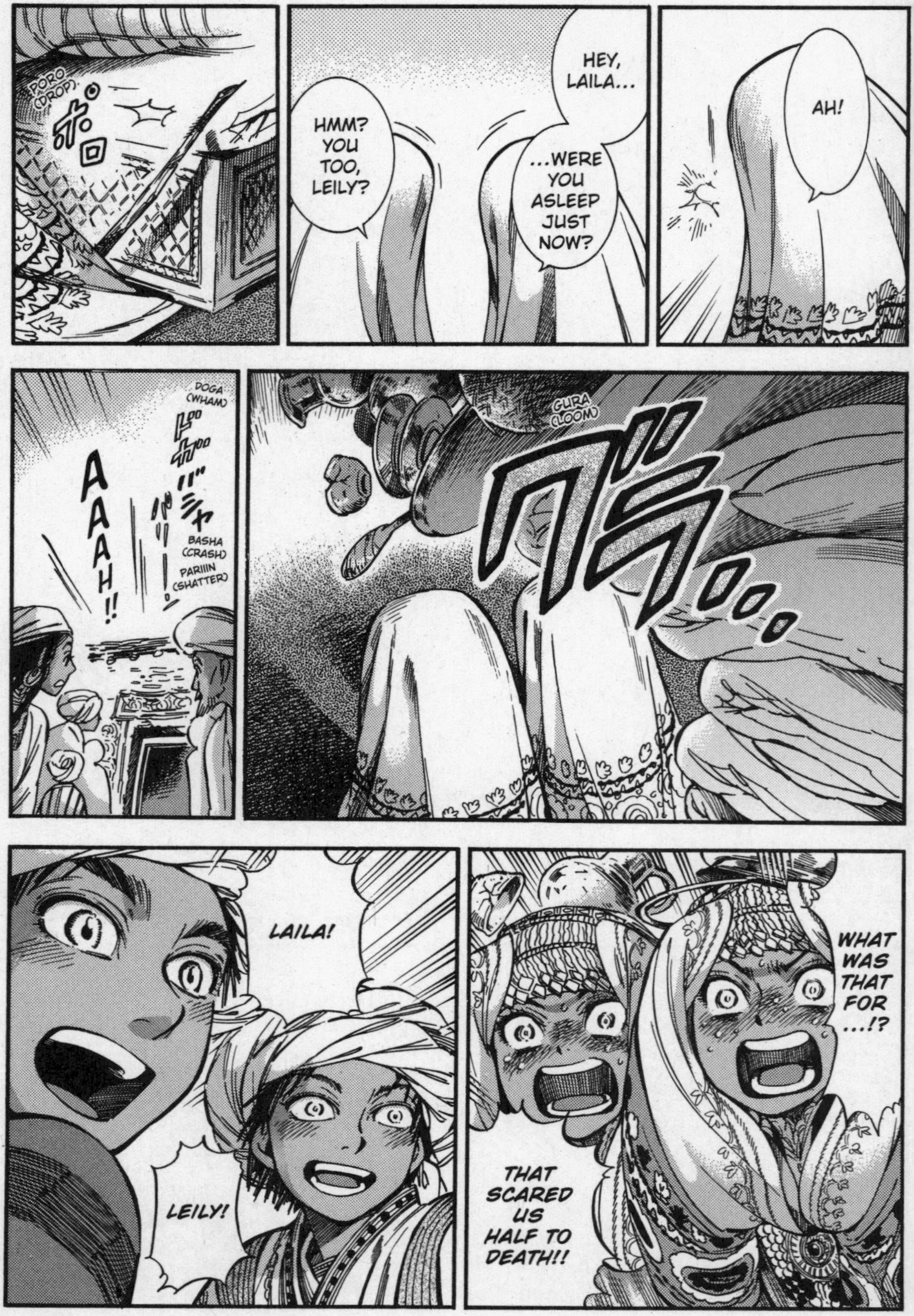
AH!
HEY, LAILA...
...WERE YOU ASLEEP JUST NOW?
HMM? YOU TOO, LEILY?
PORO (DROP)
GURA (LOOM)
DOGA (WHAM)
AAAAH!!
BASHA (CRASH)
PARIIN (SHATTER)
WHAT WAS THAT FOR...!?
THAT SCARED US HALF TO DEATH!!
LAILA!
LEILY!

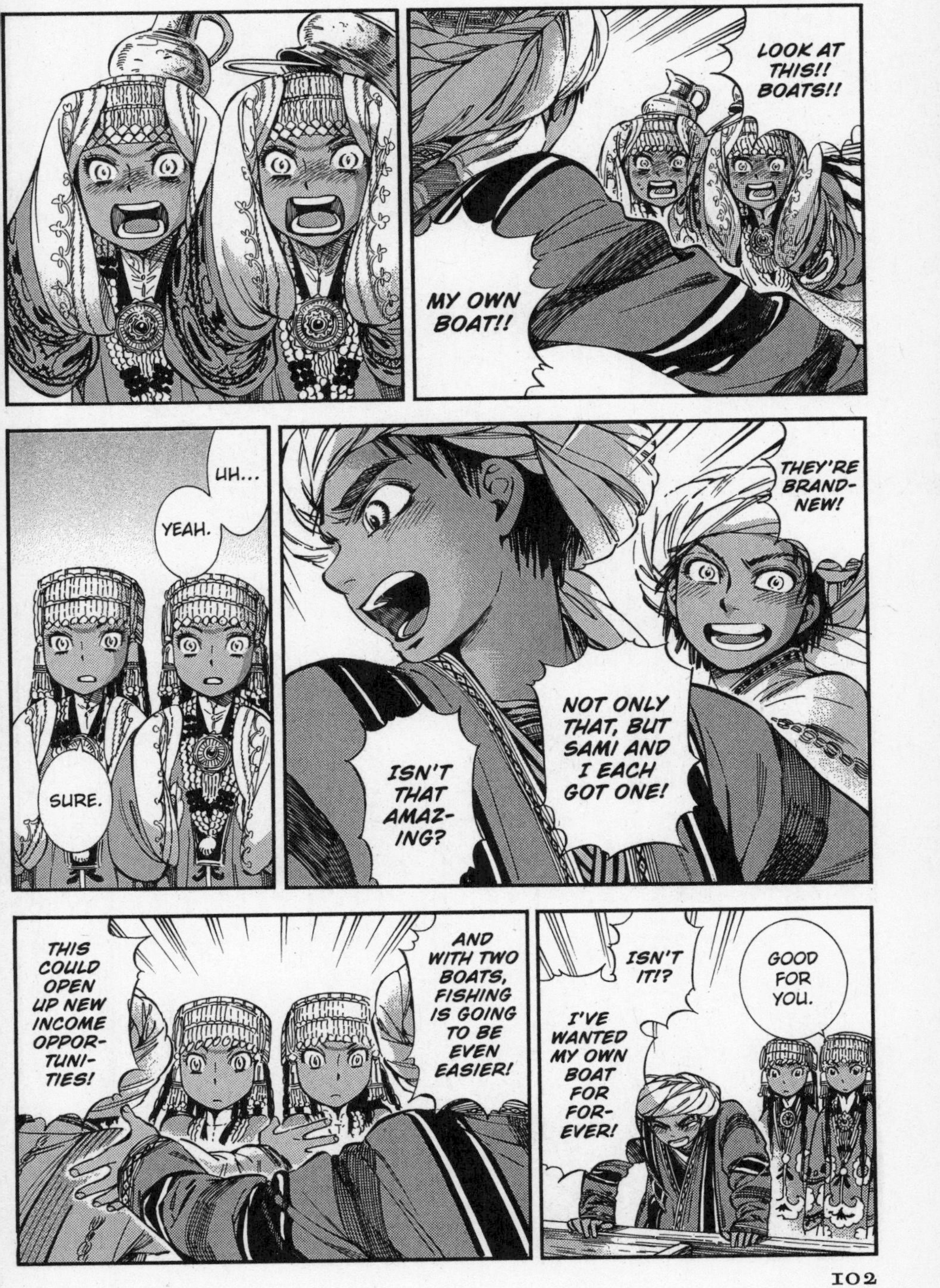
LOOK AT THIS!! BOATS!!
MY OWN BOAT!!
THEY'RE BRAND-NEW!
NOT ONLY THAT, BUT SAMI AND I EACH GOT ONE!
ISN'T THAT AMAZ-ING?
UH...
YEAH.
SURE.
GOOD FOR YOU.
ISN'T IT!?
I'VE WANTED MY OWN BOAT FOR FOR-EVER!
AND WITH TWO BOATS, FISHING IS GOING TO BE EVEN EASIER!
THIS COULD OPEN UP NEW INCOME OPPOR-TUNITIES!

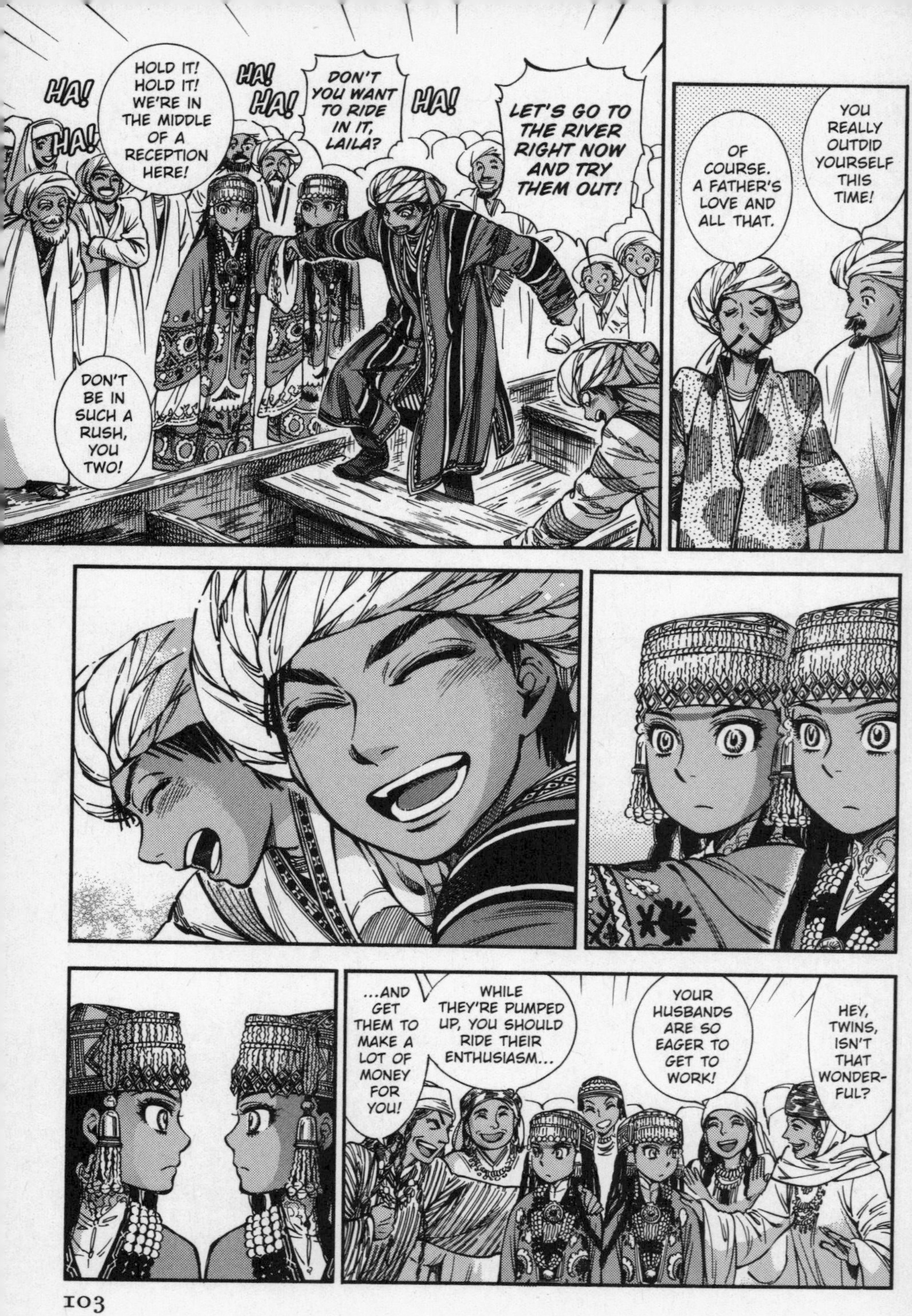
YOU REALLY OUTDID YOURSELF THIS TIME!
OF COURSE. A FATHER'S LOVE AND ALL THAT.
LET'S GO TO THE RIVER RIGHT NOW AND TRY THEM OUT!
HA!
DON'T YOU WANT TO RIDE IN IT, LAILA?
HA! HA!
HOLD IT! HOLD IT! WE'RE IN THE MIDDLE OF A RECEPTION HERE!
HA! HA!
DON'T BE IN SUCH A RUSH, YOU TWO!
HEY, TWINS, ISN'T THAT WONDERFUL?
YOUR HUSBANDS ARE SO EAGER TO GET TO WORK!
WHILE THEY'RE PUMPED UP, YOU SHOULD RIDE THEIR ENTHUSIASM...
...AND GET THEM TO MAKE A LOT OF MONEY FOR YOU!

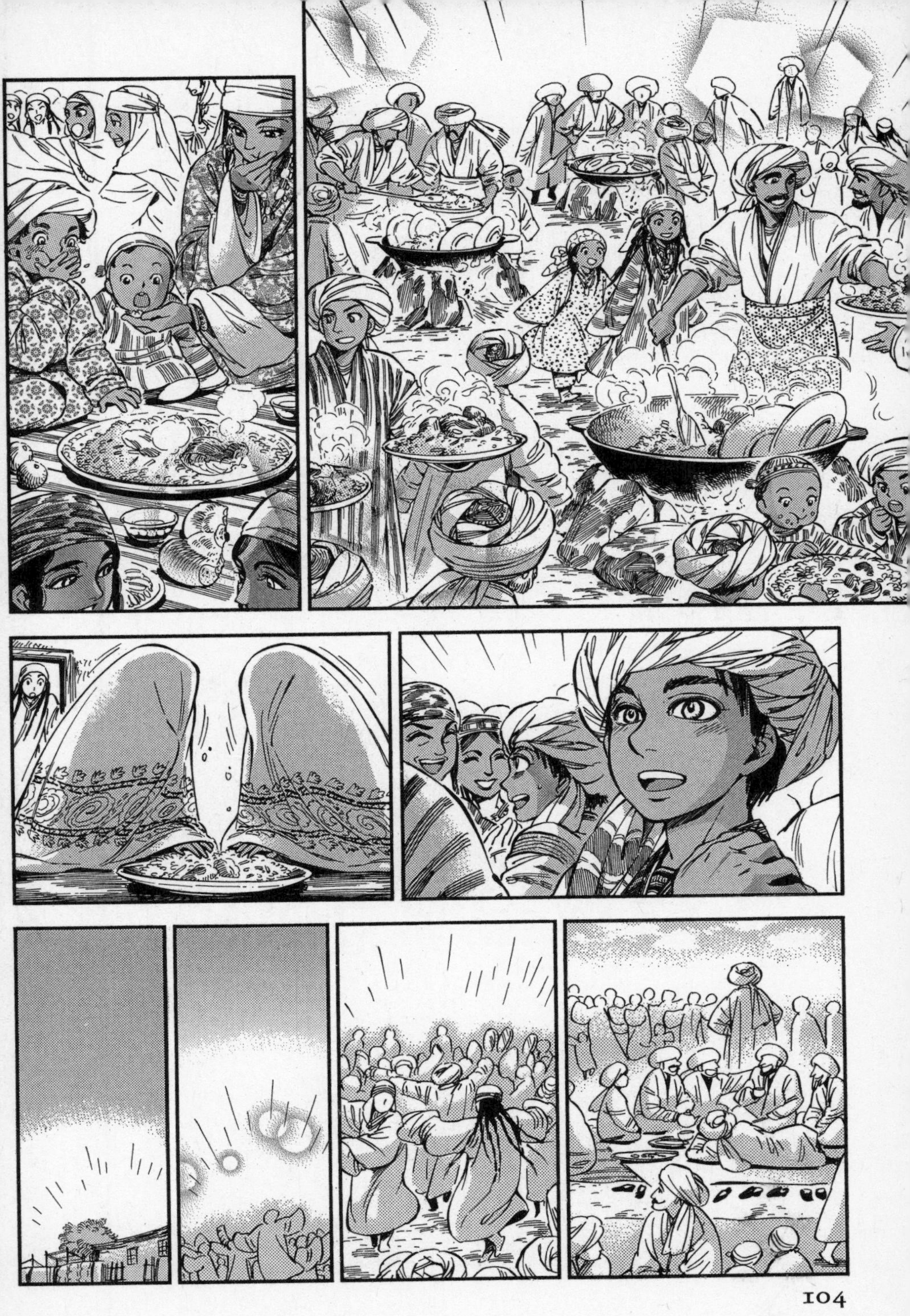

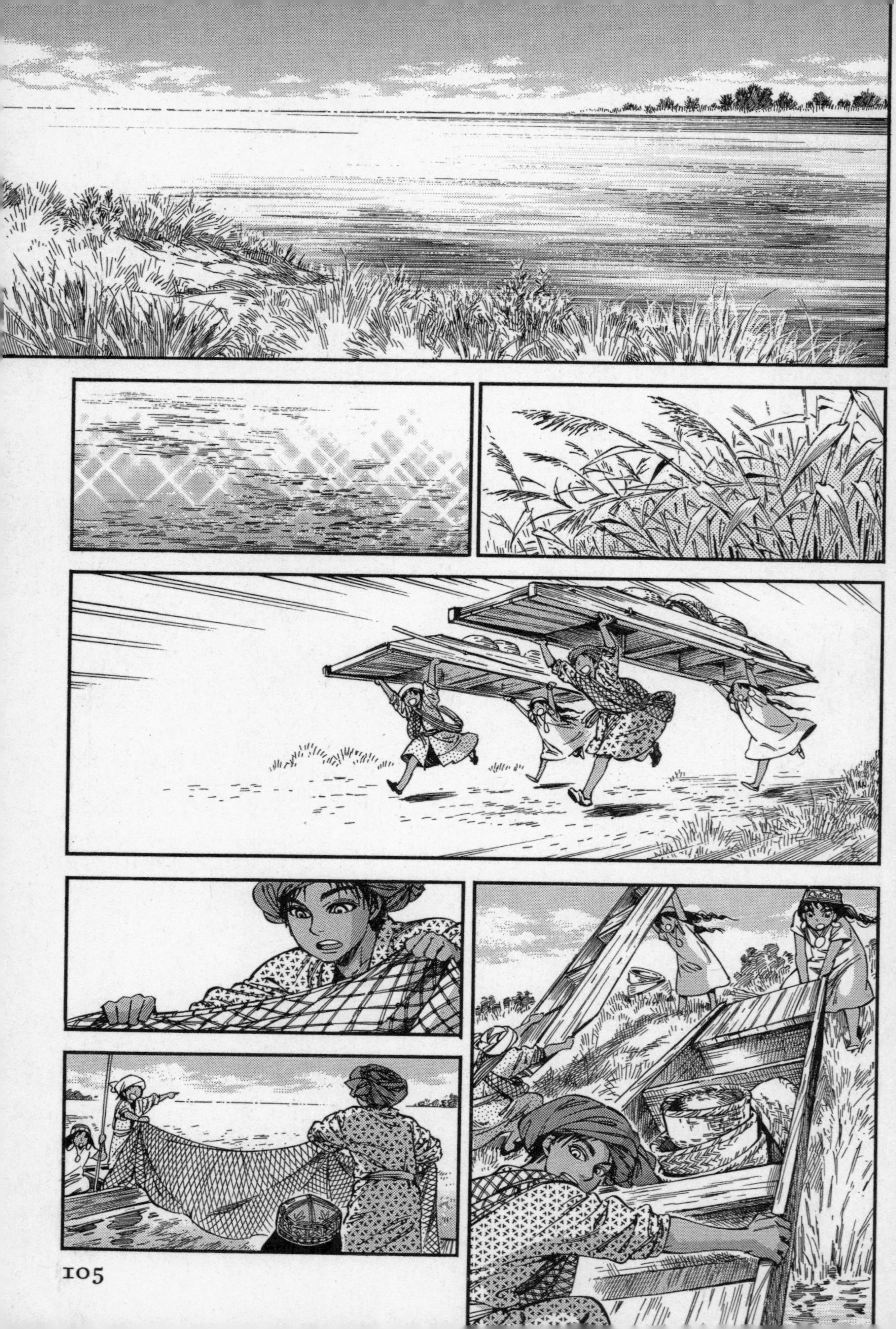

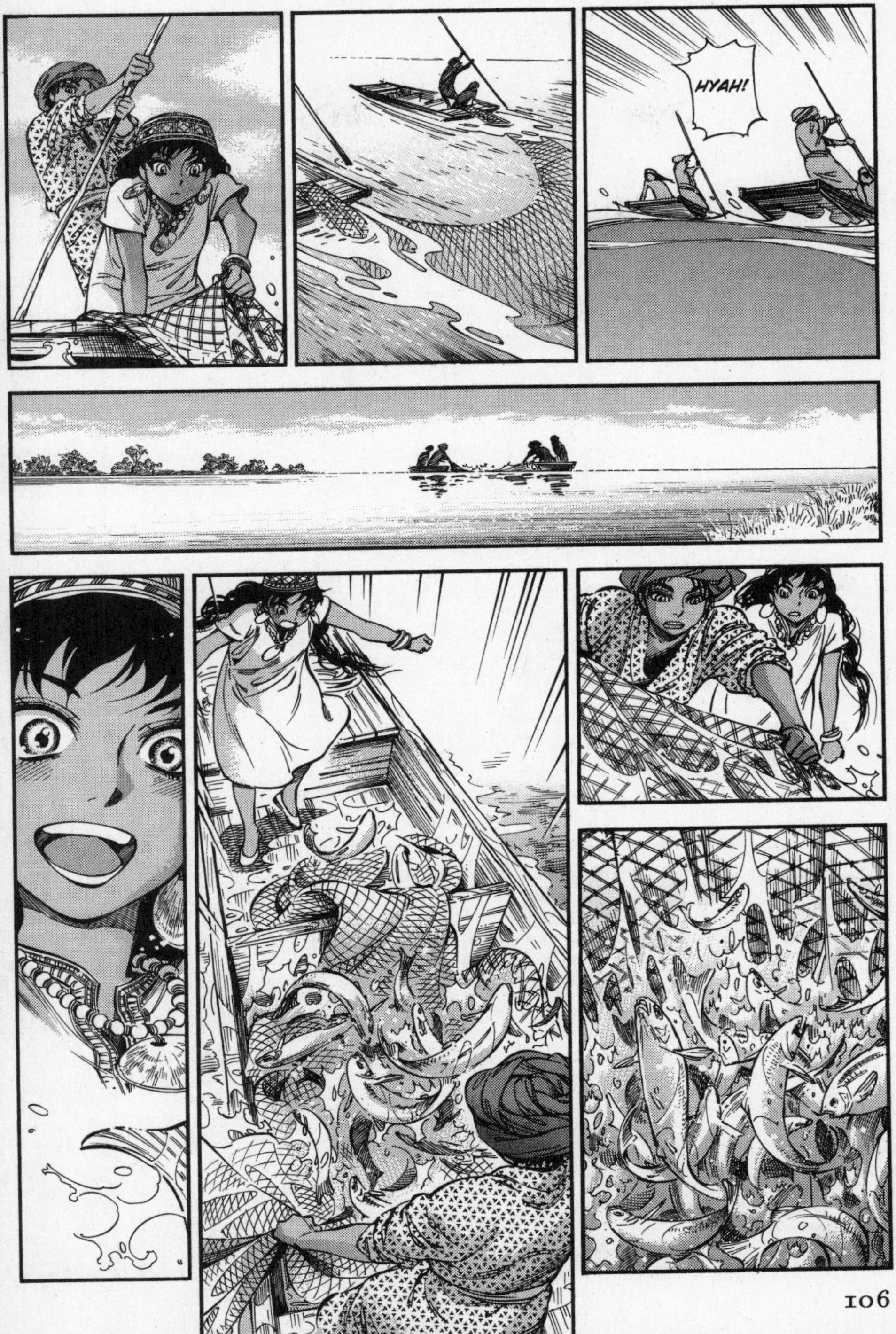
HYAH!

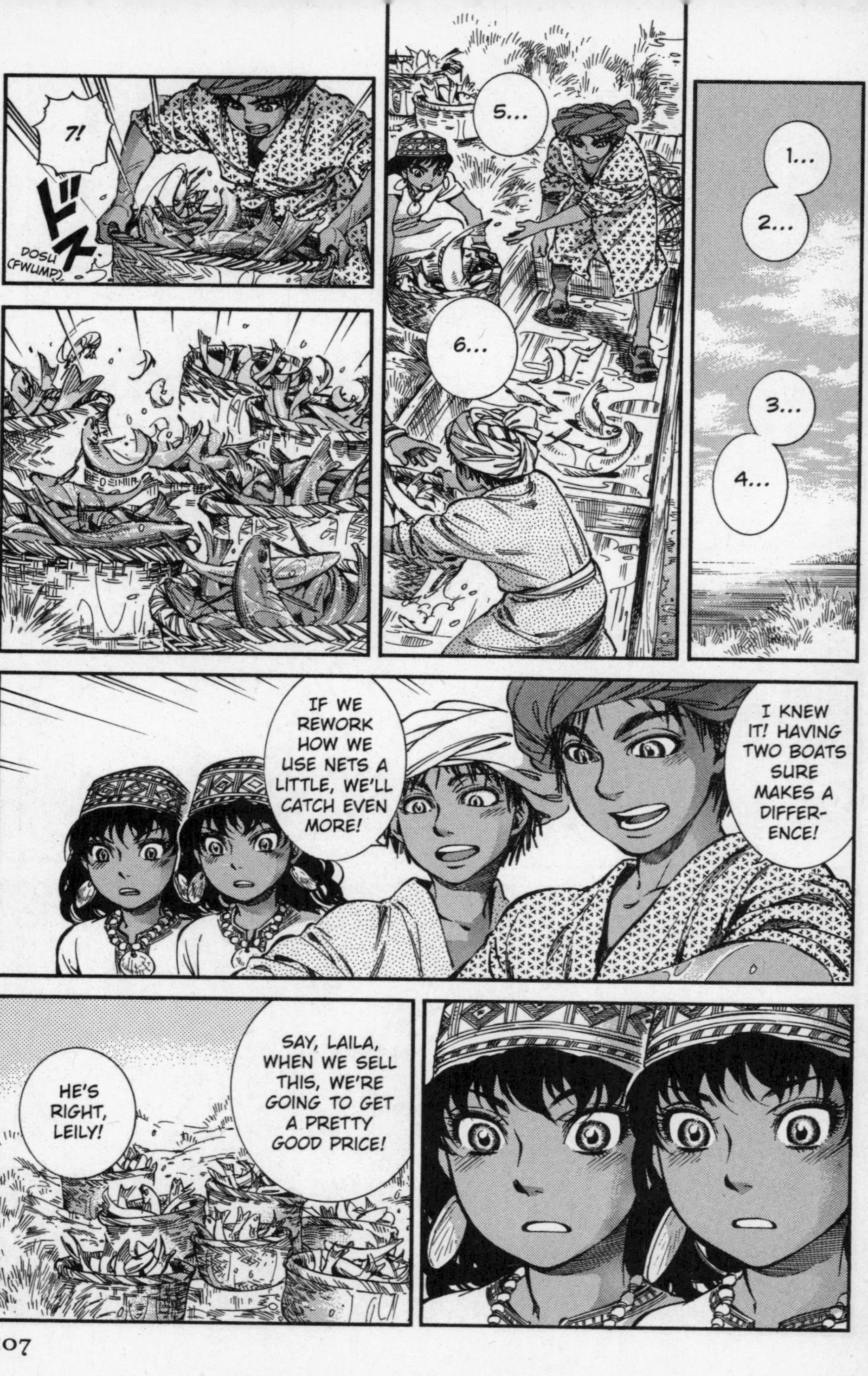
1...
2...
3...
4...
5...
6...
7!
ドス
DOSU (FWUMP)
I KNEW IT! HAVING TWO BOATS SURE MAKES A DIFFERENCE!
IF WE REWORK HOW WE USE NETS A LITTLE, WE'LL CATCH EVEN MORE!
SAY, LAILA, WHEN WE SELL THIS, WE'RE GOING TO GET A PRETTY GOOD PRICE!
HE'S RIGHT, LEILY!

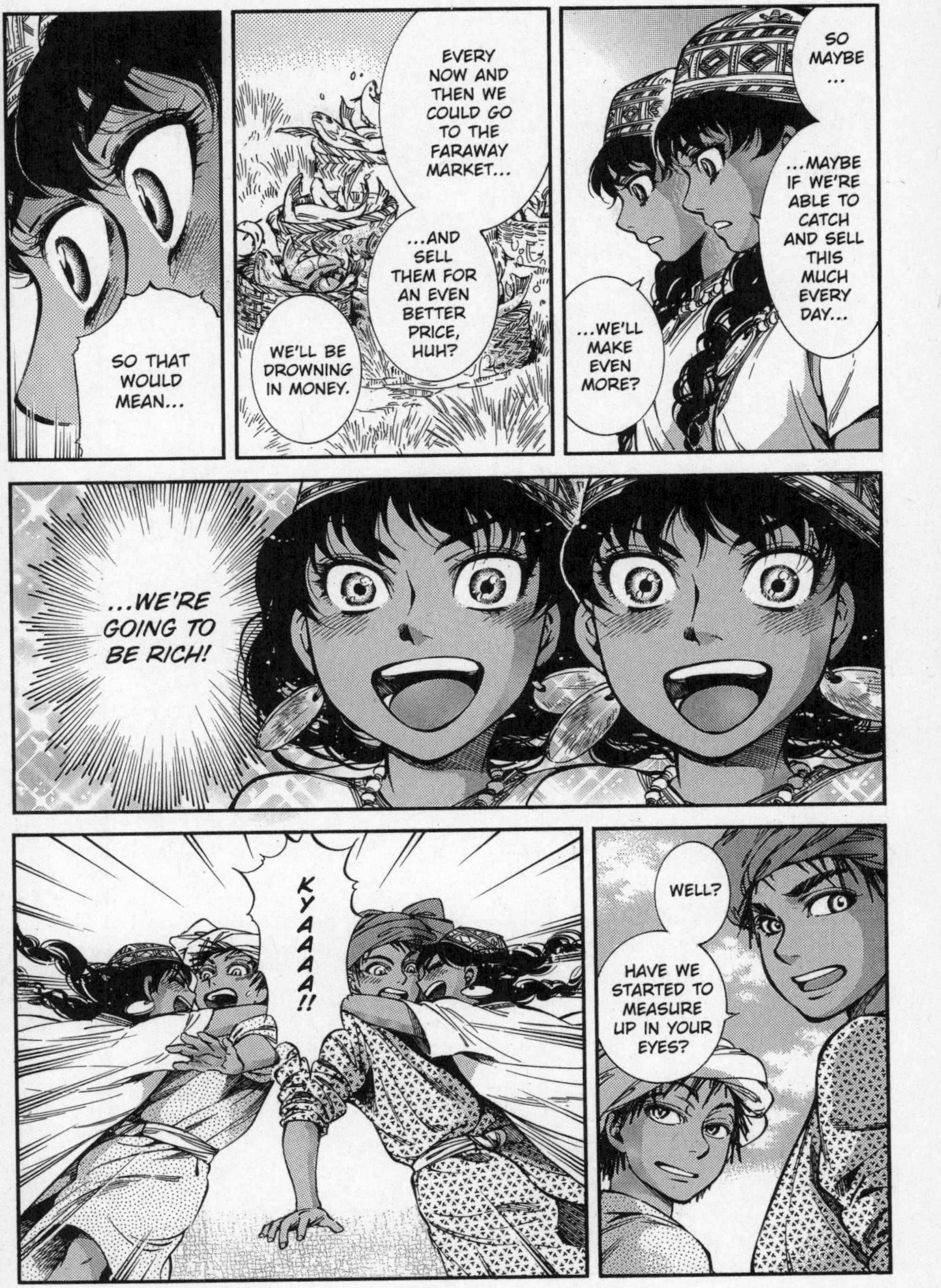
SO MAYBE ...
...MAYBE IF WE'RE ABLE TO CATCH AND SELL THIS MUCH EVERY DAY...
...WE'LL MAKE EVEN MORE?
EVERY NOW AND THEN WE COULD GO TO THE FARAWAY MARKET...
...AND SELL THEM FOR AN EVEN BETTER PRICE, HUH?
WE'LL BE DROWNING IN MONEY.
SO THAT WOULD MEAN...
...WE'RE GOING TO BE RICH!
WELL?
HAVE WE STARTED TO MEASURE UP IN YOUR EYES?
KYAAAA!!

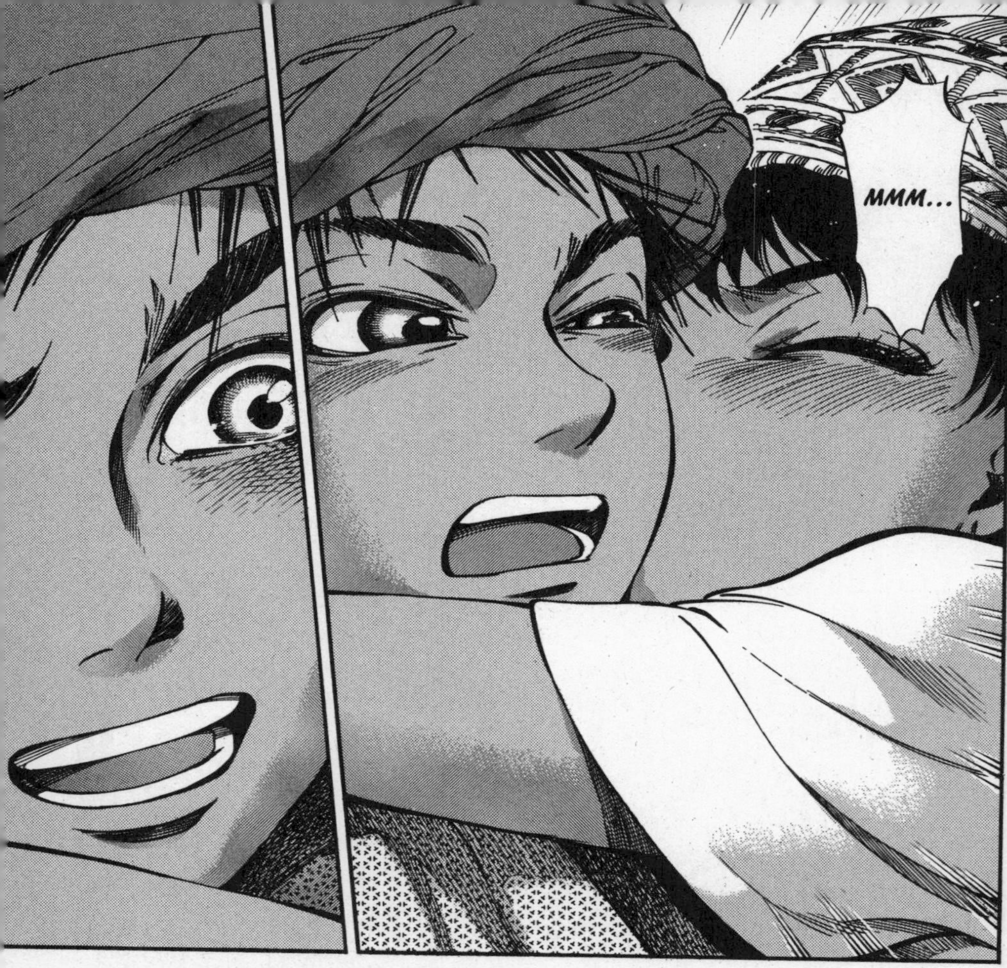
MMM...

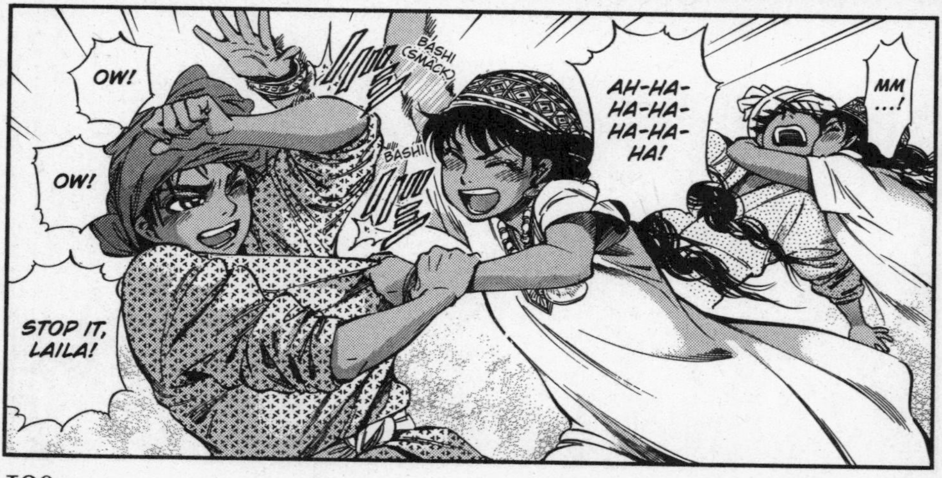
MM ...!
AH-HA-HA-HA-HA-HA-HA!
BASHI (SMACK)
BASHI
OW!
OW!
STOP IT, LAILA!

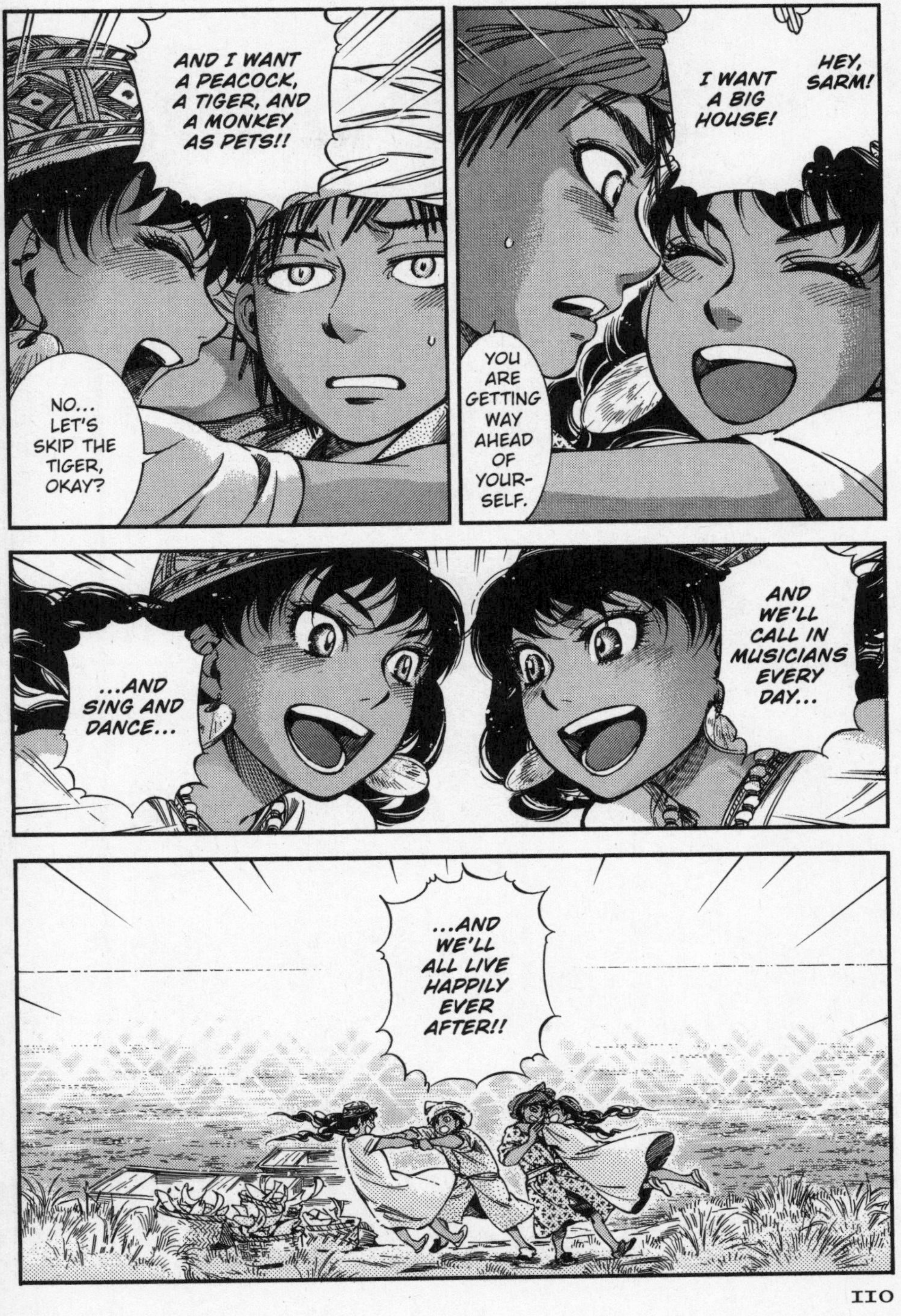
HEY, SARM!
I WANT A BIG HOUSE!
YOU ARE GETTING WAY AHEAD OF YOURSELF.
AND I WANT A PEACOCK, A TIGER, AND A MONKEY AS PETS!!
NO... LET'S SKIP THE TIGER, OKAY?
AND WE'LL CALL IN MUSICIANS EVERY DAY...
...AND SING AND DANCE...
...AND WE'LL ALL LIVE HAPPILY EVER AFTER!!

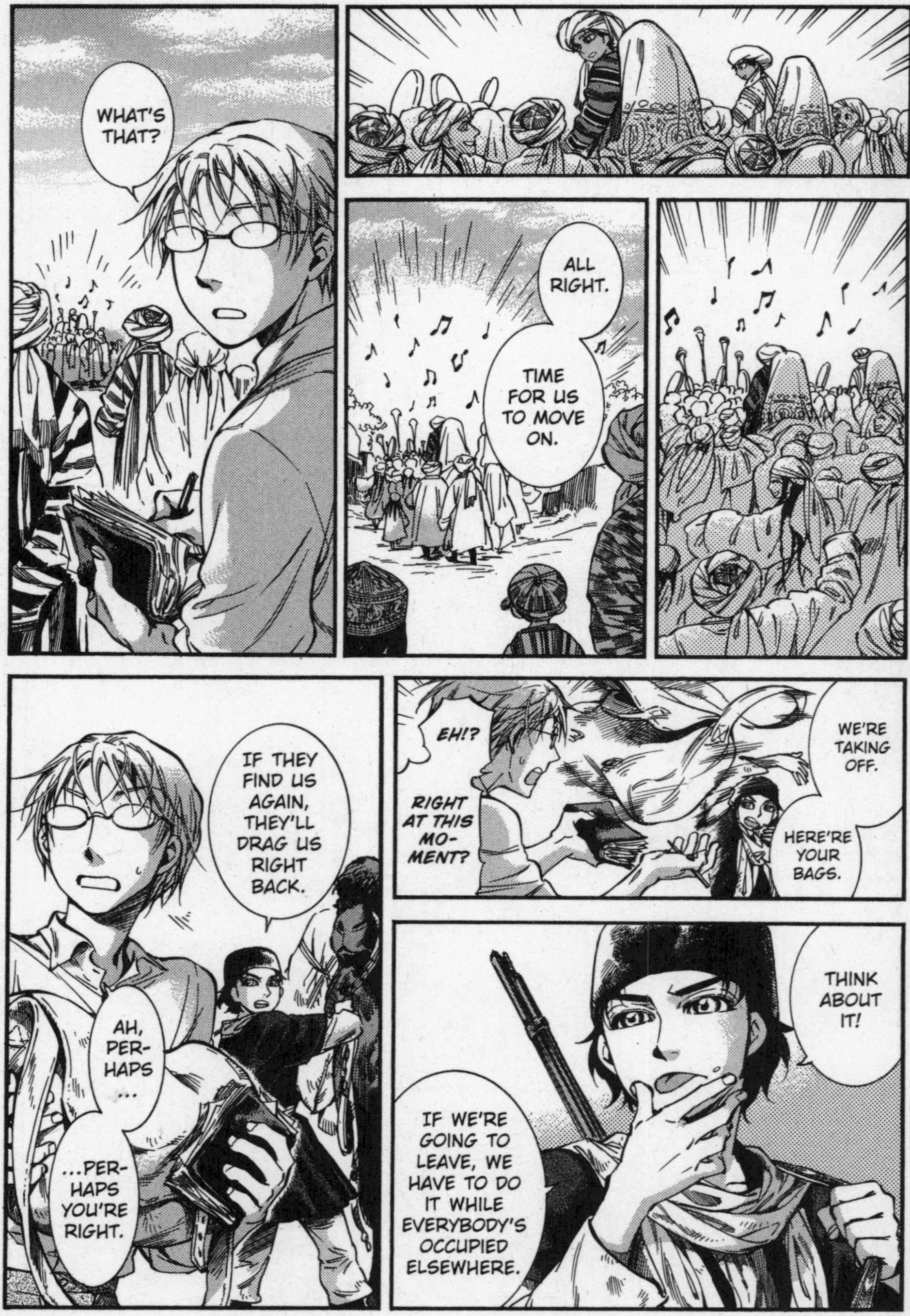
ALL RIGHT.
TIME FOR US TO MOVE ON.
WHAT'S THAT?
WE'RE TAKING OFF.
HERE'RE YOUR BAGS.
EH!?
RIGHT AT THIS MO-MENT?
THINK ABOUT IT!
IF WE'RE GOING TO LEAVE, WE HAVE TO DO IT WHILE EVERYBODY'S OCCUPIED ELSEWHERE.
IF THEY FIND US AGAIN, THEY'LL DRAG US RIGHT BACK.
AH, PER-HAPS...
...PER-HAPS YOU'RE RIGHT.

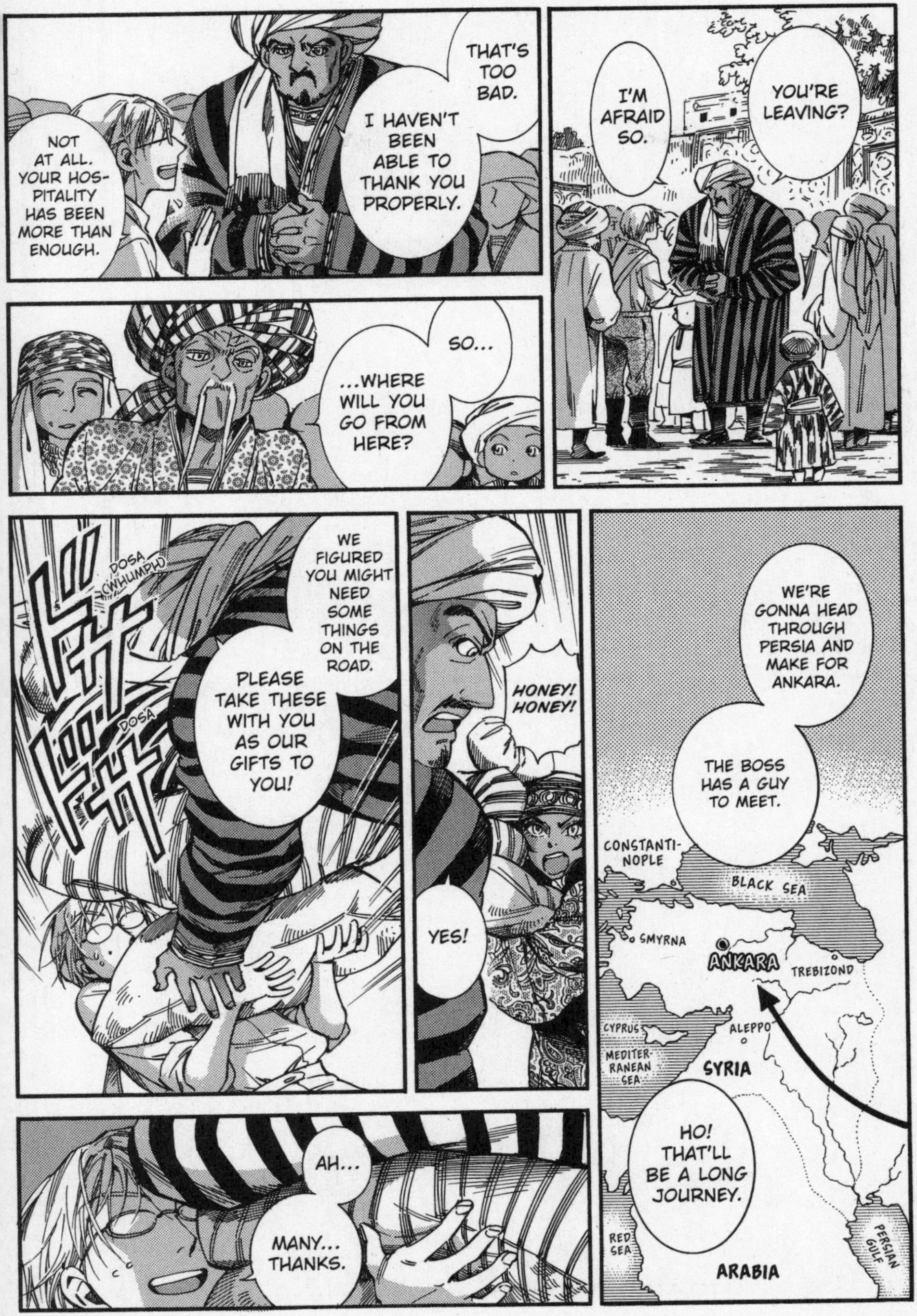
YOU'RE LEAVING?
I'M AFRAID SO.
THAT'S TOO BAD.
I HAVEN'T BEEN ABLE TO THANK YOU PROPERLY.
NOT AT ALL. YOUR HOSPITALITY HAS BEEN MORE THAN ENOUGH.
SO...
...WHERE WILL YOU GO FROM HERE?
WE'RE GONNA HEAD THROUGH PERSIA AND MAKE FOR ANKARA.
THE BOSS HAS A GUY TO MEET.
HO! THAT'LL BE A LONG JOURNEY.
CONSTANTINOPLE
BLACK SEA
SMYRNA
ANKARA
TREBIZOND
CYPRUS
ALEPPO
MEDITERRANEAN SEA
SYRIA
RED SEA
ARABIA
PERSIAN GULF
HONEY! HONEY!
YES!
WE FIGURED YOU MIGHT NEED SOME THINGS ON THE ROAD.
PLEASE TAKE THESE WITH YOU AS OUR GIFTS TO YOU!
DOSA (WHUMPH)
DOSA
AH...
MANY... THANKS.

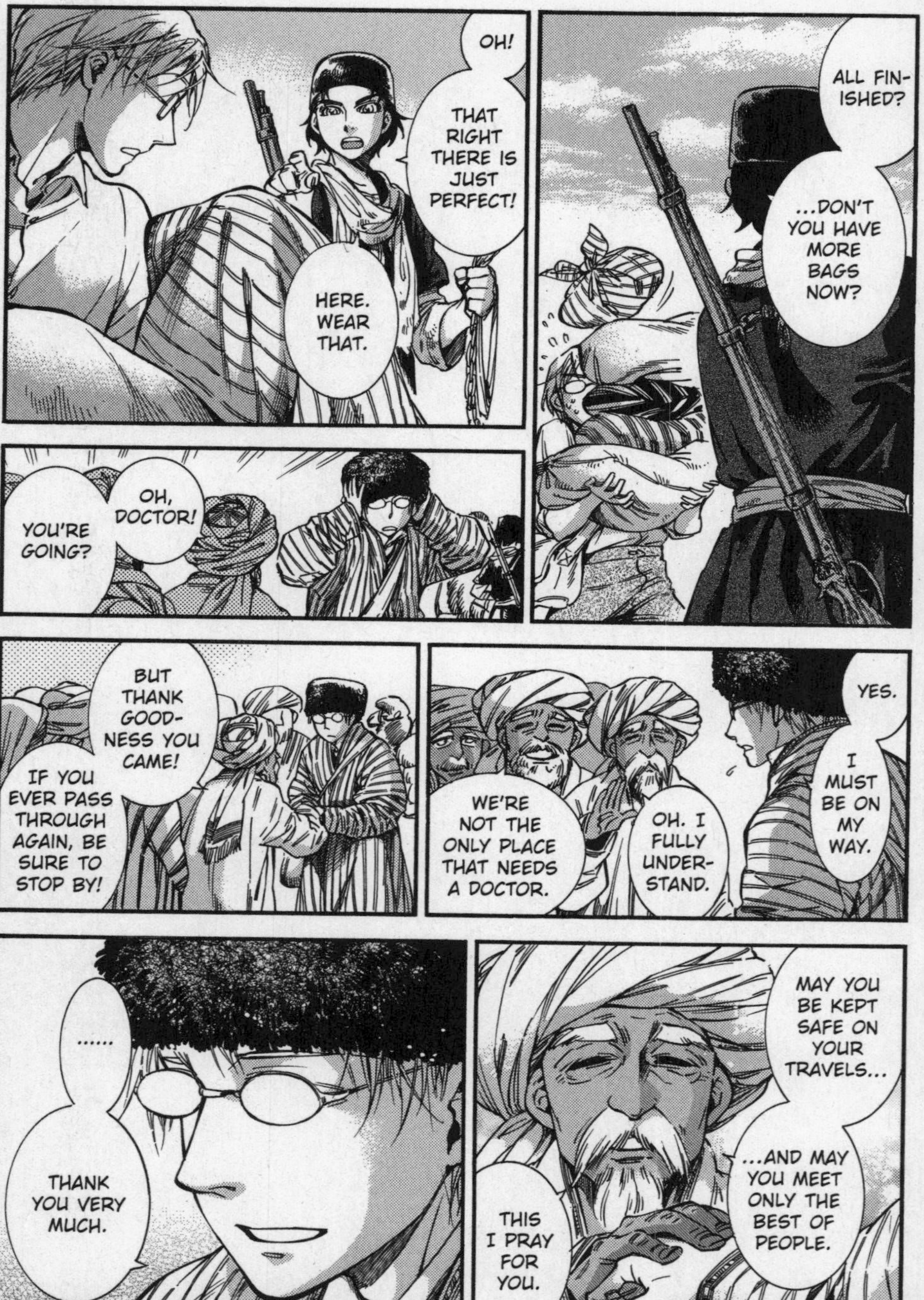
ALL FIN-ISHED?
...DON'T YOU HAVE MORE BAGS NOW?
OH!
THAT RIGHT THERE IS JUST PERFECT!
HERE. WEAR THAT.
OH, DOCTOR!
YOU'RE GOING?
YES.
I MUST BE ON MY WAY.
OH. I FULLY UNDER-STAND.
WE'RE NOT THE ONLY PLACE THAT NEEDS A DOCTOR.
BUT THANK GOOD-NESS YOU CAME!
IF YOU EVER PASS THROUGH AGAIN, BE SURE TO STOP BY!
MAY YOU BE KEPT SAFE ON YOUR TRAVELS...
...AND MAY YOU MEET ONLY THE BEST OF PEOPLE.
THIS I PRAY FOR YOU.
......
THANK YOU VERY MUCH.

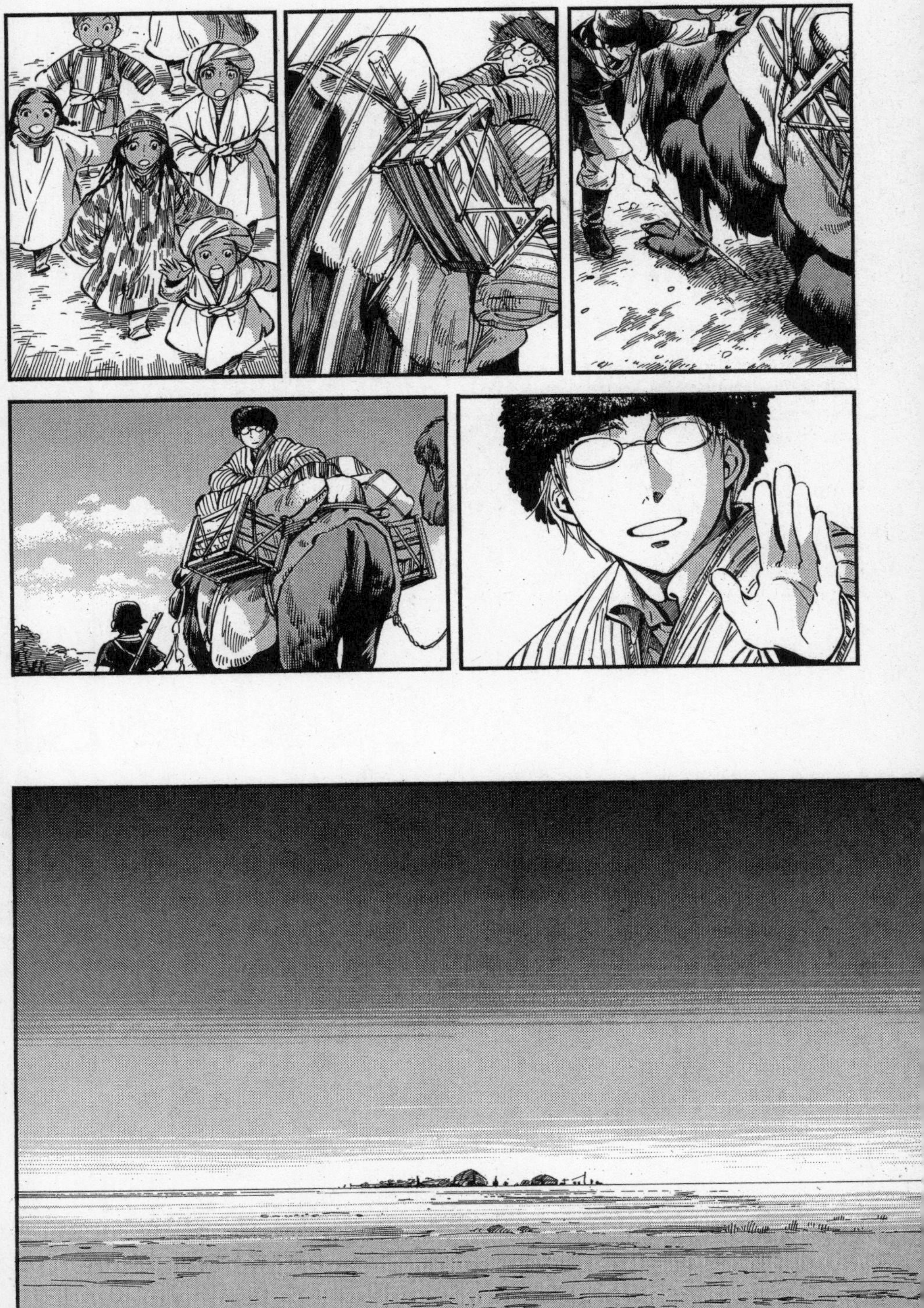

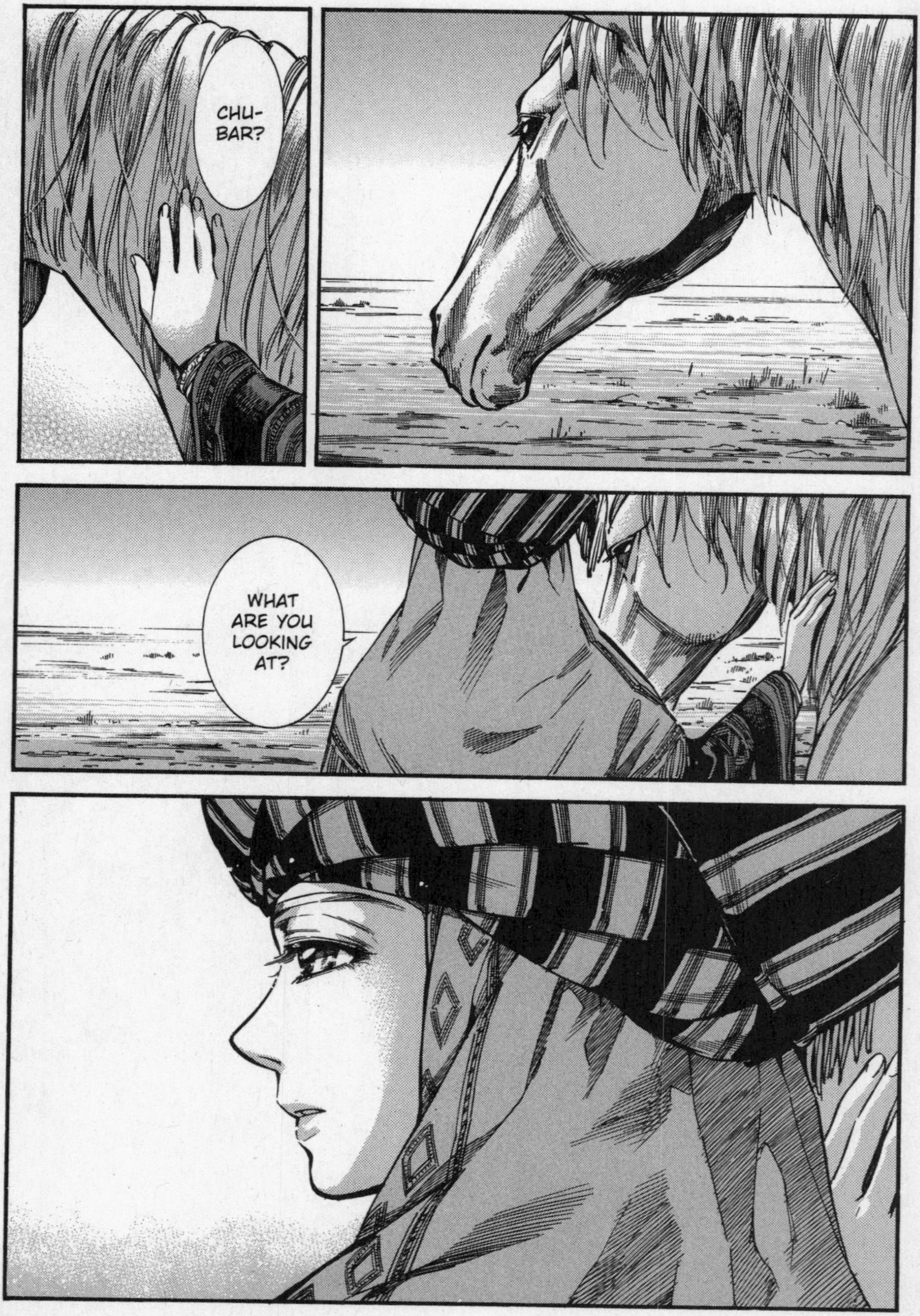
CHU-BAR?
WHAT ARE YOU LOOKING AT?

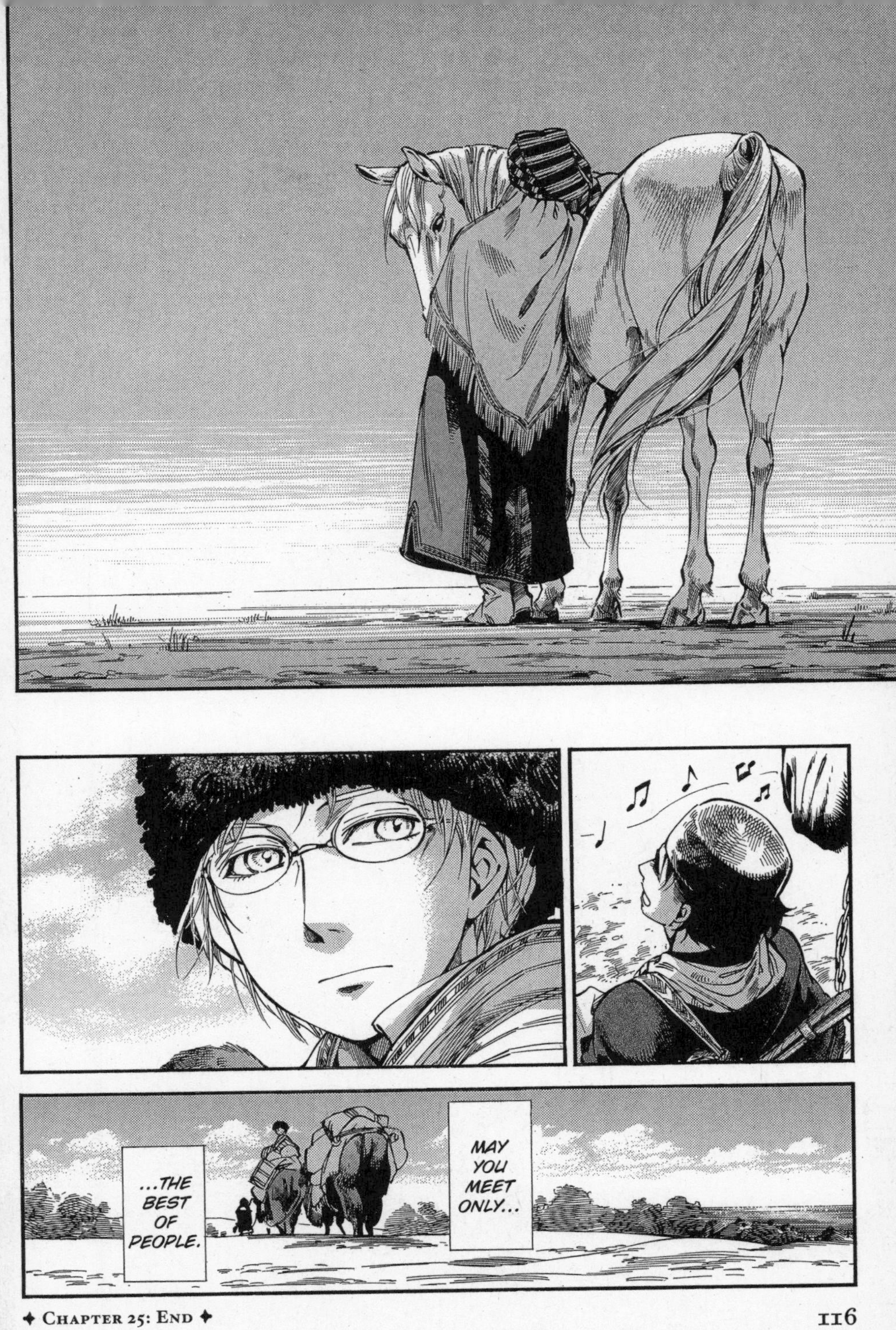
MAY YOU MEET ONLY...
...THE BEST OF PEOPLE.

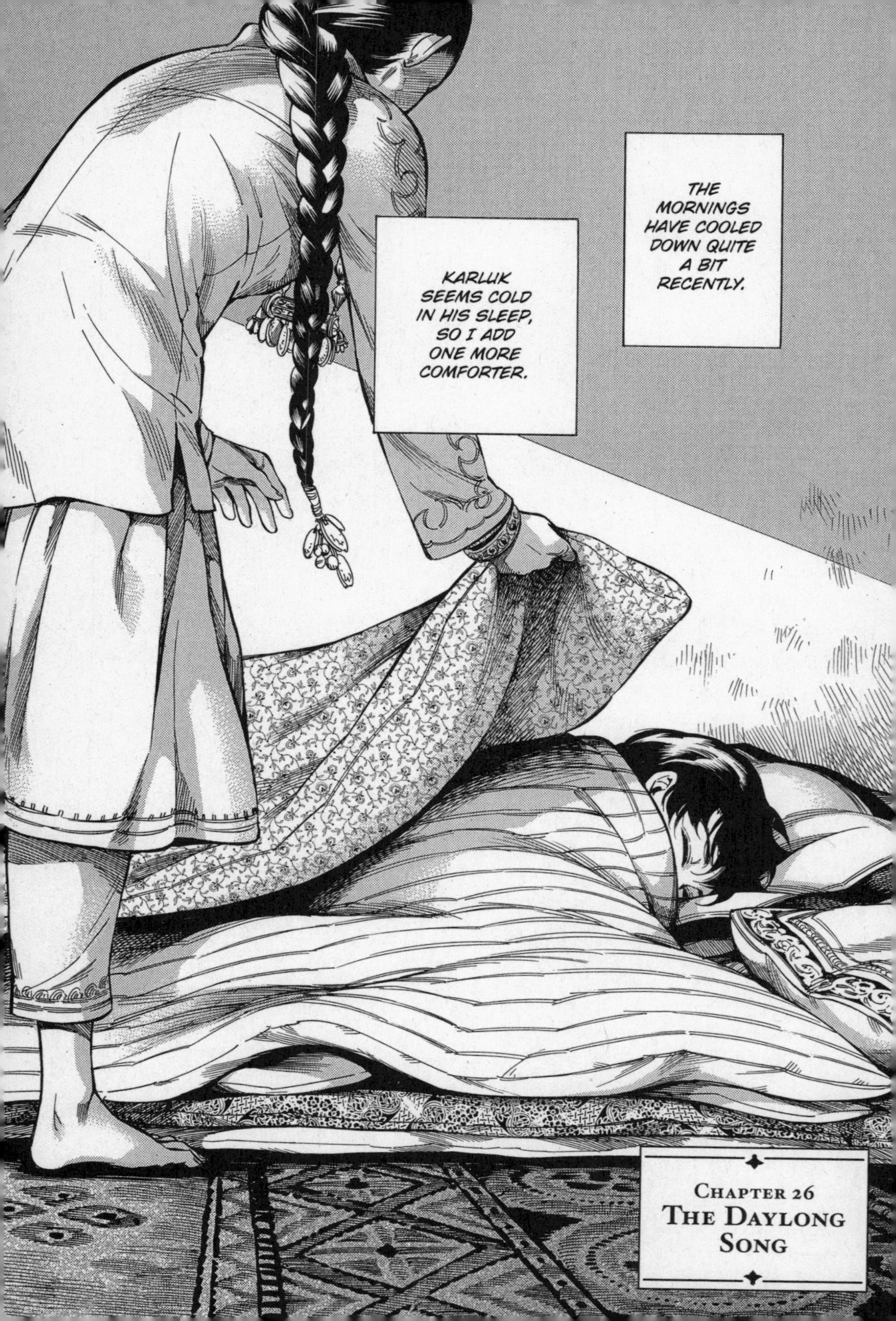
THE MORNINGS HAVE COOLED DOWN QUITE A BIT RECENTLY.
KARLUK SEEMS COLD IN HIS SLEEP, SO I ADD ONE MORE COMFORTER.
CHAPTER 26
THE DAYLONG SONG

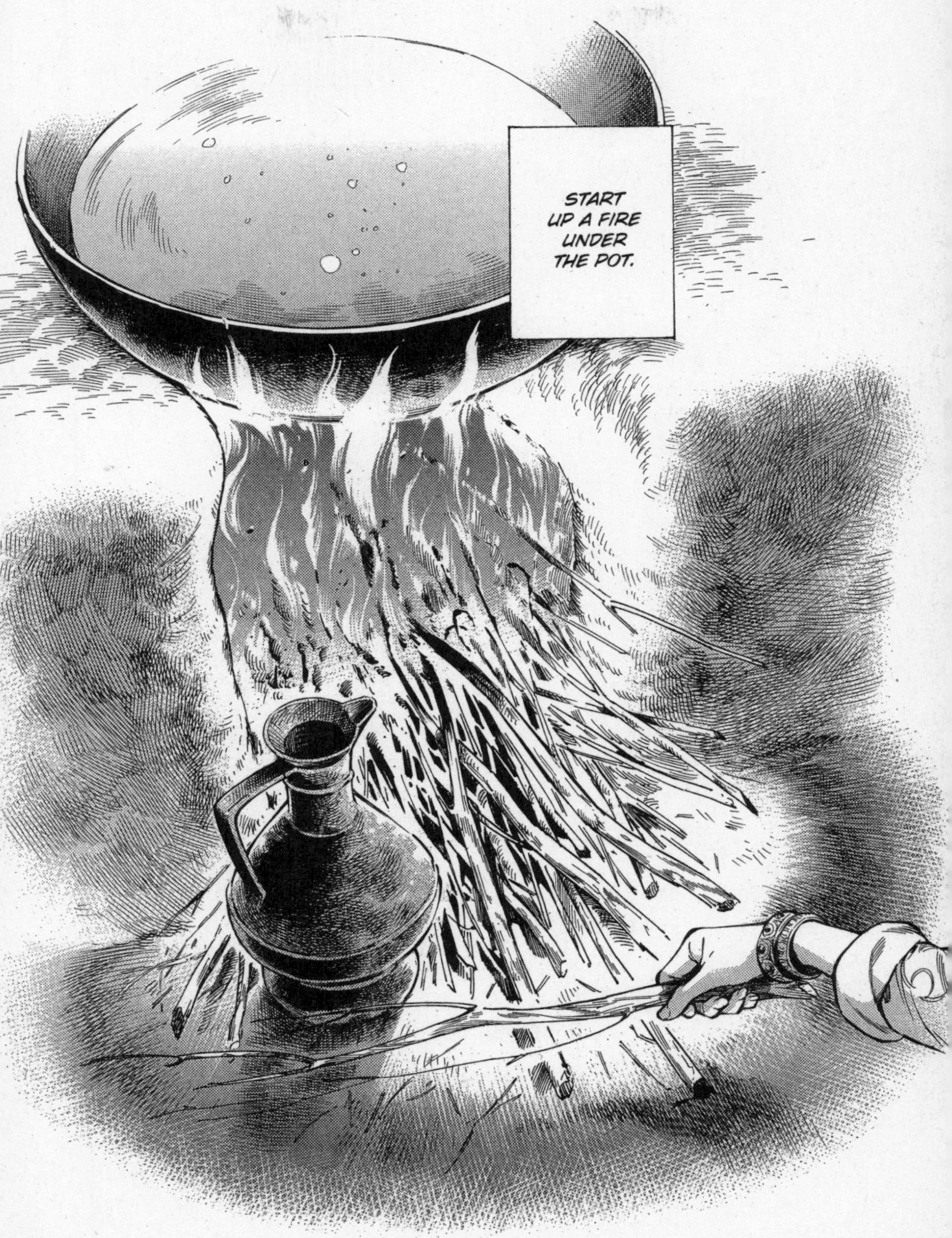
START
UP A FIRE
UNDER
THE POT.

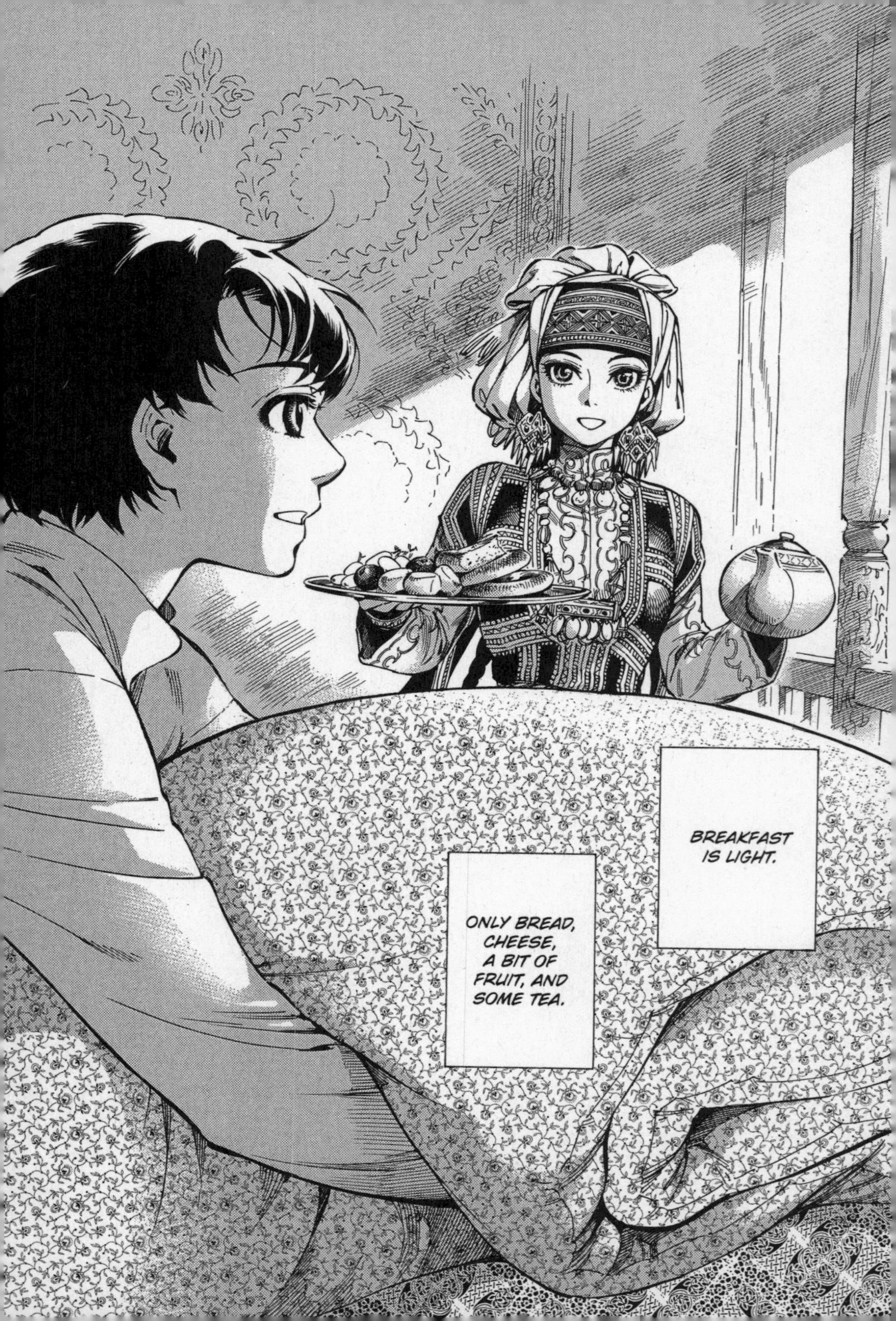
BREAKFAST IS LIGHT.
ONLY BREAD, CHEESE, A BIT OF FRUIT, AND SOME TEA.

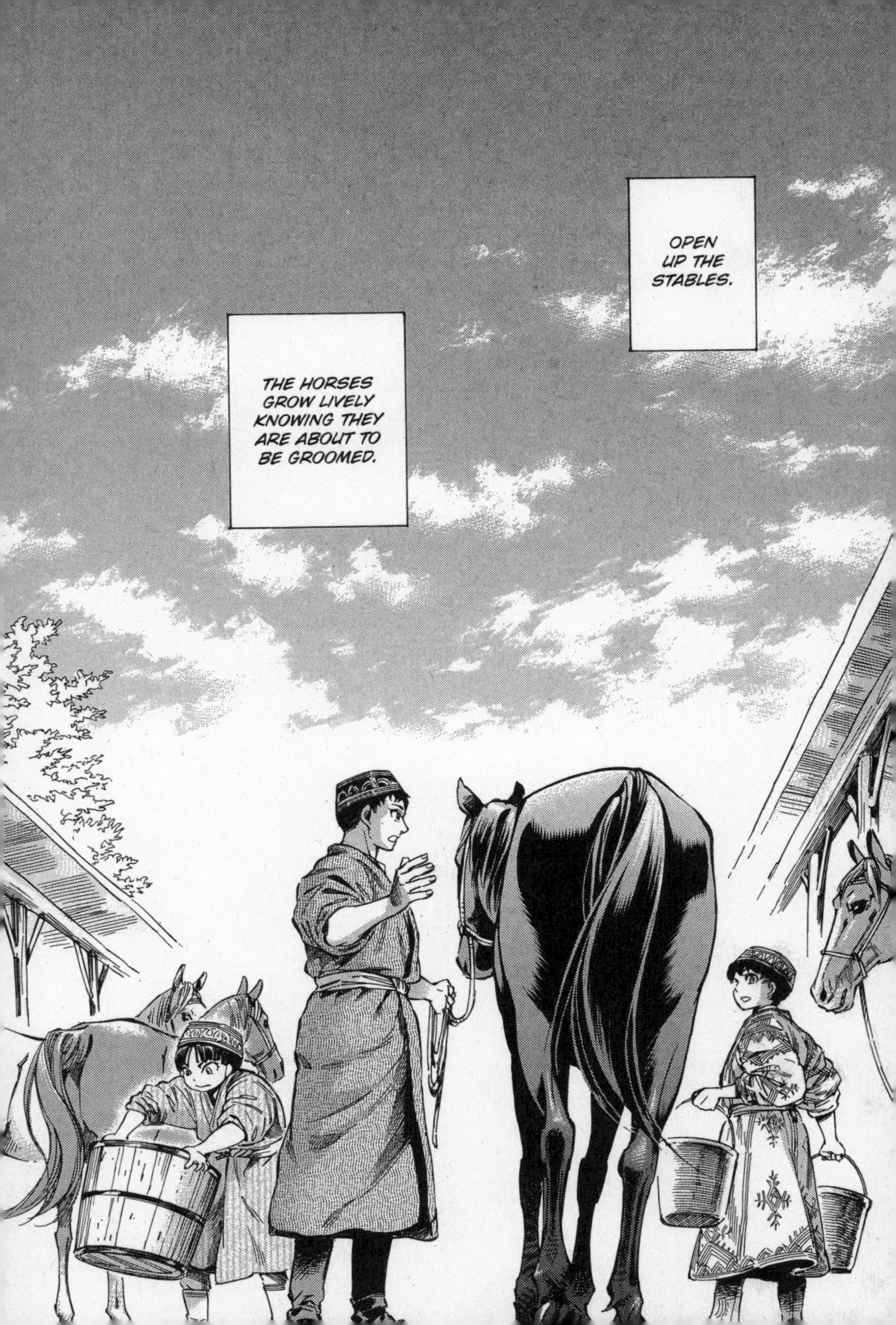
OPEN UP THE STABLES.
THE HORSES GROW LIVELY KNOWING THEY ARE ABOUT TO BE GROOMED.

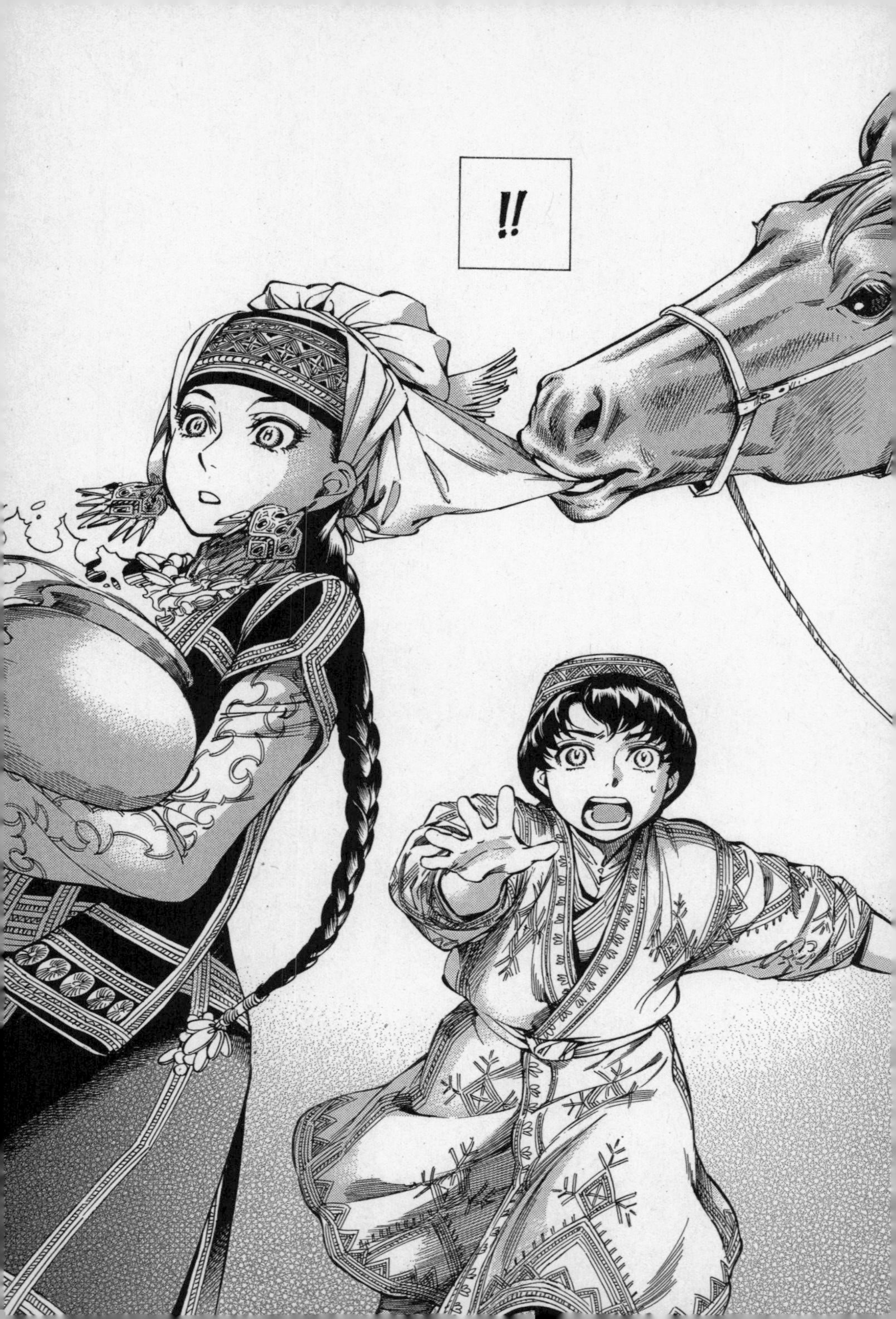
!!

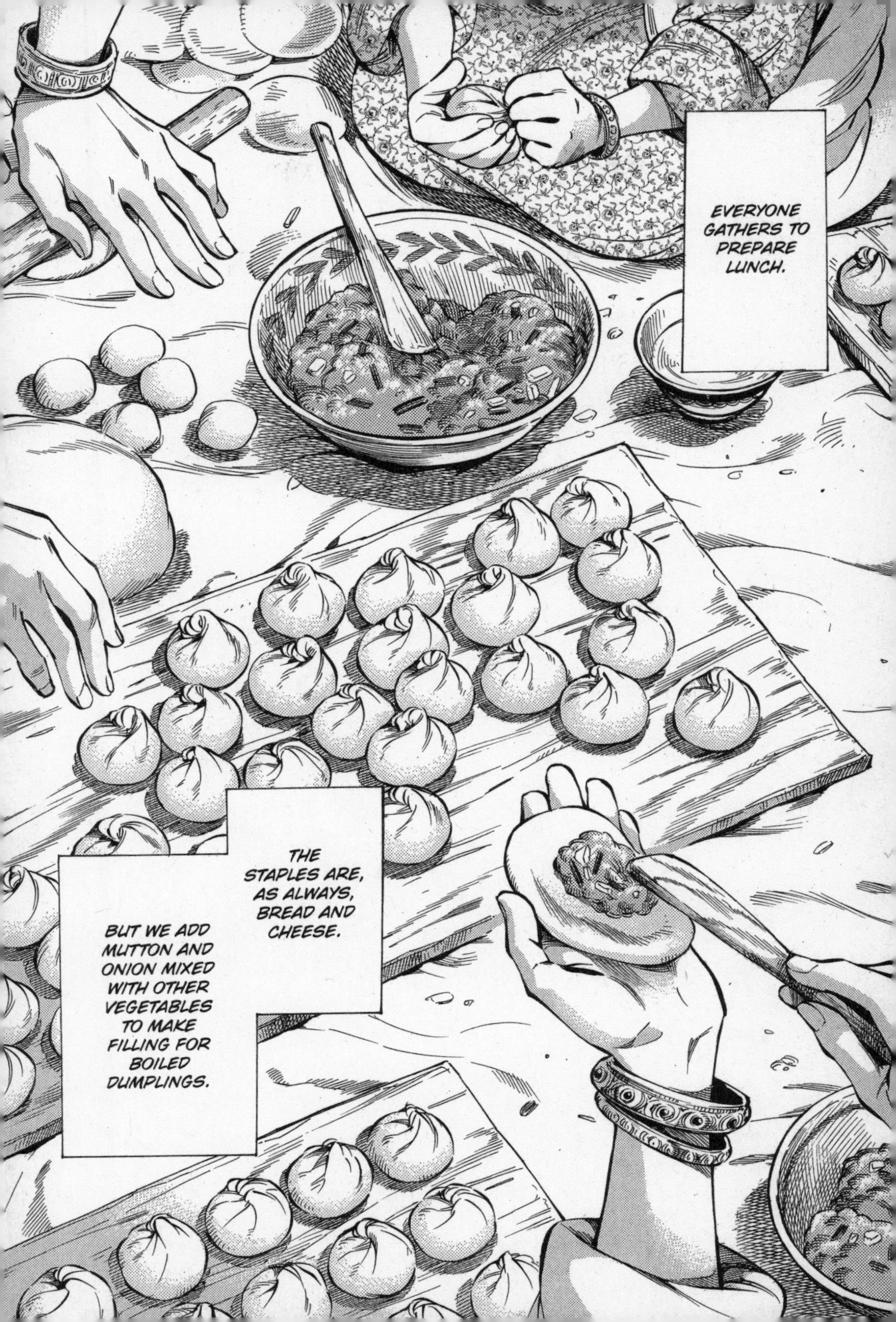
EVERYONE GATHERS TO PREPARE LUNCH.
THE STAPLES ARE, AS ALWAYS, BREAD AND CHEESE.
BUT WE ADD MUTTON AND ONION MIXED WITH OTHER VEGETABLES TO MAKE FILLING FOR BOILED DUMPLINGS.

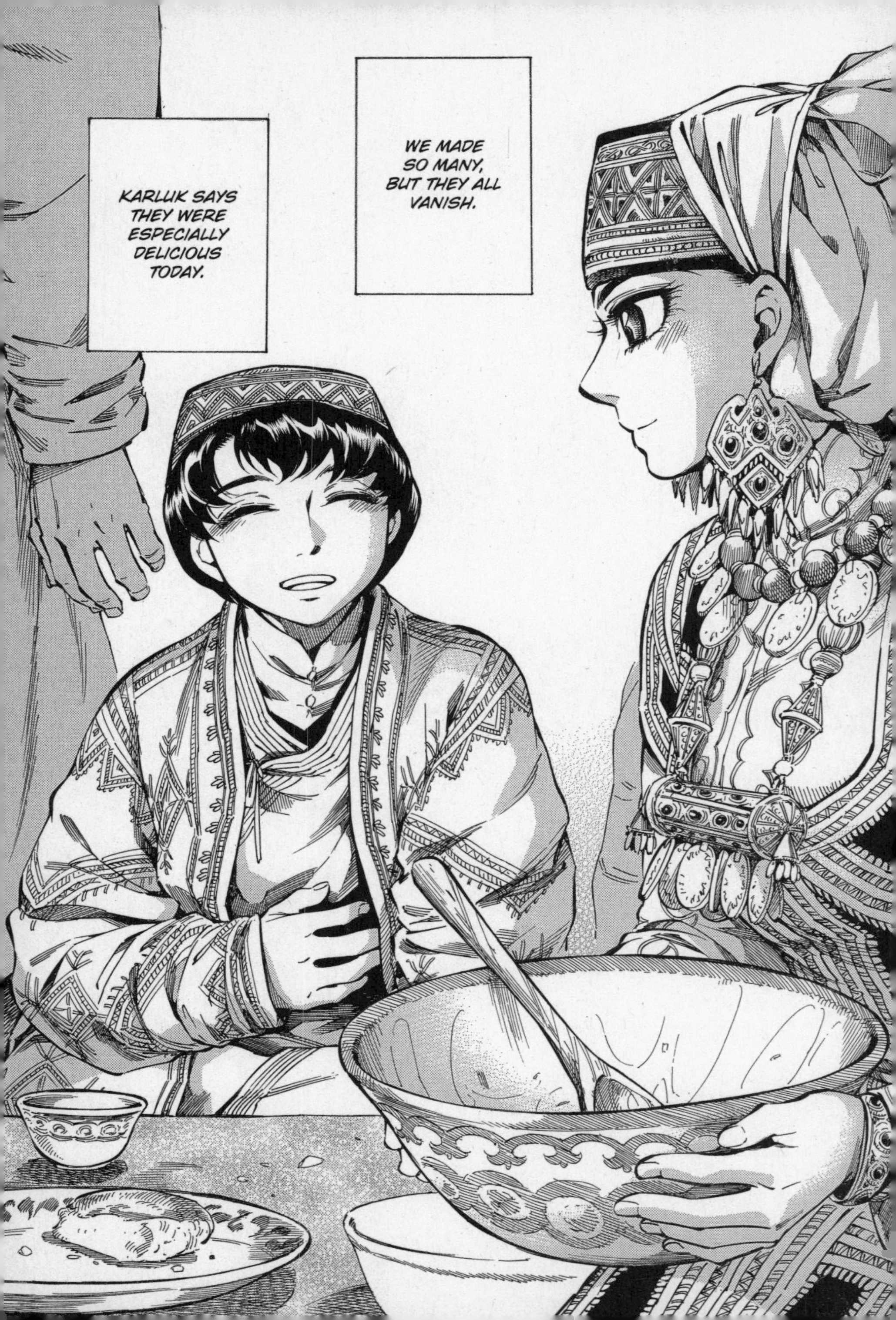
WE MADE SO MANY, BUT THEY ALL VANISH.
KARLUK SAYS THEY WERE ESPECIALLY DELICIOUS TODAY.

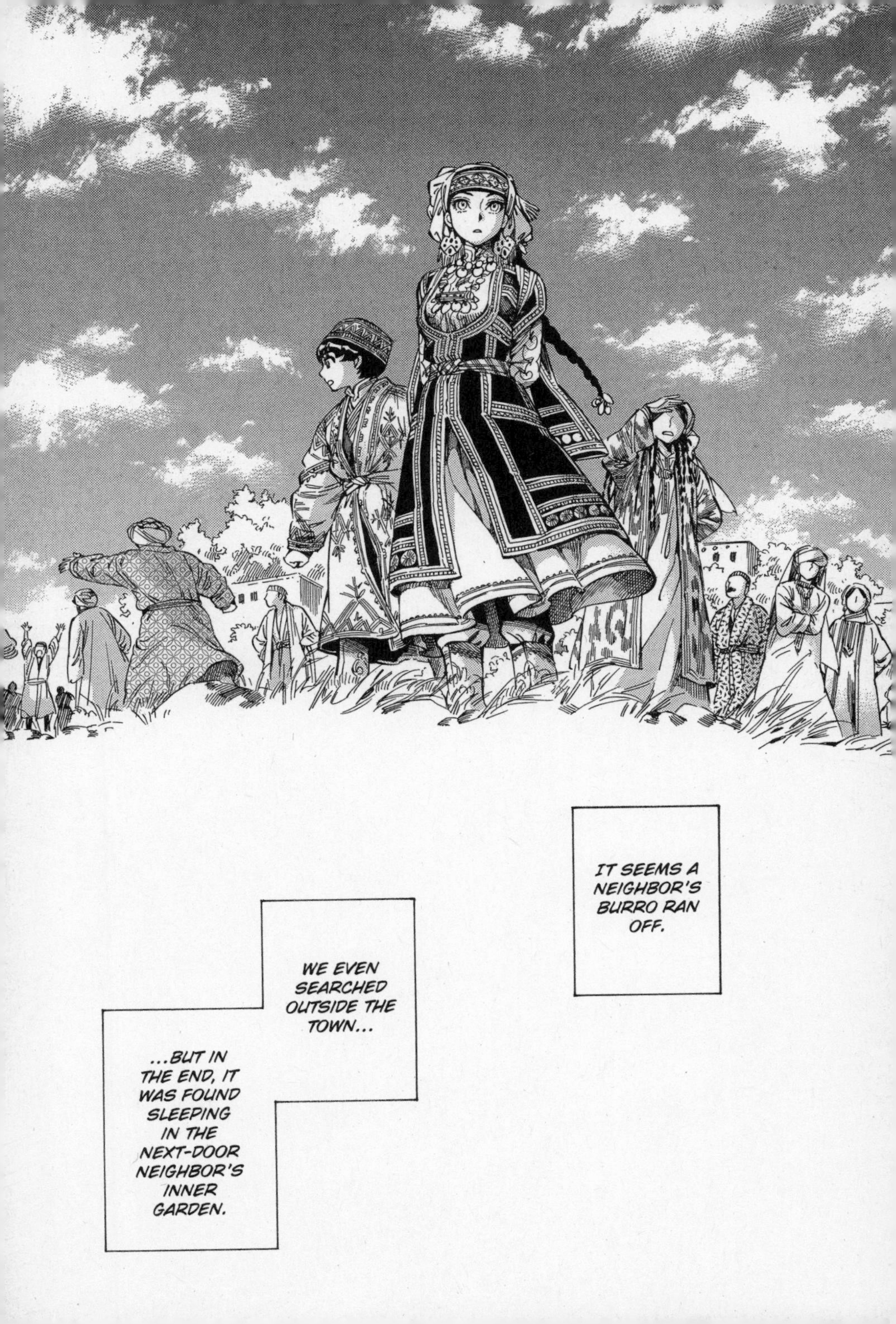
IT SEEMS A NEIGHBOR'S BURRO RAN OFF.
WE EVEN SEARCHED OUTSIDE THE TOWN...
...BUT IN THE END, IT WAS FOUND SLEEPING IN THE NEXT-DOOR NEIGHBOR'S INNER GARDEN.

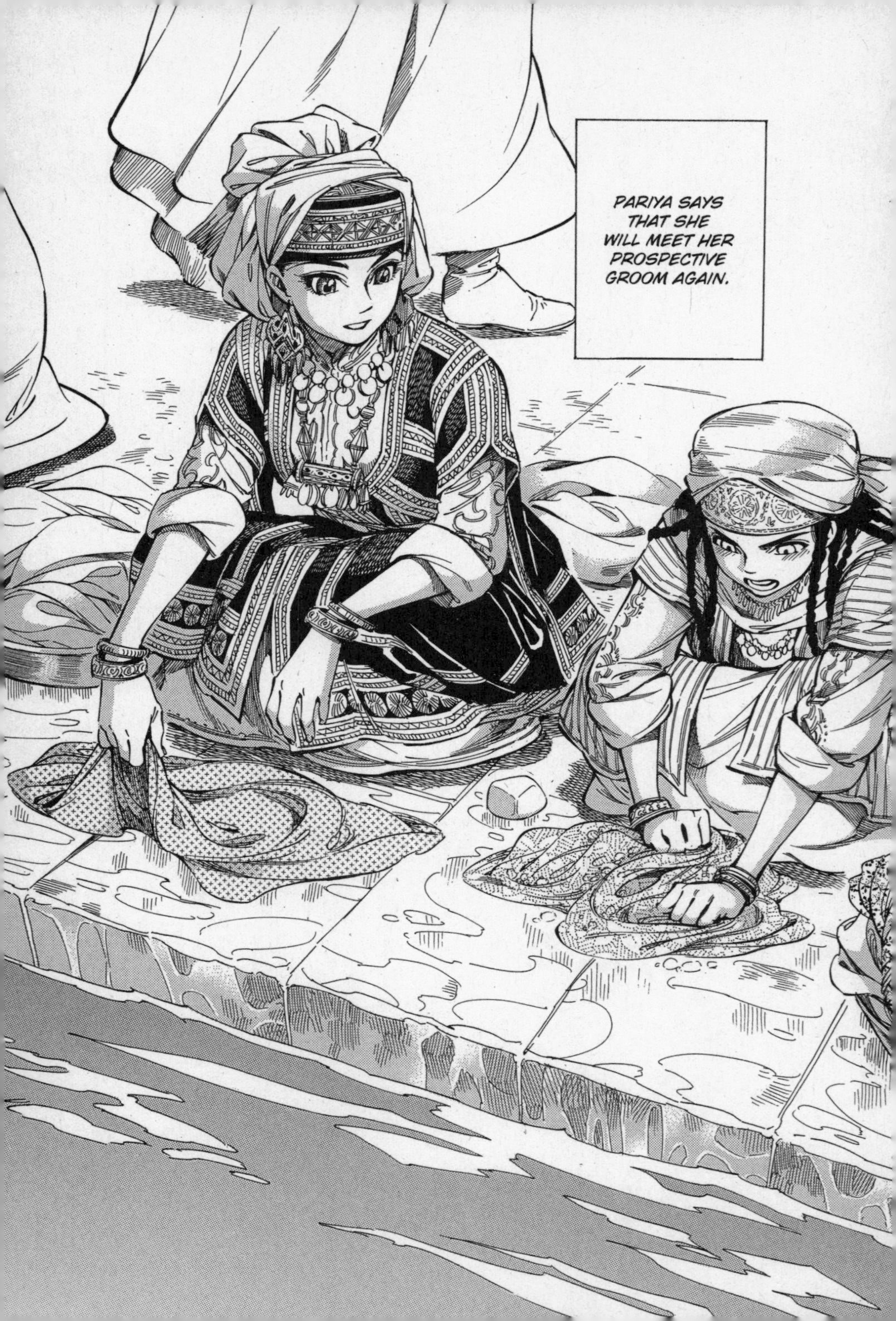
PARIYA SAYS THAT SHE WILL MEET HER PROSPECTIVE GROOM AGAIN.

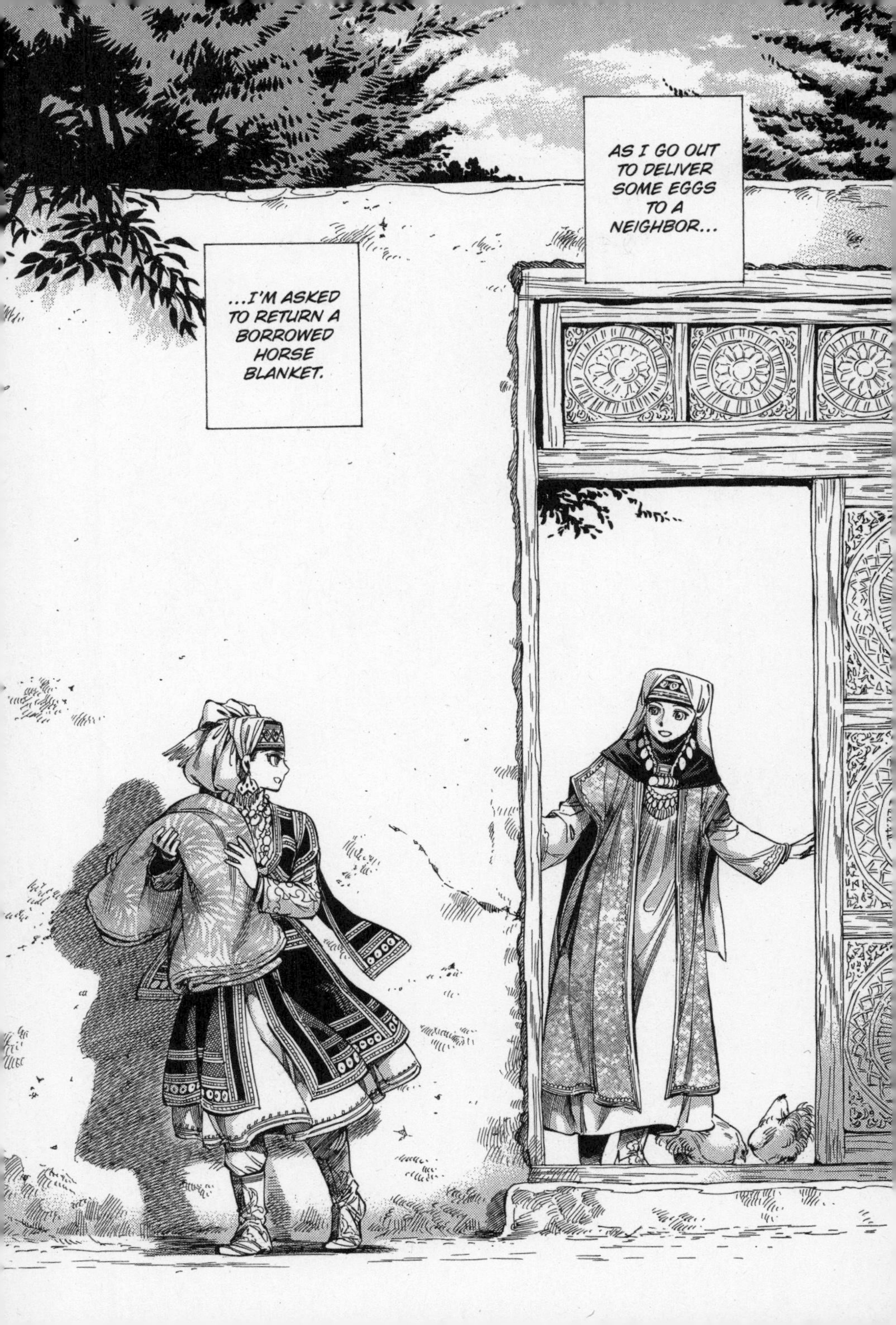
AS I GO OUT TO DELIVER SOME EGGS TO A NEIGHBOR...
...I'M ASKED TO RETURN A BORROWED HORSE BLANKET.

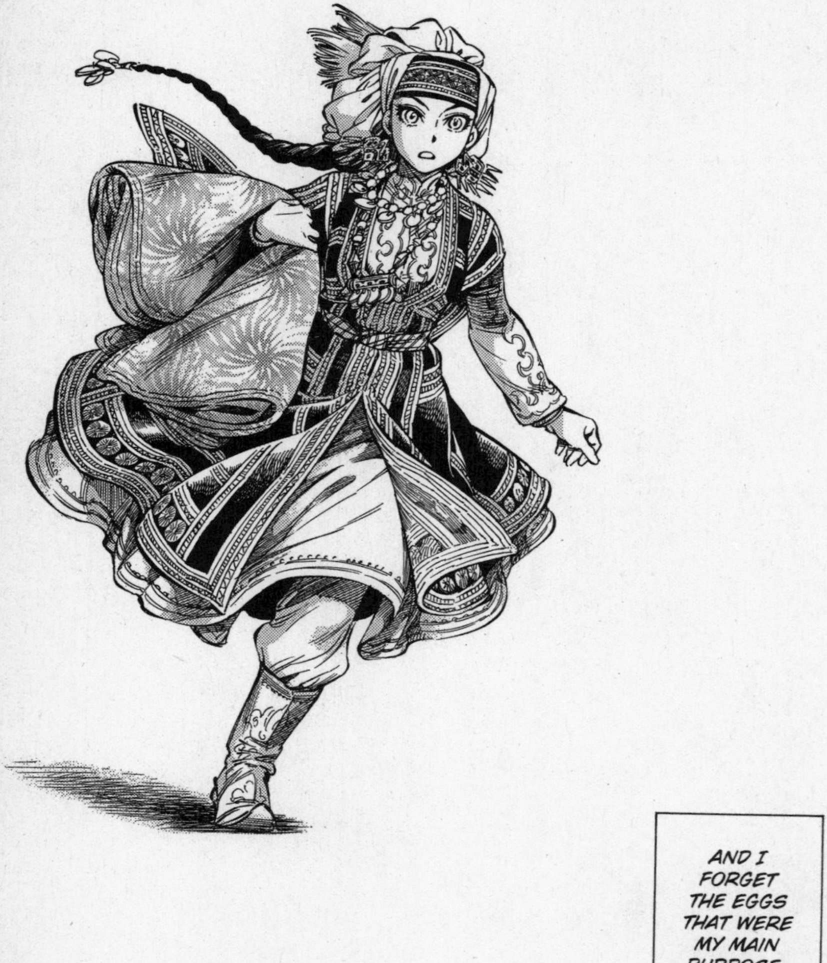
AND I FORGET THE EGGS THAT WERE MY MAIN PURPOSE.

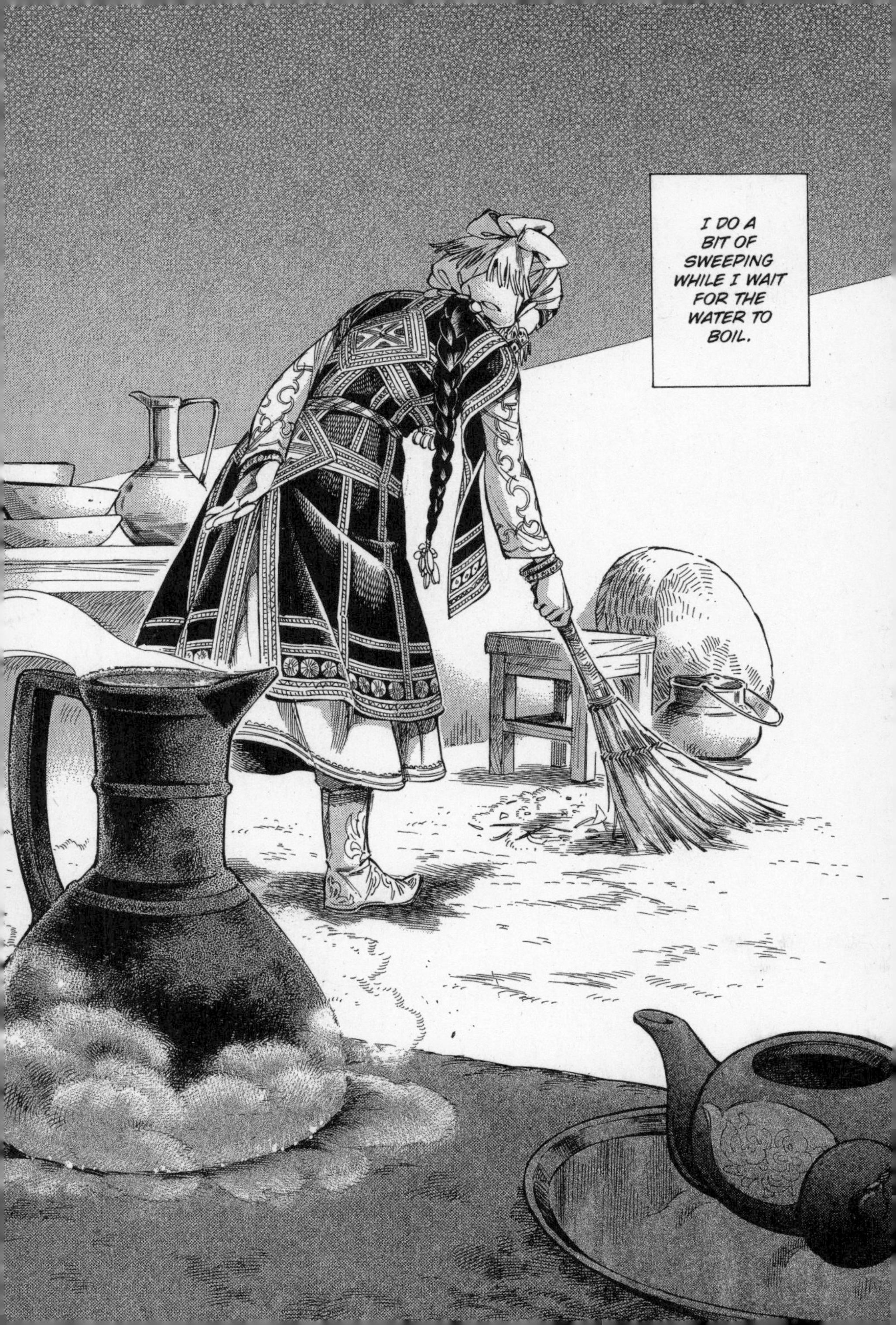
I DO A BIT OF SWEEPING WHILE I WAIT FOR THE WATER TO BOIL.

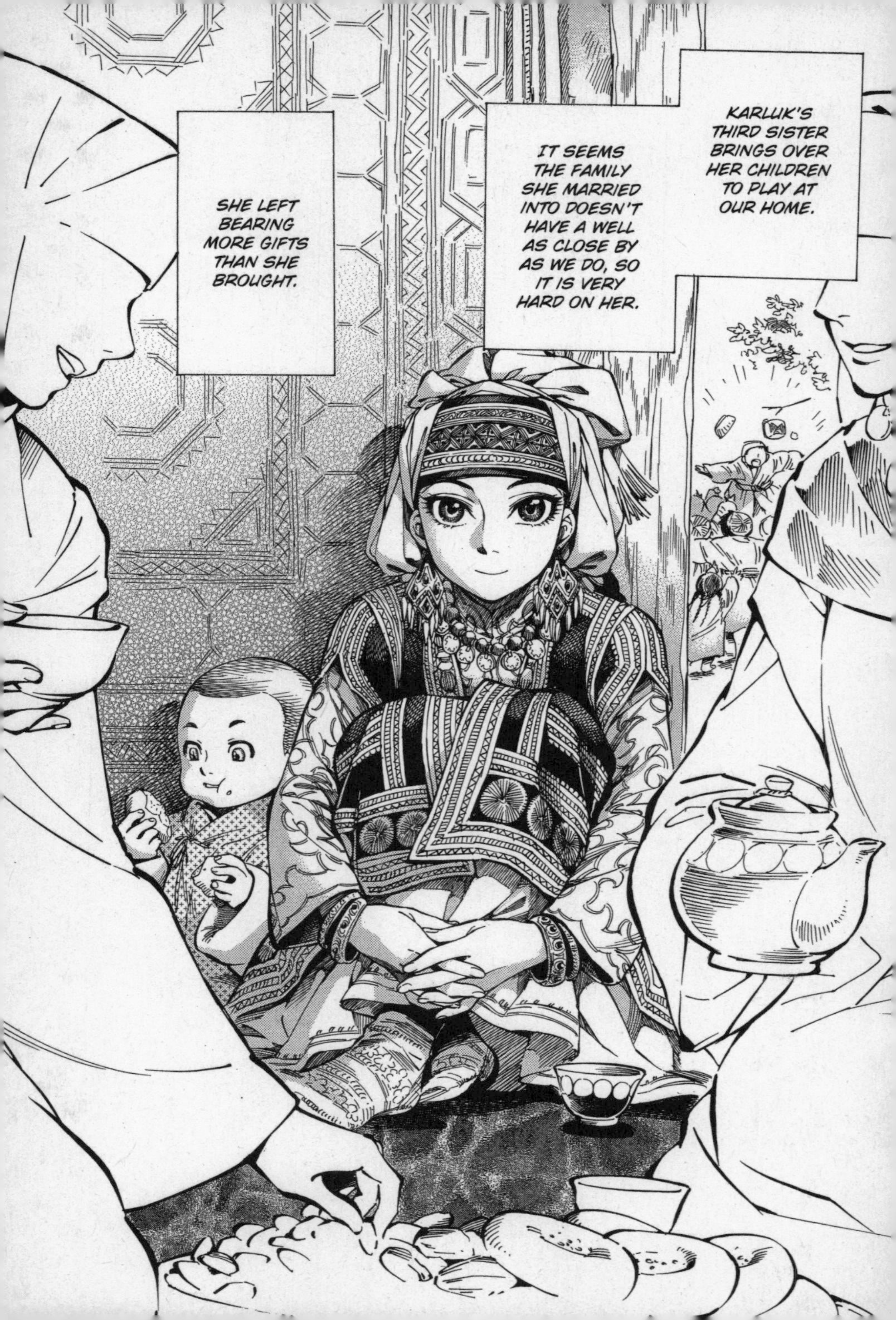
KARLUK'S THIRD SISTER BRINGS OVER HER CHILDREN TO PLAY AT OUR HOME.
IT SEEMS THE FAMILY SHE MARRIED INTO DOESN'T HAVE A WELL AS CLOSE BY AS WE DO, SO IT IS VERY HARD ON HER.
SHE LEFT BEARING MORE GIFTS THAN SHE BROUGHT.

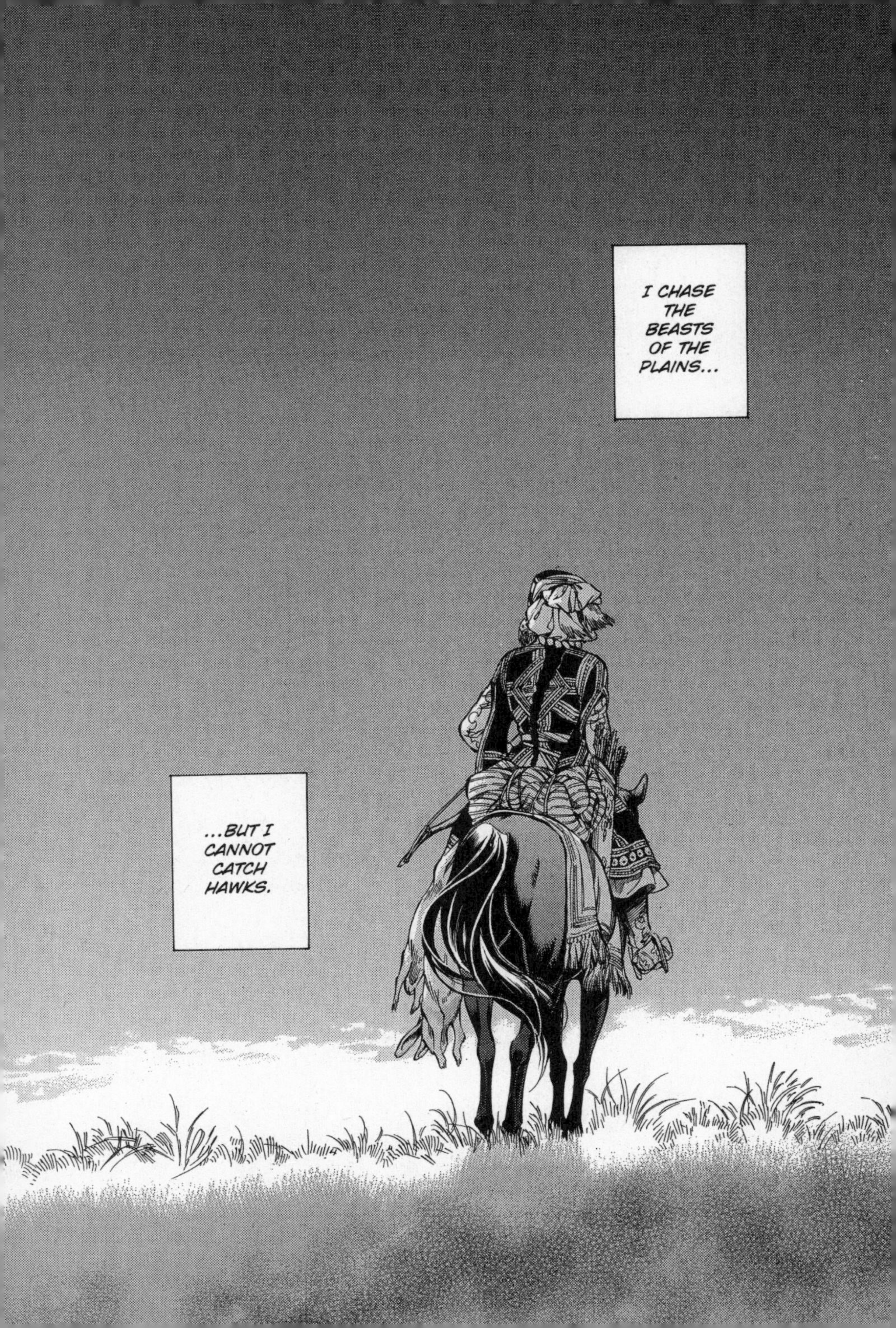
I CHASE THE BEASTS OF THE PLAINS...
...BUT I CANNOT CATCH HAWKS.

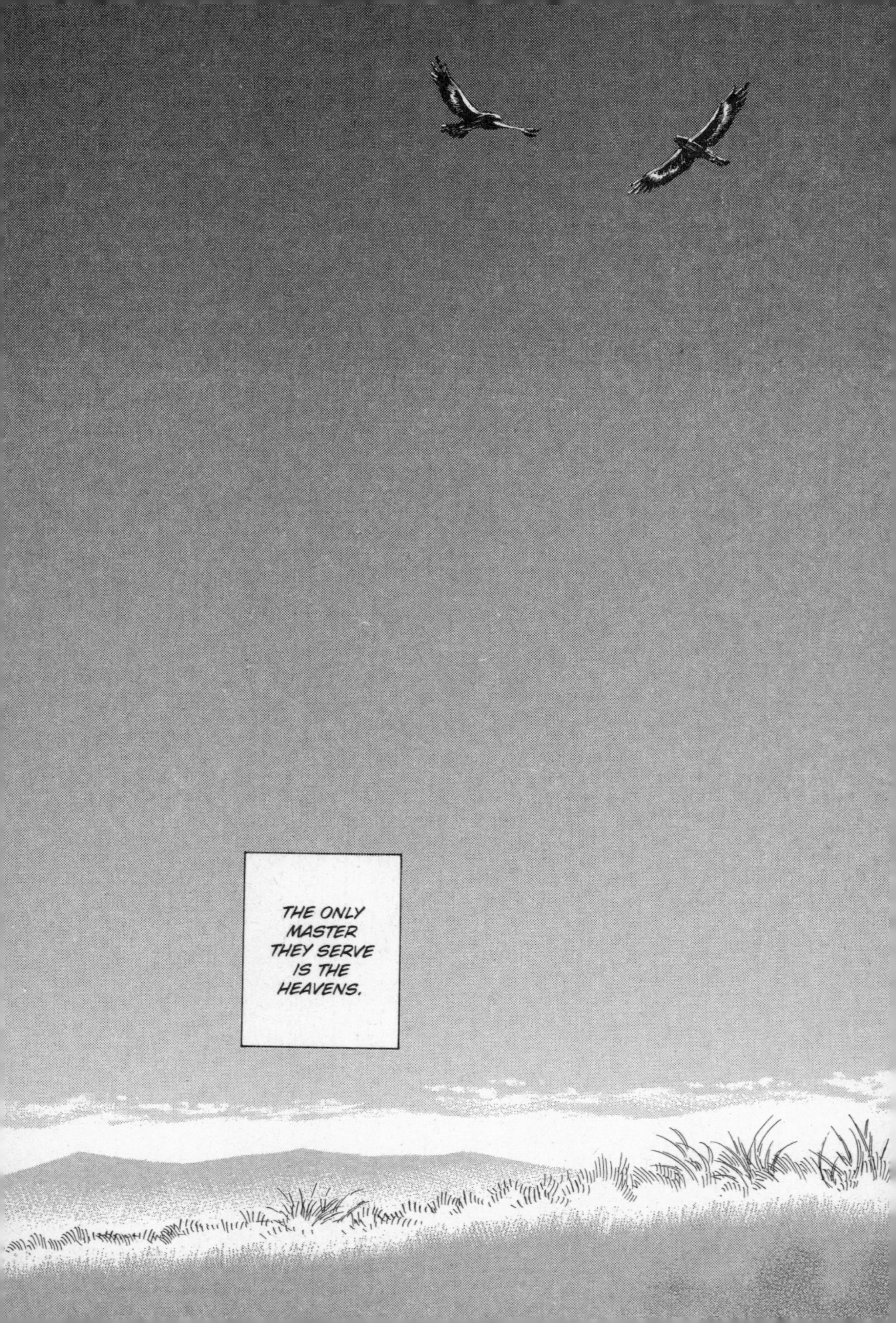
THE ONLY MASTER THEY SERVE IS THE HEAVENS.

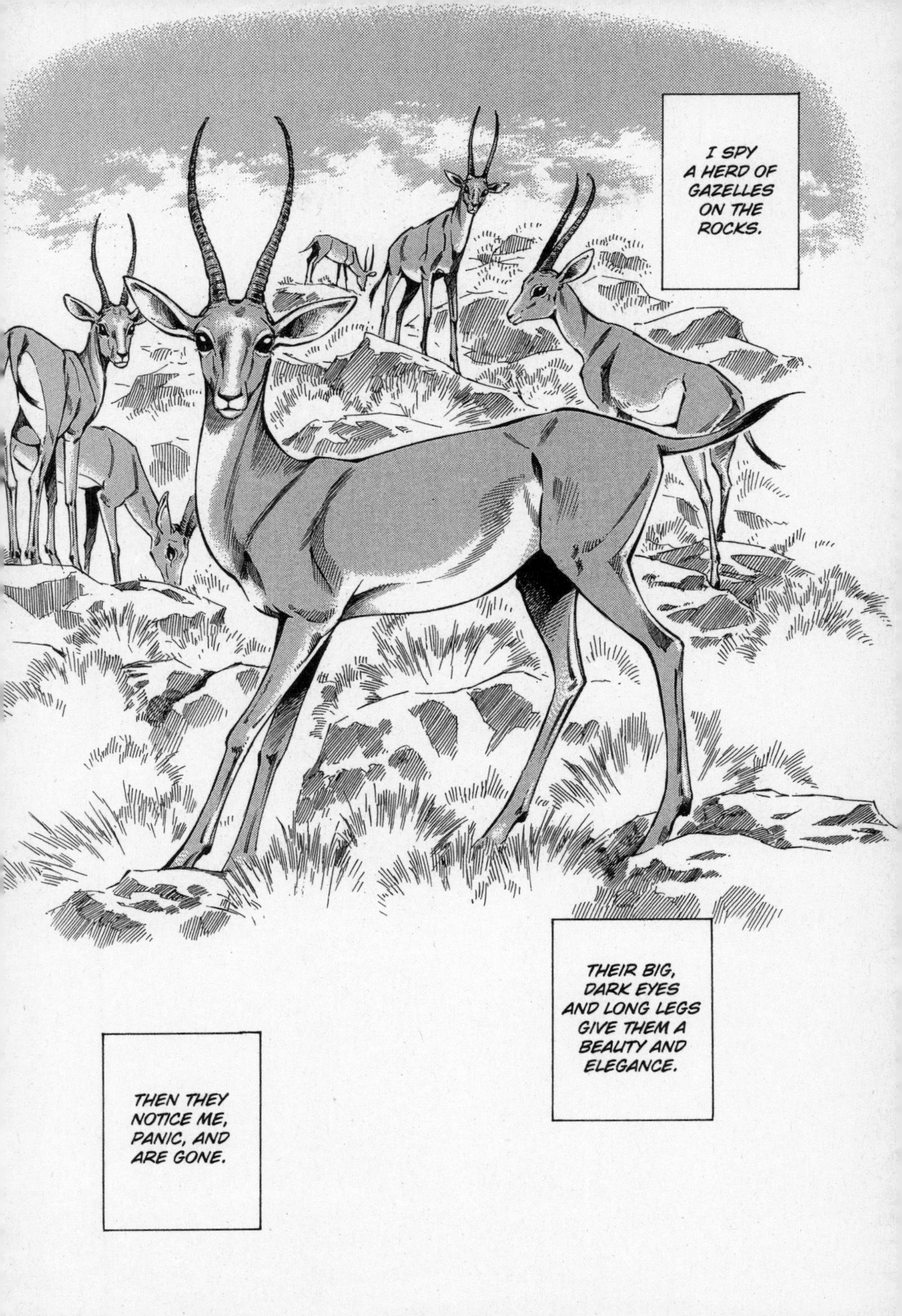
I SPY A HERD OF GAZELLES ON THE ROCKS.
THEIR BIG, DARK EYES AND LONG LEGS GIVE THEM A BEAUTY AND ELEGANCE.
THEN THEY NOTICE ME, PANIC, AND ARE GONE.

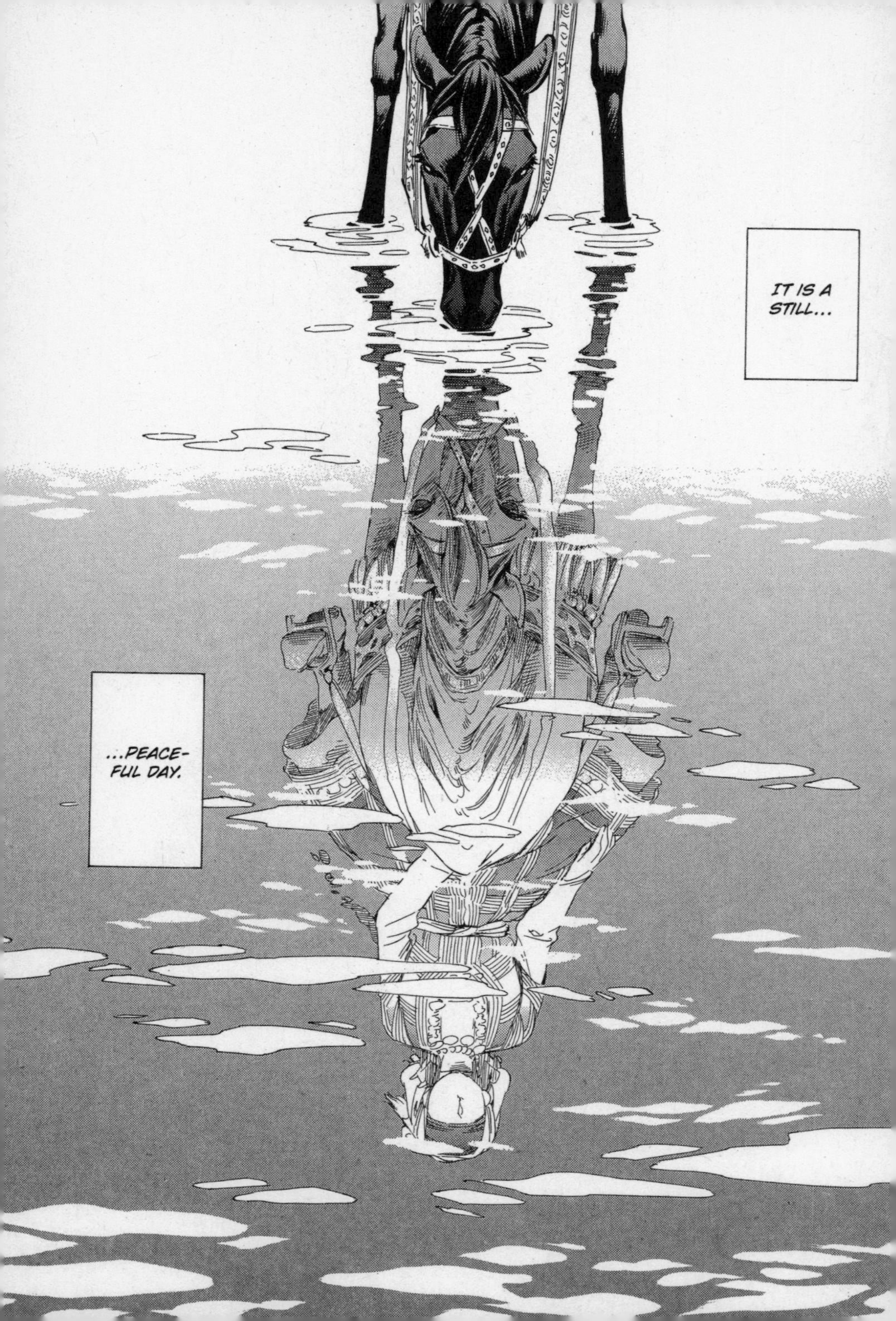
IT IS A STILL...
...PEACE-FUL DAY.

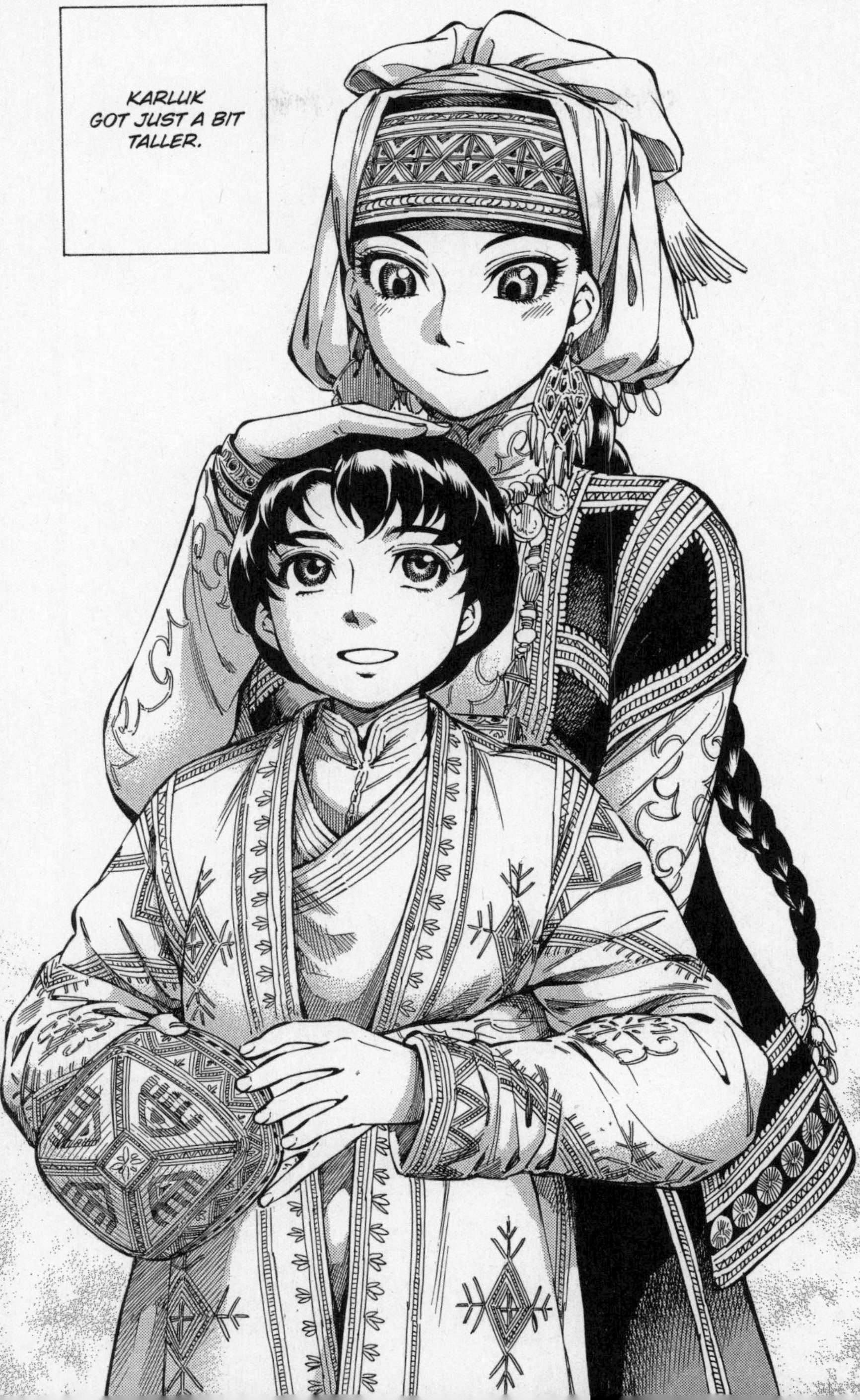
KARLUK GOT JUST A BIT TALLER.

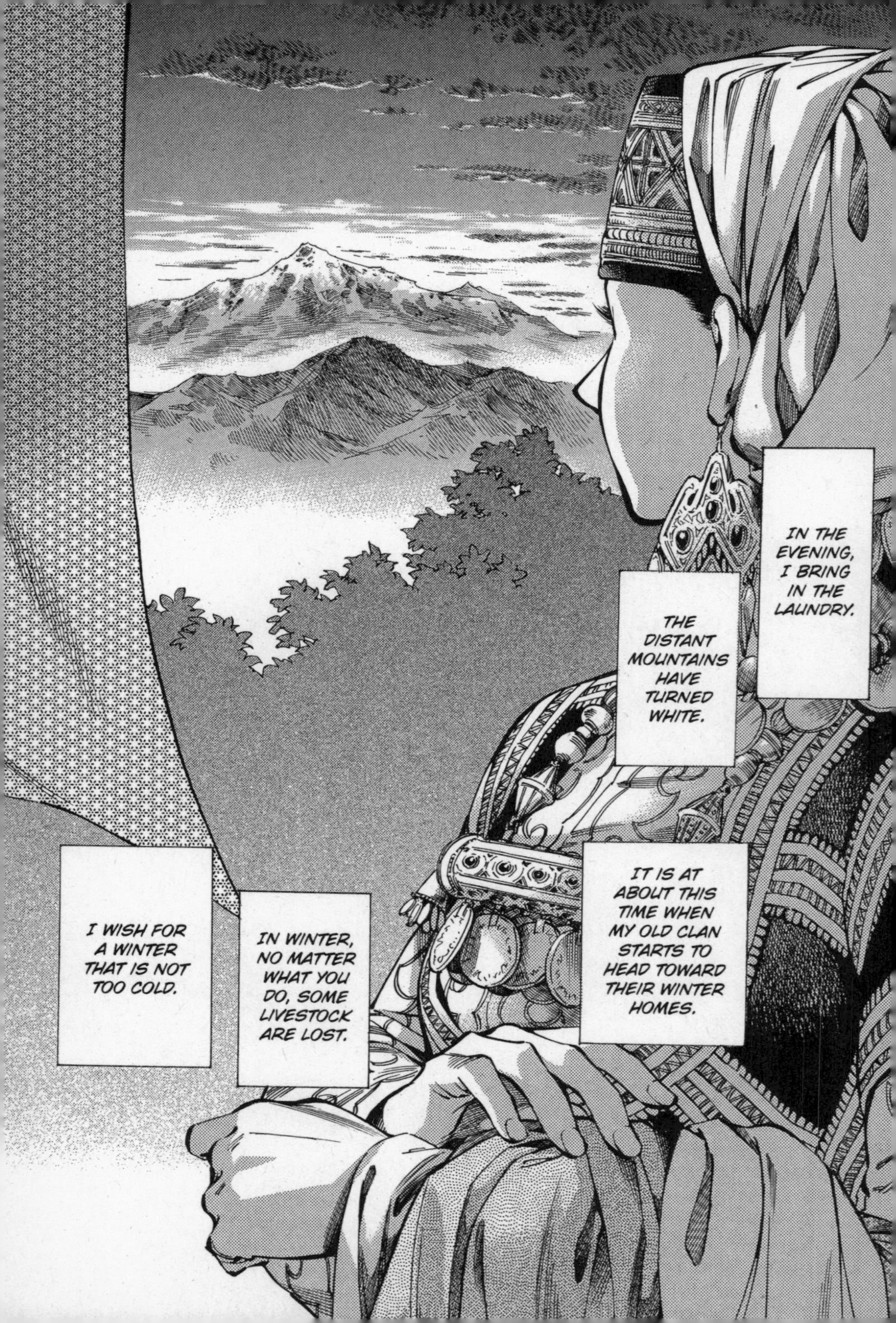
IN THE EVENING, I BRING IN THE LAUNDRY.
THE DISTANT MOUNTAINS HAVE TURNED WHITE.
IT IS AT ABOUT THIS TIME WHEN MY OLD CLAN STARTS TO HEAD TOWARD THEIR WINTER HOMES.
IN WINTER, NO MATTER WHAT YOU DO, SOME LIVESTOCK ARE LOST.
I WISH FOR A WINTER THAT IS NOT TOO COLD.

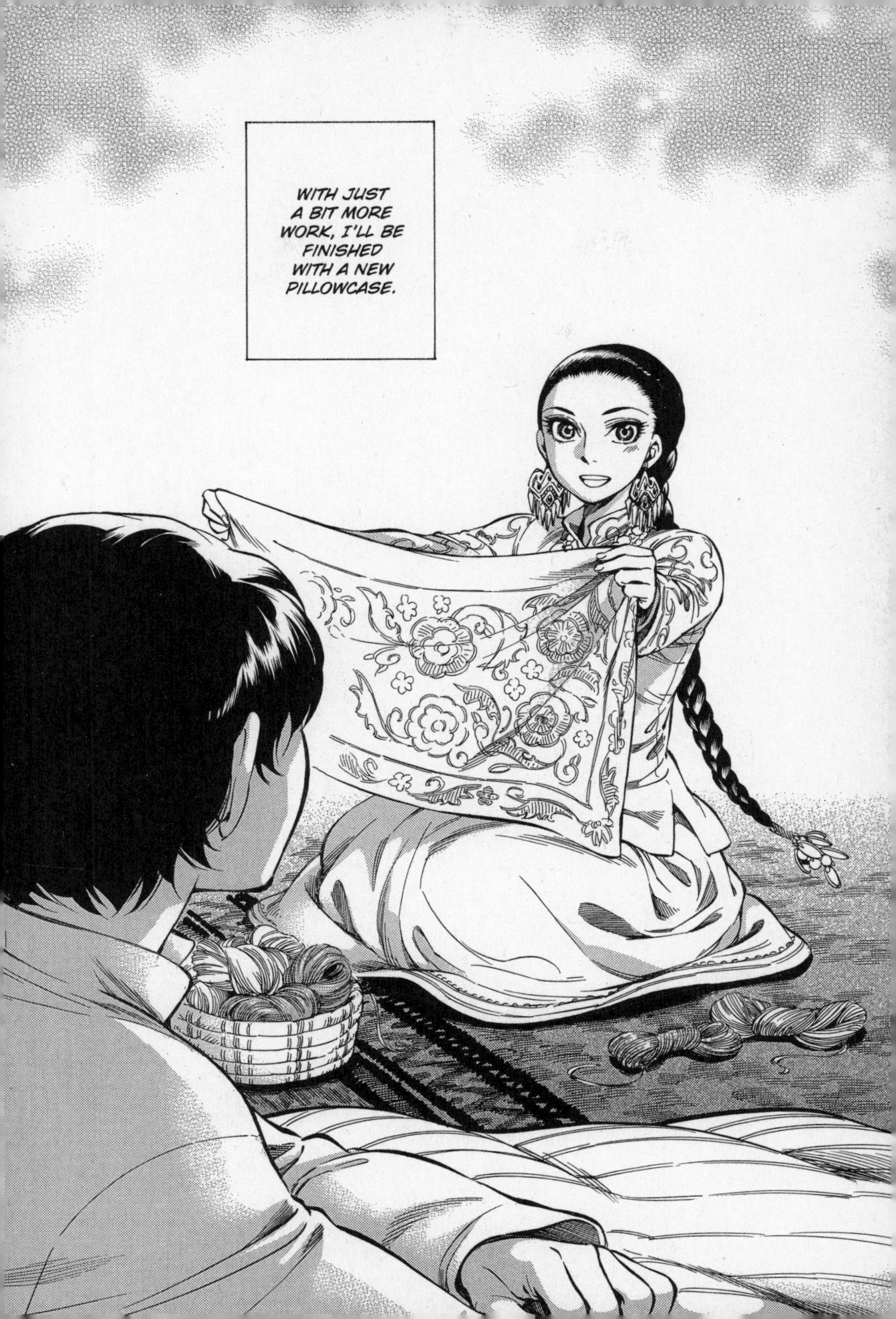
WITH JUST A BIT MORE WORK, I'LL BE FINISHED WITH A NEW PILLOWCASE.

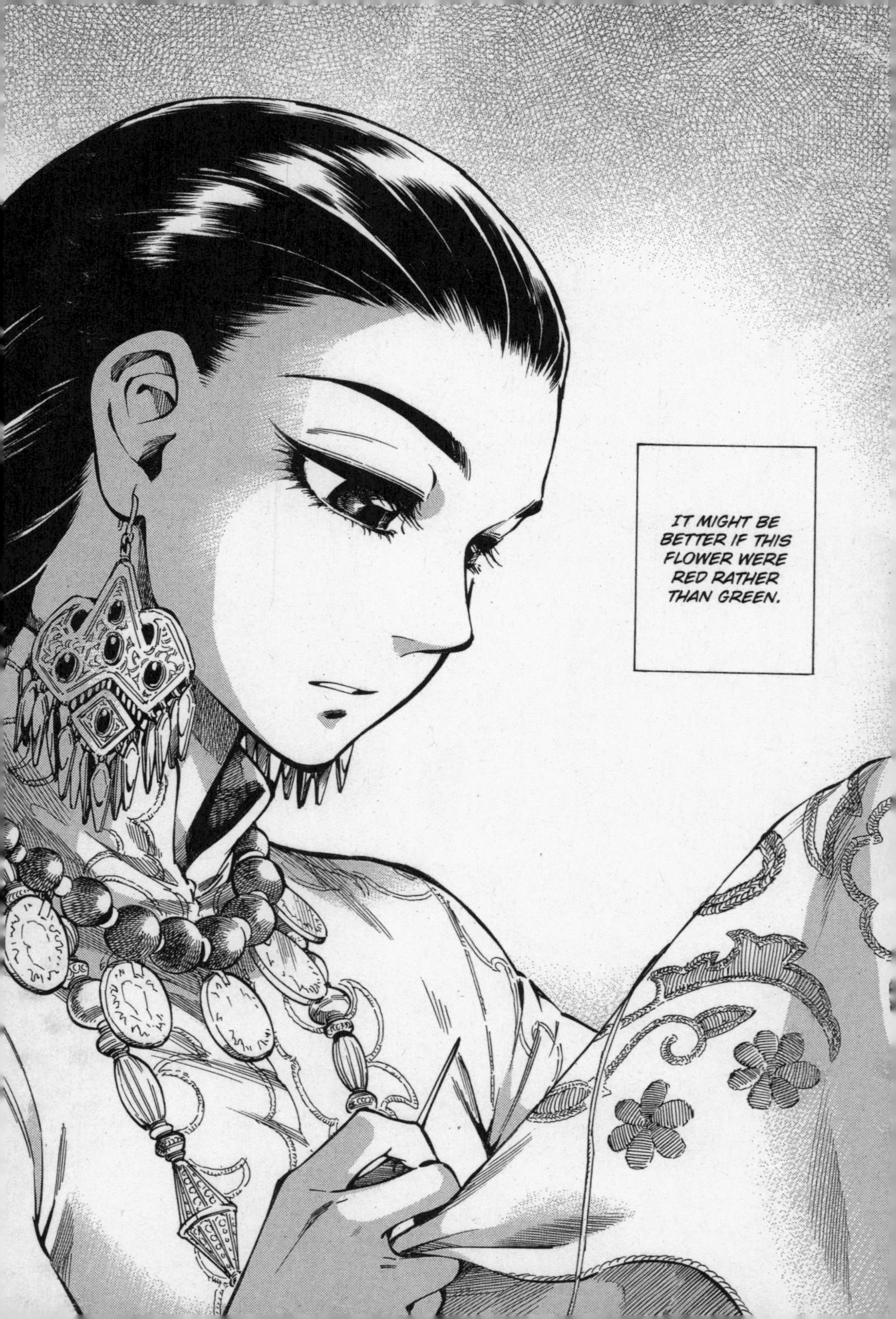
IT MIGHT BE BETTER IF THIS FLOWER WERE RED RATHER THAN GREEN.

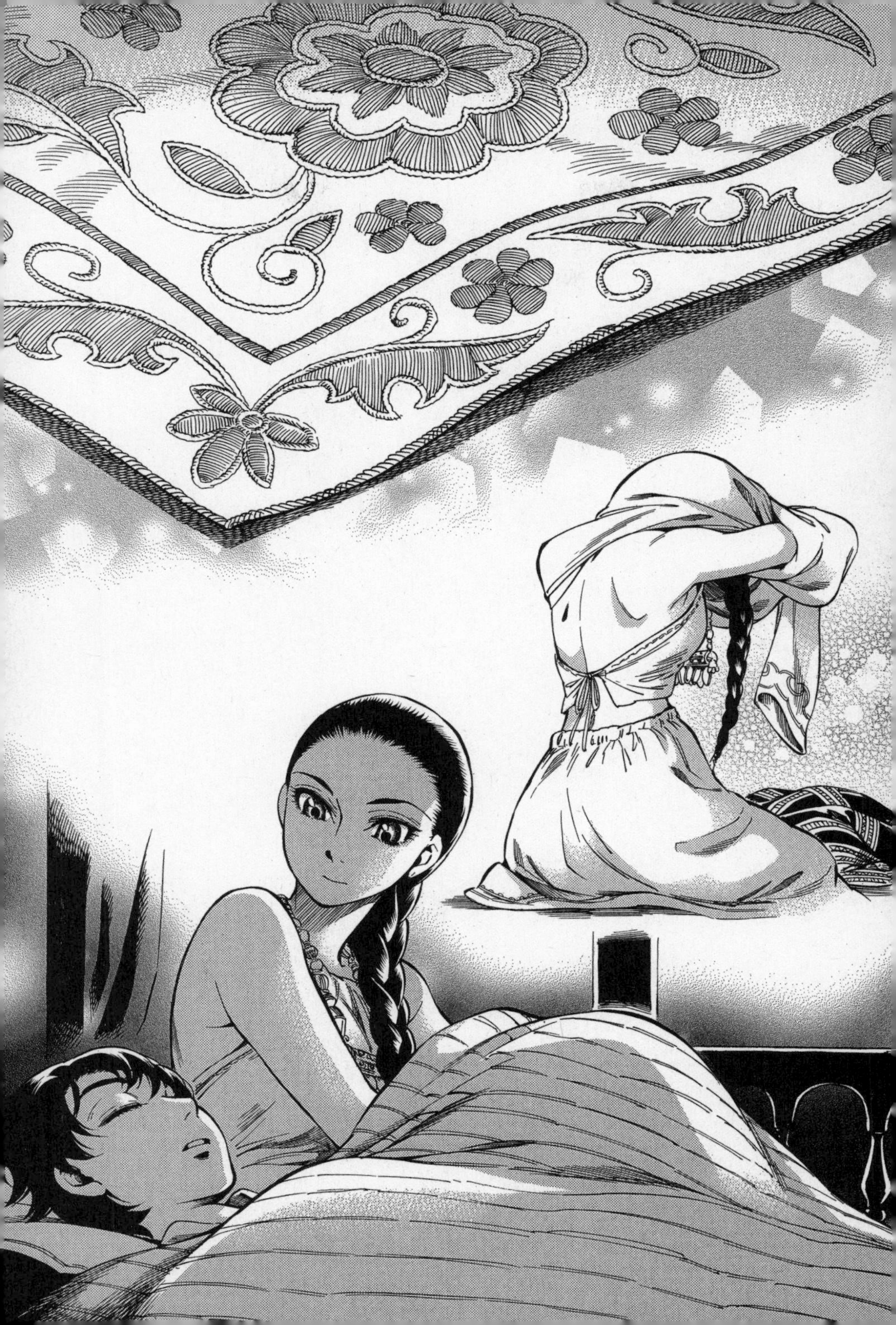

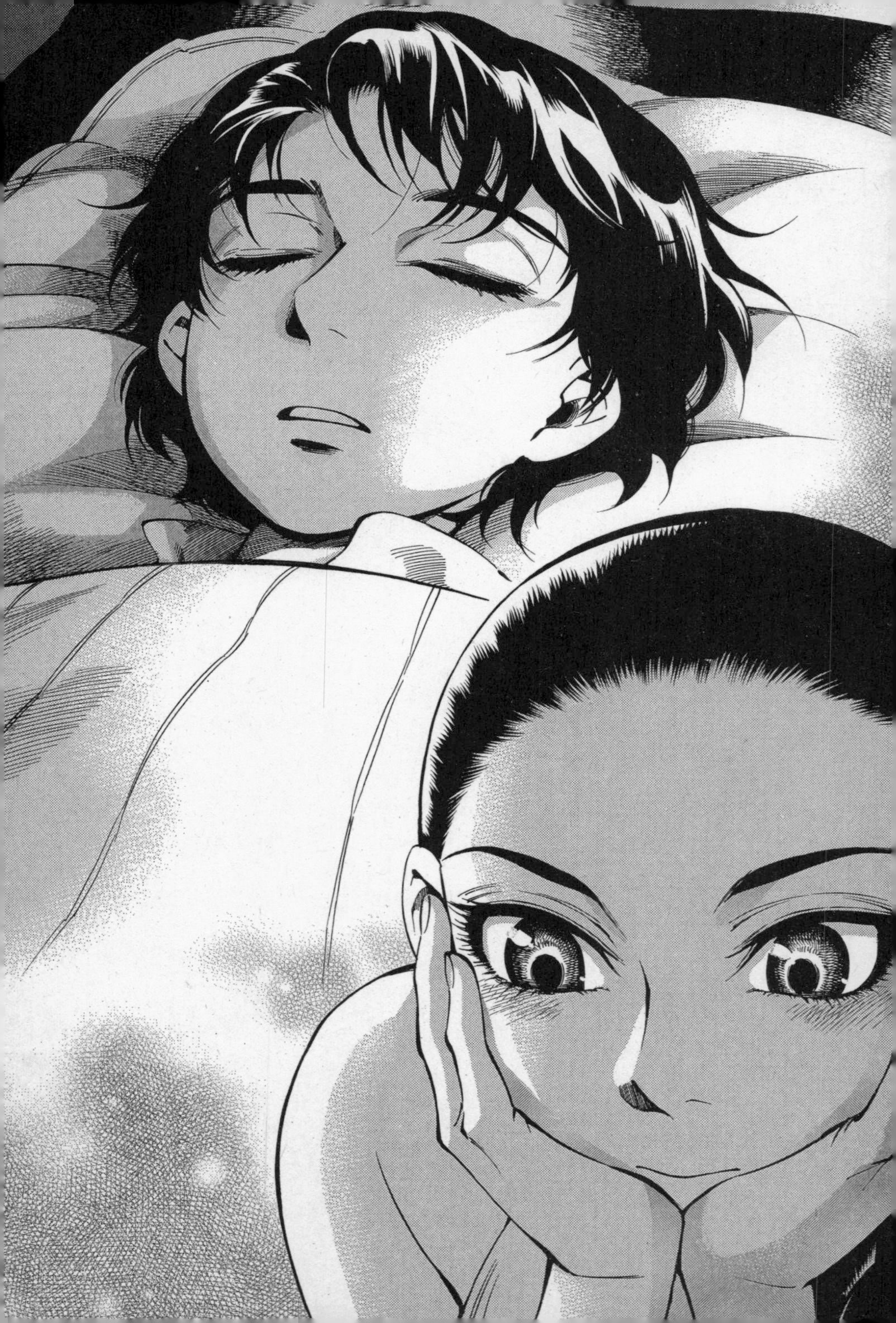

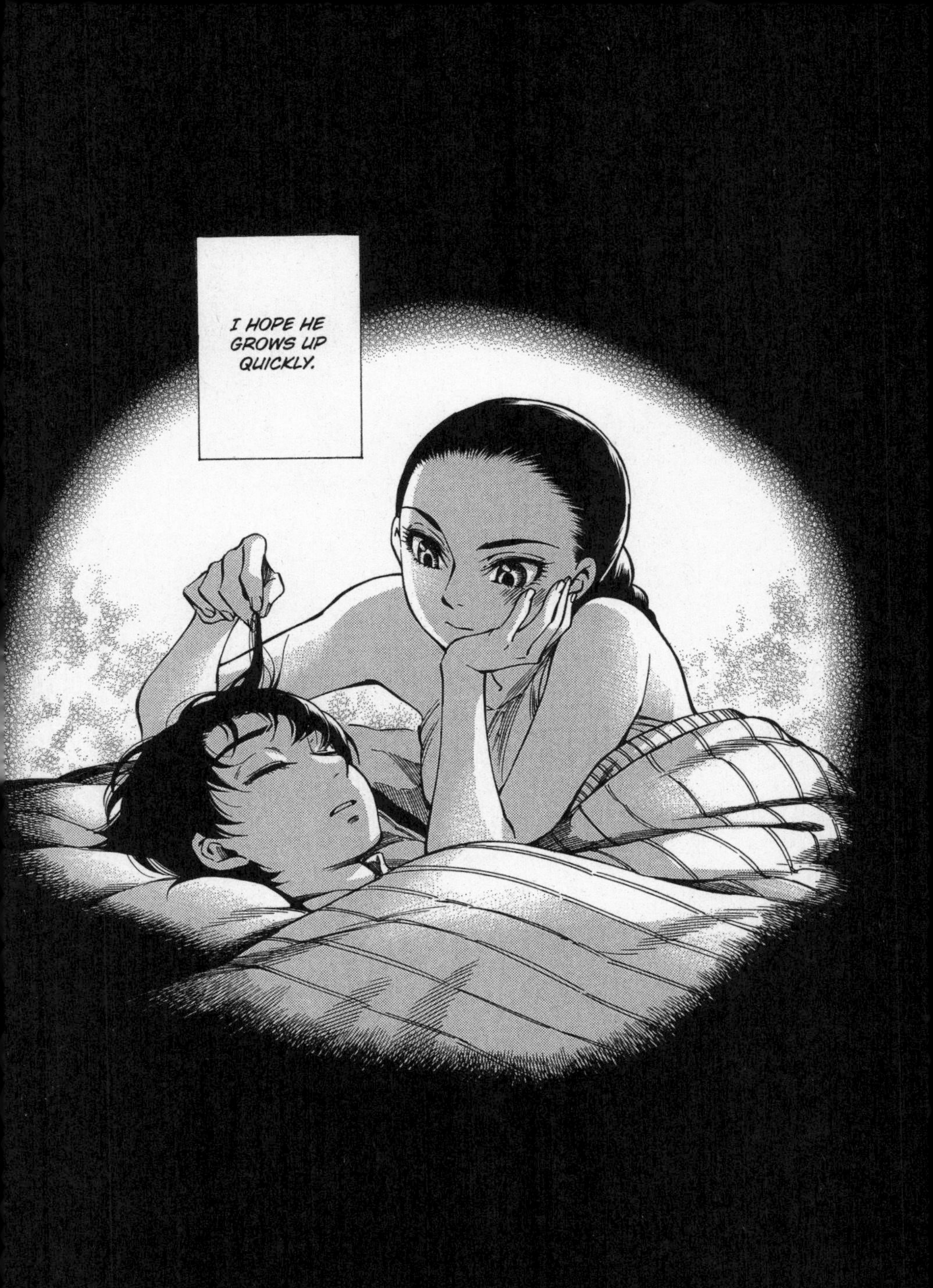
I HOPE HE GROWS UP QUICKLY.

◆CHAPTER 26: END◆

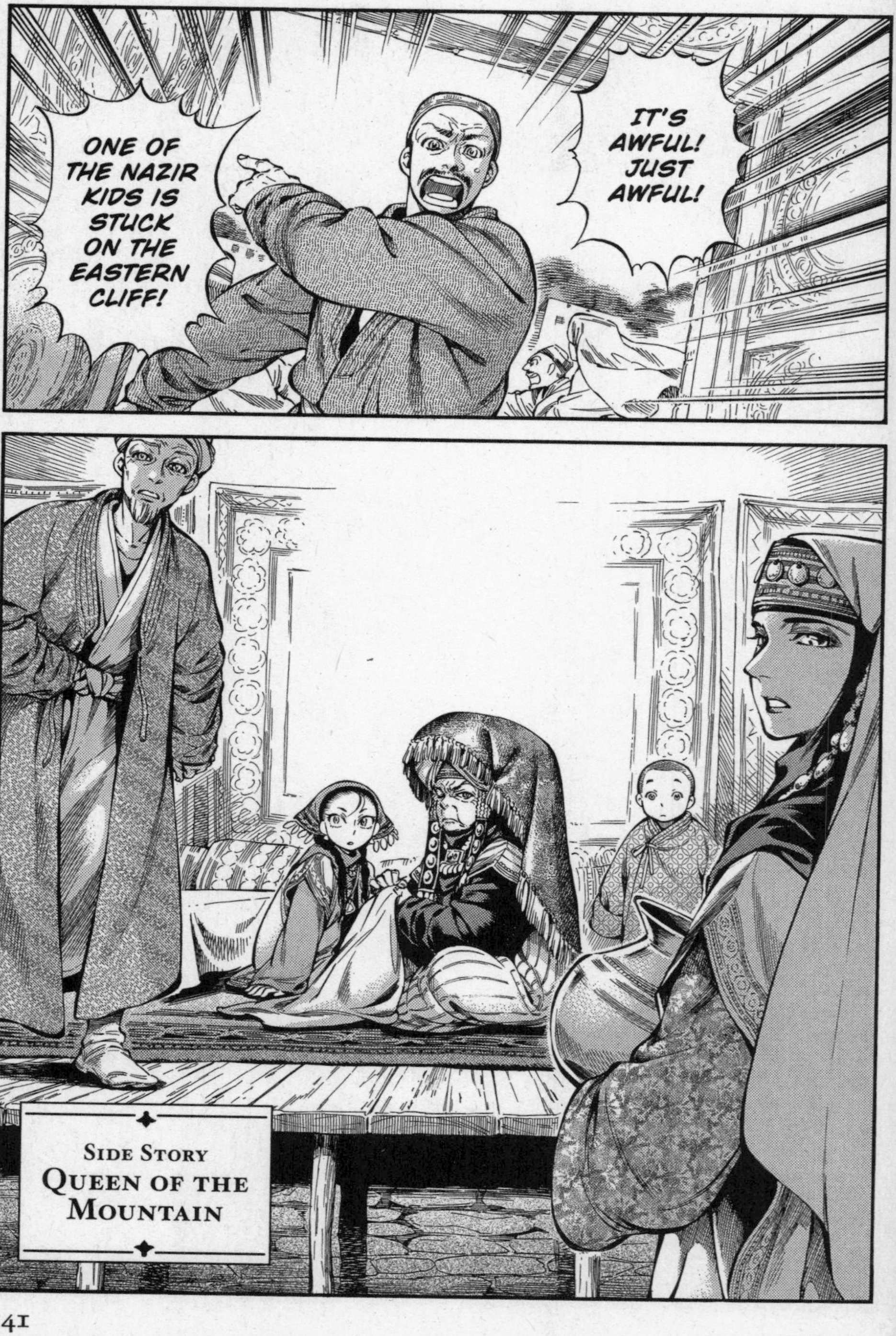
IT'S AWFUL! JUST AWFUL!
ONE OF THE NAZIR KIDS IS STUCK ON THE EASTERN CLIFF!
SIDE STORY QUEEN OF THE MOUNTAIN

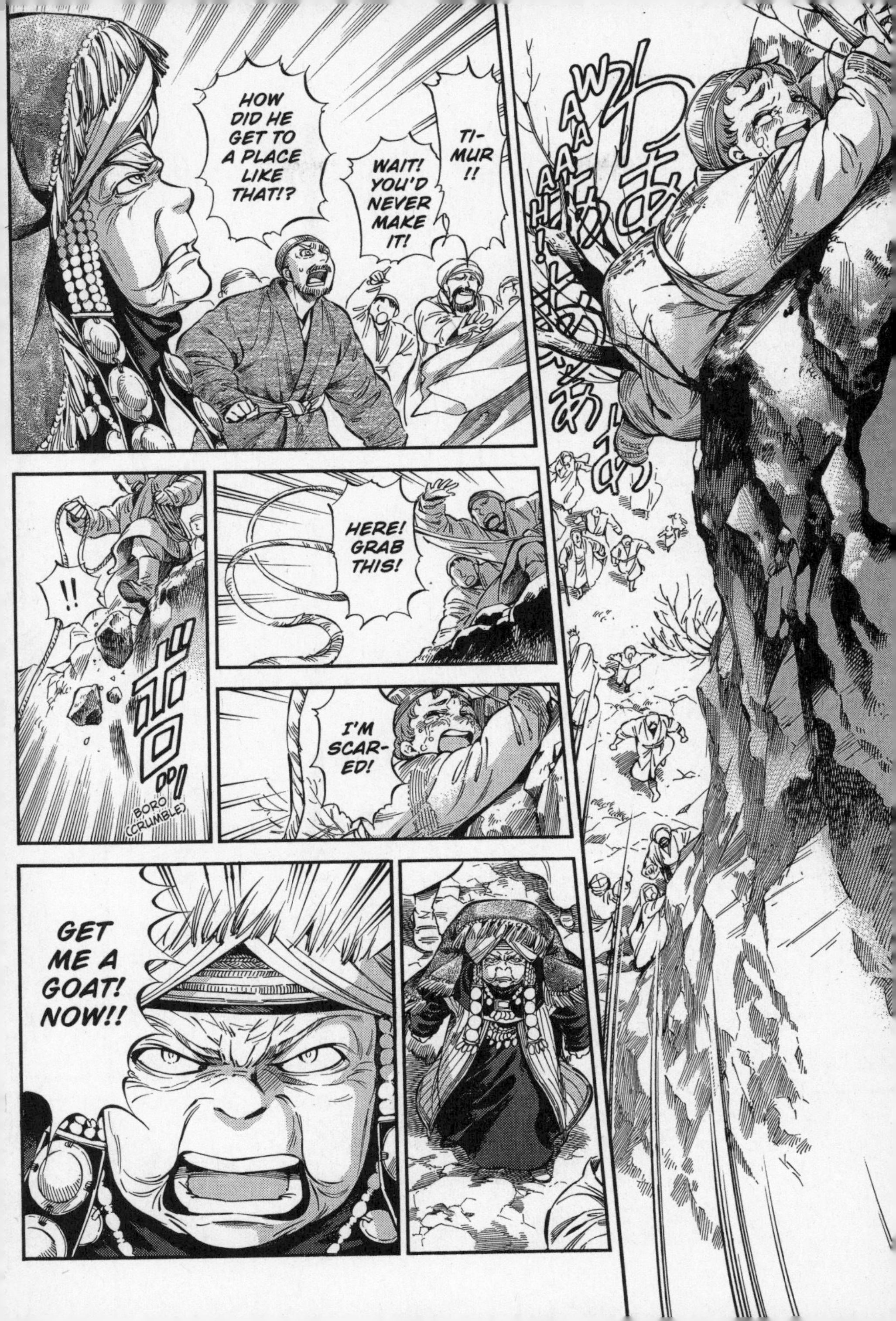
WAAAAH!
TI-MUR!!
WAIT! YOU'D NEVER MAKE IT!
HOW DID HE GET TO A PLACE LIKE THAT!?
HERE! GRAB THIS!
I'M SCARED!
!!
BORO (CRUMBLE)
GET ME A GOAT! NOW!!

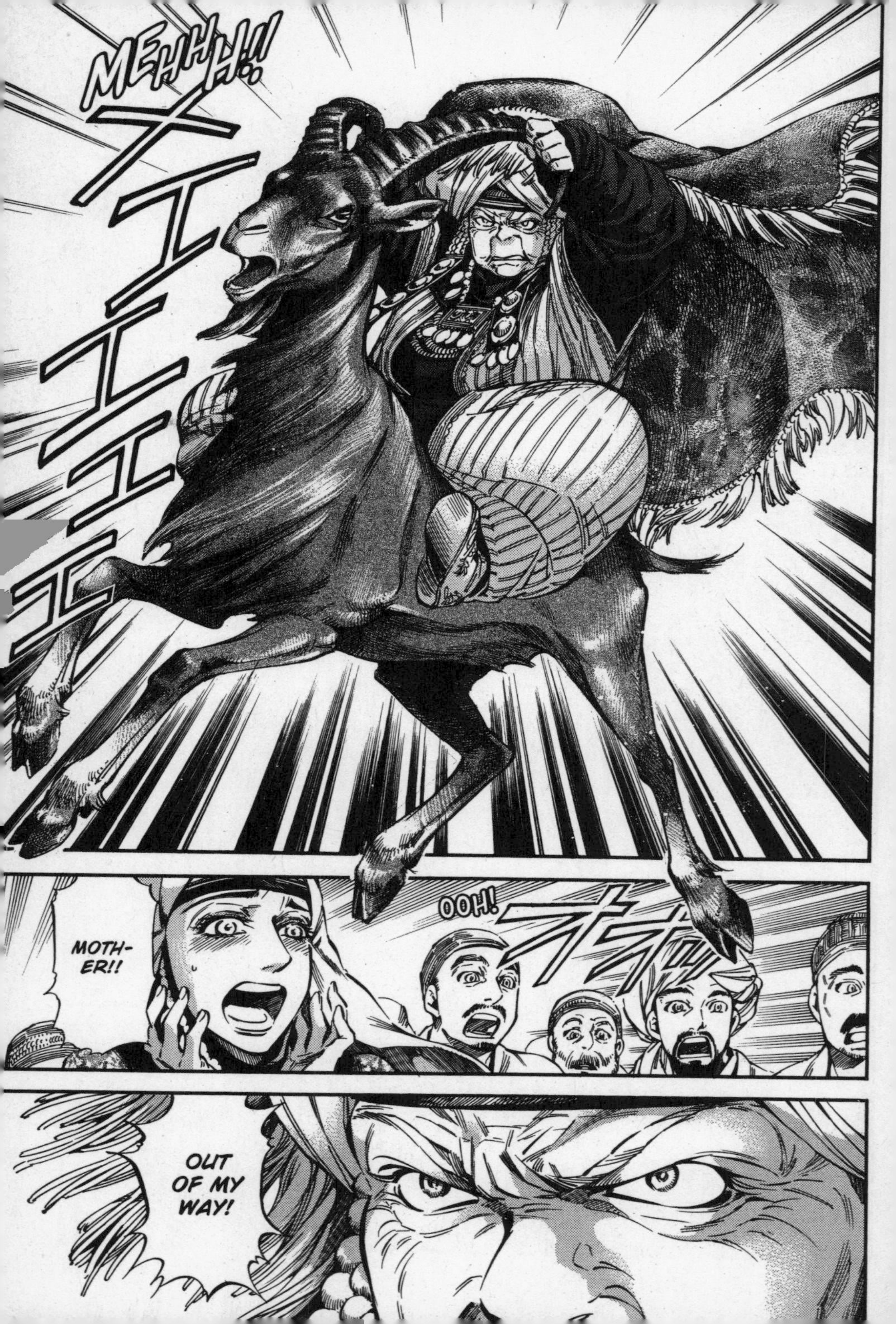
MEHHH!!
OOH!
MOTH-ER!!
OUT OF MY WAY!

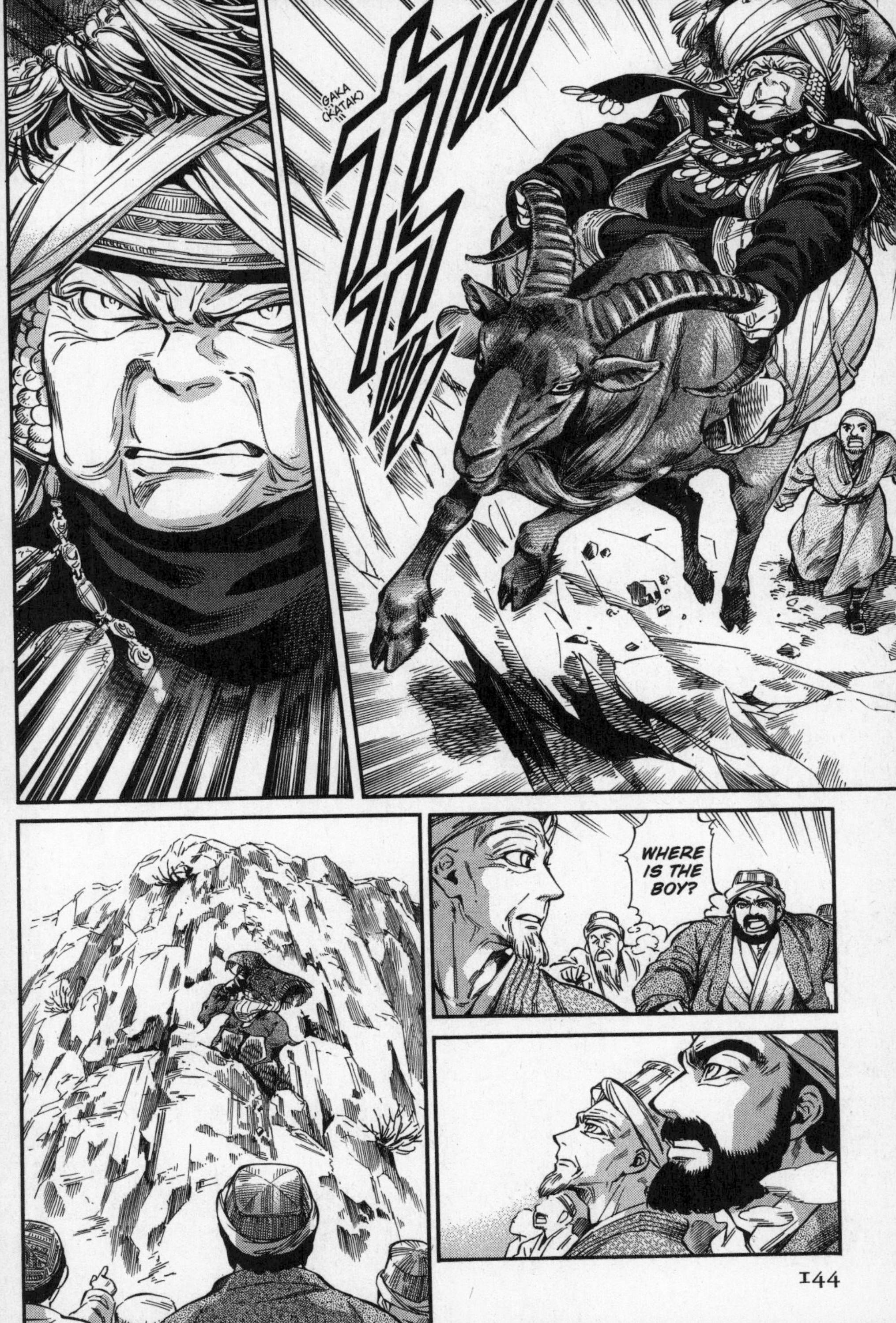
GAKA (KATAK)
WHERE IS THE BOY?

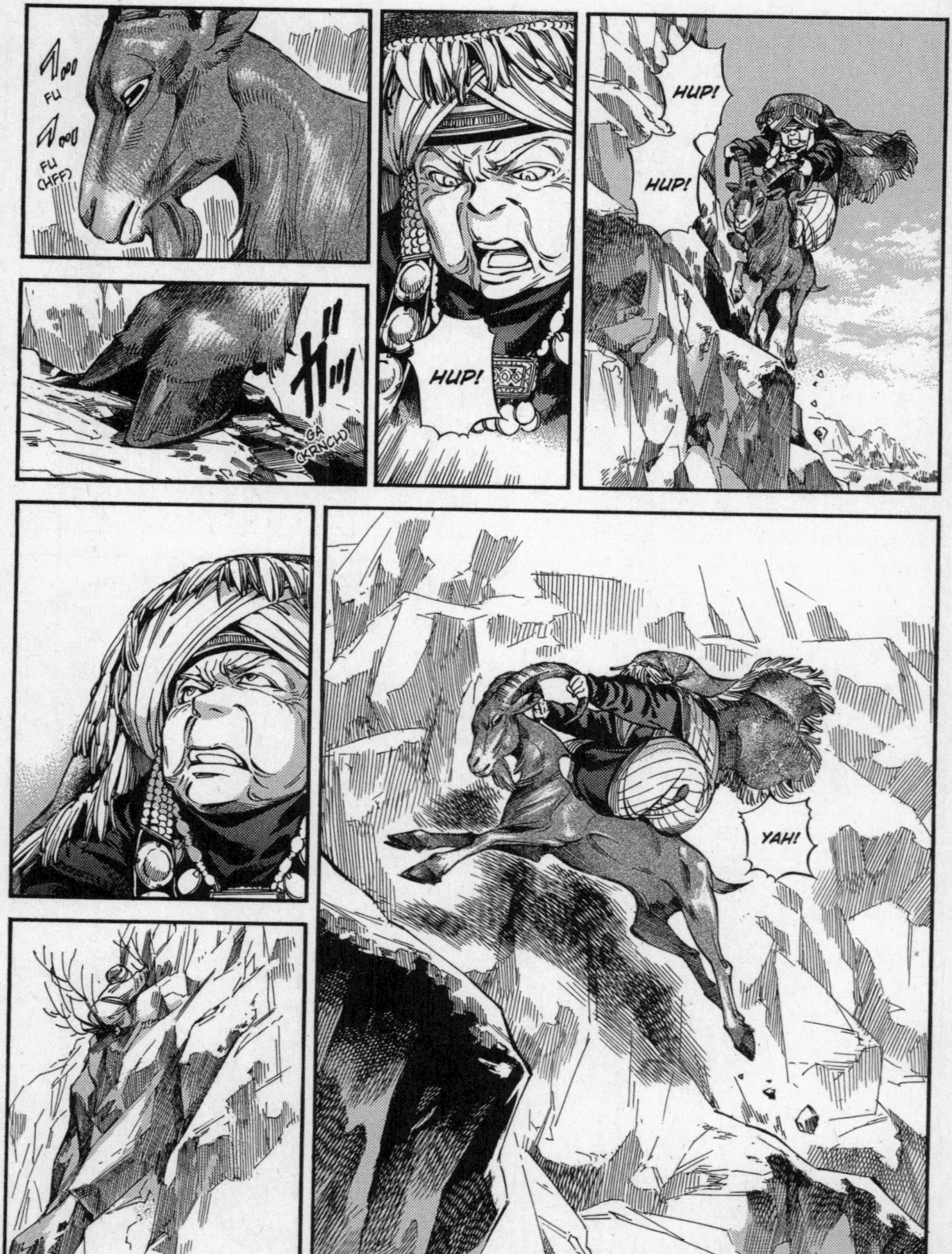
HUP!
HUP!
HUP!
FU
FU (HFF)
GA (KRNCH)
YAH!

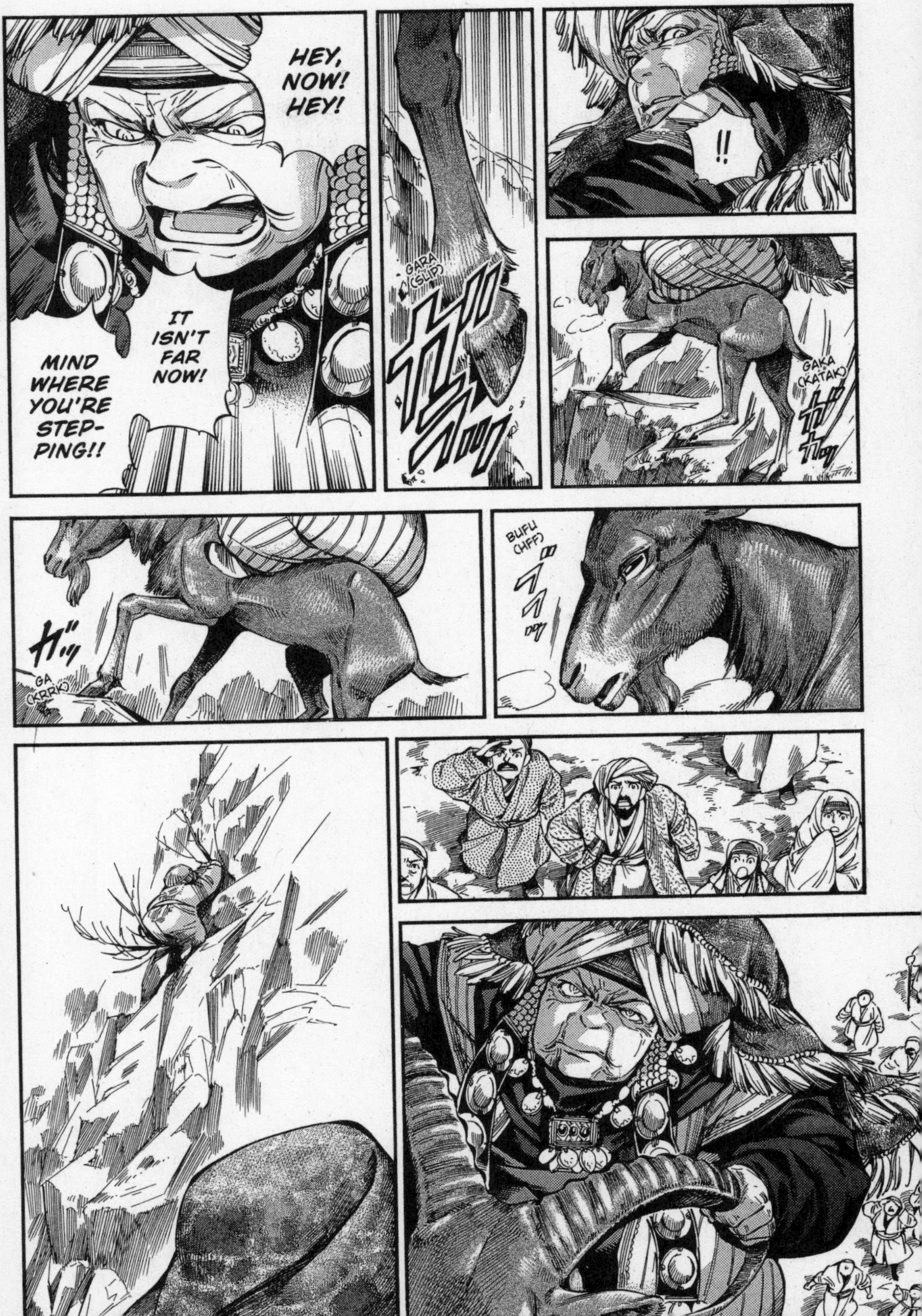
!!
GAKA (KATAK)
GARA (SLIP)
HEY, NOW! HEY!
IT ISN'T FAR NOW!
MIND WHERE YOU'RE STEP-PING!!
BUFU (HFF)
GA (KRRK)

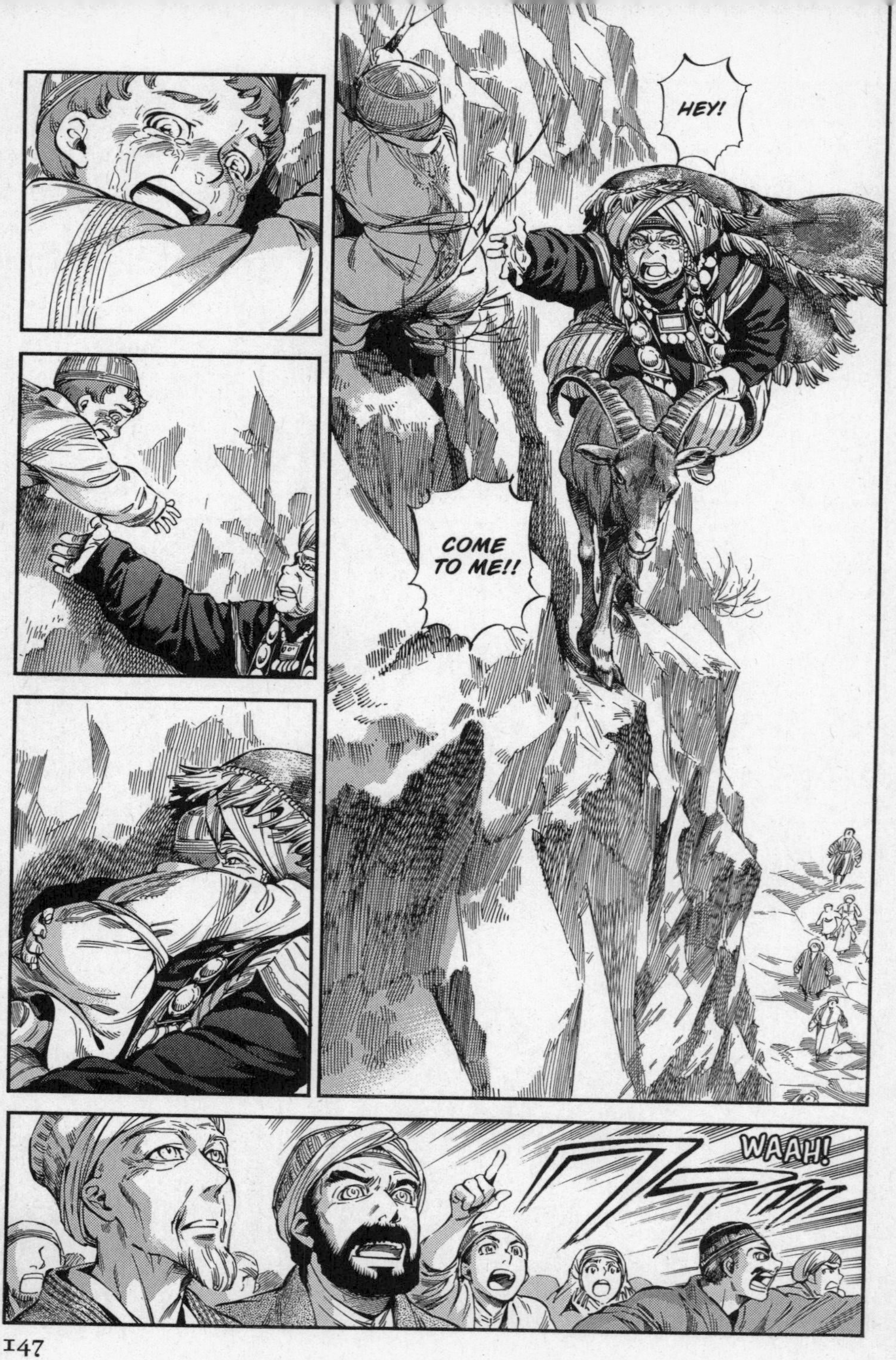
HEY!
COME TO ME!!
WAAH!

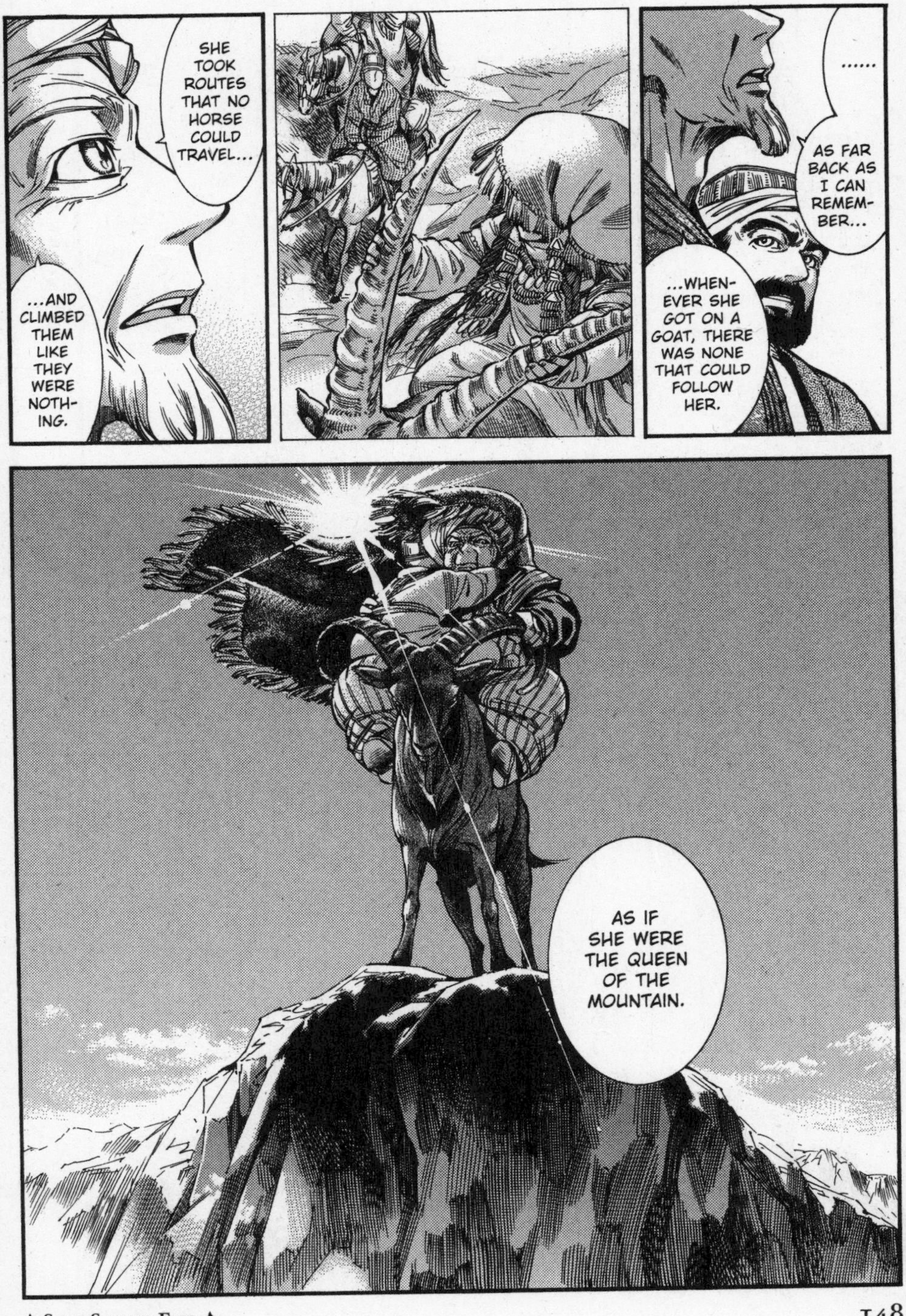
......
AS FAR BACK AS I CAN REMEMBER...
...WHENEVER SHE GOT ON A GOAT, THERE WAS NONE THAT COULD FOLLOW HER.
SHE TOOK ROUTES THAT NO HORSE COULD TRAVEL...
...AND CLIMBED THEM LIKE THEY WERE NOTHING.
AS IF SHE WERE THE QUEEN OF THE MOUNTAIN.

✦ SIDE STORY: END ✦

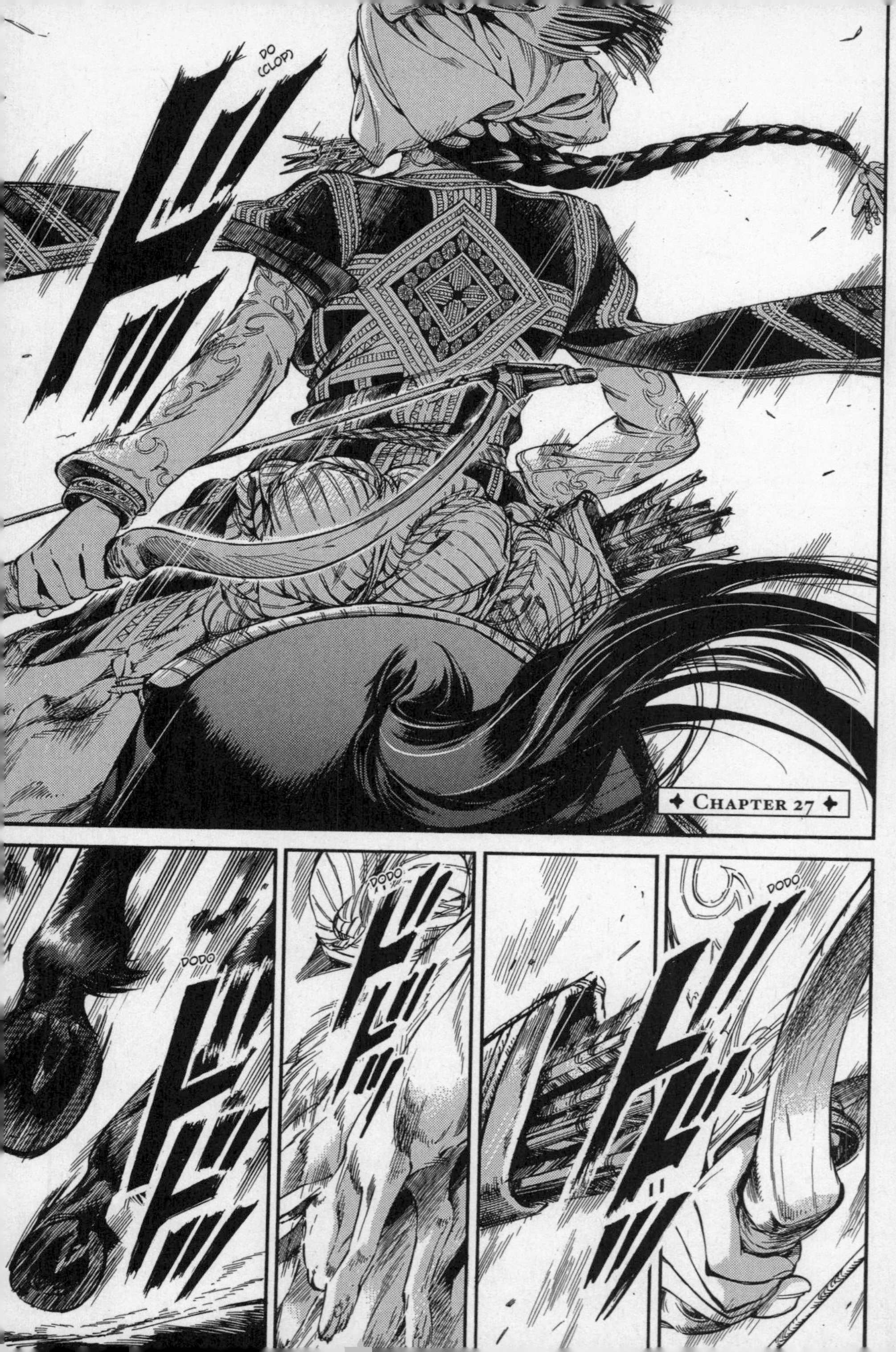
DO (CLOP)
Chapter 27
DODO
DODO
DODO

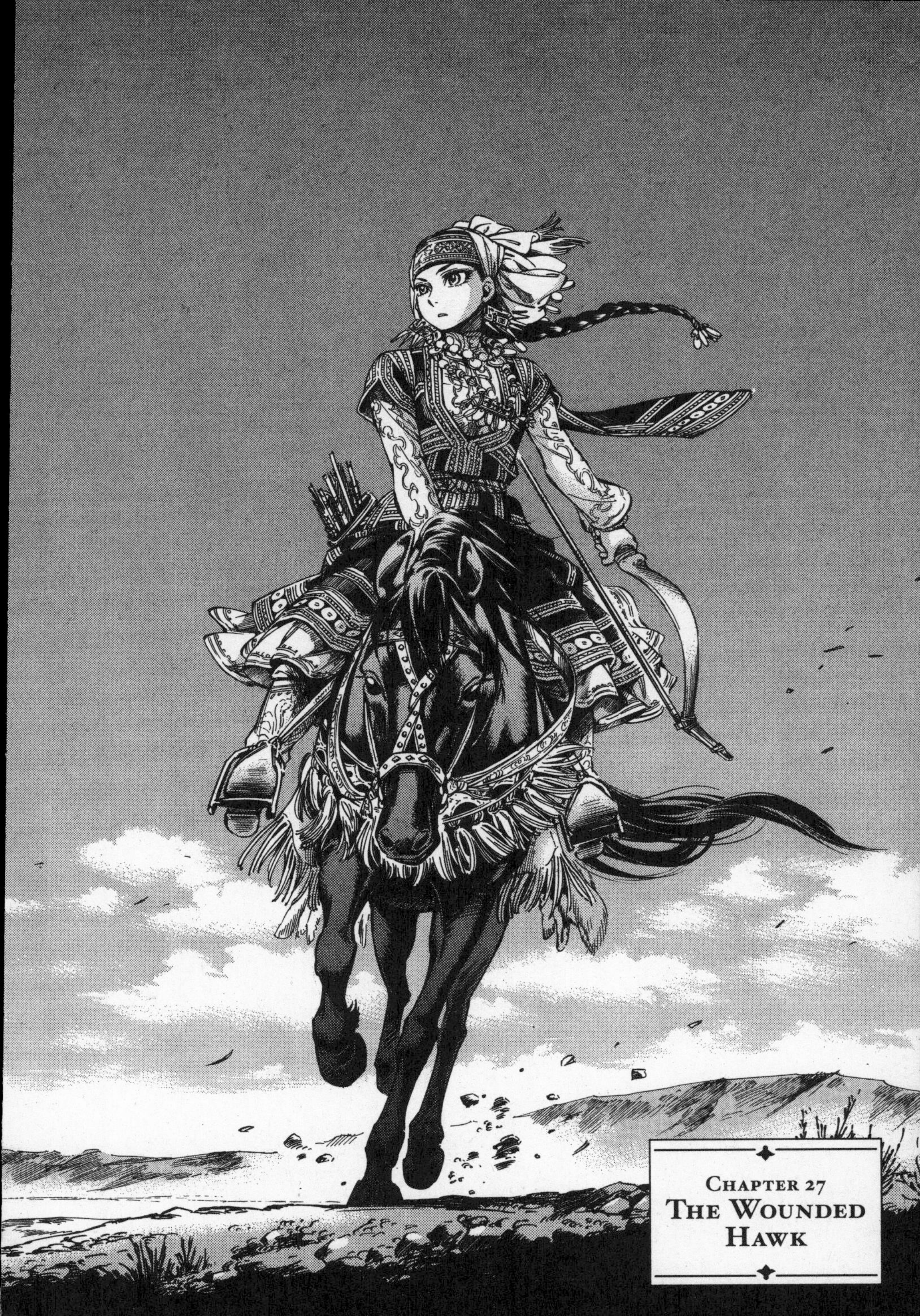

Chapter 27
The Wounded Hawk

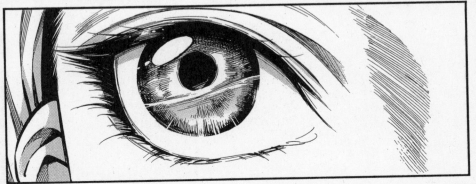

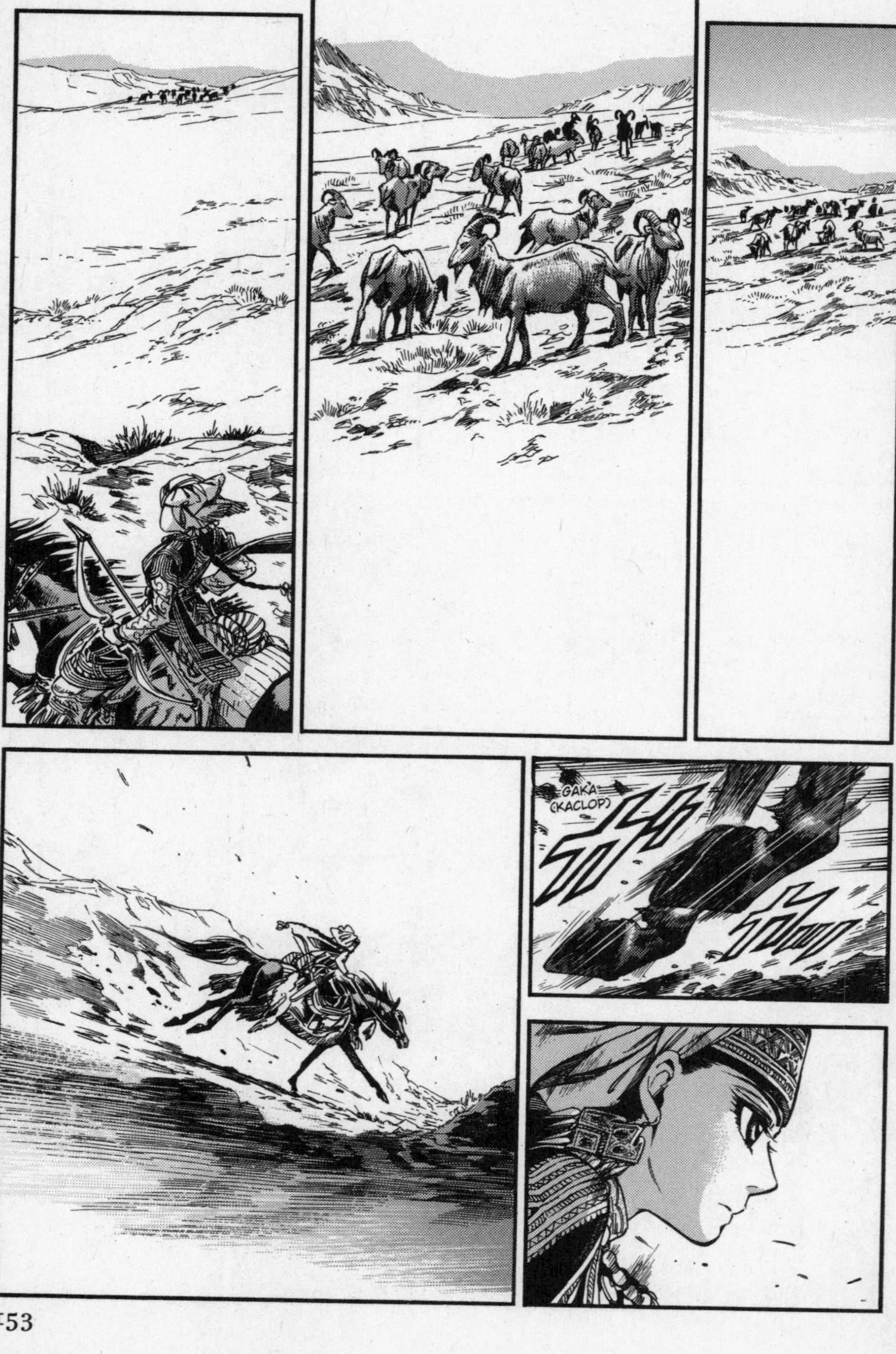
GAKA
(KACLOP)

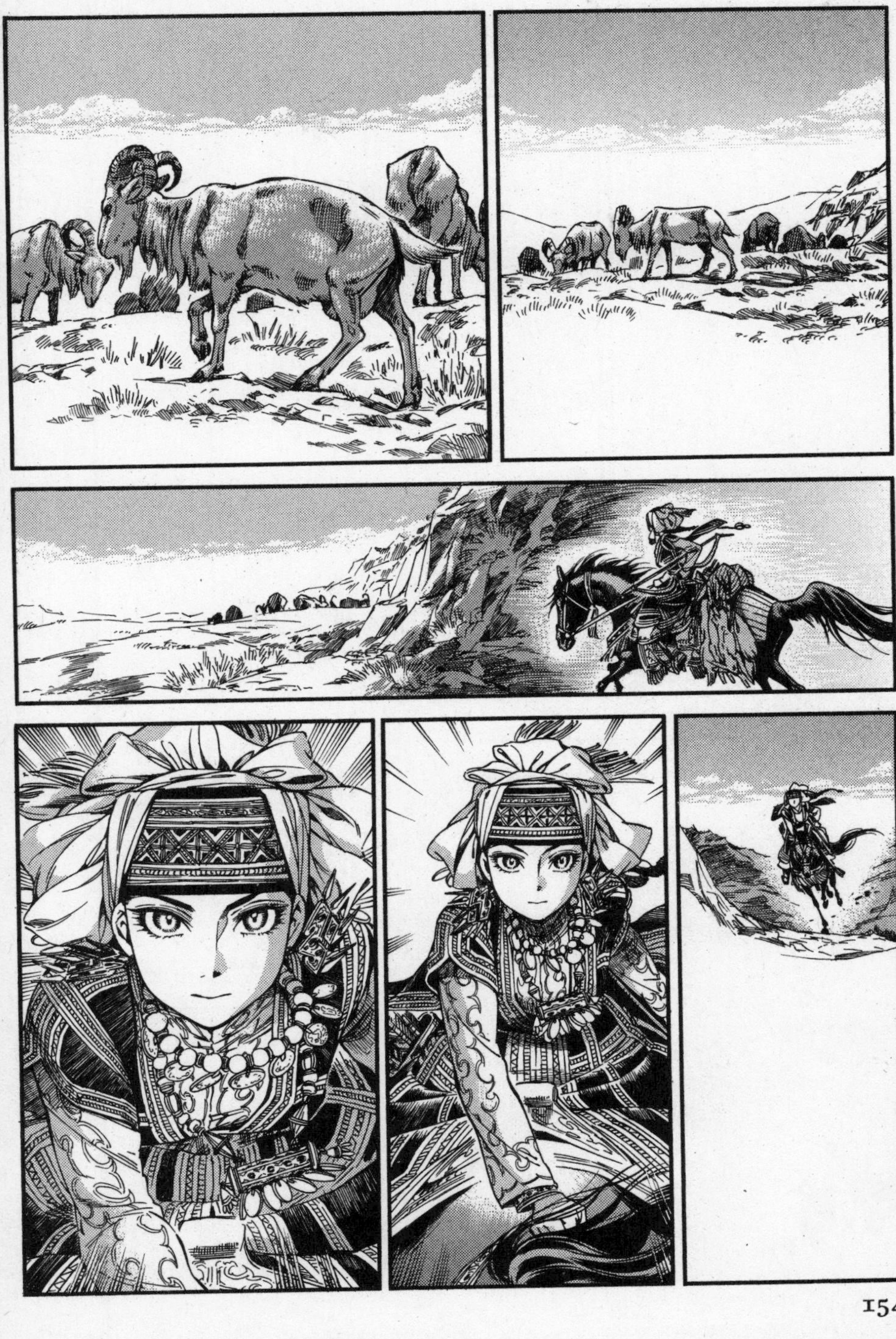

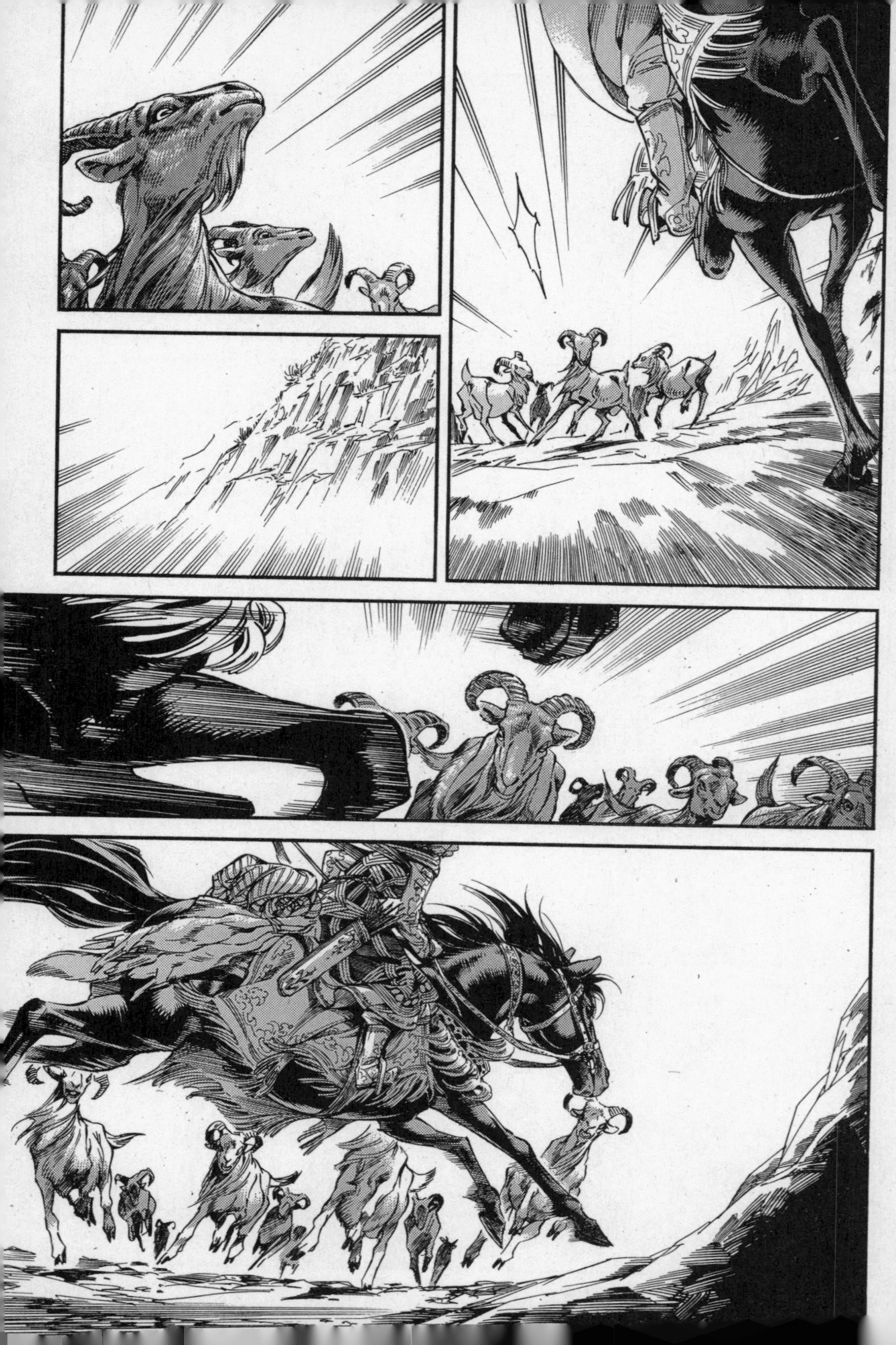

DODODODO
(RRRUMBLE)

ド ド ド ド

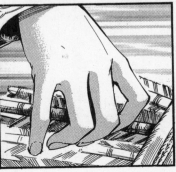

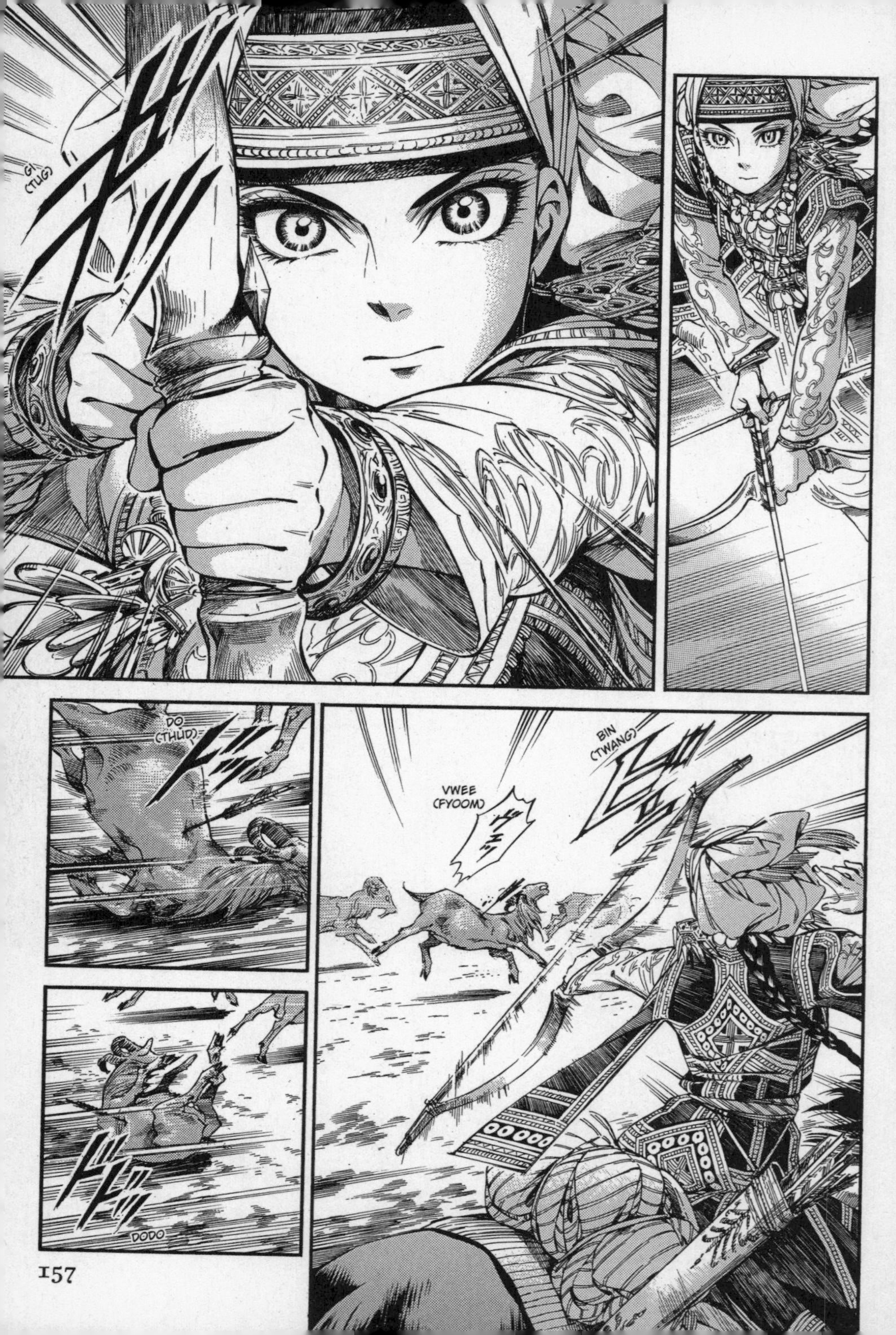
GI
(TUG)
BIN
(TWANG)
VWEE
(FYOOM)
DO
(THUD)
DODO

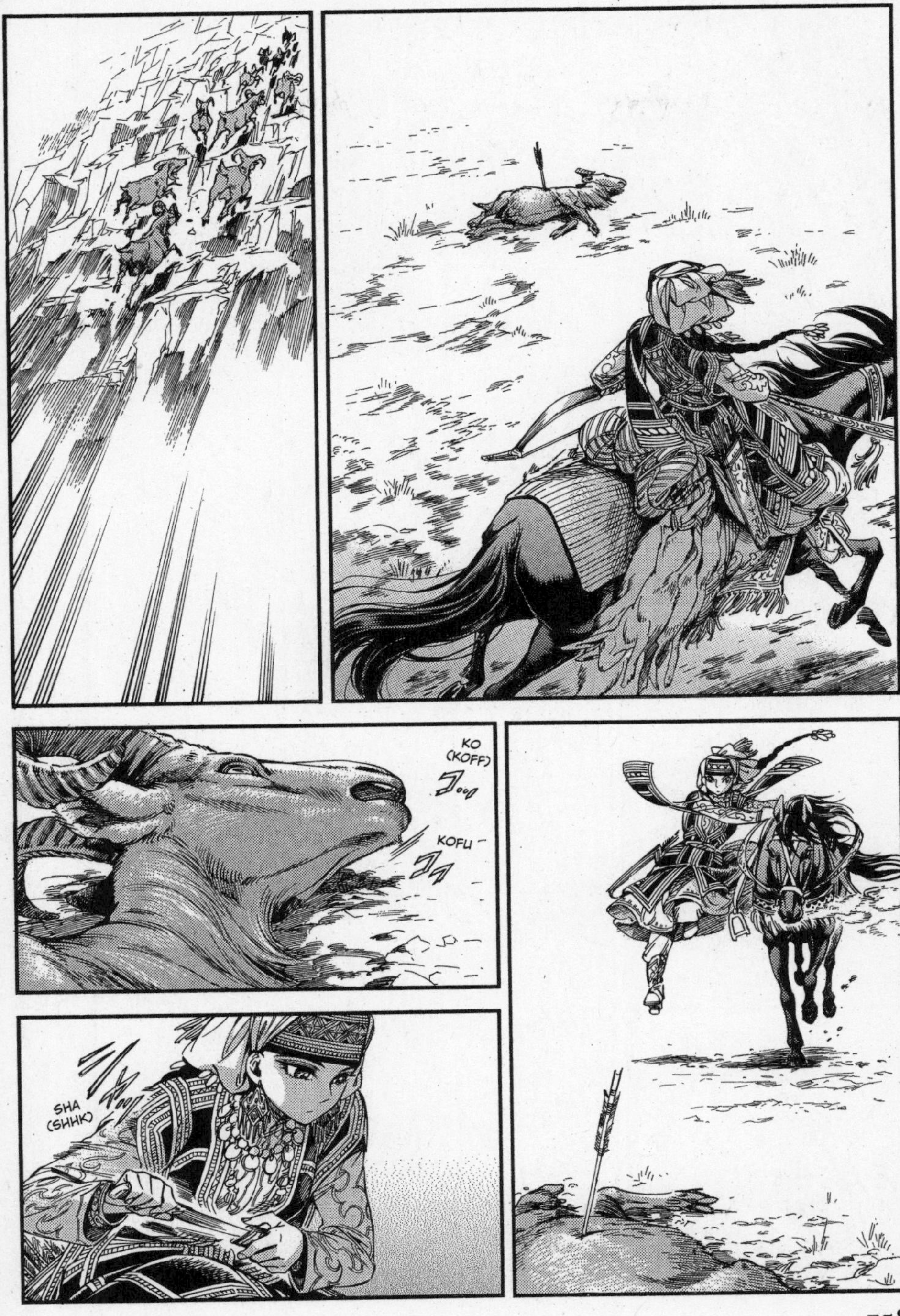
KO (KOFF)
KOFU
SHA (SHHK)

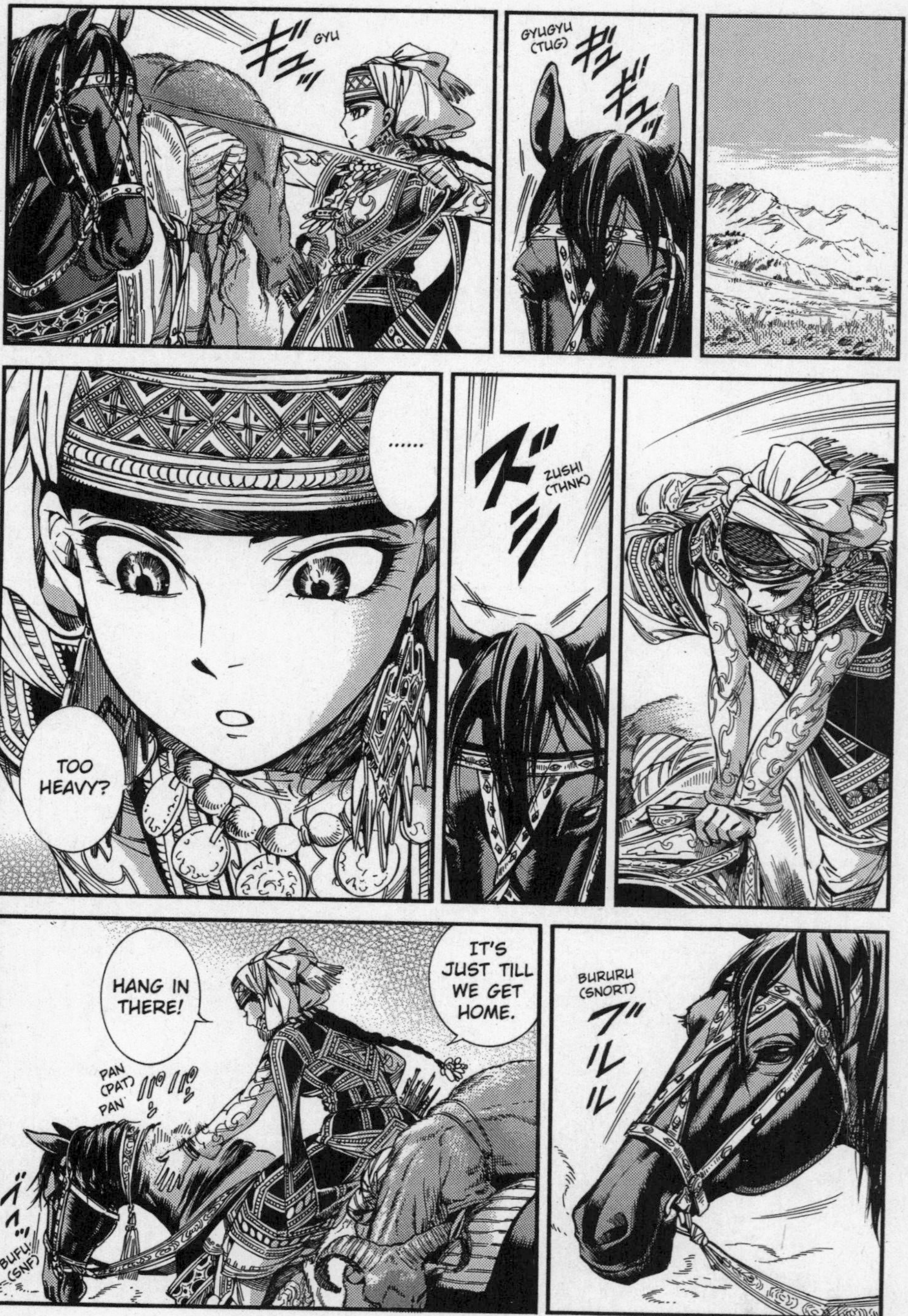
GYUGYU (TUG)
GYU
ZUSHI (THNK)
......
TOO HEAVY?
BURURU (SNORT)
IT'S JUST TILL WE GET HOME.
HANG IN THERE!
PAN (PAT) PAN
BUFU! (SNF)

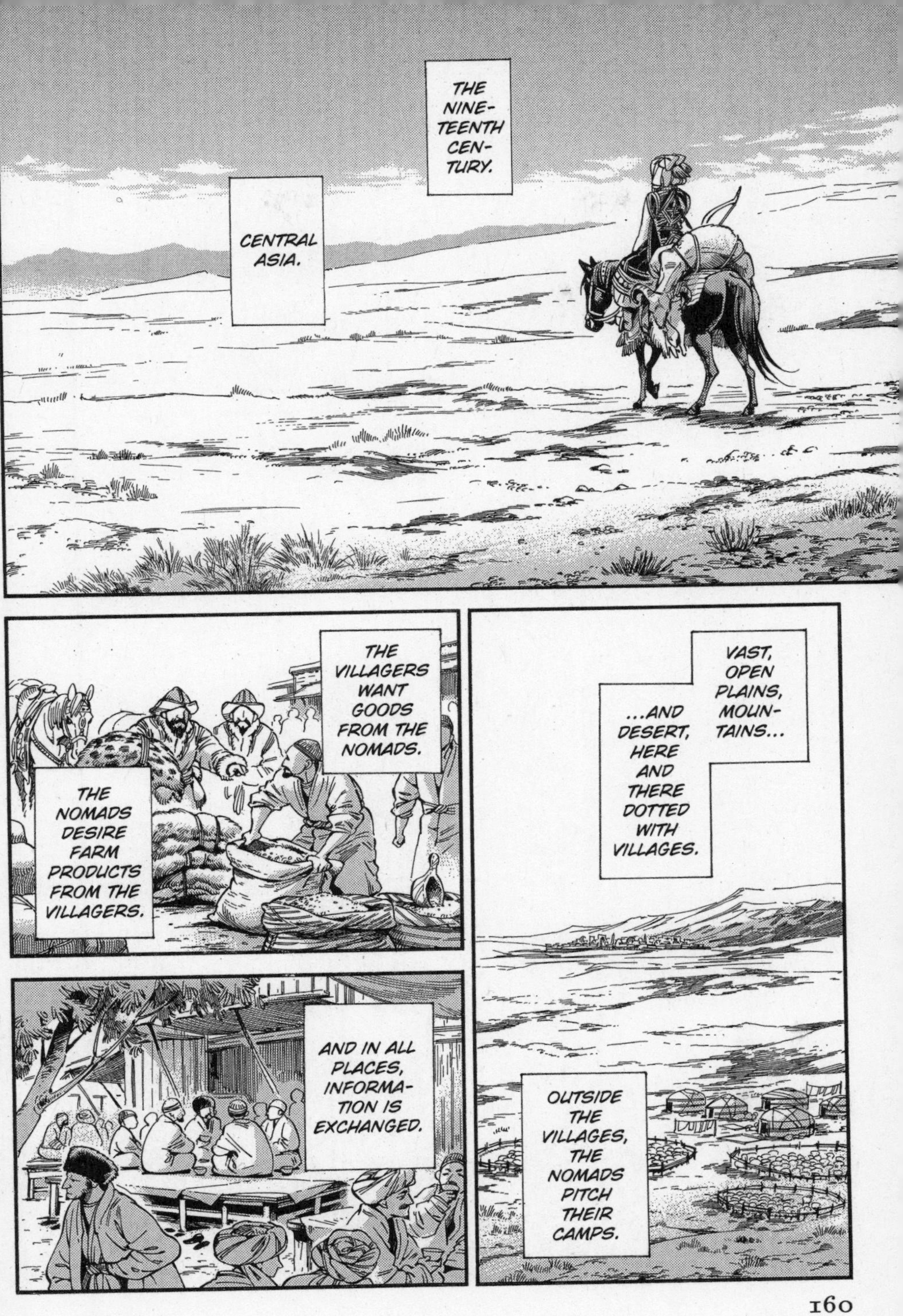
THE NINETEENTH CENTURY.
CENTRAL ASIA.
VAST, OPEN PLAINS, MOUNTAINS...
...AND DESERT, HERE AND THERE DOTTED WITH VILLAGES.
OUTSIDE THE VILLAGES, THE NOMADS PITCH THEIR CAMPS.
THE VILLAGERS WANT GOODS FROM THE NOMADS.
THE NOMADS DESIRE FARM PRODUCTS FROM THE VILLAGERS.
AND IN ALL PLACES, INFORMATION IS EXCHANGED.

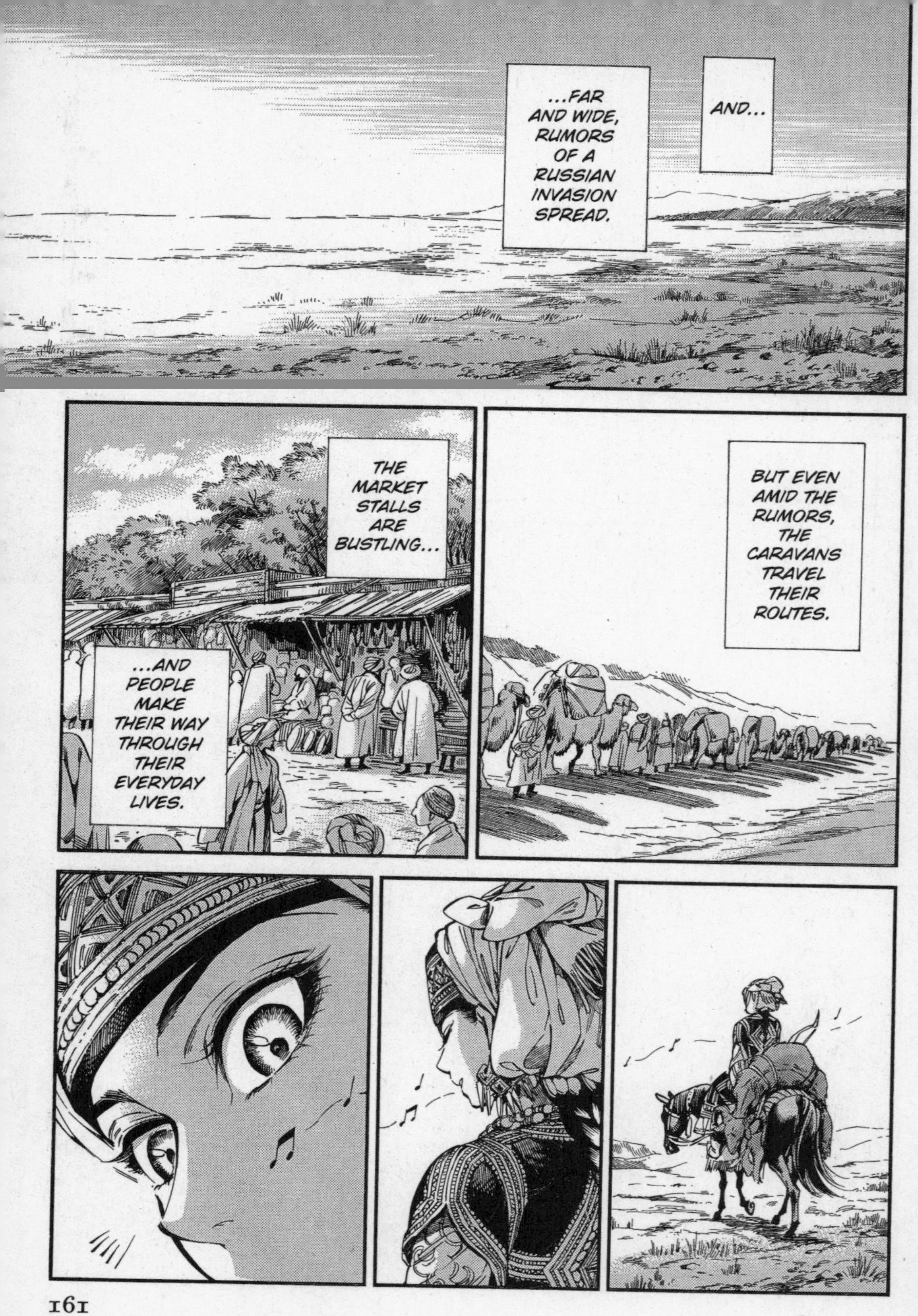
AND...
...FAR AND WIDE, RUMORS OF A RUSSIAN INVASION SPREAD.
BUT EVEN AMID THE RUMORS, THE CARAVANS TRAVEL THEIR ROUTES.
THE MARKET STALLS ARE BUSTLING...
...AND PEOPLE MAKE THEIR WAY THROUGH THEIR EVERYDAY LIVES.

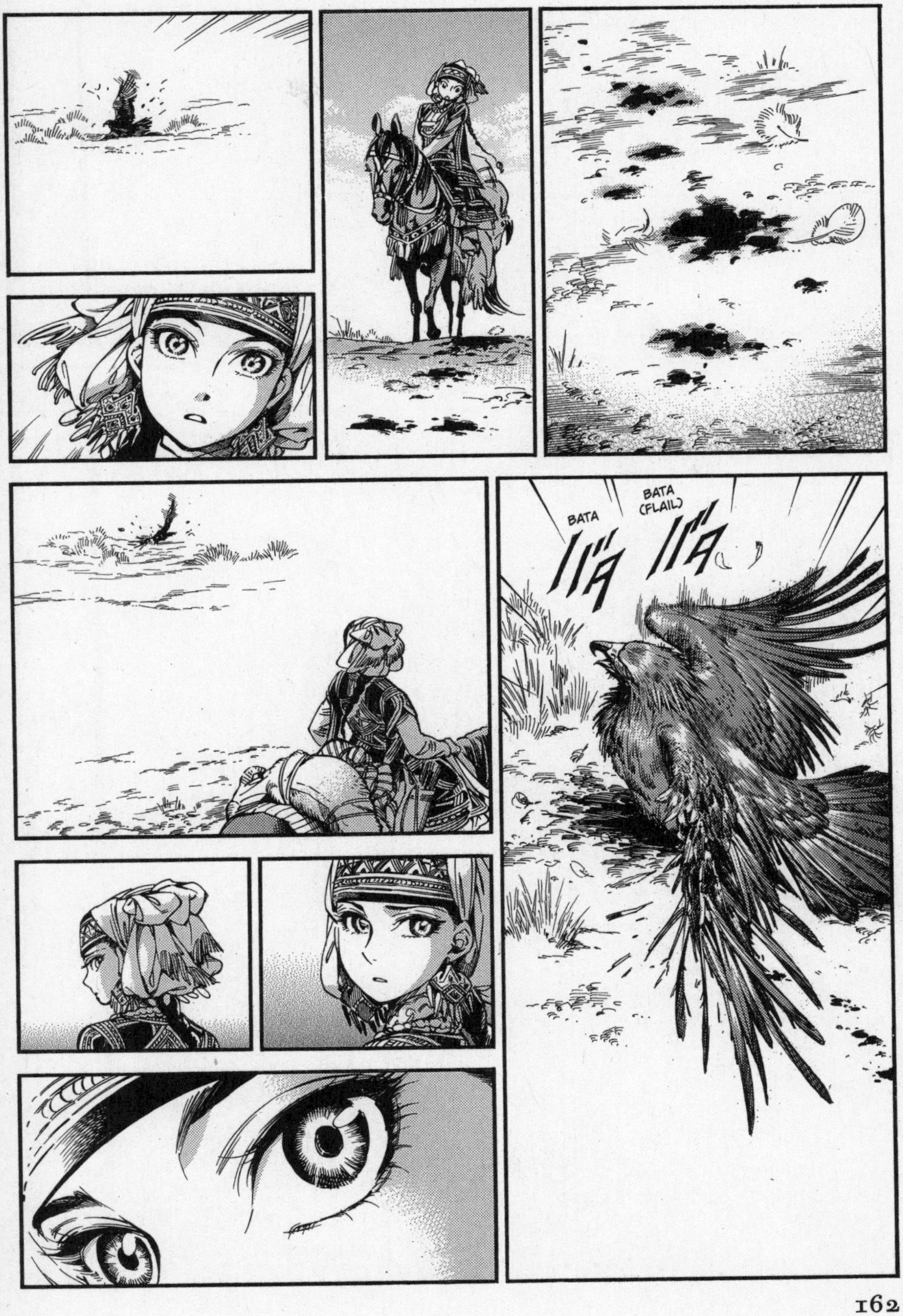
BATA
BATA (FLAIL)
バタ
バタ

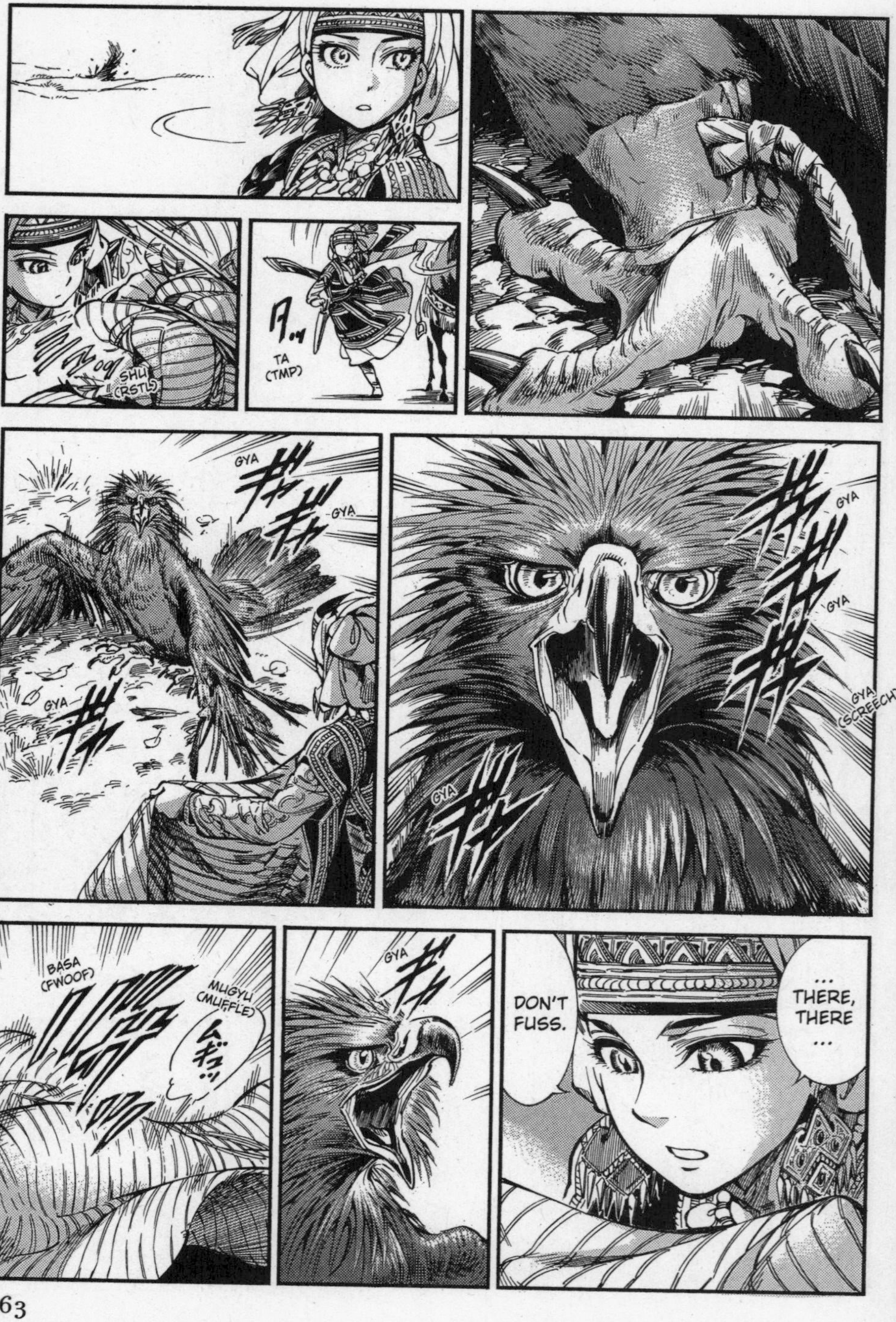
TA (TMP)
SHU (RSTL)
GYA
GYA
GYA (SCREECH)
GYA
GYA
GYA
GYA
... THERE, THERE ...
DON'T FUSS.
GYA
BASA (FWOOF)
MUGYU (MUFFLE)

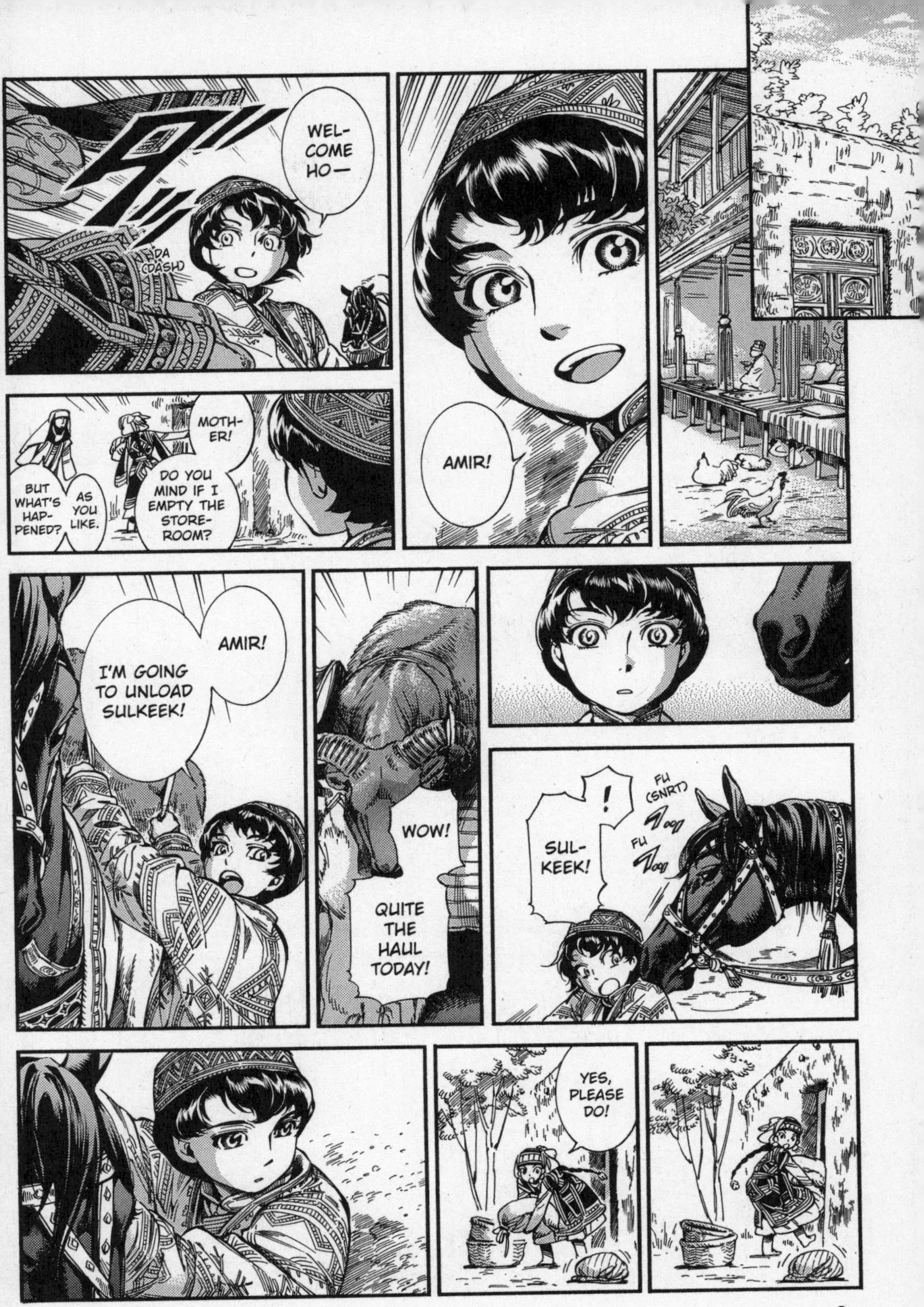
AMIR!
WELCOME HO—
DA (DASH)
MOTHER!
DO YOU MIND IF I EMPTY THE STOREROOM?
AS YOU LIKE.
BUT WHAT'S HAPPENED?
!
SULKEEK!
FU (SNRT)
FU
WOW!
QUITE THE HAUL TODAY!
AMIR!
I'M GOING TO UNLOAD SULKEEK!
YES, PLEASE DO!

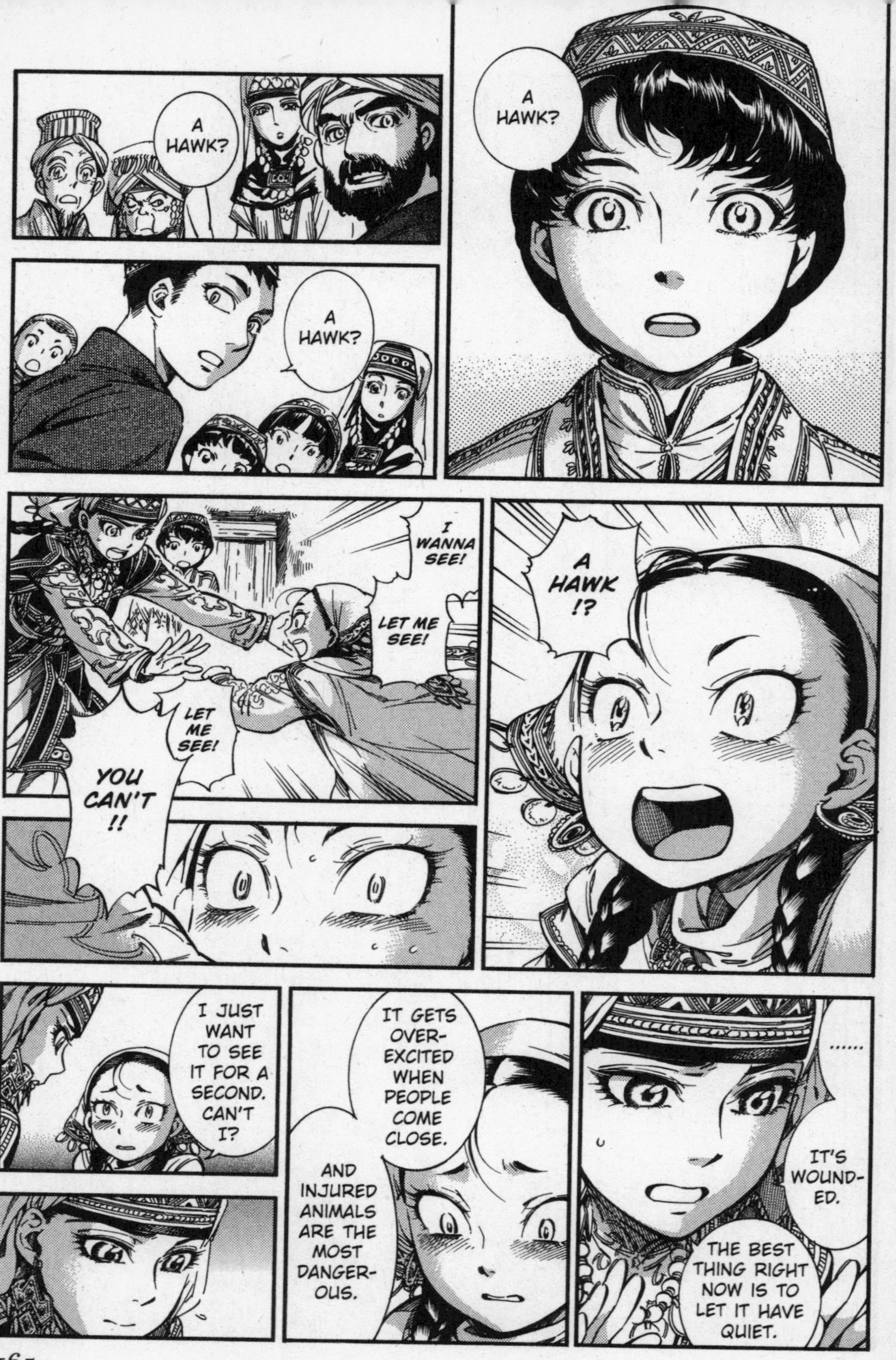
A HAWK?
A HAWK?
A HAWK?
A HAWK!?
I WANNA SEE!
LET ME SEE!
LET ME SEE!
YOU CAN'T!!
......
IT'S WOUNDED.
THE BEST THING RIGHT NOW IS TO LET IT HAVE QUIET.
IT GETS OVER-EXCITED WHEN PEOPLE COME CLOSE.
AND INJURED ANIMALS ARE THE MOST DANGEROUS.
I JUST WANT TO SEE IT FOR A SECOND. CAN'T I?

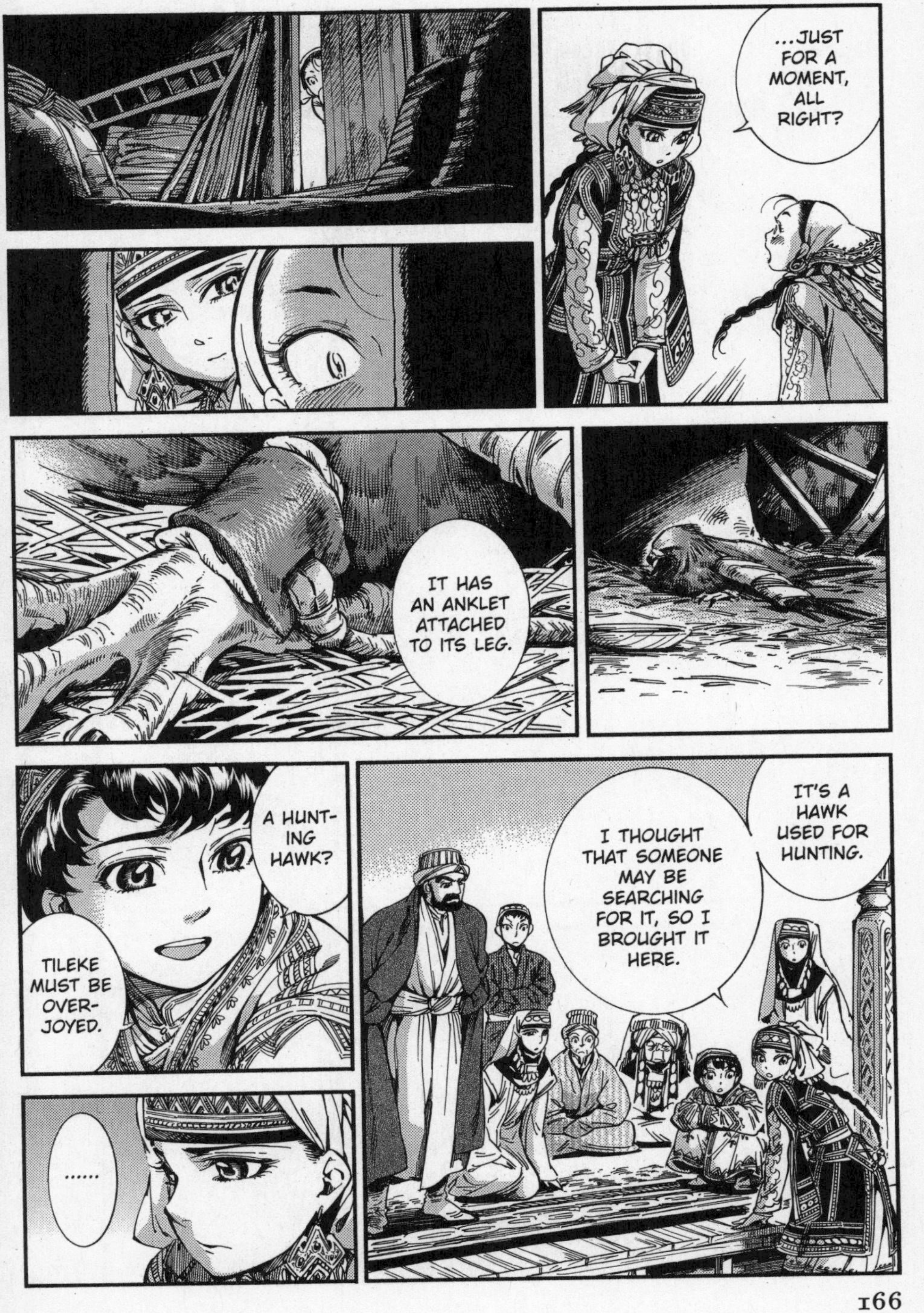
...JUST FOR A MOMENT, ALL RIGHT?
IT HAS AN ANKLET ATTACHED TO ITS LEG.
IT'S A HAWK USED FOR HUNTING.
I THOUGHT THAT SOMEONE MAY BE SEARCHING FOR IT, SO I BROUGHT IT HERE.
A HUNT-ING HAWK?
TILEKE MUST BE OVER-JOYED.
......

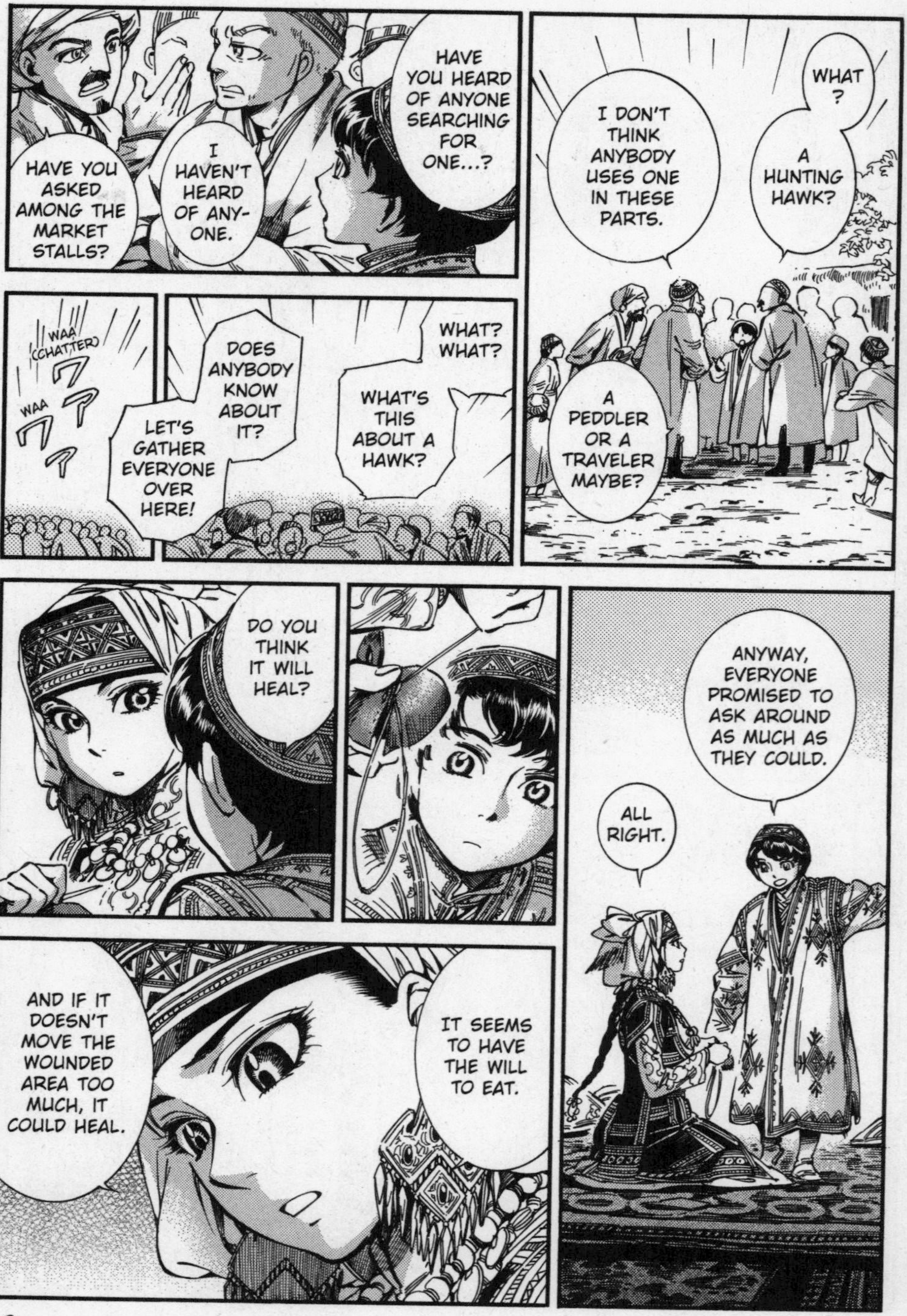
WHAT? A HUNTING HAWK?
I DON'T THINK ANYBODY USES ONE IN THESE PARTS.
A PEDDLER OR A TRAVELER MAYBE?
HAVE YOU HEARD OF ANYONE SEARCHING FOR ONE...?
I HAVEN'T HEARD OF ANY-ONE.
HAVE YOU ASKED AMONG THE MARKET STALLS?
WHAT? WHAT?
WHAT'S THIS ABOUT A HAWK?
DOES ANYBODY KNOW ABOUT IT?
LET'S GATHER EVERYONE OVER HERE!
WAA (CHATTER) ワァ
WAA ワァ
ANYWAY, EVERYONE PROMISED TO ASK AROUND AS MUCH AS THEY COULD.
ALL RIGHT.
DO YOU THINK IT WILL HEAL?
IT SEEMS TO HAVE THE WILL TO EAT.
AND IF IT DOESN'T MOVE THE WOUNDED AREA TOO MUCH, IT COULD HEAL.

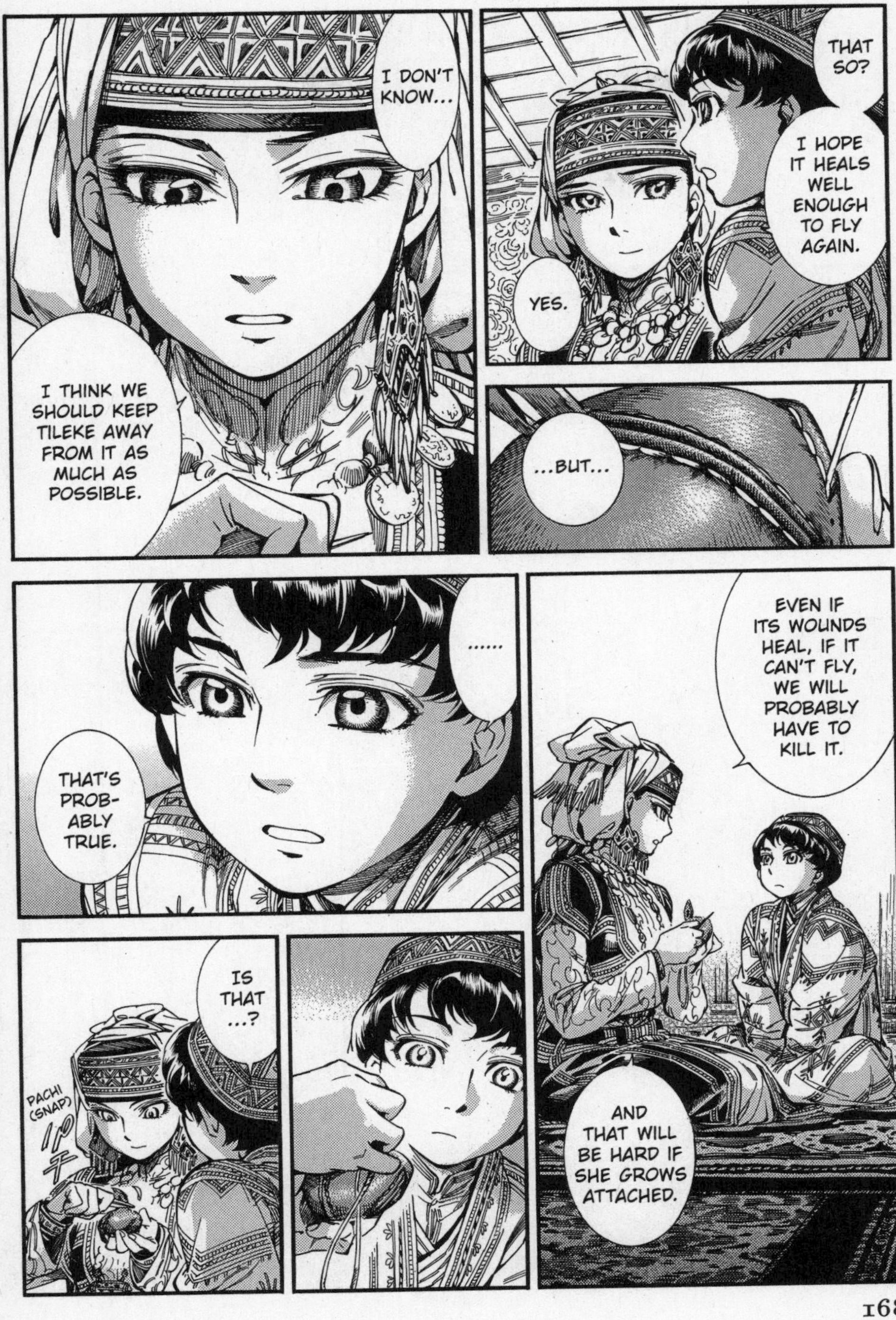
THAT SO?
I HOPE IT HEALS WELL ENOUGH TO FLY AGAIN.
YES.
...BUT...
I DON'T KNOW...
I THINK WE SHOULD KEEP TILEKE AWAY FROM IT AS MUCH AS POSSIBLE.
EVEN IF ITS WOUNDS HEAL, IF IT CAN'T FLY, WE WILL PROBABLY HAVE TO KILL IT.
AND THAT WILL BE HARD IF SHE GROWS ATTACHED.
......
THAT'S PROB-ABLY TRUE.
IS THAT ...?
PACHI (SNAP)

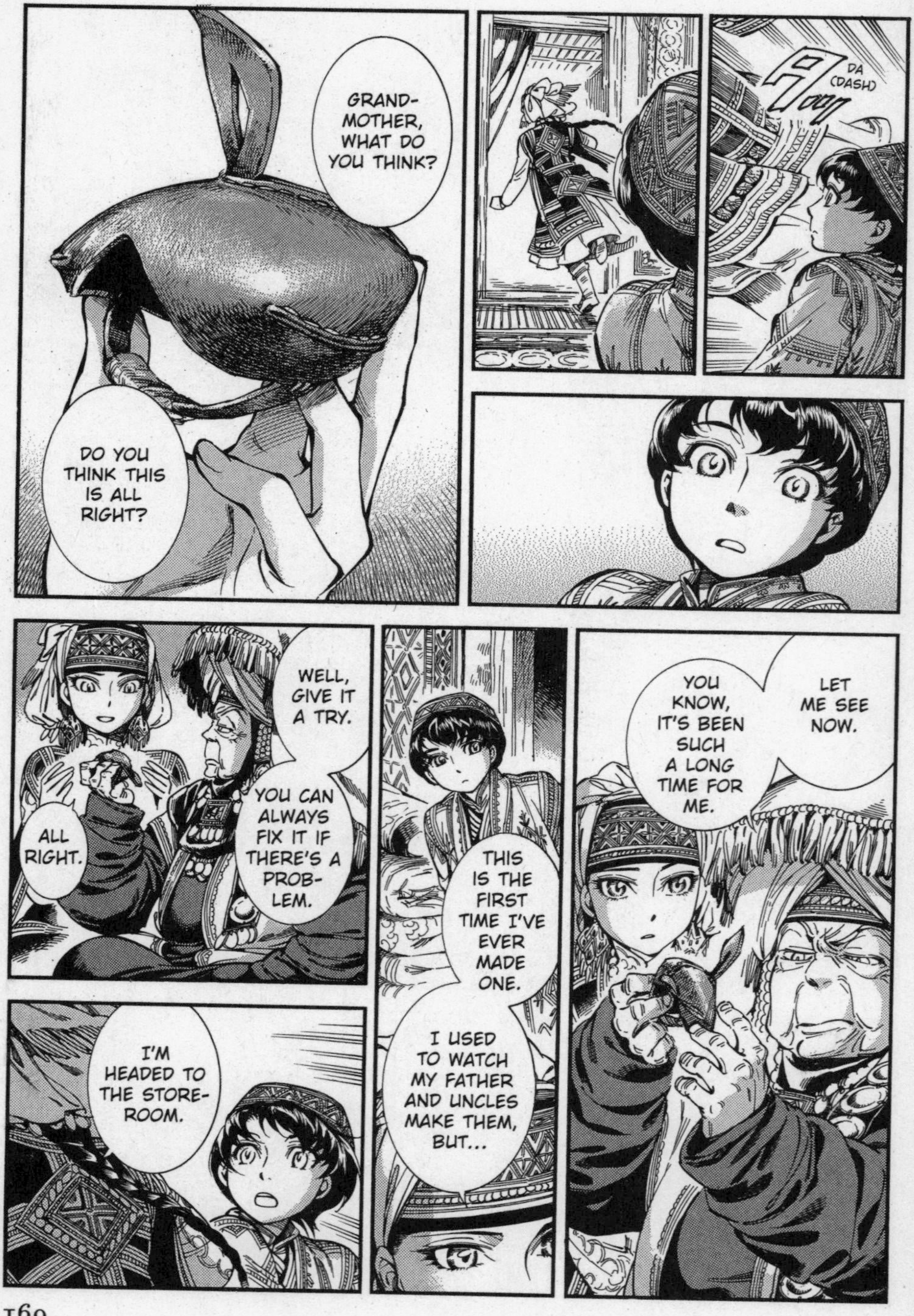
DA (DASH)
GRAND-MOTHER, WHAT DO YOU THINK?
DO YOU THINK THIS IS ALL RIGHT?
LET ME SEE NOW.
YOU KNOW, IT'S BEEN SUCH A LONG TIME FOR ME.
THIS IS THE FIRST TIME I'VE EVER MADE ONE.
WELL, GIVE IT A TRY.
YOU CAN ALWAYS FIX IT IF THERE'S A PROB-LEM.
ALL RIGHT.
I USED TO WATCH MY FATHER AND UNCLES MAKE THEM, BUT...
I'M HEADED TO THE STORE-ROOM.

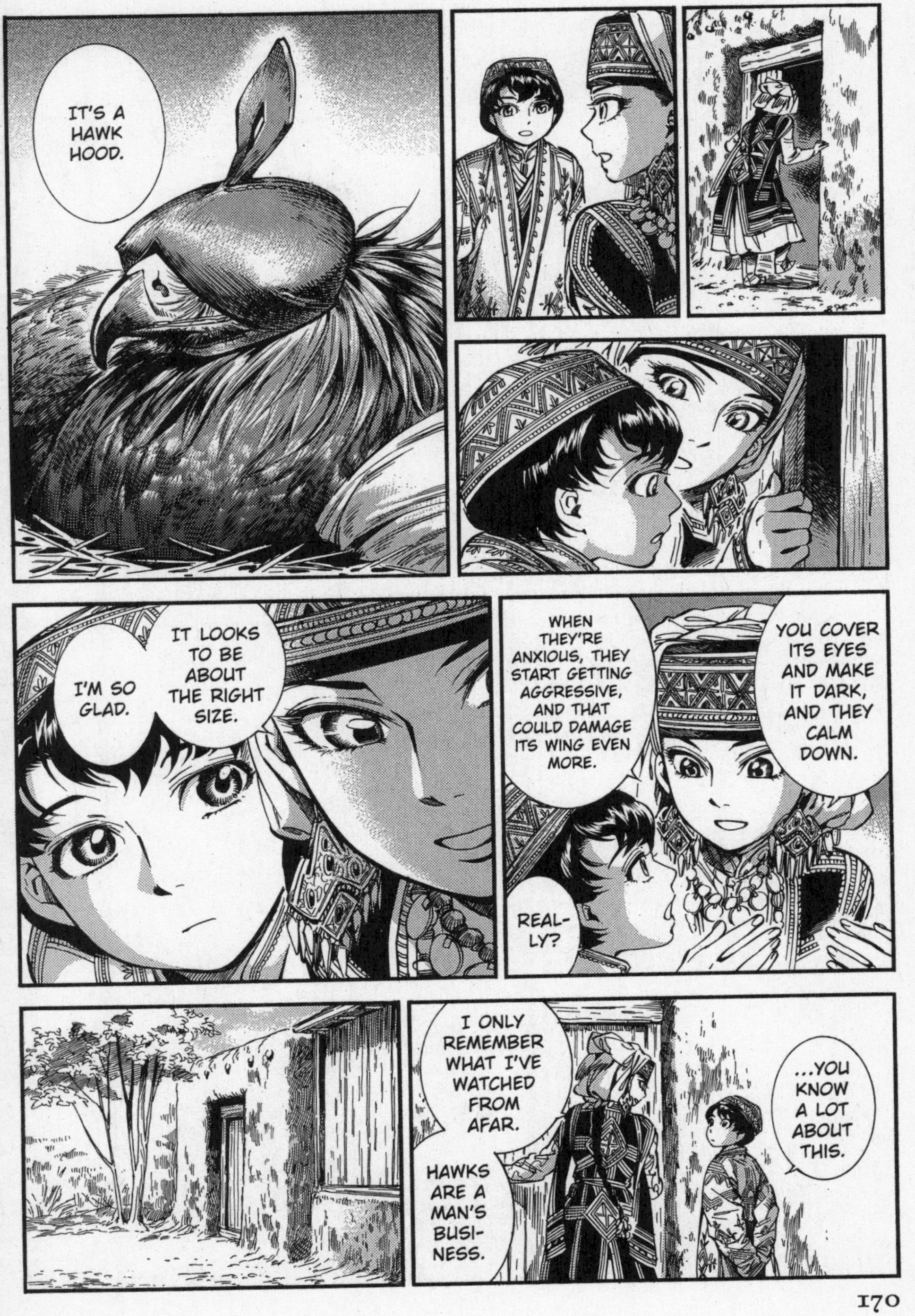
IT'S A HAWK HOOD.
YOU COVER ITS EYES AND MAKE IT DARK, AND THEY CALM DOWN.
WHEN THEY'RE ANXIOUS, THEY START GETTING AGGRESSIVE, AND THAT COULD DAMAGE ITS WING EVEN MORE.
REAL-LY?
IT LOOKS TO BE ABOUT THE RIGHT SIZE.
I'M SO GLAD.
...YOU KNOW A LOT ABOUT THIS.
I ONLY REMEMBER WHAT I'VE WATCHED FROM AFAR.
HAWKS ARE A MAN'S BUSI-NESS.

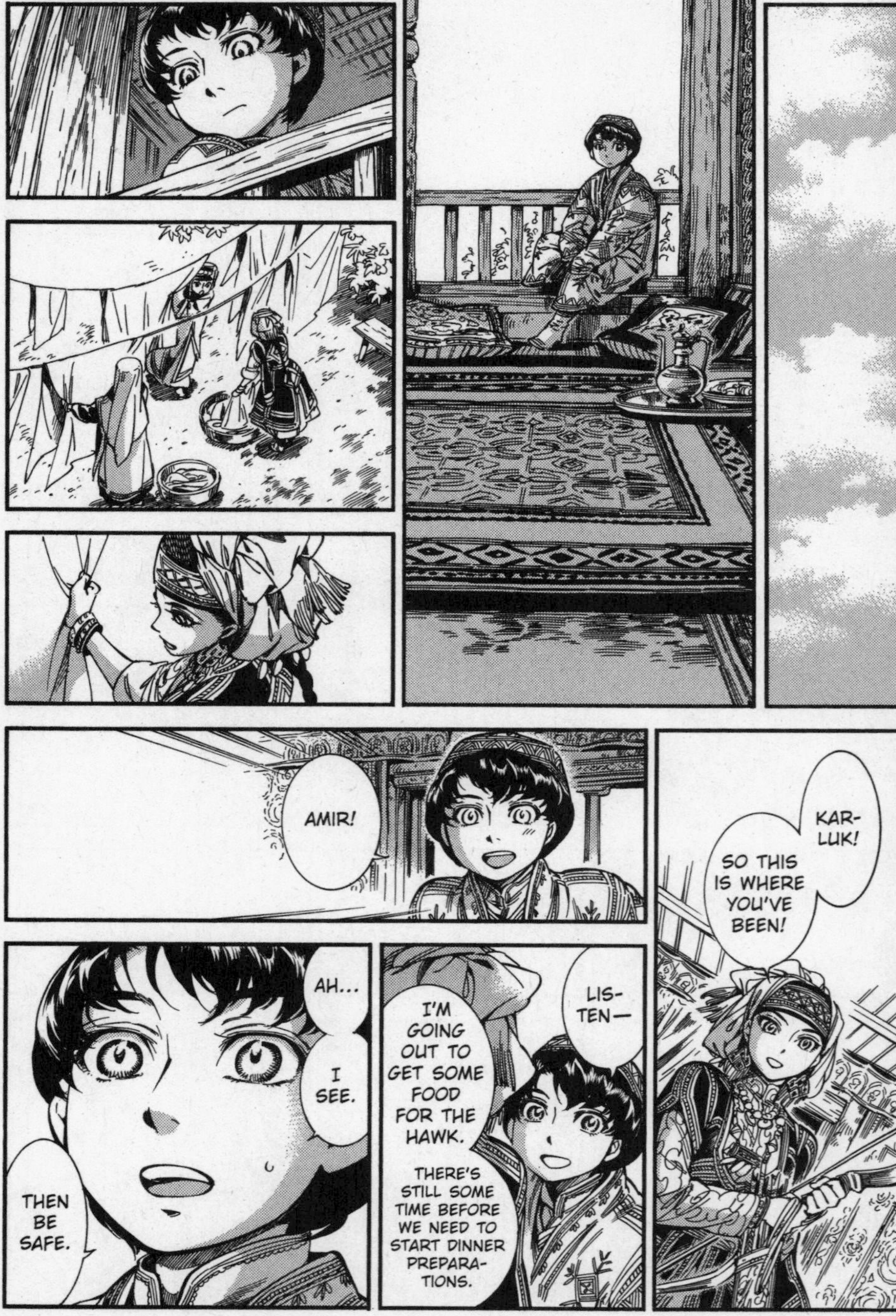
KAR-LUK!
SO THIS IS WHERE YOU'VE BEEN!
AMIR!
LIS-TEN—
I'M GOING OUT TO GET SOME FOOD FOR THE HAWK.
THERE'S STILL SOME TIME BEFORE WE NEED TO START DINNER PREPARATIONS.
AH...
I SEE.
THEN BE SAFE.

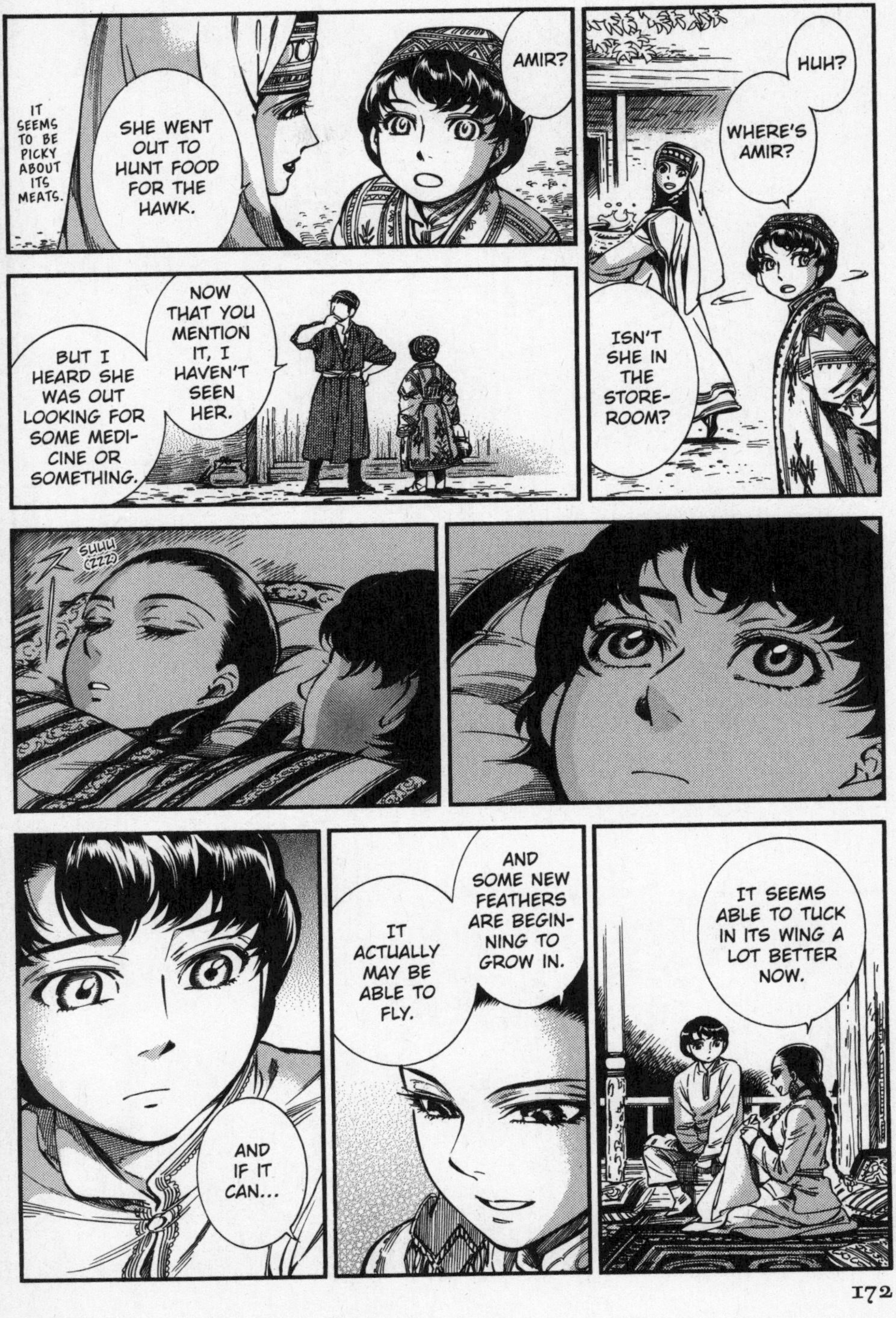
HUH?
WHERE'S AMIR?
ISN'T SHE IN THE STORE-ROOM?
AMIR?
SHE WENT OUT TO HUNT FOOD FOR THE HAWK.
IT SEEMS TO BE PICKY ABOUT ITS MEATS.
NOW THAT YOU MENTION IT, I HAVEN'T SEEN HER.
BUT I HEARD SHE WAS OUT LOOKING FOR SOME MEDI-CINE OR SOMETHING.
SUUU (ZZZ)
IT SEEMS ABLE TO TUCK IN ITS WING A LOT BETTER NOW.
AND SOME NEW FEATHERS ARE BEGIN-NING TO GROW IN.
IT ACTUALLY MAY BE ABLE TO FLY.
AND IF IT CAN...

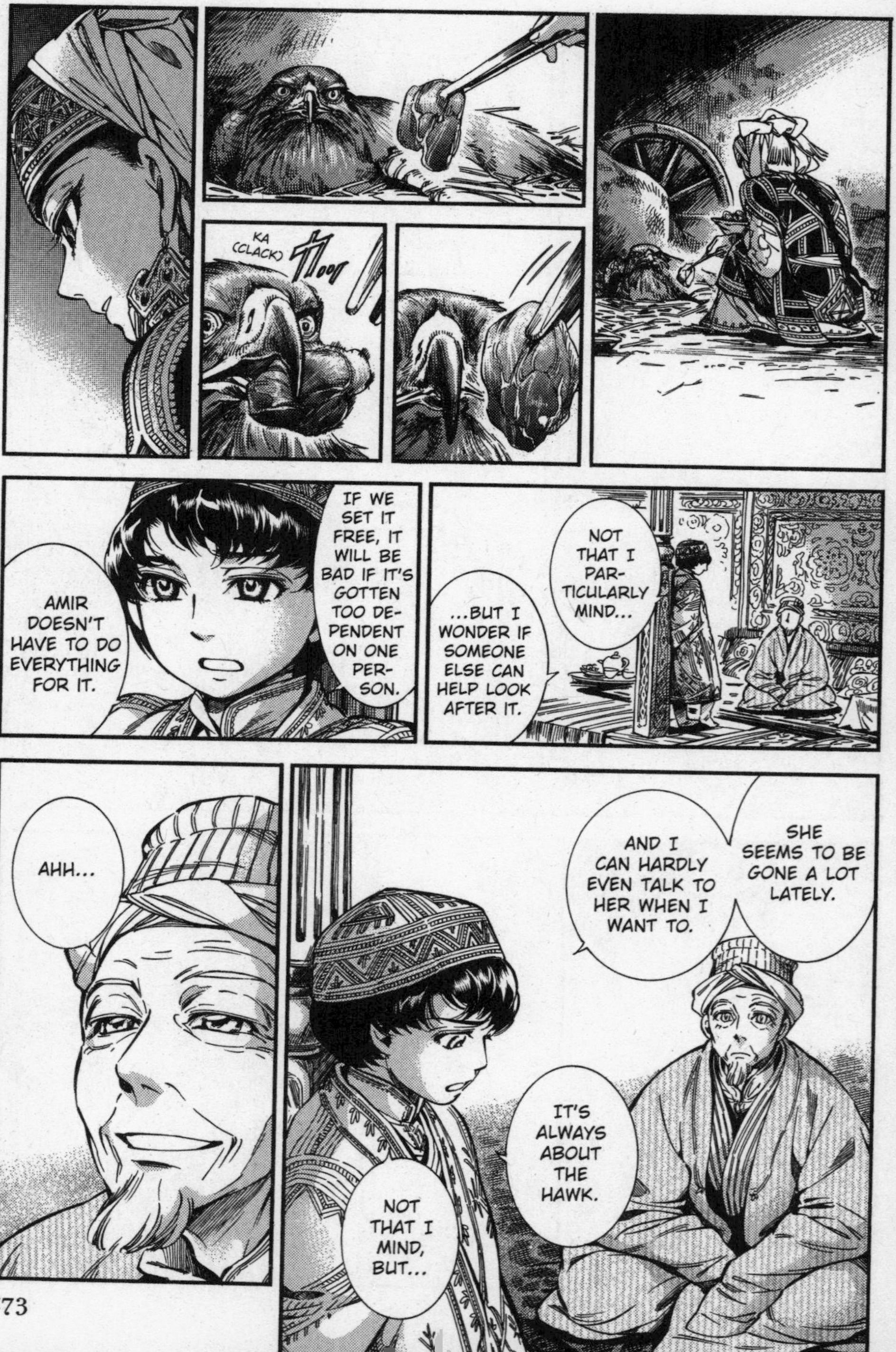
KA (CLACK)
NOT THAT I PAR-TICULARLY MIND...
...BUT I WONDER IF SOMEONE ELSE CAN HELP LOOK AFTER IT.
IF WE SET IT FREE, IT WILL BE BAD IF IT'S GOTTEN TOO DE-PENDENT ON ONE PER-SON.
AMIR DOESN'T HAVE TO DO EVERYTHING FOR IT.
SHE SEEMS TO BE GONE A LOT LATELY.
AND I CAN HARDLY EVEN TALK TO HER WHEN I WANT TO.
IT'S ALWAYS ABOUT THE HAWK.
NOT THAT I MIND, BUT...
AHH...

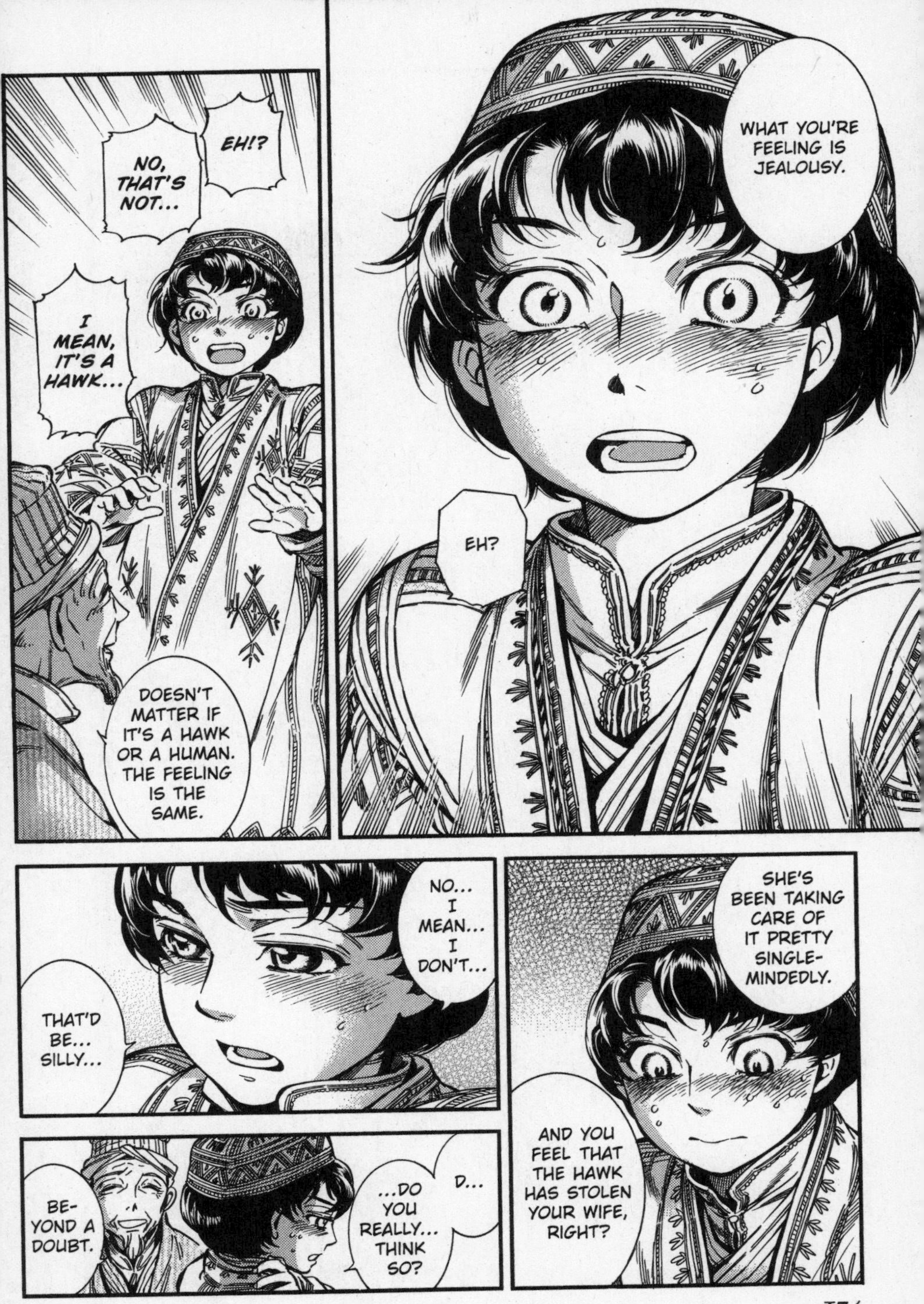
WHAT YOU'RE FEELING IS JEALOUSY.
EH?
EH!?
NO, THAT'S NOT...
I MEAN, IT'S A HAWK...
DOESN'T MATTER IF IT'S A HAWK OR A HUMAN. THE FEELING IS THE SAME.
SHE'S BEEN TAKING CARE OF IT PRETTY SINGLE-MINDEDLY.
AND YOU FEEL THAT THE HAWK HAS STOLEN YOUR WIFE, RIGHT?
NO... I MEAN... I DON'T...
THAT'D BE... SILLY...
D...
...DO YOU REALLY... THINK SO?
BE-YOND A DOUBT.

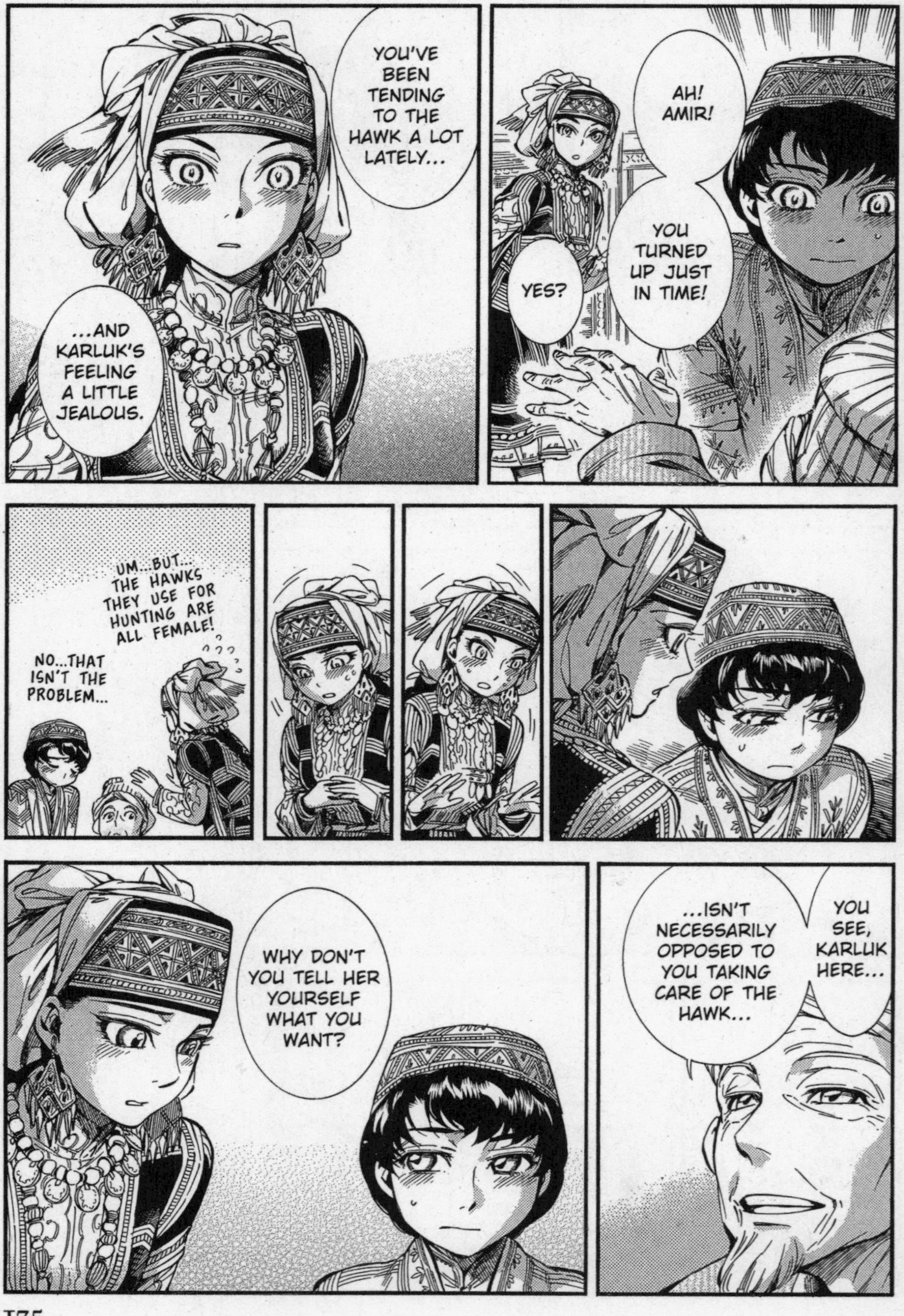
AH! AMIR!
YOU TURNED UP JUST IN TIME!
YES?
YOU'VE BEEN TENDING TO THE HAWK A LOT LATELY...
...AND KARLUK'S FEELING A LITTLE JEALOUS.
UM...BUT... THE HAWKS THEY USE FOR HUNTING ARE ALL FEMALE!
NO...THAT ISN'T THE PROBLEM...
YOU SEE, KARLUK HERE...
...ISN'T NECESSARILY OPPOSED TO YOU TAKING CARE OF THE HAWK...
WHY DON'T YOU TELL HER YOURSELF WHAT YOU WANT?

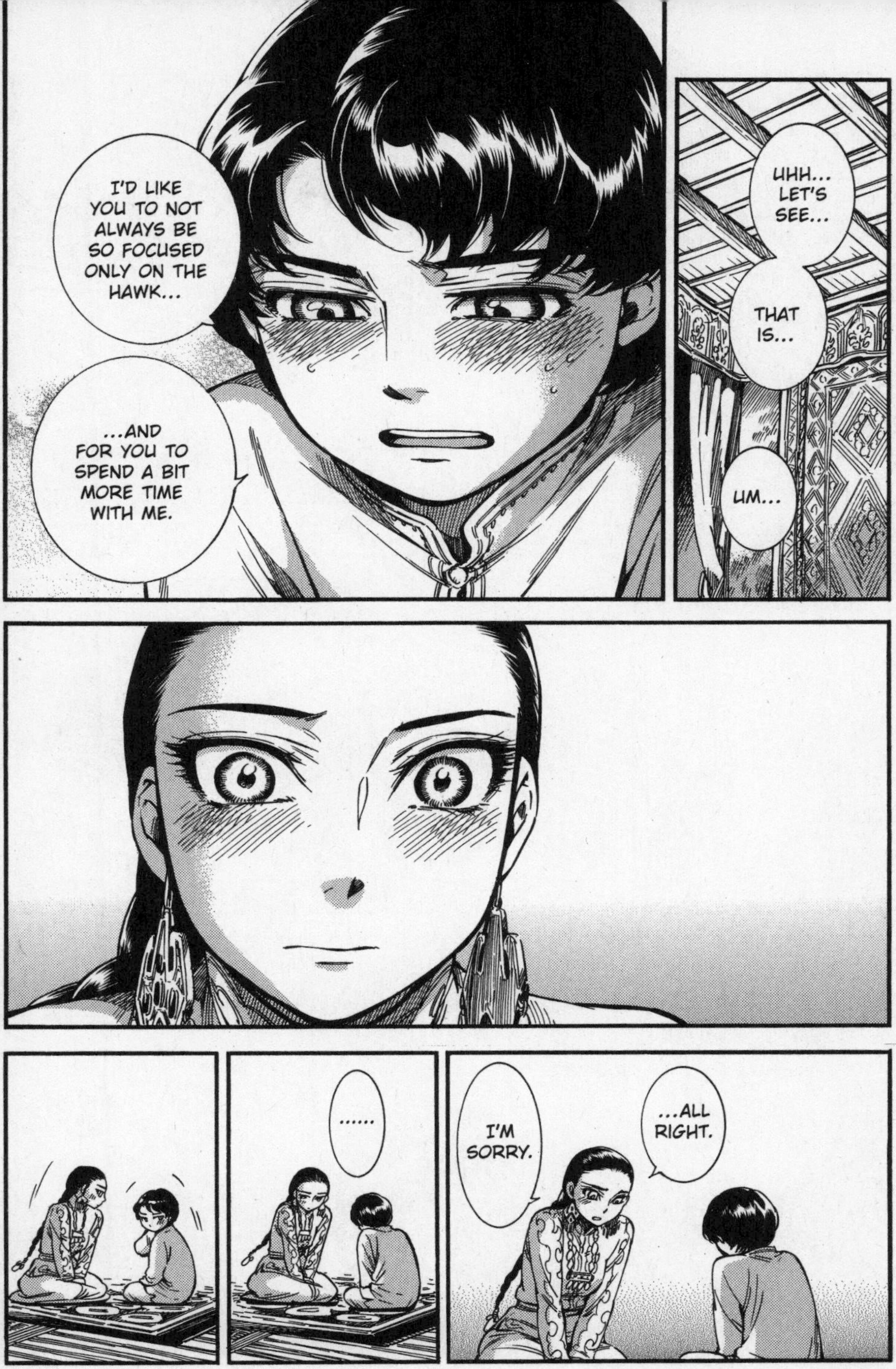
UHH... LET'S SEE...
THAT IS...
UM...
I'D LIKE YOU TO NOT ALWAYS BE SO FOCUSED ONLY ON THE HAWK...
...AND FOR YOU TO SPEND A BIT MORE TIME WITH ME.
...ALL RIGHT.
I'M SORRY.
......

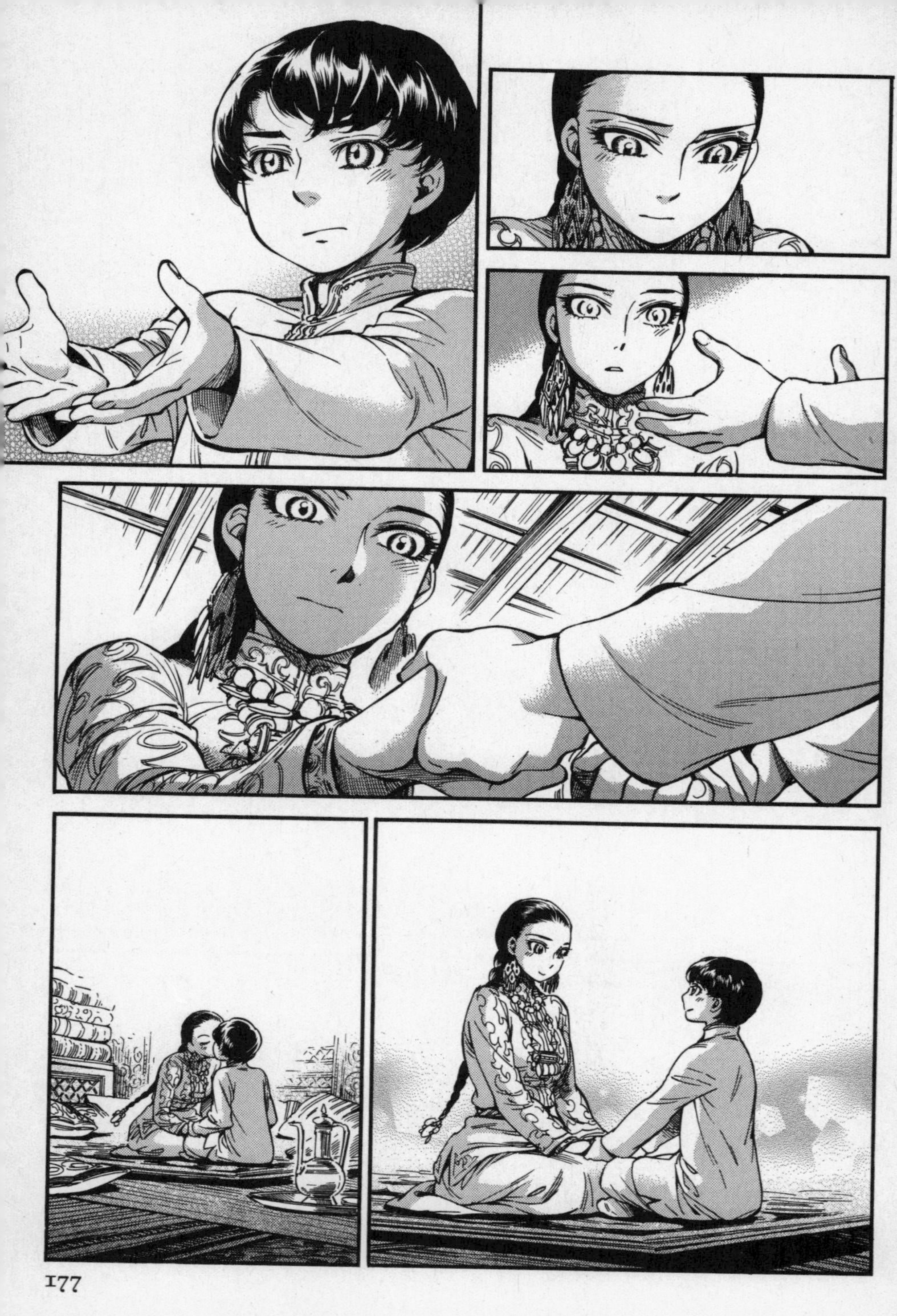

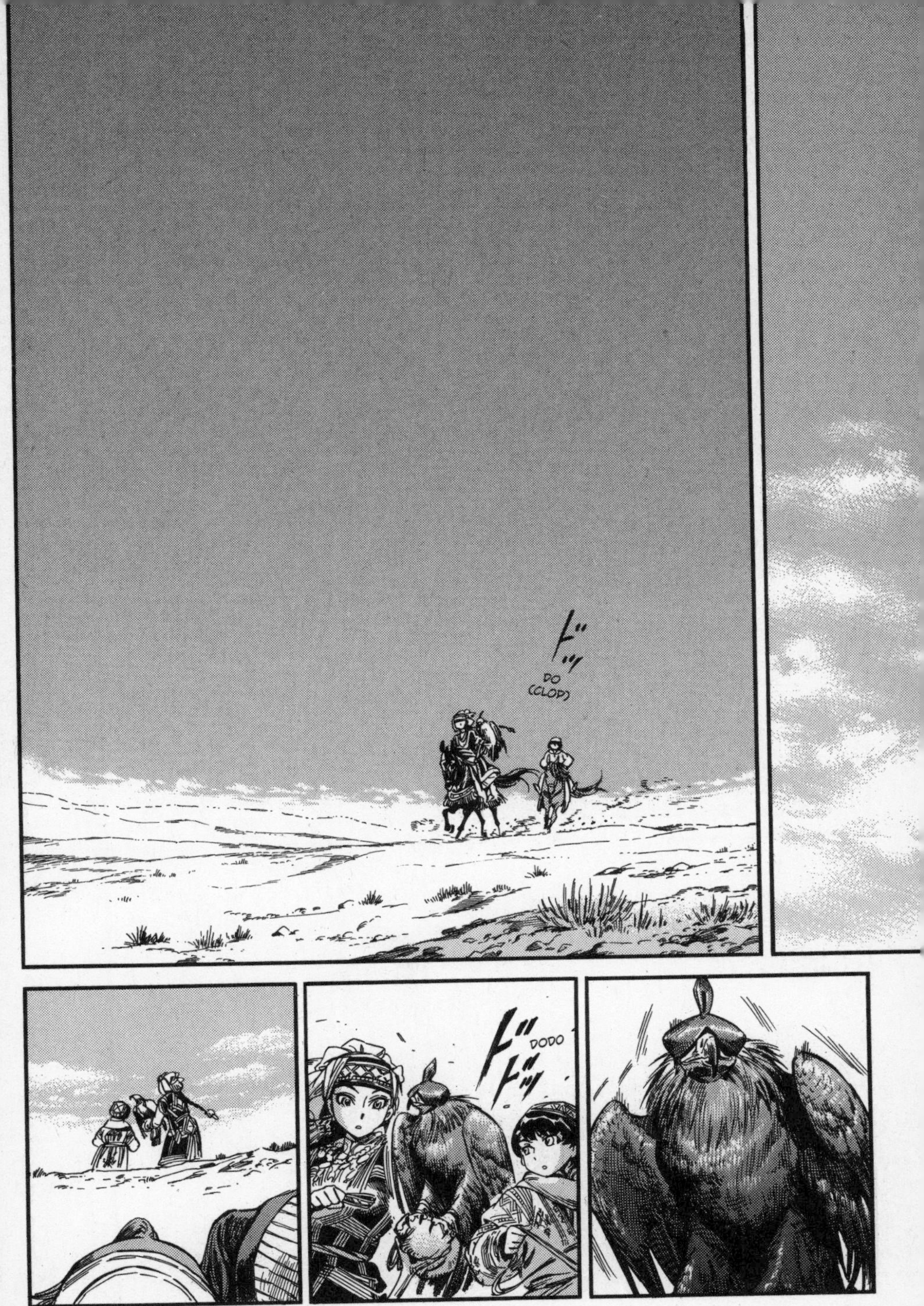
ドッ
DO
(CLOP)
ドドッ
DODO

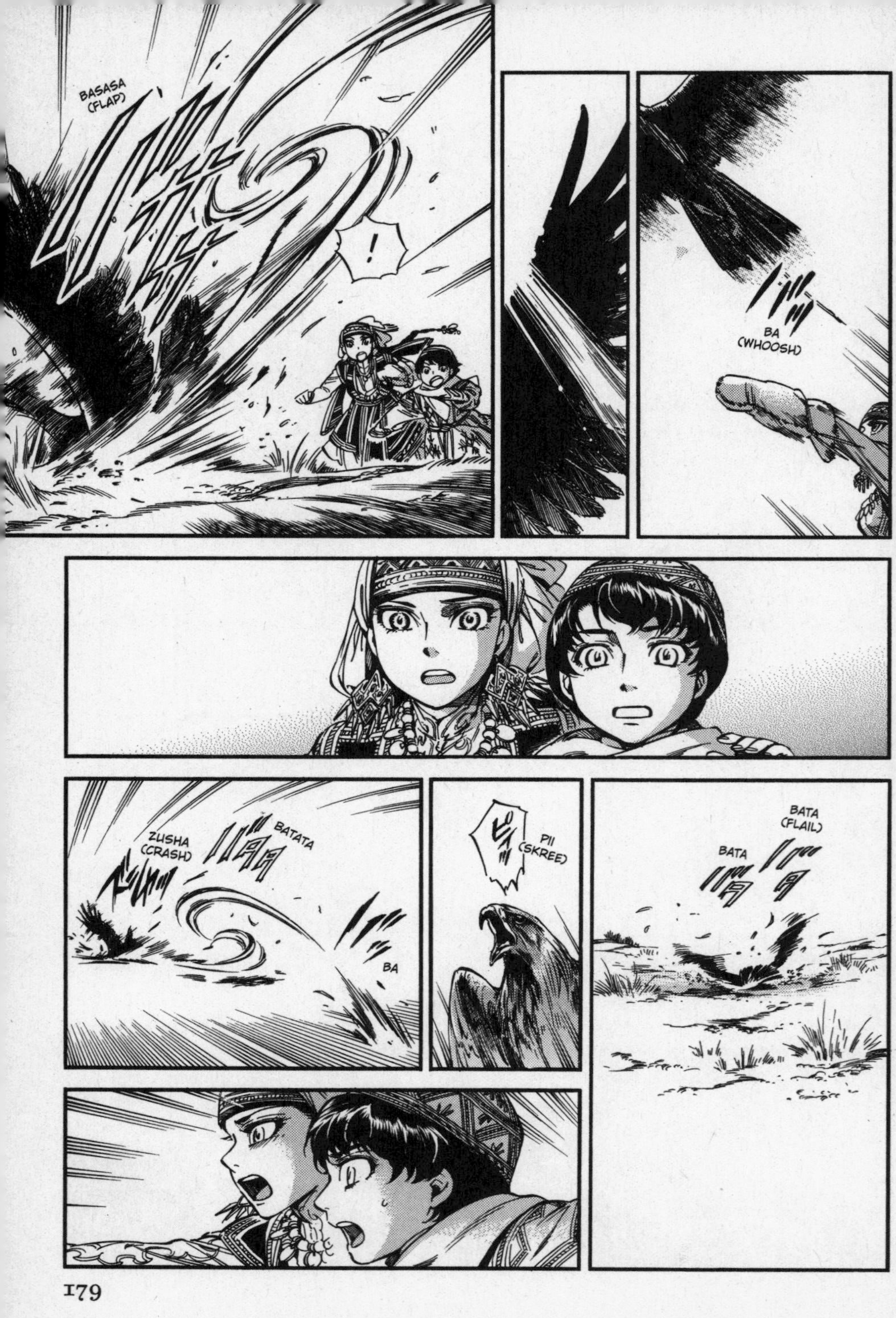
BA (WHOOSH)
BASASA (FLAP)
!
BATA (FLAIL)
BATA
PII (SKREE)
BATATA
ZUSHA (CRASH)
BA

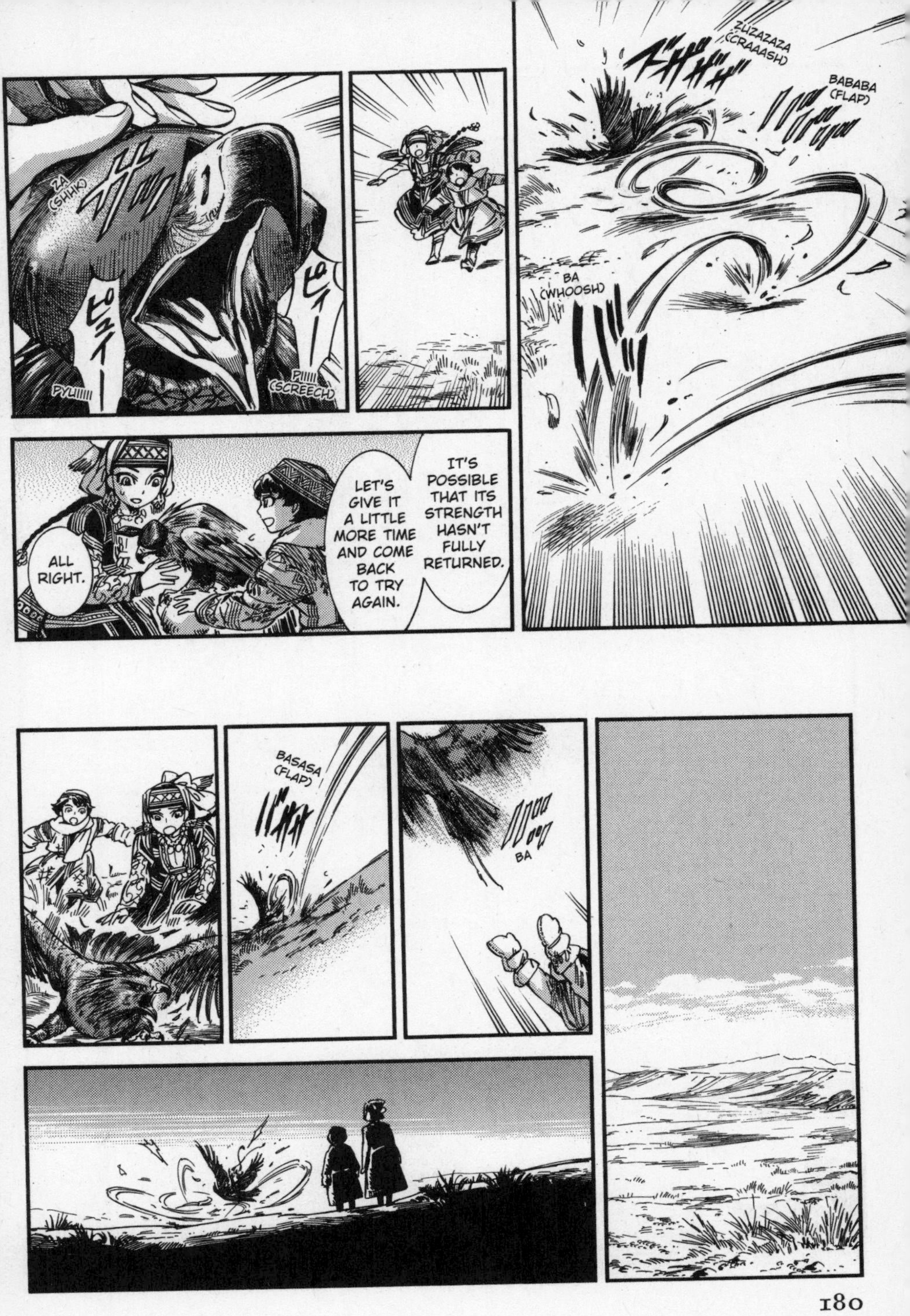
ZUZAZAZA (CRAAASH)
BABABA (FLAP)
BA (WHOOSH)
ZA (SHHK)
PI!!!!! (SCREECH)
PYU!!!!!!
IT'S POSSIBLE THAT ITS STRENGTH HASN'T FULLY RETURNED.
LET'S GIVE IT A LITTLE MORE TIME AND COME BACK TO TRY AGAIN.
ALL RIGHT.
BA
BASASA (FLAP)

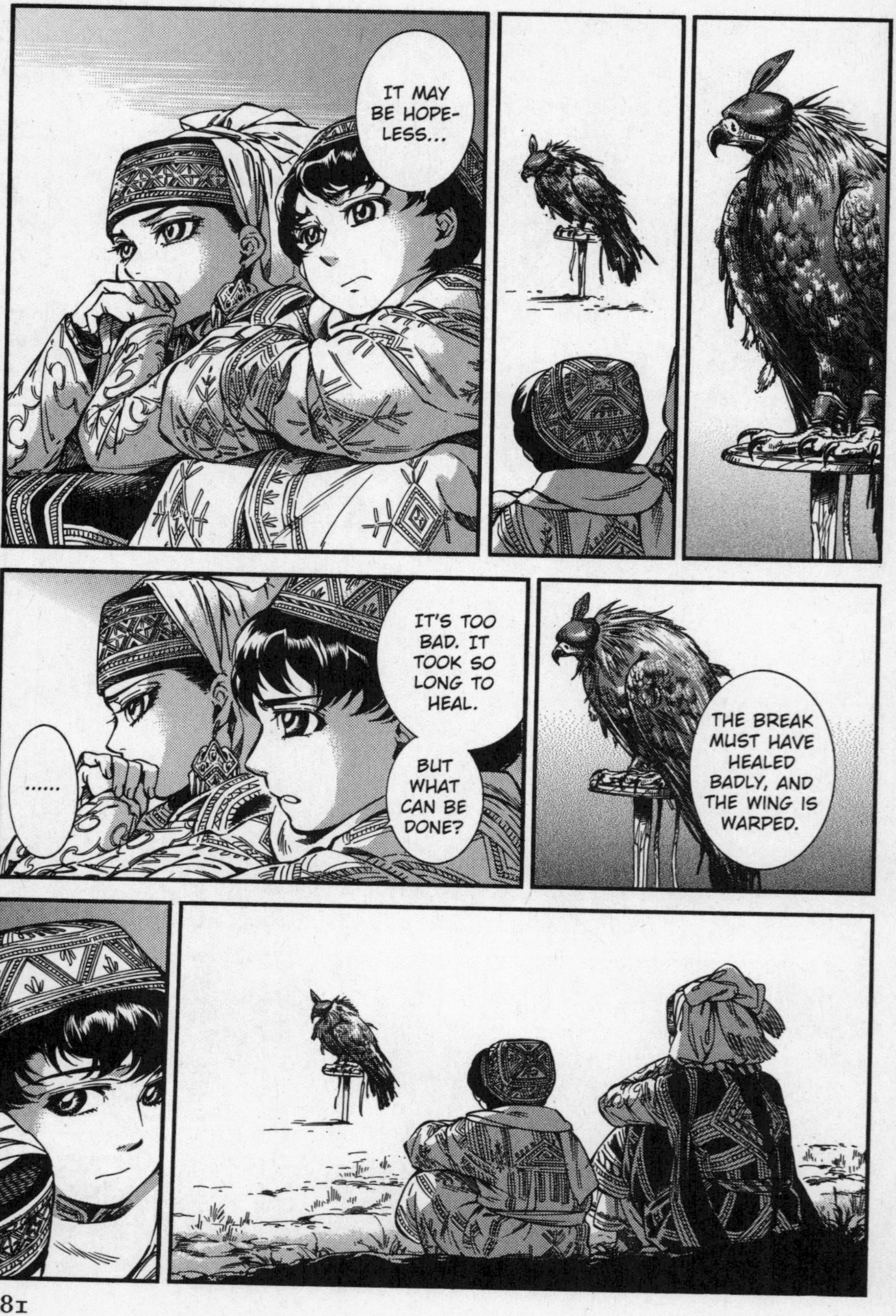
IT MAY BE HOPE-LESS...
THE BREAK MUST HAVE HEALED BADLY, AND THE WING IS WARPED.
IT'S TOO BAD. IT TOOK SO LONG TO HEAL.
BUT WHAT CAN BE DONE?
......

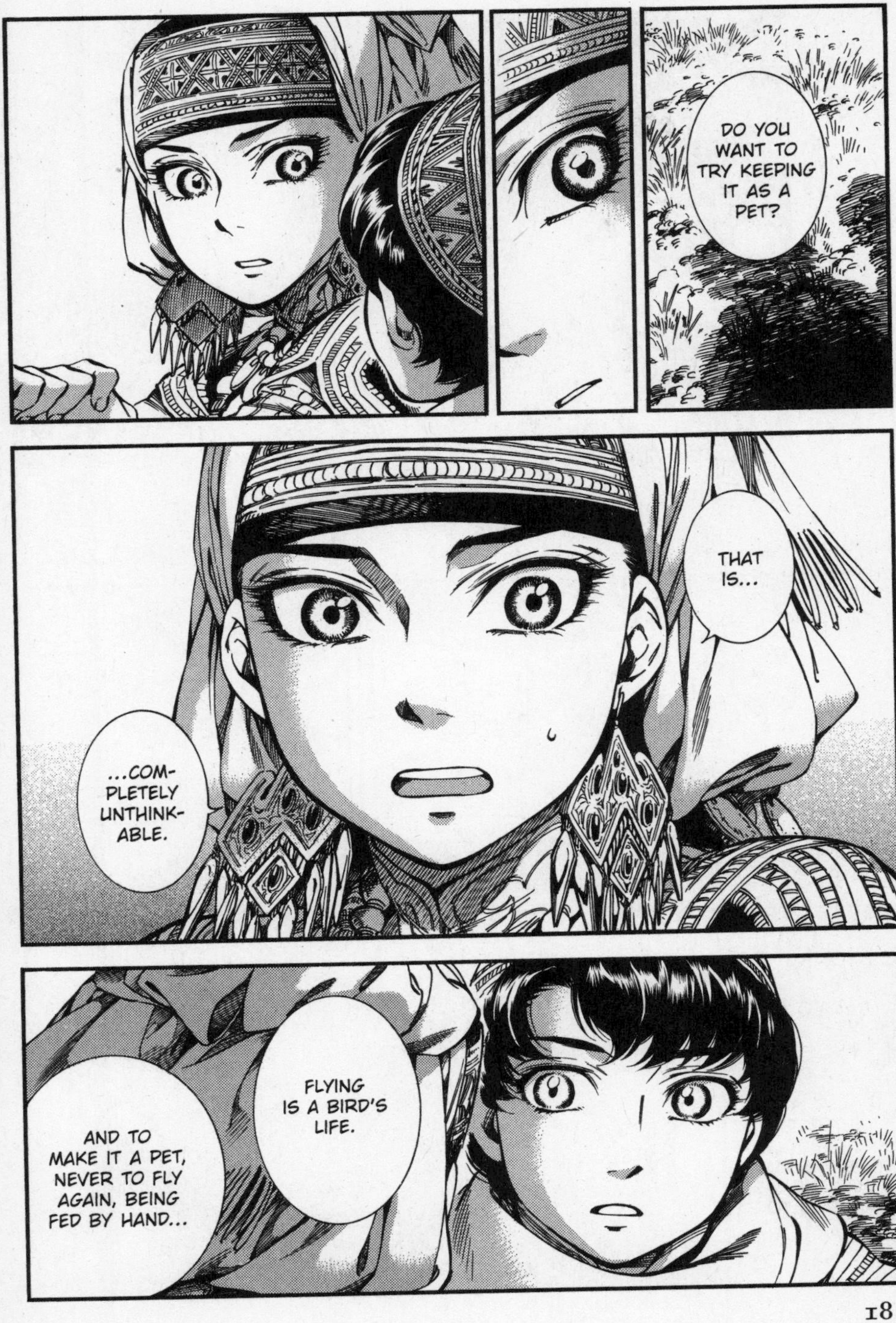
DO YOU WANT TO TRY KEEPING IT AS A PET?
THAT IS...
...COM-PLETELY UNTHINK-ABLE.
FLYING IS A BIRD'S LIFE.
AND TO MAKE IT A PET, NEVER TO FLY AGAIN, BEING FED BY HAND...

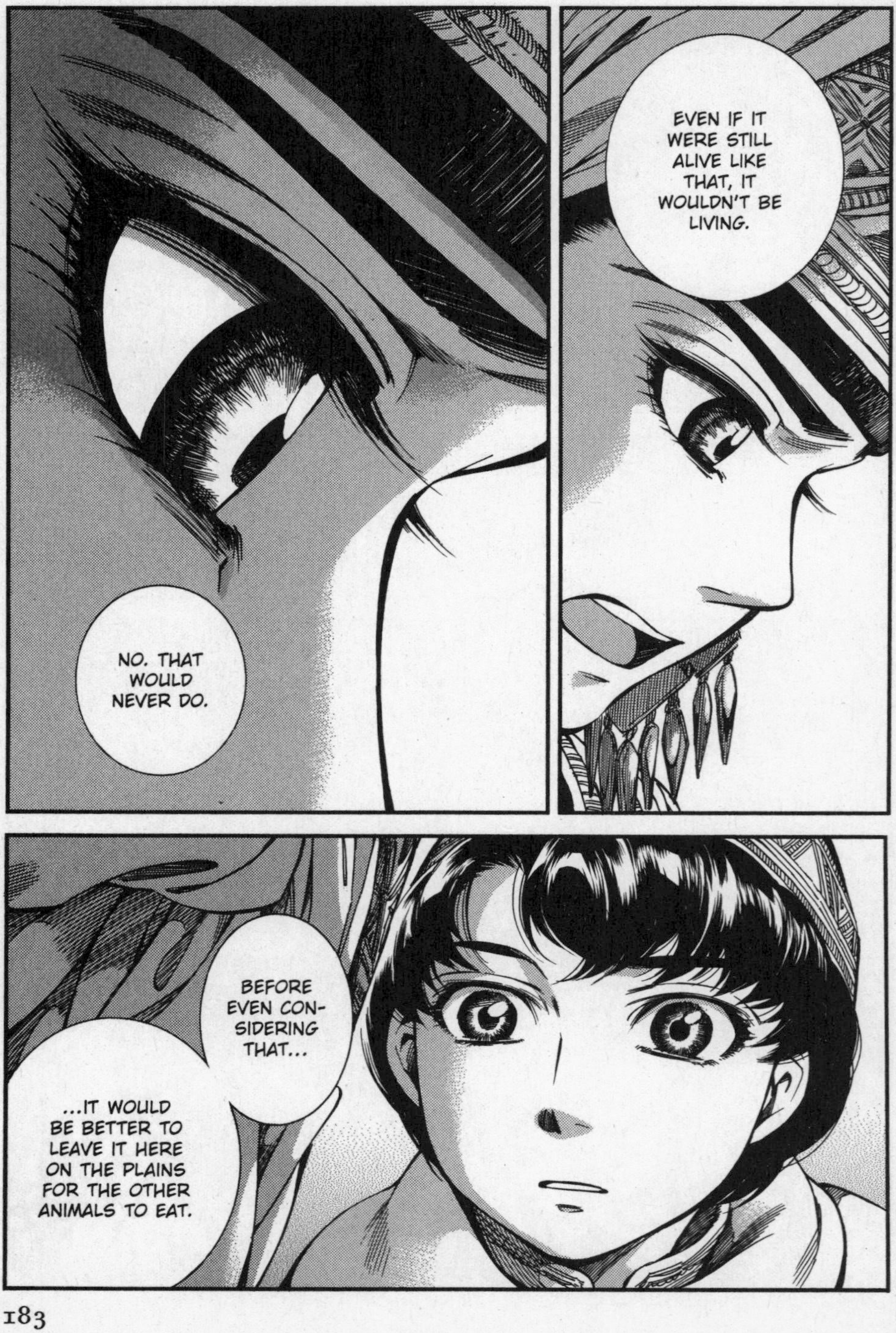
EVEN IF IT WERE STILL ALIVE LIKE THAT, IT WOULDN'T BE LIVING.
NO. THAT WOULD NEVER DO.
BEFORE EVEN CON-SIDERING THAT...
...IT WOULD BE BETTER TO LEAVE IT HERE ON THE PLAINS FOR THE OTHER ANIMALS TO EAT.

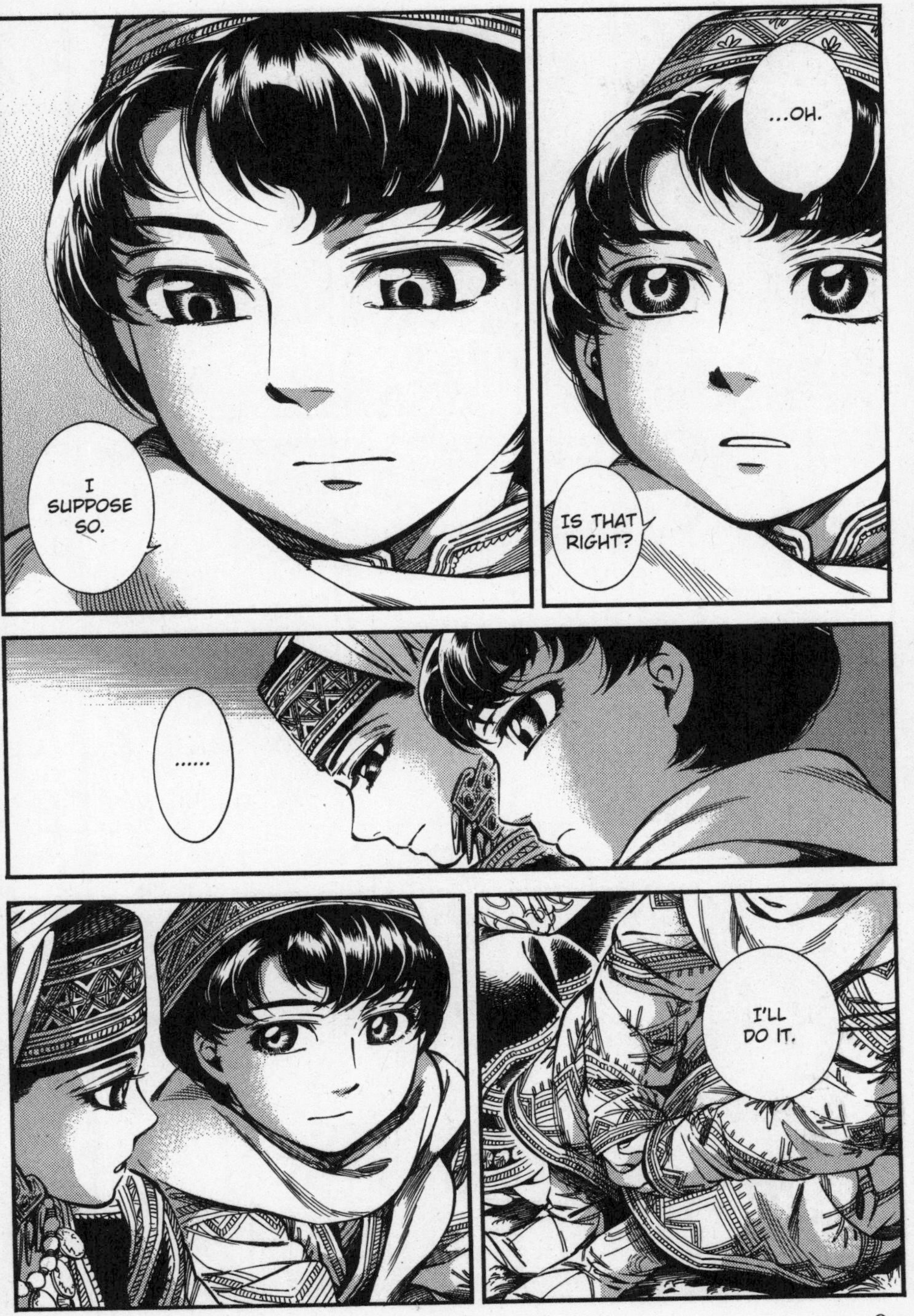
...OH.
IS THAT RIGHT?
I SUPPOSE SO.
......
I'LL DO IT.

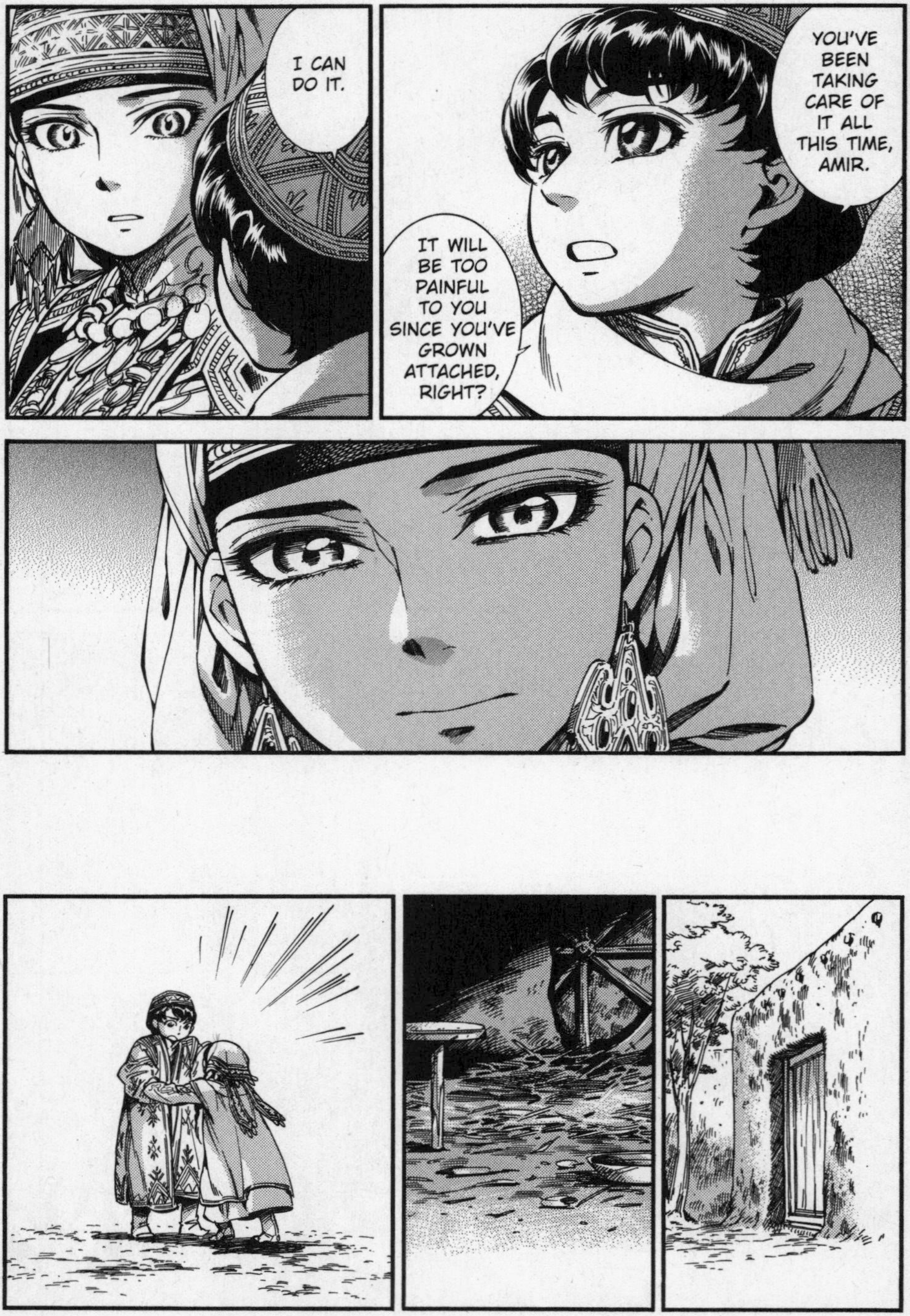
YOU'VE BEEN TAKING CARE OF IT ALL THIS TIME, AMIR.
IT WILL BE TOO PAINFUL TO YOU SINCE YOU'VE GROWN ATTACHED, RIGHT?
I CAN DO IT.

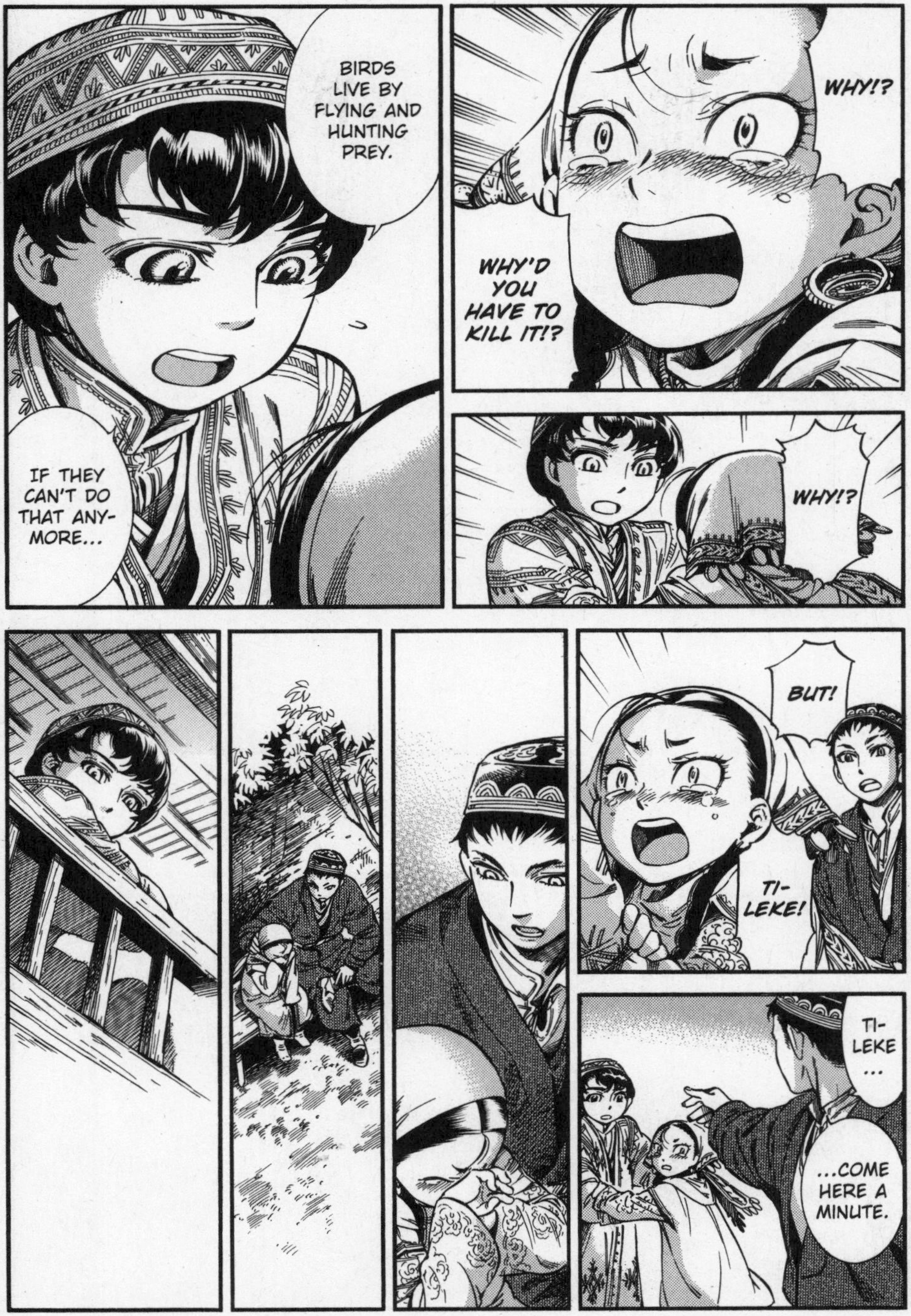
WHY!?
WHY'D YOU HAVE TO KILL IT!?
WHY!?
BIRDS LIVE BY FLYING AND HUNTING PREY.
IF THEY CAN'T DO THAT ANY-MORE...
BUT!
TI-LEKE!
TI-LEKE...
...COME HERE A MINUTE.

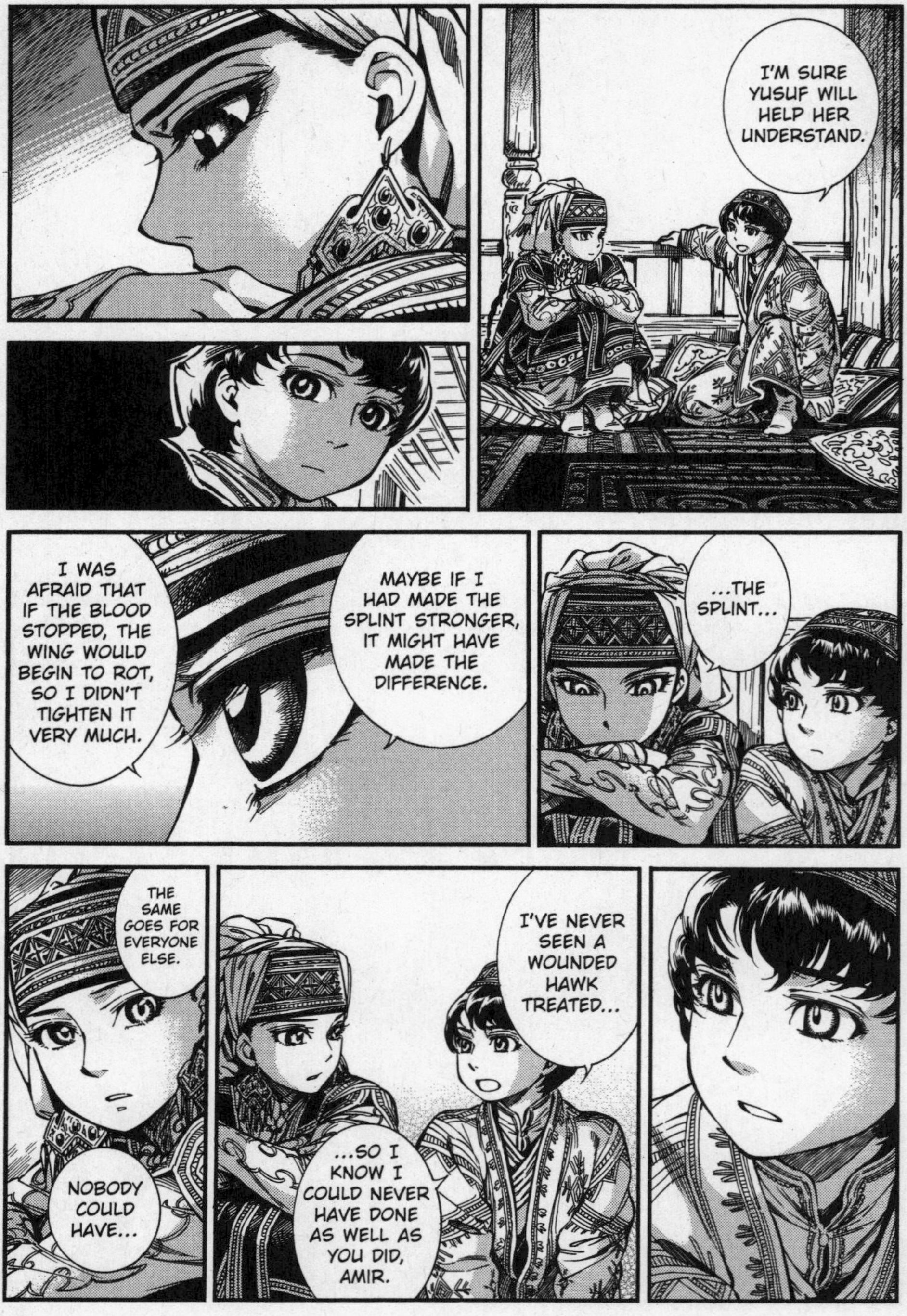
I'M SURE YUSUF WILL HELP HER UNDERSTAND.
...THE SPLINT...
MAYBE IF I HAD MADE THE SPLINT STRONGER, IT MIGHT HAVE MADE THE DIFFERENCE.
I WAS AFRAID THAT IF THE BLOOD STOPPED, THE WING WOULD BEGIN TO ROT, SO I DIDN'T TIGHTEN IT VERY MUCH.
I'VE NEVER SEEN A WOUNDED HAWK TREATED...
...SO I KNOW I COULD NEVER HAVE DONE AS WELL AS YOU DID, AMIR.
THE SAME GOES FOR EVERYONE ELSE.
NOBODY COULD HAVE...

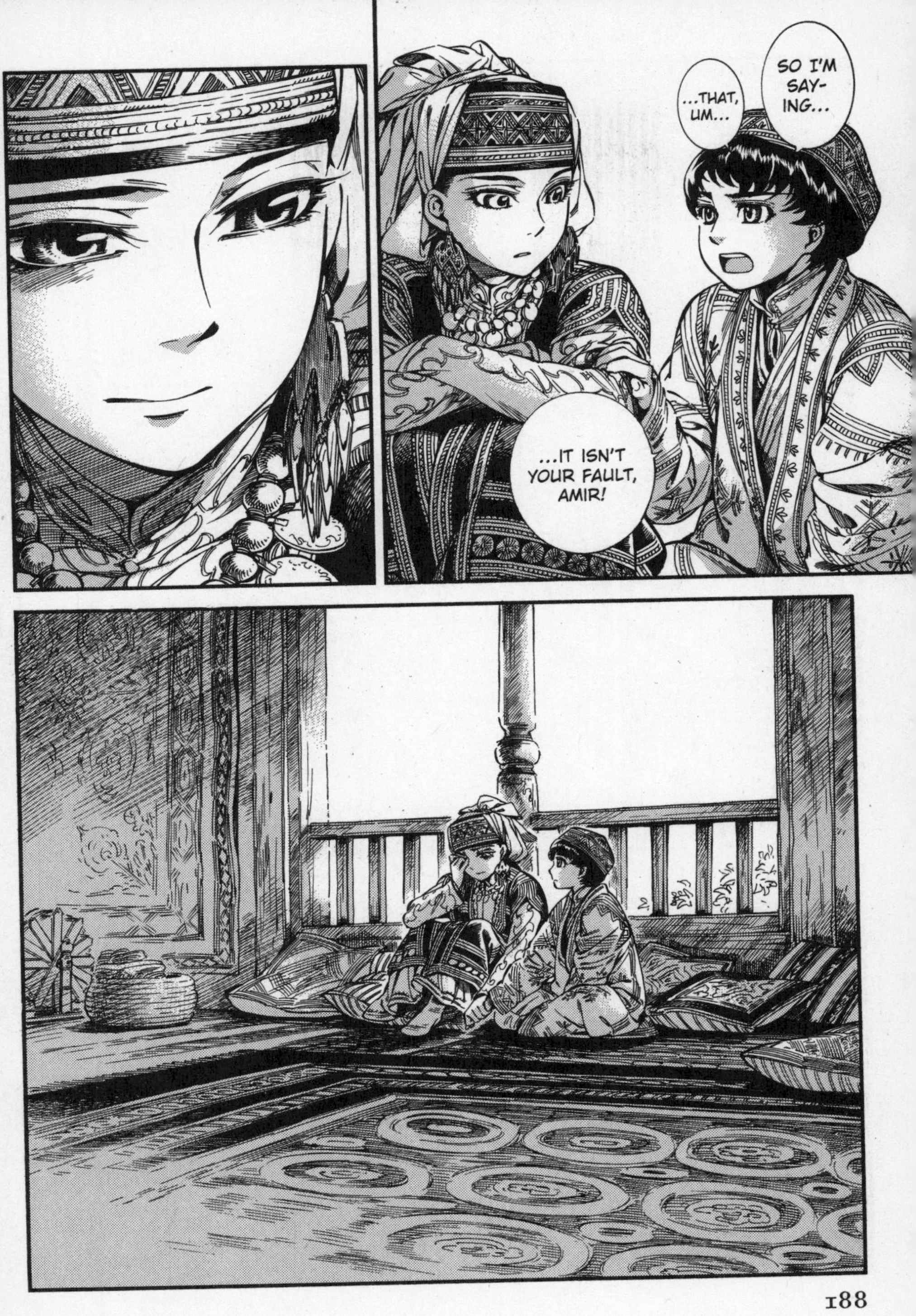
SO I'M SAY-ING...
...THAT, UM...
...IT ISN'T YOUR FAULT, AMIR!

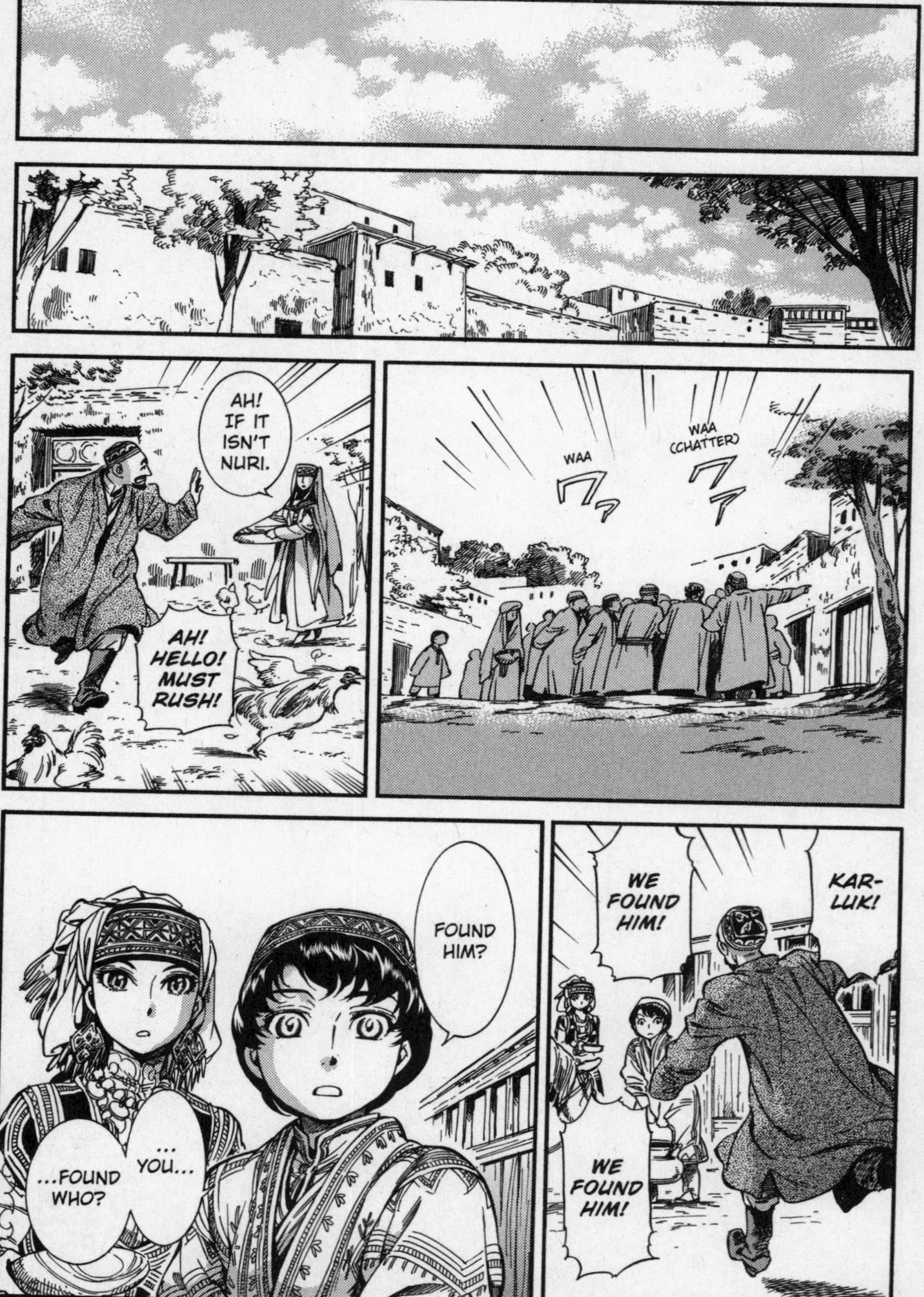
WAA (CHATTER)
ワァ
WAA
ワァ
AH! IF IT ISN'T NURI.
AH! HELLO! MUST RUSH!
KAR-LUK!
WE FOUND HIM!
WE FOUND HIM!
FOUND HIM?
... YOU...
...FOUND WHO?

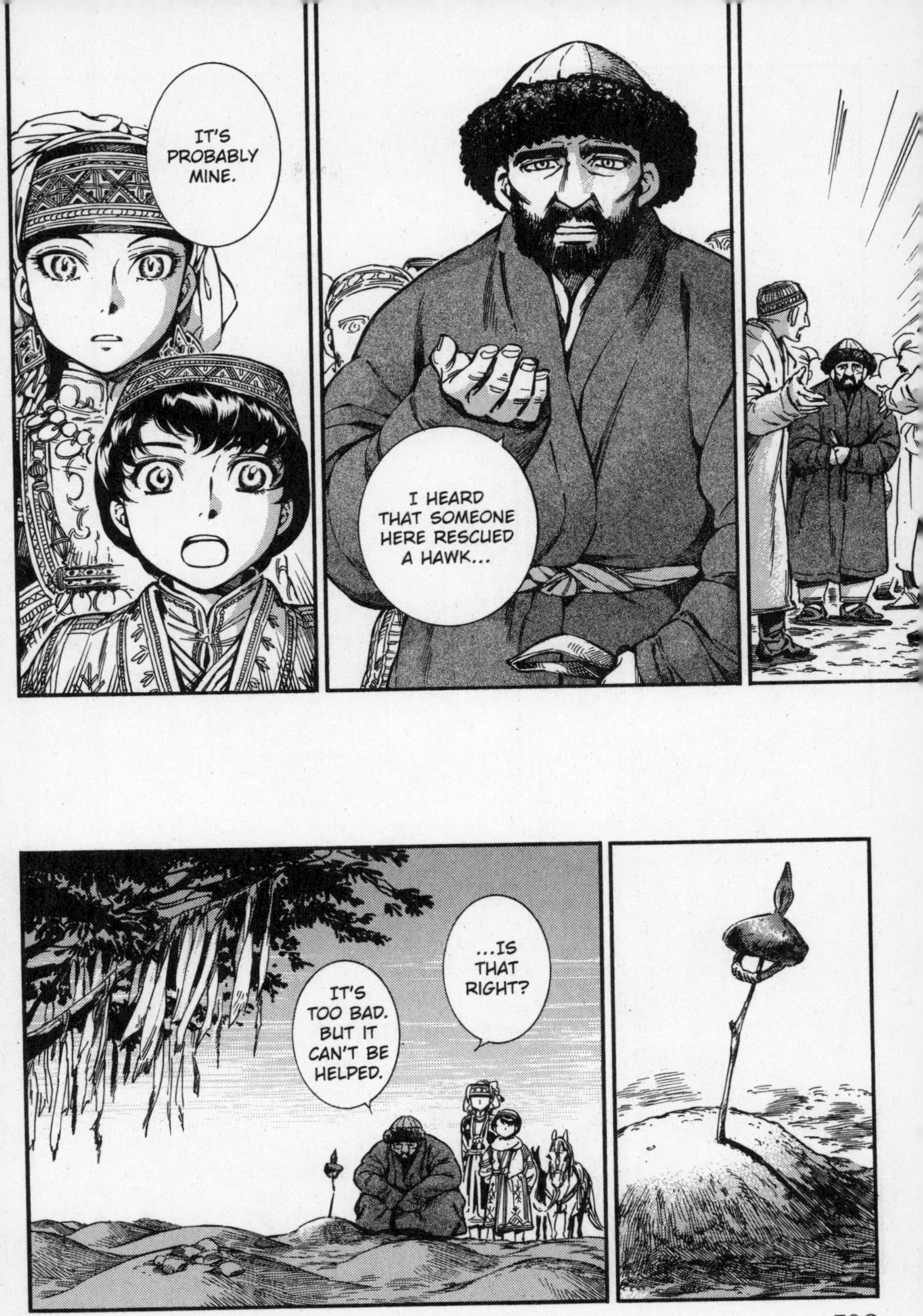
I HEARD THAT SOMEONE HERE RESCUED A HAWK...
IT'S PROBABLY MINE.
...IS THAT RIGHT?
IT'S TOO BAD. BUT IT CAN'T BE HELPED.

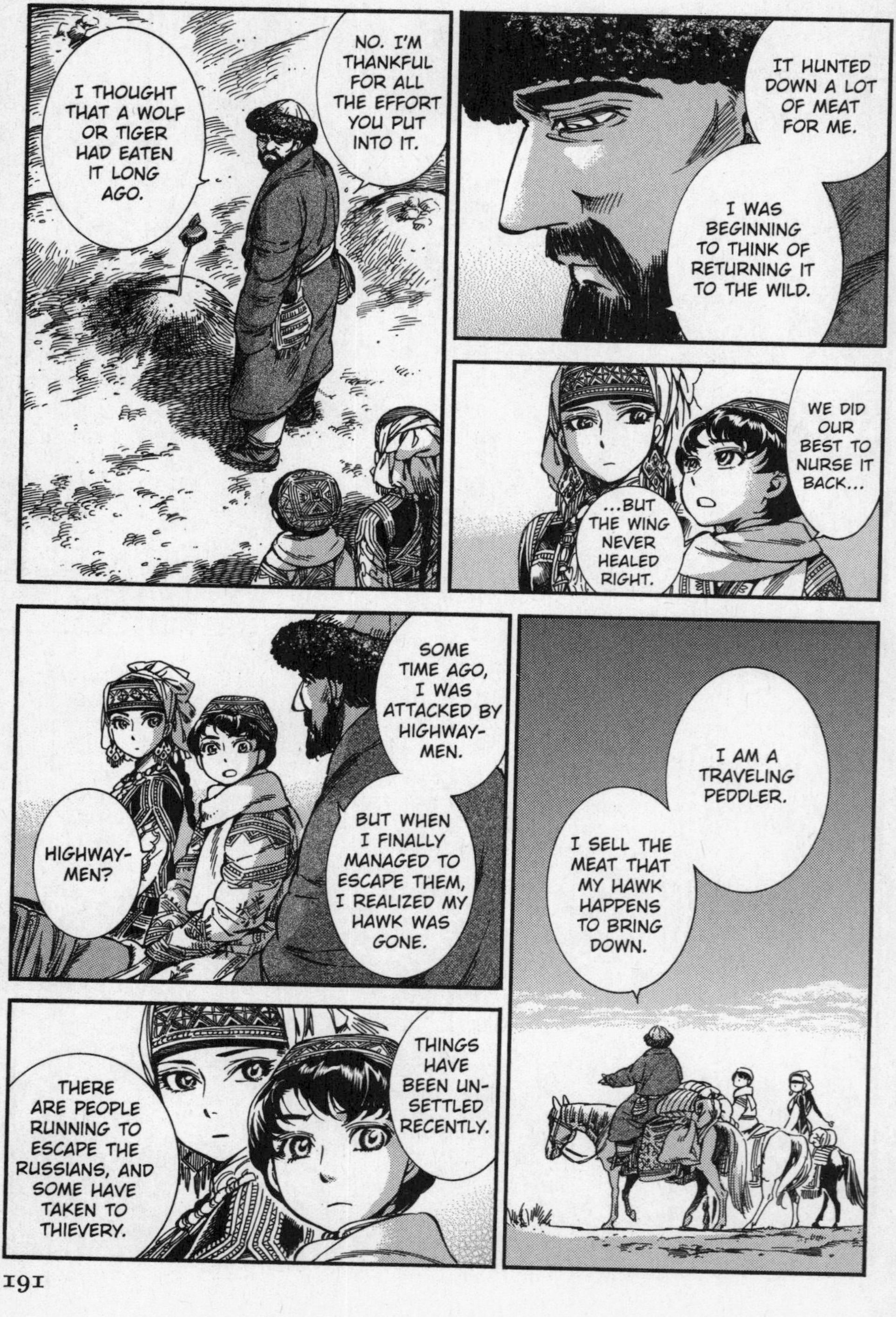
IT HUNTED DOWN A LOT OF MEAT FOR ME.
I WAS BEGINNING TO THINK OF RETURNING IT TO THE WILD.
WE DID OUR BEST TO NURSE IT BACK...
...BUT THE WING NEVER HEALED RIGHT.
NO. I'M THANKFUL FOR ALL THE EFFORT YOU PUT INTO IT.
I THOUGHT THAT A WOLF OR TIGER HAD EATEN IT LONG AGO.
I AM A TRAVELING PEDDLER.
I SELL THE MEAT THAT MY HAWK HAPPENS TO BRING DOWN.
SOME TIME AGO, I WAS ATTACKED BY HIGHWAY-MEN.
BUT WHEN I FINALLY MANAGED TO ESCAPE THEM, I REALIZED MY HAWK WAS GONE.
HIGHWAY-MEN?
THINGS HAVE BEEN UN-SETTLED RECENTLY.
THERE ARE PEOPLE RUNNING TO ESCAPE THE RUSSIANS, AND SOME HAVE TAKEN TO THIEVERY.

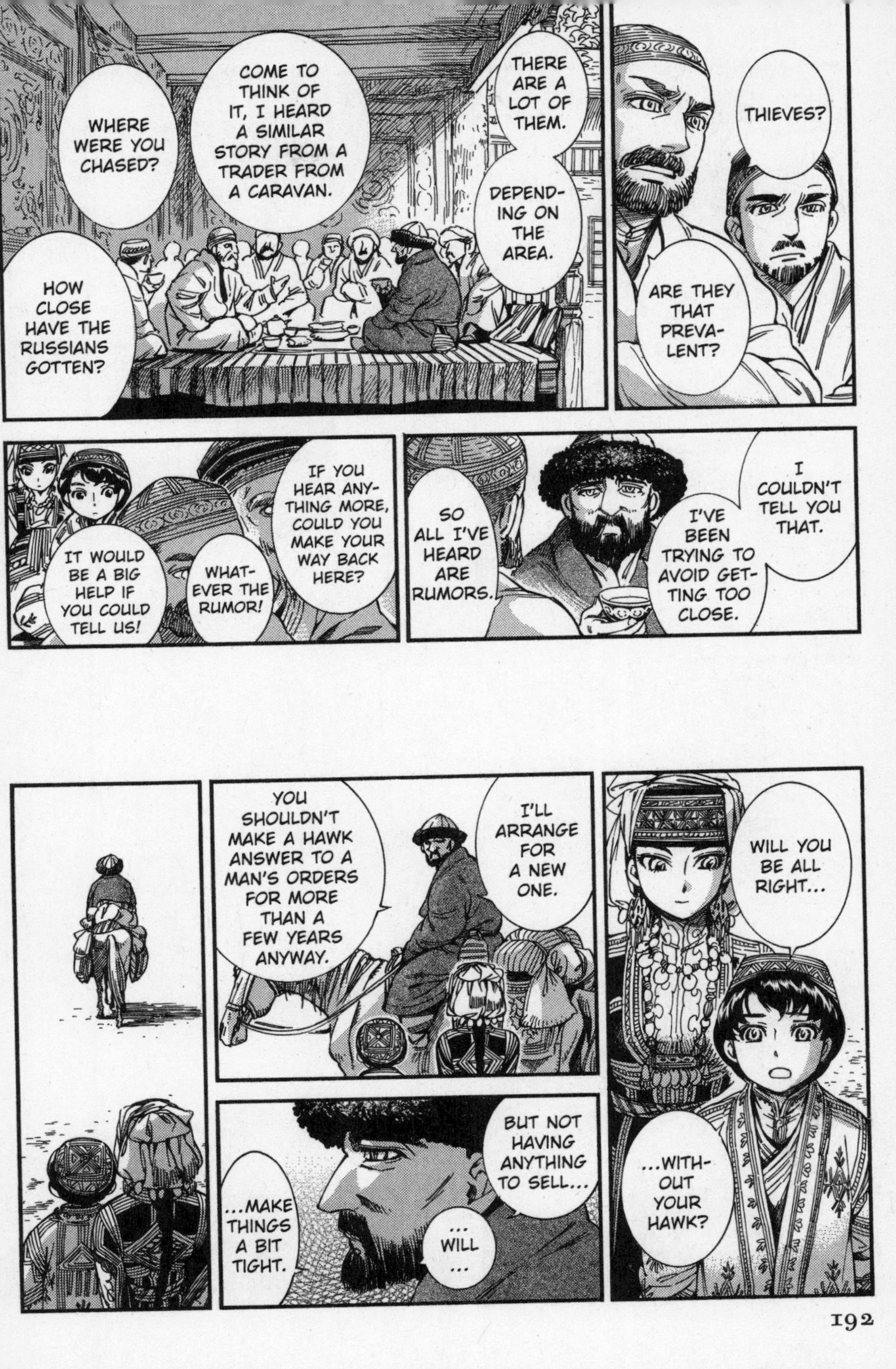
THIEVES?
ARE THEY THAT PREVALENT?
THERE ARE A LOT OF THEM.
DEPENDING ON THE AREA.
COME TO THINK OF IT, I HEARD A SIMILAR STORY FROM A TRADER FROM A CARAVAN.
WHERE WERE YOU CHASED?
HOW CLOSE HAVE THE RUSSIANS GOTTEN?
I COULDN'T TELL YOU THAT.
I'VE BEEN TRYING TO AVOID GETTING TOO CLOSE.
SO ALL I'VE HEARD ARE RUMORS.
IF YOU HEAR ANYTHING MORE, COULD YOU MAKE YOUR WAY BACK HERE?
WHATEVER THE RUMOR!
IT WOULD BE A BIG HELP IF YOU COULD TELL US!
WILL YOU BE ALL RIGHT...
...WITHOUT YOUR HAWK?
I'LL ARRANGE FOR A NEW ONE.
YOU SHOULDN'T MAKE A HAWK ANSWER TO A MAN'S ORDERS FOR MORE THAN A FEW YEARS ANYWAY.
BUT NOT HAVING ANYTHING TO SELL...
...WILL...
...MAKE THINGS A BIT TIGHT.

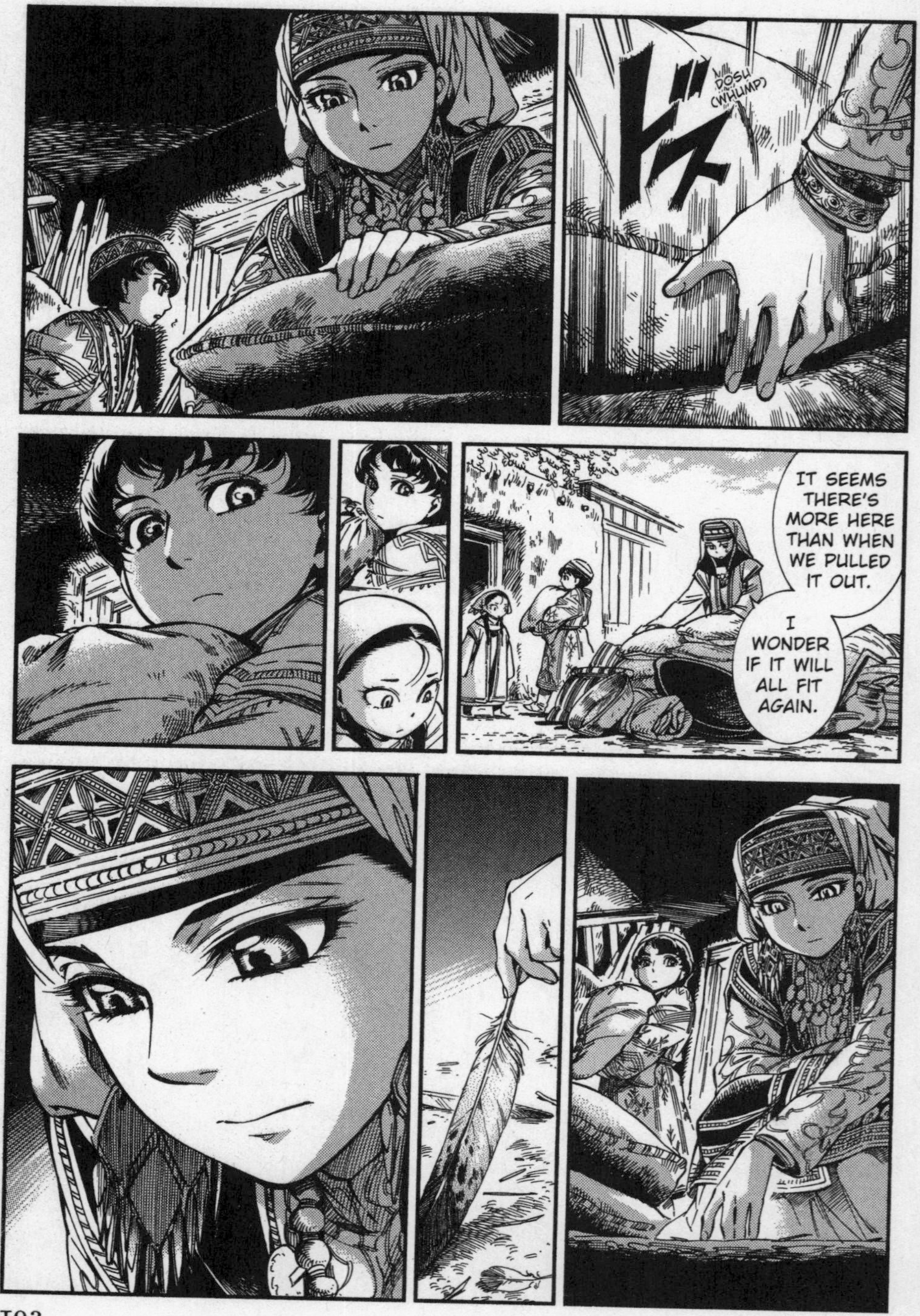
ドス
DOSU (WHUMP)
IT SEEMS THERE'S MORE HERE THAN WHEN WE PULLED IT OUT.
I WONDER IF IT WILL ALL FIT AGAIN.

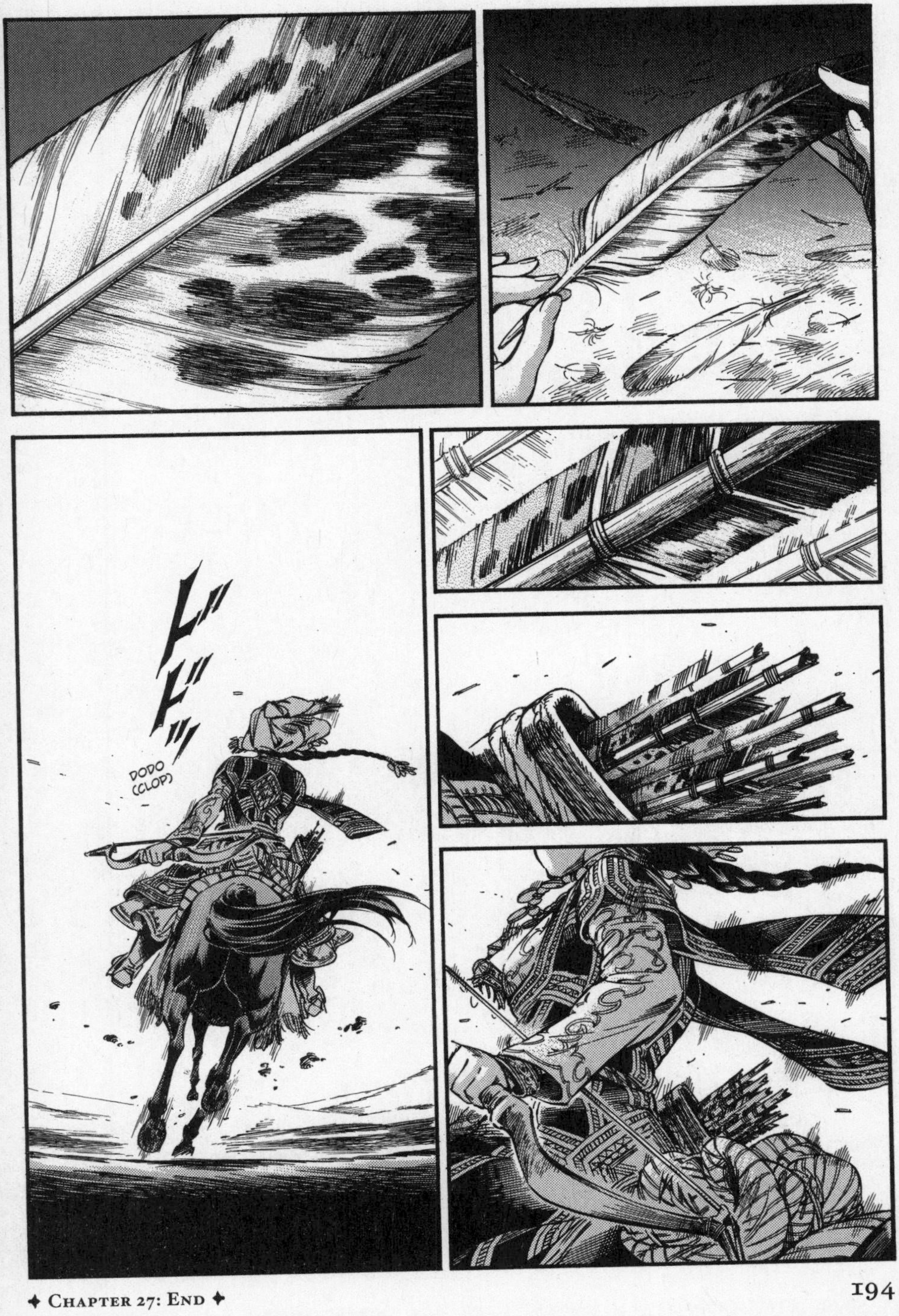
DODO
(CLOP)

✦ Chapter 27: End ✦

Afterword

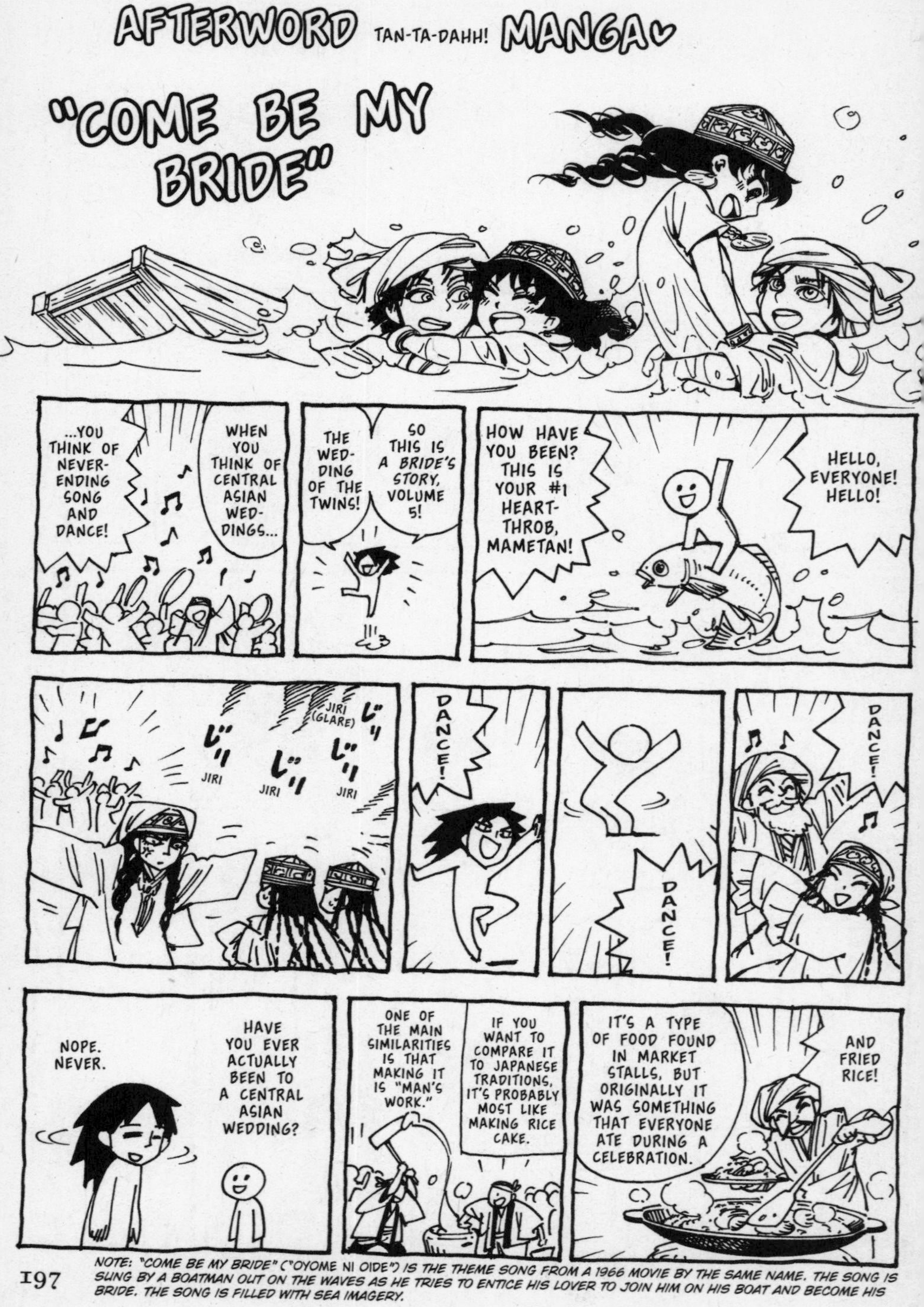
AFTERWORD TAN-TA-DAHH! MANGA
"COME BE MY BRIDE"
HELLO, EVERYONE! HELLO!
HOW HAVE YOU BEEN? THIS IS YOUR #1 HEART-THROB, MAMETAN!
SO THIS IS A BRIDE'S STORY, VOLUME 5!
THE WEDDING OF THE TWINS!
WHEN YOU THINK OF CENTRAL ASIAN WEDDINGS...
...YOU THINK OF NEVER-ENDING SONG AND DANCE!
DANCE!
DANCE!
DANCE!
じり JIRI (GLARE)
じり JIRI
じり JIRI
じり JIRI
AND FRIED RICE!
IT'S A TYPE OF FOOD FOUND IN MARKET STALLS, BUT ORIGINALLY IT WAS SOMETHING THAT EVERYONE ATE DURING A CELEBRATION.
IF YOU WANT TO COMPARE IT TO JAPANESE TRADITIONS, IT'S PROBABLY MOST LIKE MAKING RICE CAKE.
ONE OF THE MAIN SIMILARITIES IS THAT MAKING IT IS "MAN'S WORK."
HAVE YOU EVER ACTUALLY BEEN TO A CENTRAL ASIAN WEDDING?
NOPE. NEVER.

NOTE: "COME BE MY BRIDE" ("OYOME NI OIDE") IS THE THEME SONG FROM A 1966 MOVIE BY THE SAME NAME. THE SONG IS SUNG BY A BOATMAN OUT ON THE WAVES AS HE TRIES TO ENTICE HIS LOVER TO JOIN HIM ON HIS BOAT AND BECOME HIS BRIDE. THE SONG IS FILLED WITH SEA IMAGERY.

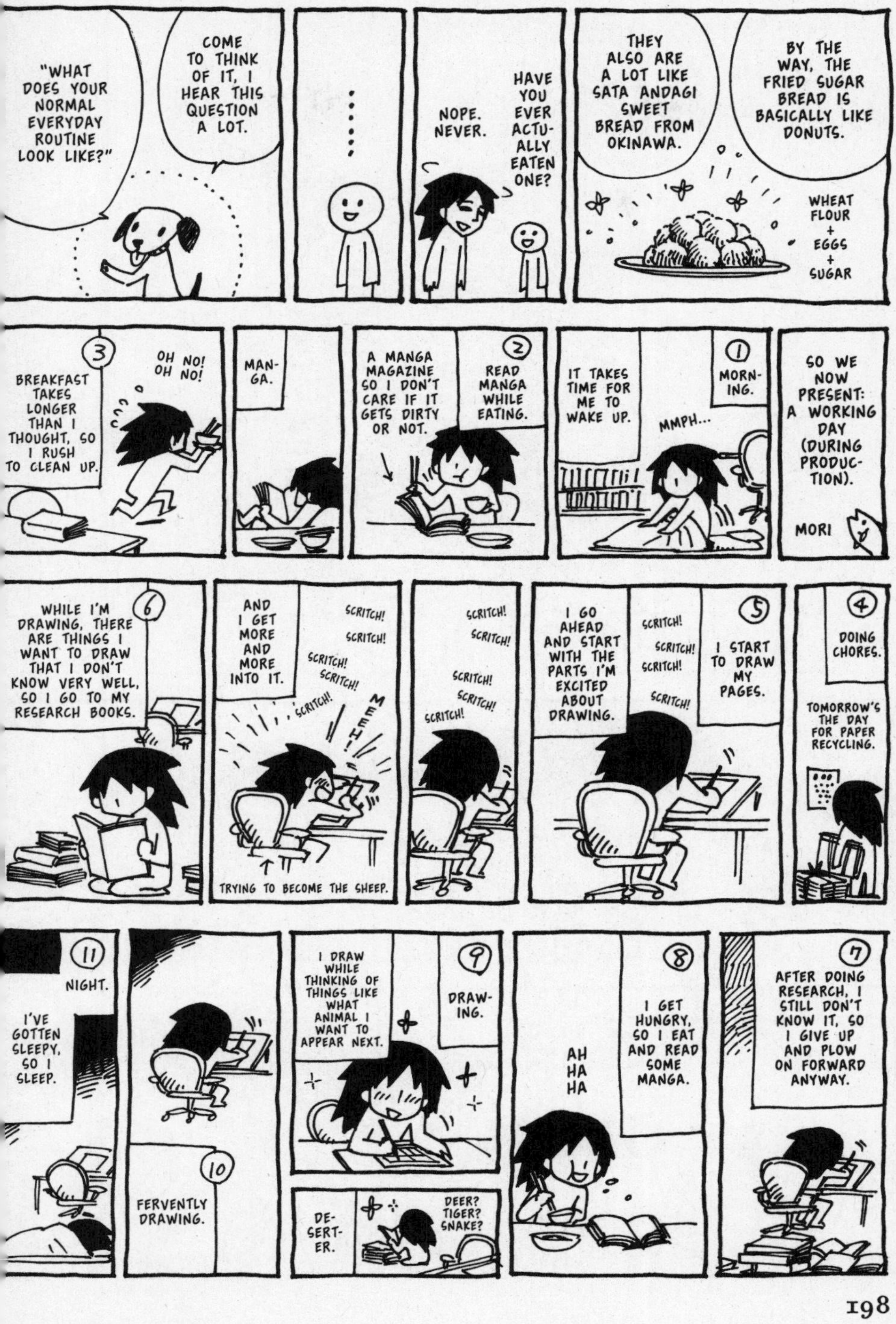
BY THE WAY, THE FRIED SUGAR BREAD IS BASICALLY LIKE DONUTS.
THEY ALSO ARE A LOT LIKE SATA ANDAGI SWEET BREAD FROM OKINAWA.
WHEAT FLOUR + EGGS + SUGAR
HAVE YOU EVER ACTUALLY EATEN ONE?
NOPE. NEVER.
......
COME TO THINK OF IT, I HEAR THIS QUESTION A LOT.
"WHAT DOES YOUR NORMAL EVERYDAY ROUTINE LOOK LIKE?"
SO WE NOW PRESENT: A WORKING DAY (DURING PRODUCTION).
MORI
1
MORNING.
IT TAKES TIME FOR ME TO WAKE UP.
MMPH...
2
READ MANGA WHILE EATING.
A MANGA MAGAZINE SO I DON'T CARE IF IT GETS DIRTY OR NOT.
MANGA.
3
OH NO! OH NO!
BREAKFAST TAKES LONGER THAN I THOUGHT, SO I RUSH TO CLEAN UP.
4
DOING CHORES.
TOMORROW'S THE DAY FOR PAPER RECYCLING.
5
I START TO DRAW MY PAGES.
SCRITCH!
SCRITCH!
SCRITCH!
SCRITCH!
I GO AHEAD AND START WITH THE PARTS I'M EXCITED ABOUT DRAWING.
SCRITCH!
SCRITCH!
SCRITCH!
SCRITCH!
SCRITCH!
SCRITCH!
SCRITCH!
AND I GET MORE AND MORE INTO IT.
SCRITCH!
SCRITCH!
SCRITCH!
MEEH!
TRYING TO BECOME THE SHEEP.
6
WHILE I'M DRAWING, THERE ARE THINGS I WANT TO DRAW THAT I DON'T KNOW VERY WELL, SO I GO TO MY RESEARCH BOOKS.
7
AFTER DOING RESEARCH, I STILL DON'T KNOW IT, SO I GIVE UP AND PLOW ON FORWARD ANYWAY.
8
I GET HUNGRY, SO I EAT AND READ SOME MANGA.
AH HA HA
9
DRAWING.
I DRAW WHILE THINKING OF THINGS LIKE WHAT ANIMAL I WANT TO APPEAR NEXT.
DEER? TIGER? SNAKE?
DE-SERT-ER.
10
FERVENTLY DRAWING.
11
NIGHT.
I'VE GOTTEN SLEEPY, SO I SLEEP.

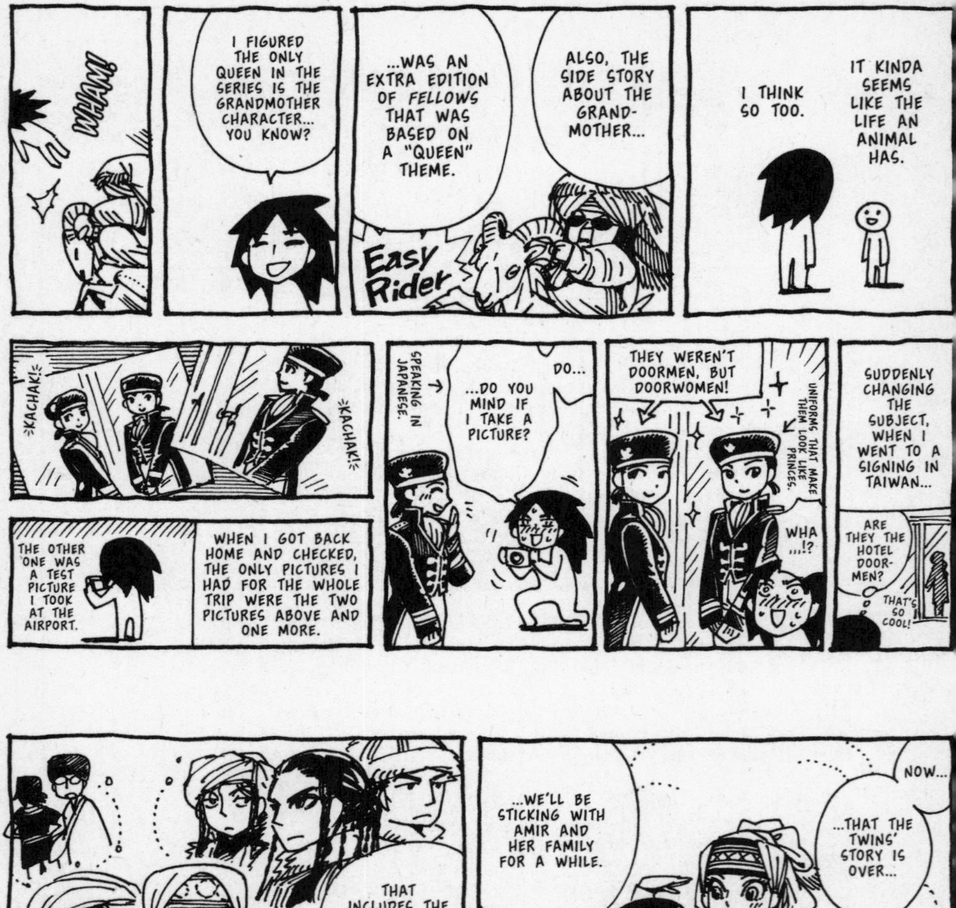
IT KINDA SEEMS LIKE THE LIFE AN ANIMAL HAS.
I THINK SO TOO.
ALSO, THE SIDE STORY ABOUT THE GRAND-MOTHER...
...WAS AN EXTRA EDITION OF *FELLOWS* THAT WAS BASED ON A "QUEEN" THEME.
Easy Rider
I FIGURED THE ONLY QUEEN IN THE SERIES IS THE GRANDMOTHER CHARACTER... YOU KNOW?
WHAM!
SUDDENLY CHANGING THE SUBJECT, WHEN I WENT TO A SIGNING IN TAIWAN...
ARE THEY THE HOTEL DOORMEN?
THAT'S SO COOL!
THEY WEREN'T DOORMEN, BUT DOORWOMEN!
UNIFORMS THAT MAKE THEM LOOK LIKE PRINCES.
WHA...!?
DO...
...DO YOU MIND IF I TAKE A PICTURE?
SPEAKING IN JAPANESE.
KACHAK!
KACHAK!
WHEN I GOT BACK HOME AND CHECKED, THE ONLY PICTURES I HAD FOR THE WHOLE TRIP WERE THE TWO PICTURES ABOVE AND ONE MORE.
THE OTHER ONE WAS A TEST PICTURE I TOOK AT THE AIRPORT.
NOW...
...THAT THE TWINS' STORY IS OVER...
...WE'LL BE STICKING WITH AMIR AND HER FAMILY FOR A WHILE.
THAT INCLUDES THE STORIES OF THESE GUYS, AND THOSE PEOPLE, AND...
SO LET'S MEET AGAIN IN THE NEXT VOLUME!
THANK YOU SO MUCH FOR READING THIS ONE!
GOOD-BYE! GOOD-BYE!
WHAT HAPPENED TO THE "LOVE TORNADO"?
IT WAS A WEATHER FORECAST. THOSE ARE WRONG ALL THE TIME.
WOW! YOU'RE MEAN!
APOLO-GIZE TO THE WEATH-ER PEOPLE!
THE END

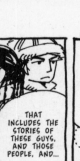

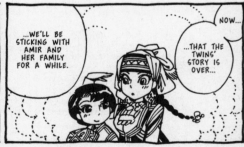

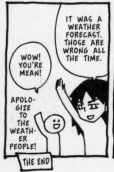

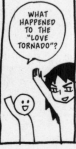

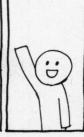

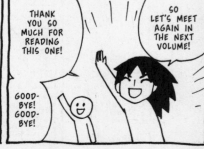

A BRIDE'S STORY ⑤

Kaoru Mori

Translation: William Flanagan

Lettering: Abigail Blackman

A BRIDE'S STORY Volume 5 © 2013 Kaoru Mori All rights reserved. First published in Japan in 2013 by ENTERBRAIN, INC., Tokyo. English translation rights arranged with ENTERBRAIN, INC. through Tuttle-Mori Agency, Inc., Tokyo.

Translation © 2013 by Hachette Book Group

Yen Press
Hachette Book Group
237 Park Avenue, New York, NY 10017

www.HachetteBookGroup.com • www.YenPress.com

Yen Press is an imprint of Hachette Book Group, Inc. The Yen Press name and logo are trademarks of Hachette Book Group, Inc.

First Yen Press Edition: September 2013

ISBN: 978-0-316-24309-4

10 9 8 7 6 5 4 3 2 1

BVG

Printed in the United States of America

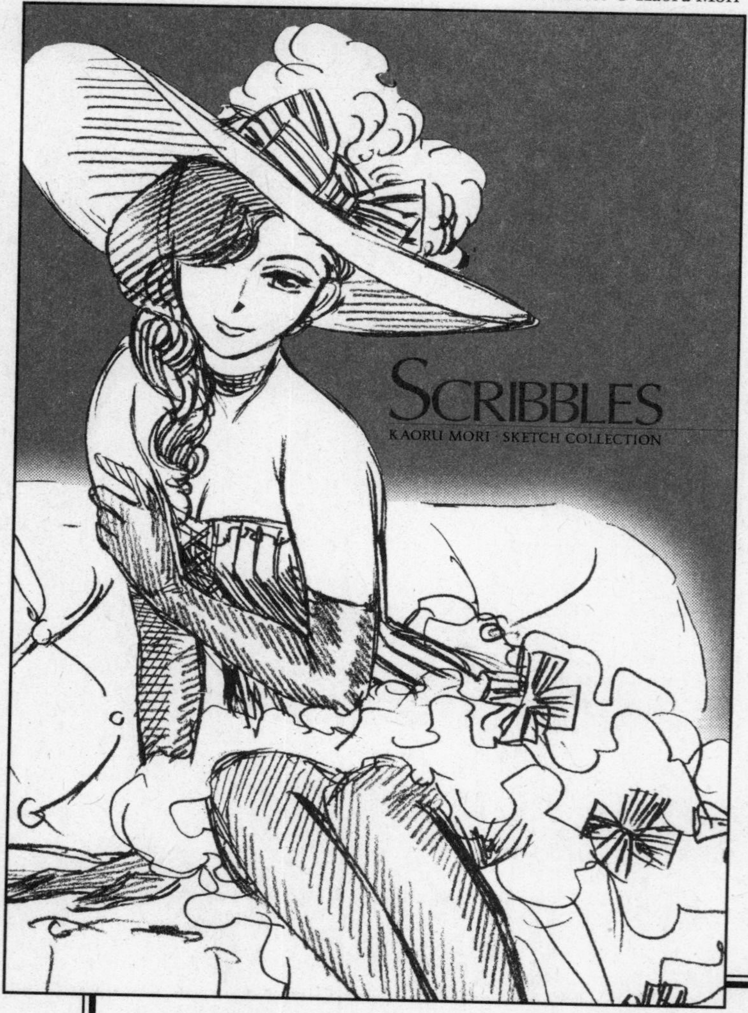
SCRIBBLES
KAORU MORI · SKETCH COLLECTION

***Read on to enjoy selections from Kaoru Mori's sketch collection,* Scribbles.**

For more of Kaoru Mori's sketches, short stories, and more, look for* Kaoru Mori: Anything and Something, *now available from Yen Press!

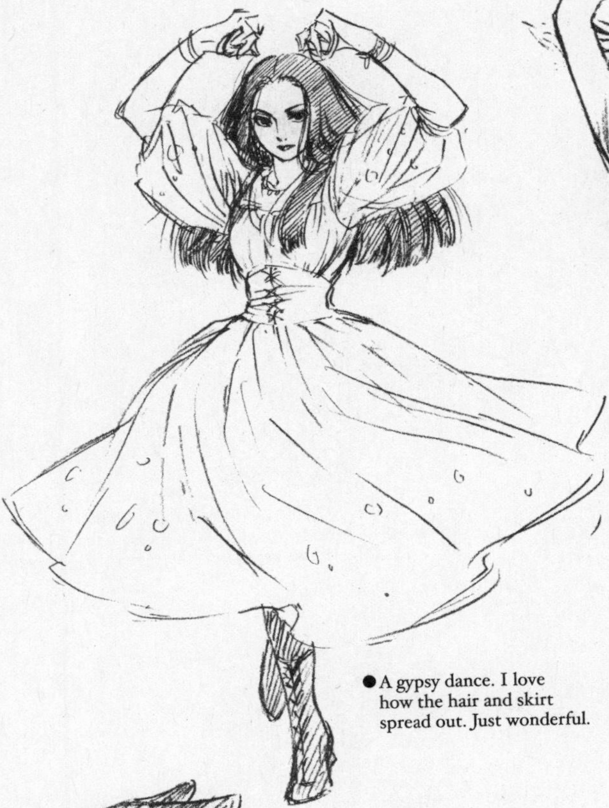

● A gypsy dance. I love how the hair and skirt spread out. Just wonderful.

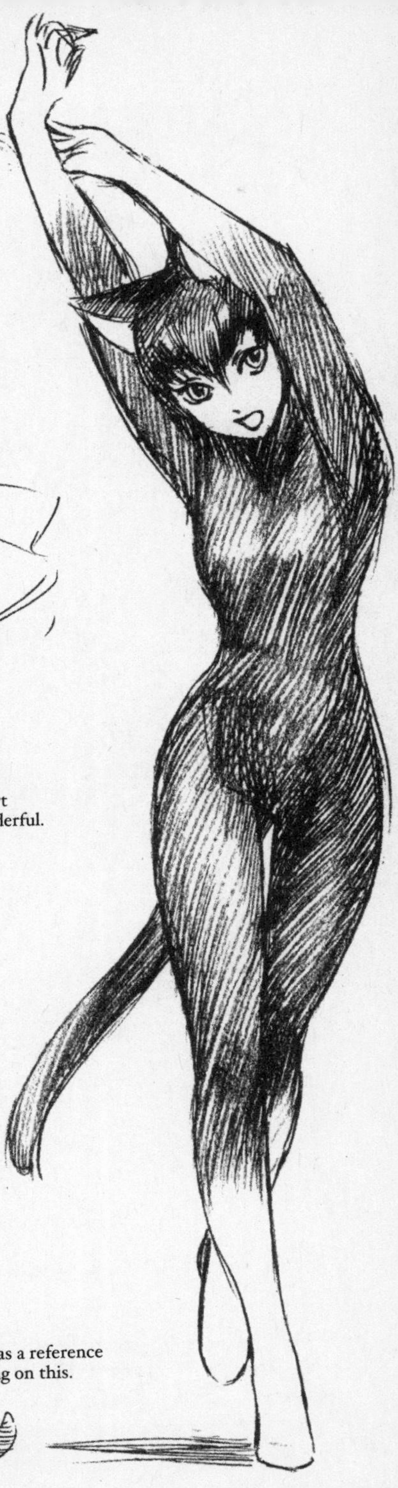

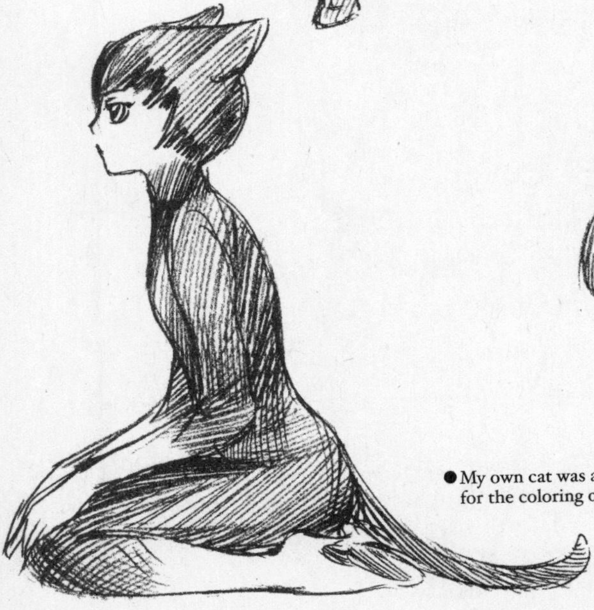

● My own cat was a reference for the coloring on this.

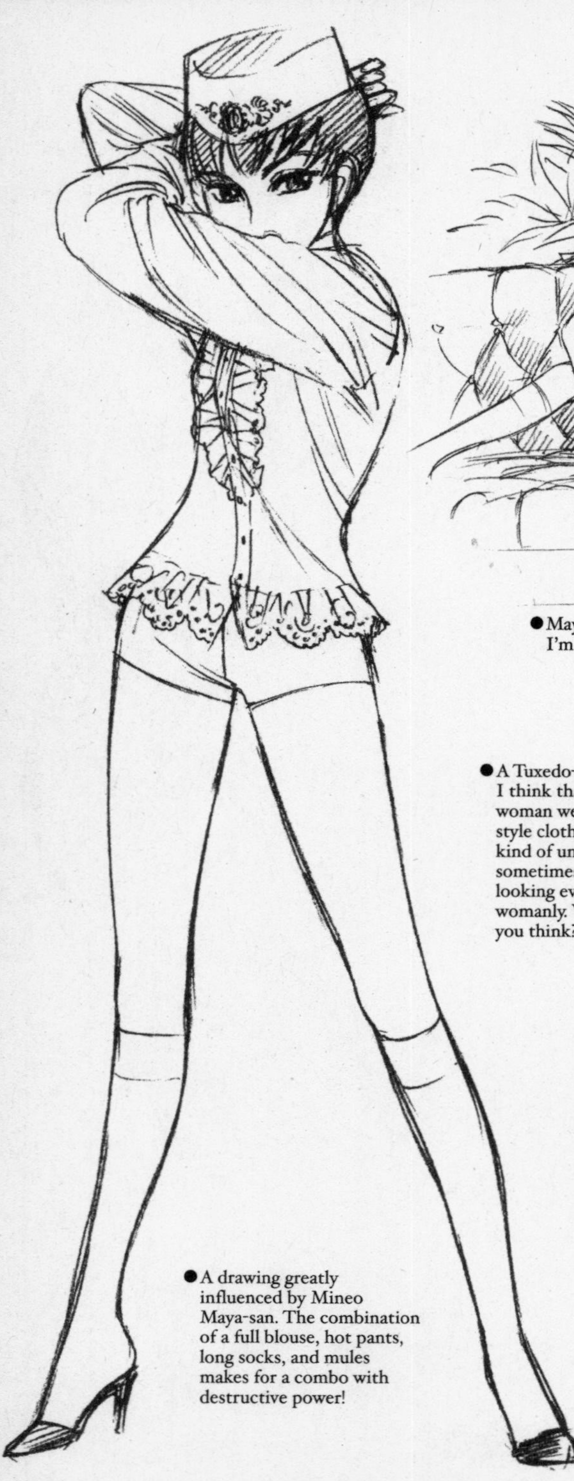

● A drawing greatly influenced by Mineo Maya-san. The combination of a full blouse, hot pants, long socks, and mules makes for a combo with destructive power!

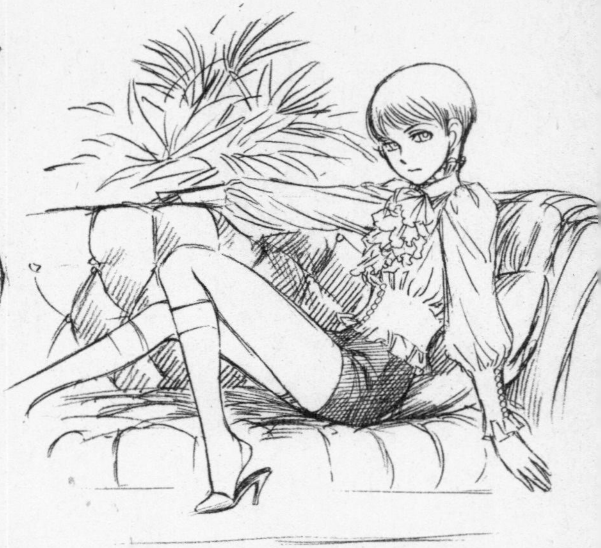

● Maya-san Style No. 2. If you want my opinion, I'm a fan of this type of clothing for young women.

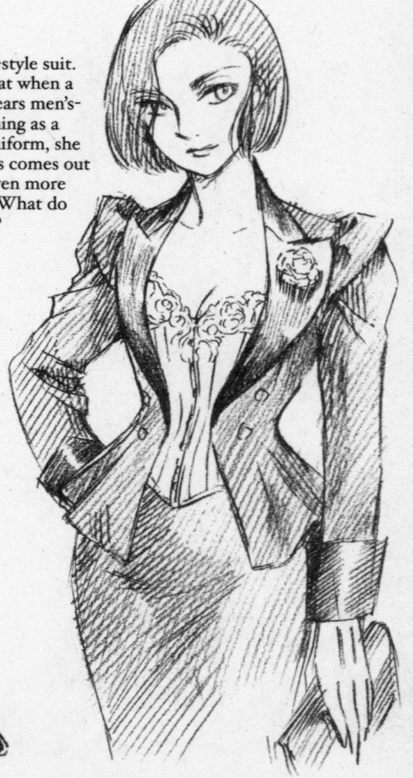

● A Tuxedo-style suit. I think that when a woman wears men's-style clothing as a kind of uniform, she sometimes comes out looking even more womanly. What do you think?

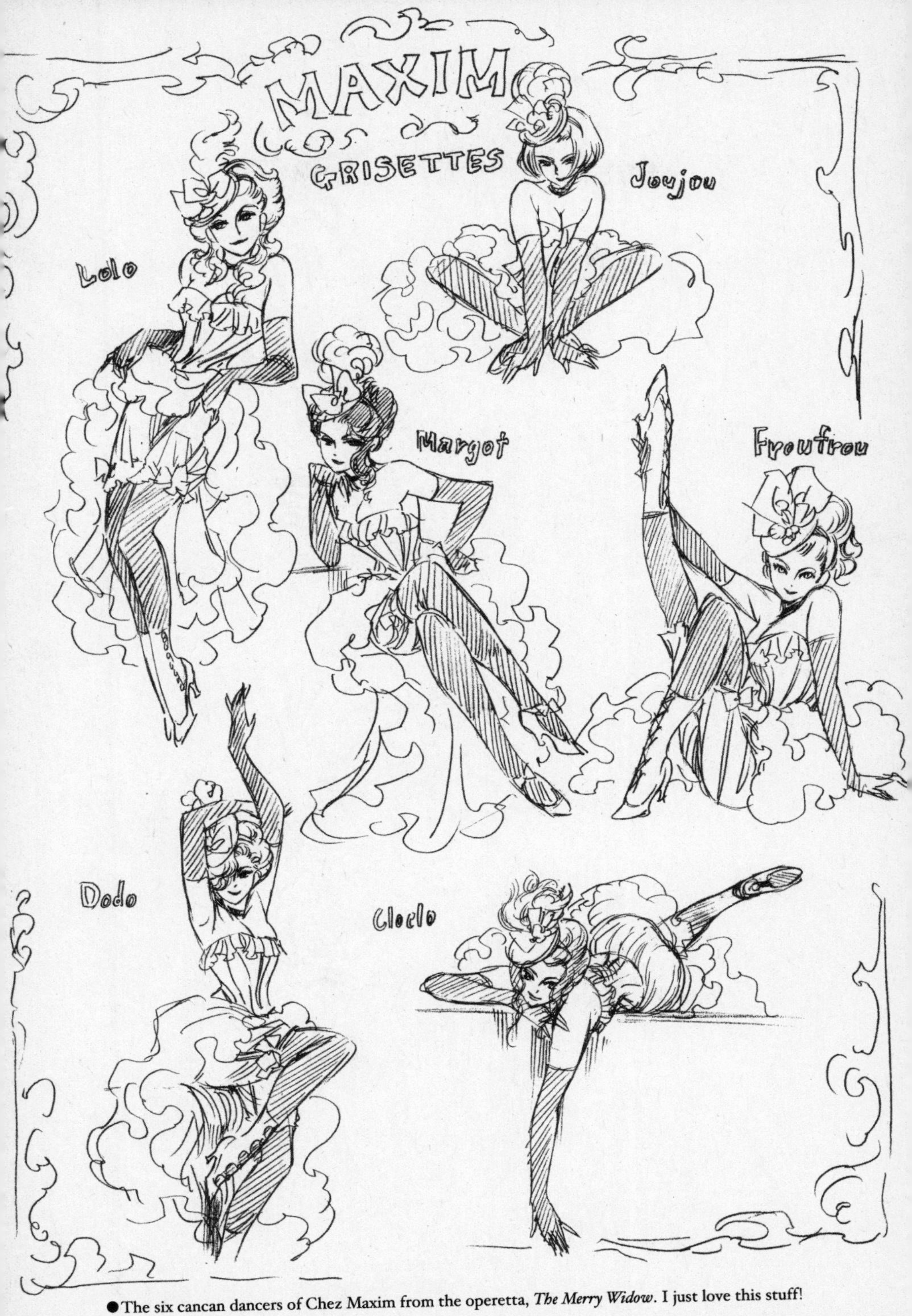
MAXIM
GRISETTES
Joujou
Lolo
Margot
Froufrou
Dodo
Cloclo

●The six cancan dancers of Chez Maxim from the operetta, *The Merry Widow*. I just love this stuff!

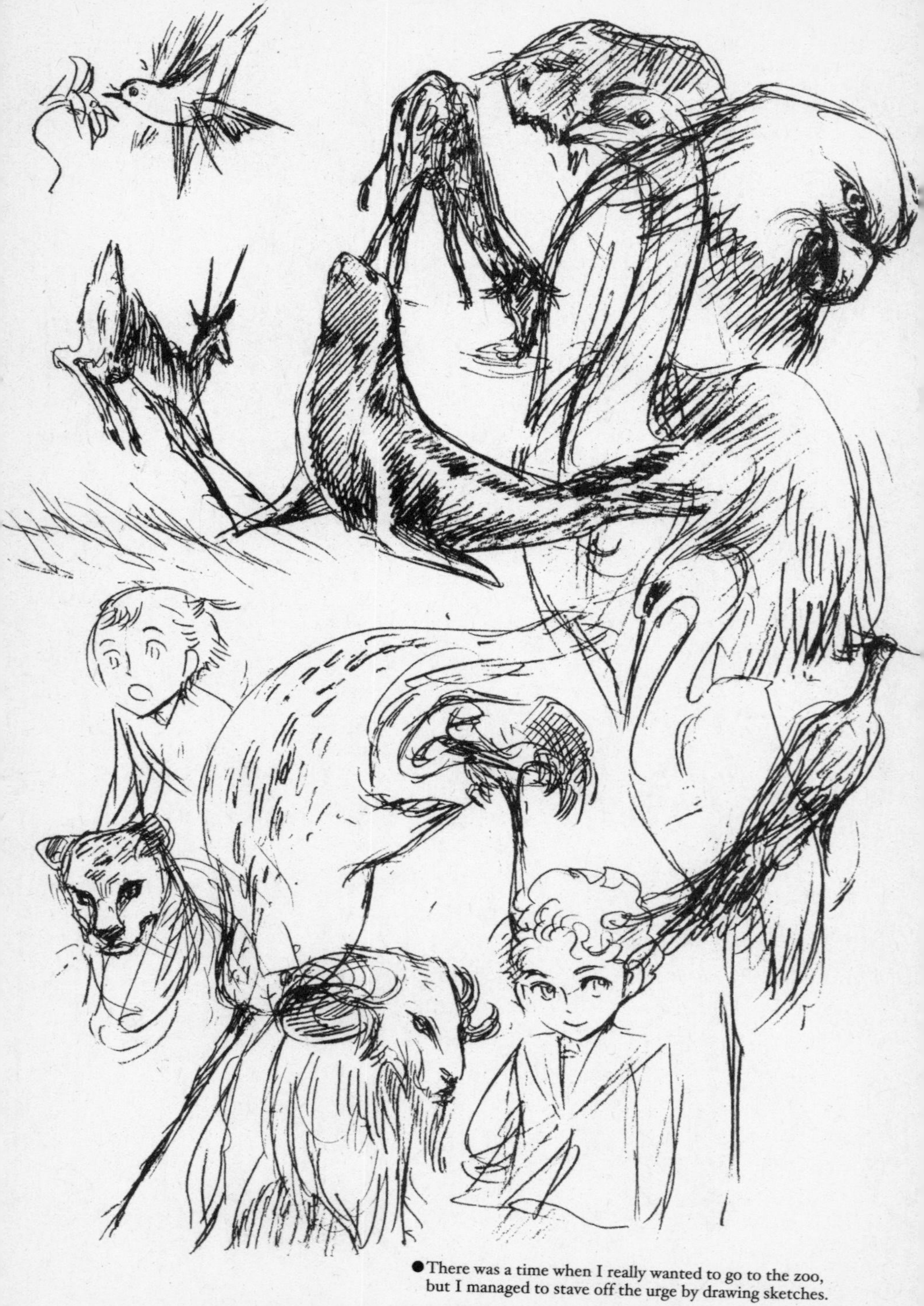

●There was a time when I really wanted to go to the zoo, but I managed to stave off the urge by drawing sketches.

●Every now and then when I board a train, I see a Korean schoolgirl in *jeogori* uniform. She's so cute that I get the urge to start following her. I don't follow her, though.

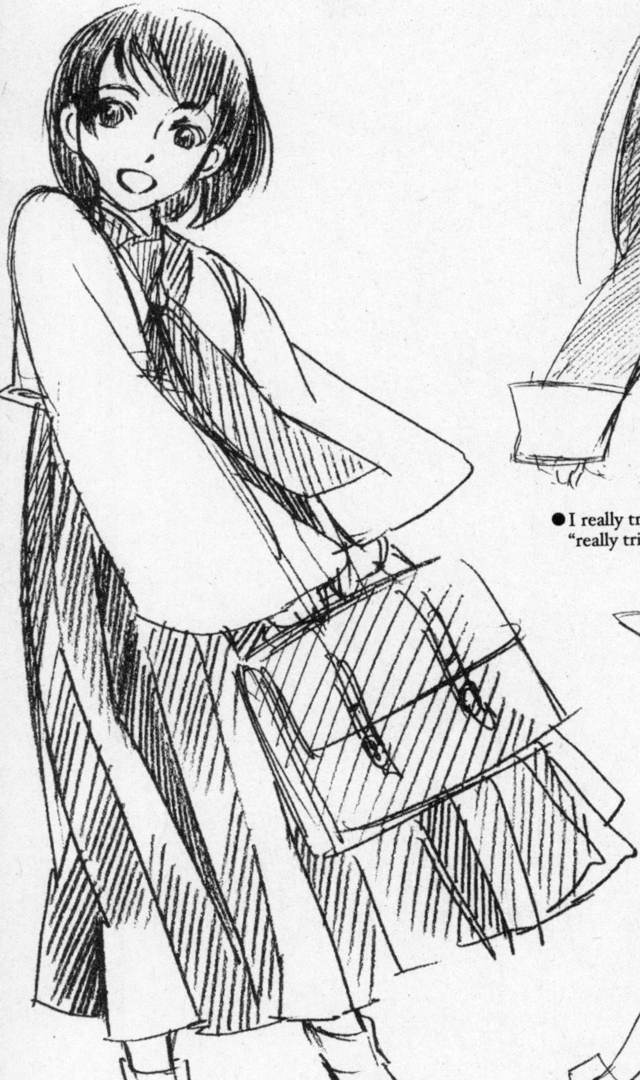

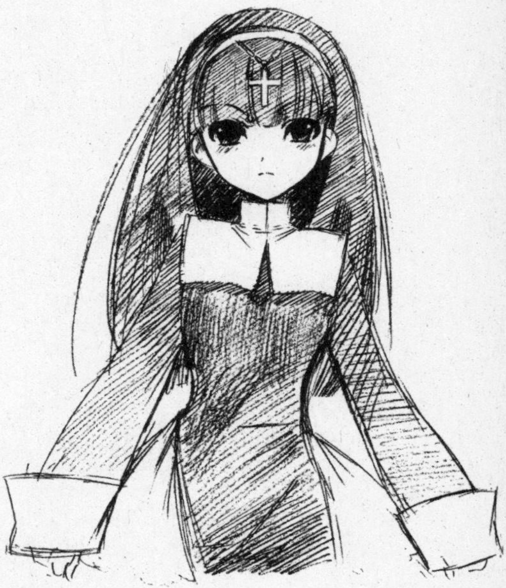

●I really tried to do a *moe* picture, but I think the "really tried" translated into "tried too hard."

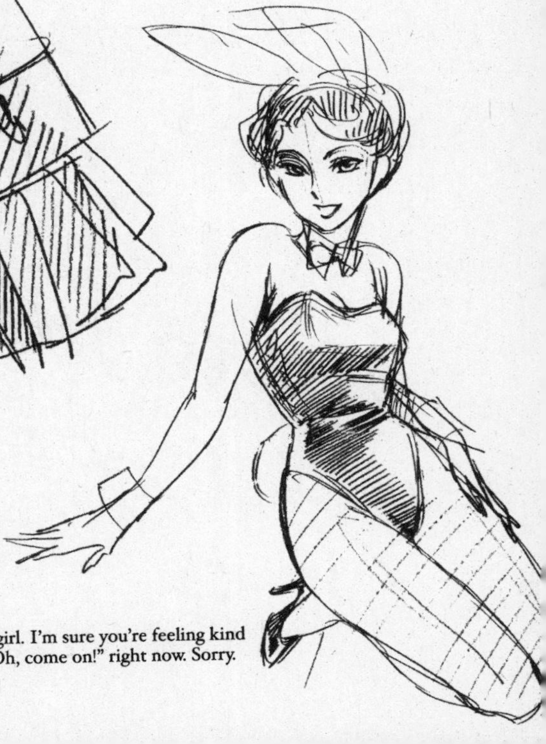

●A bunny girl. I'm sure you're feeling kind of like, "Oh, come on!" right now. Sorry.

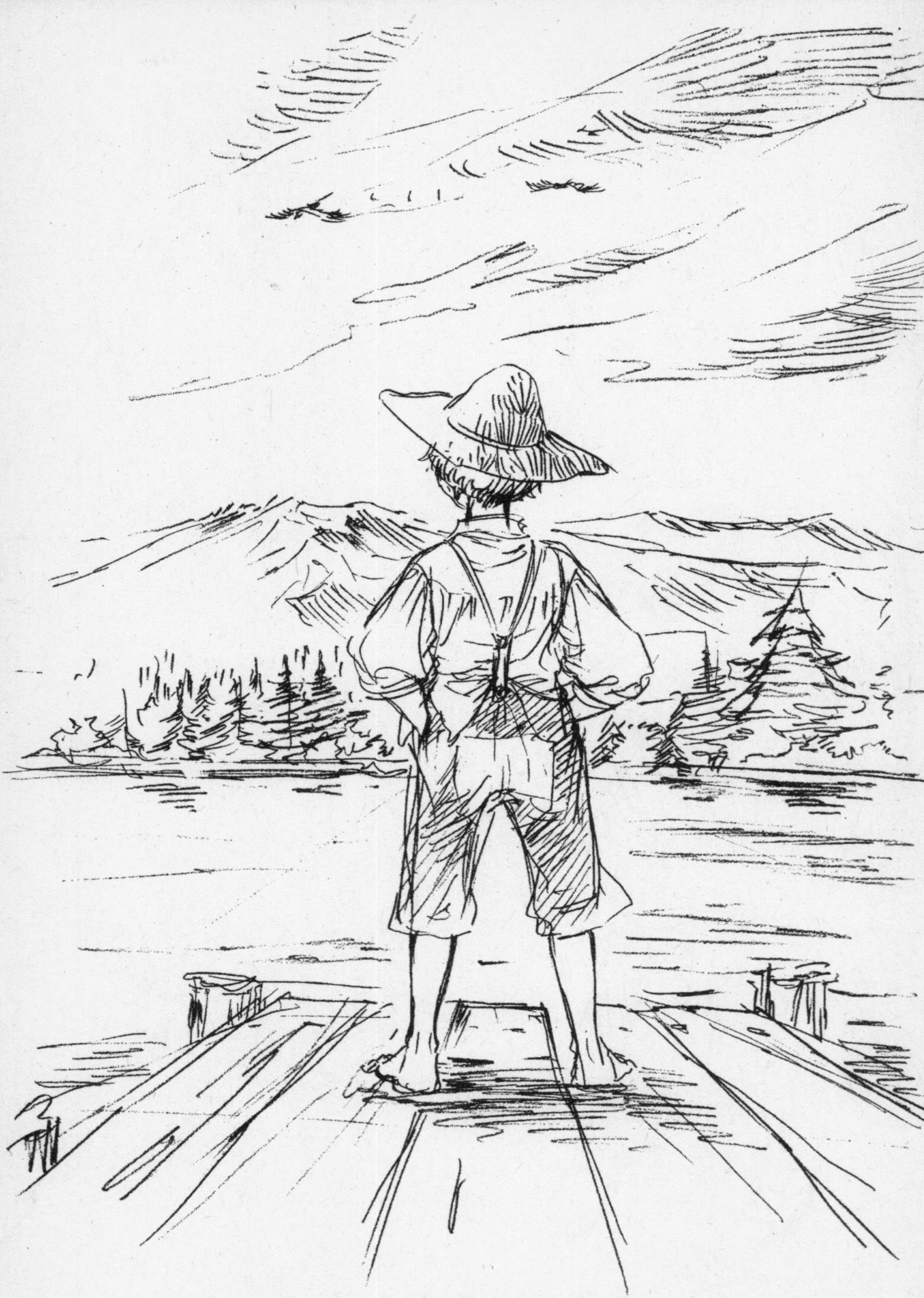

● Tom Sawyer!

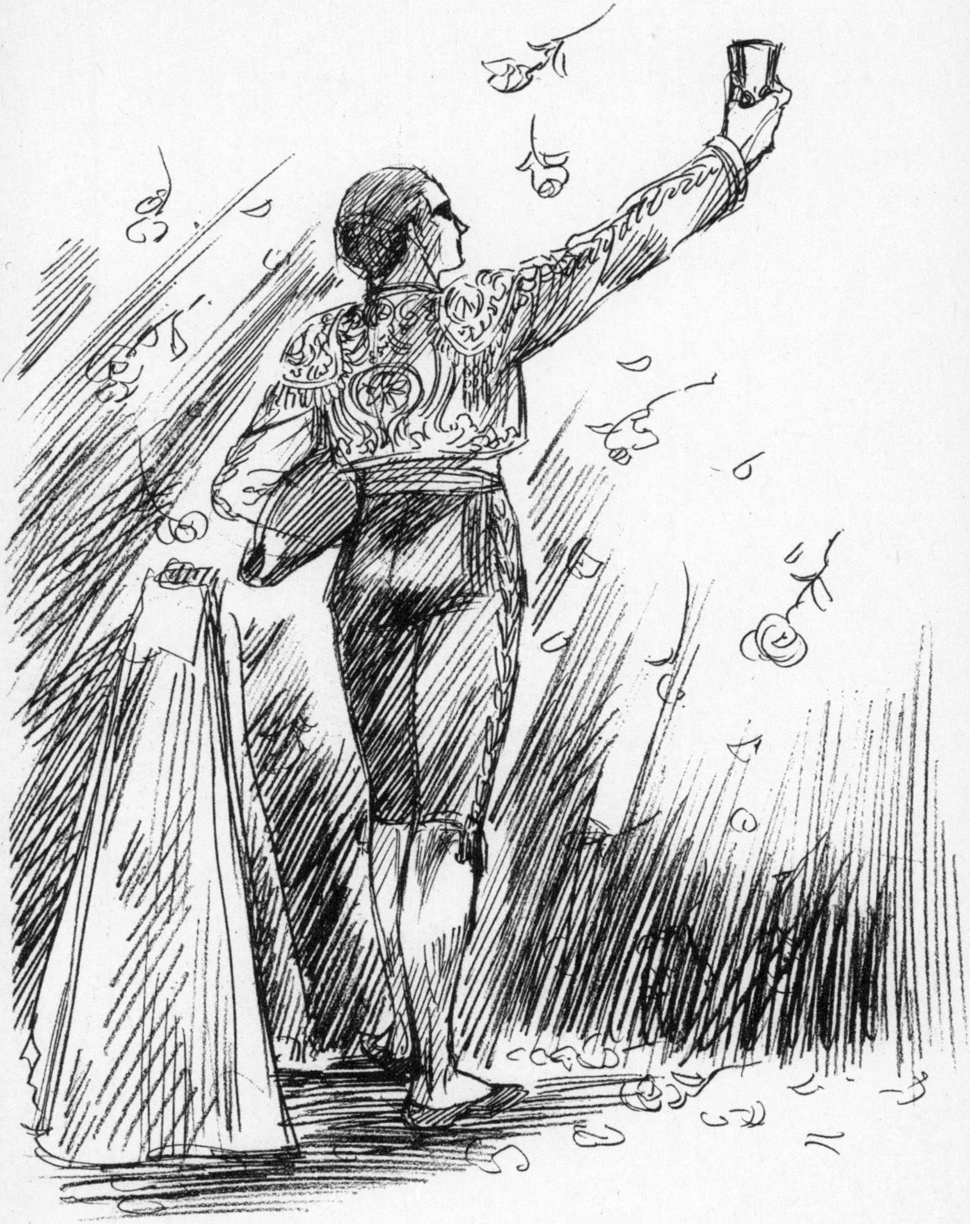

● The "Toréador Song" from Bizet's *Carmen.* It's hugely famous, but no matter how many times I listen, I still think it's fabulous. "Toréador, en garde!!"